5—

Praise for Christopher Reich's

THE TAKE

"Make sure your seat belt is fastened and your tray table is up—this is one hard-and-fast battle royal. Tension, turmoil, and drama ooze from every page. There's not a wasted word in this high-octane game changer."

—Steve Berry, #1 bestselling author of *The Lost Order* and *The Patriot Threat*

"A fast, wild ride with no less than the balance of power in the Western world at stake." —*Parade*

"*The Take* is a slick, elegant, and gripping spy thriller of the first order. With a brilliant heist, a twisting web of secrets and intrigue, and an adrenaline-fueled plot, Reich whisked me out of my world and into his from the explosive first pages. Simon Riske is my favorite kind of hero—flawed, dark, and utterly intriguing. Fabulous!" —Lisa Unger, *New York Times* bestselling author of *The Red Hunter*

"It's *To Catch a Thief* meets Jason Bourne: a stylish, jet-propelled thriller full of intriguing characters and surprising twists. Simon Riske is a character I'll want to meet again." —Jeff Abbott, *New York Times* bestselling author of *Blame*

THE TAKE

THE TAKE

CHRISTOPHER REICH

MULHOLLAND BOOKS

Little, Brown and Company
New York Boston London

Copyright © 2018 by Christopher Reich
Excerpt from *Crown Jewel* copyright © 2019 by Christopher Reich

Hachette Book Group supports the right to free expression and the value of copyright. The purpose of copyright is to encourage writers and artists to produce the creative works that enrich our culture.

The scanning, uploading, and distribution of this book without permission is a theft of the author's intellectual property. If you would like permission to use material from the book (other than for review purposes), please contact permissions@hbgusa.com. Thank you for your support of the author's rights.

Mulholland Books / Little, Brown and Company
Hachette Book Group
1290 Avenue of the Americas, New York, NY 10104
mulhollandbooks.com

The publisher is not responsible for websites (or their content) that are not owned by the publisher.

Printed in the United States of America

Originally published in hardcover by Mulholland Books, January 2018
First Mulholland Books mass market edition, January 2019

10 9 8 7 6 5 4 3 2 1

To my mother, Babs Reich
With love

THE TAKE

CHAPTER 1

Fifty-nine seconds.

From the time the first car entered the Avenue du Général Leclerc and blocked the prince's route to the moment the assault squad regained their vehicles, hijacked the two BMW touring sedans, and departed the scene, no more than one minute had passed.

No one screamed. No shots were fired. The robbery was carried out with precision and discipline, relying on surprise, speed, and brute force, and never resorting to violence…apart from clubbing one of the prince's bodyguards.

Staring down the barrel of an AK-47, Tino Coluzzi had learned, was ample motivation to do as you are told.

Now, forty-five minutes later, standing in a wheat field thirty kilometers south of Paris, watching flames engulf the stolen vehicles, Coluzzi could finally relax. The American had been right all along.

The prince really did travel with a million euros in cash.

The convoy of sixteen BMWs had arrived punctually at six p.m. The line of black touring sedans had drawn up in single file before the entrance of the Hotel George V, the last stopping halfway up the block.

Seated at Le Fouquet's, Tino Coluzzi finished his espresso, slipped a ten-euro note beneath the saucer, and rose, taking a moment to dab the corners of his mouth. He was slim, of medium height, and elegantly dressed in a tan poplin blazer, dark slacks, and Italian driving shoes. Sunglasses shielded his eyes from the evening rays. A gambler's mustache decorated his lip. His black hair had recently been cut and was combed neatly to one side, shiny with brilliantine.

It was impossible to detect the pistol cradled beneath his left arm or the stiletto he habitually wore at his ankle. The pistol was small—a .22 but loaded with hollowpoint bullets. He used it rarely and only at close distances. He preferred the stiletto. Over the years, he'd gained an expert's dexterity with it and could insert the blade, nick the heart, and be ten paces away before his victim had the slightest inkling he'd been mortally wounded.

"The prince is paying his bill," said a voice in his earpiece. His contact in the hotel.

"Cash?"

"Of course."

"How much?"

"Hold on."

Coluzzi turned down the street toward the hotel. To look at, he appeared entirely at ease, one of Paris's perennial bachelors with too much time on his hands. The sun was shining. The smell of the River Seine, a few blocks to the south, freshened the air. A calm breeze rustled the mature linden trees planted every ten meters. No one would ever suspect he was about to steal an enormous amount of money.

Coluzzi walked slowly, pretending to admire the

goods on display in the numerous luxury boutiques. Jewelry. Dresses. Handbags. Nothing less than ten thousand euros. As if exhausted by the sheer variety of choices, he came to a halt in front of the store across the street from the hotel. Staring into the window, he caught a perfect reflection of the revolving glass doors that led into the lobby.

The Hotel George V—or the Four Seasons Hotel George V, as it was officially known these days—was one of Paris's oldest and most prestigious hotels. Located in the famed Golden Triangle of the 8th arrondissement, it was a stone's throw from the Champs-Élysées and a five-minute walk from the Arc de Triomphe. The price for a room began at eight hundred euros a night.

"Well?" asked Coluzzi. "How much?"

"One hundred twenty-two thousand euros and change."

Approximately one hundred fifty thousand dollars. Coluzzi still valued his take in American currency.

"The prince never travels with less than a million euros in cash," the American had informed him when he offered Coluzzi the job. *"He likes to drop a few hundred thousand shopping while he's in town. The rest is yours."*

They'd met in the bar of the Hôtel Costes a week earlier. The American was a sallow, fatigued-looking man with dark eyes and a nervous smile, out of place in the swank lounge. His French was nearly fluent but uneven, and he apologized incessantly for being rusty.

The target was Prince Abdul Aziz bin Saud, a fifty-year-old Saudi Arabian playboy who traveled the world with his wives and kids as cover for his philandering. He never went anywhere without at least five bodyguards, and he moved around the city in convoys of black BMW sedans. Coluzzi was to hijack the convoy as the prince drove to Orly Airport in the southern out-skirts of Paris.

"And for you?" Coluzzi had asked. *"How much?"*

"None."

"None?"

"It's not the money I'm interested in."

The American had never said where he'd gotten Coluzzi's name or, for that matter, his phone number. Coluzzi had needed one look to know he came from the shadows. All the better. He didn't trust an honest man.

A bodyguard emerged from the hotel, then another, and Coluzzi's heart picked up a beat. A moment later, both retreated inside.

False alarm.

"Where the hell is he?"

"Hold your horses. The family's all here. Just another minute."

For the past three days Coluzzi and his crew had been following the prince, his three wives, and their ten children as they spent their way across Paris. Ten thousand euros for a handbag at Hermès. Twenty thousand for a dress at Chanel. Thirty thousand for a diamond-encrusted watch at Cartier. (A gift for the prince's oldest son, age twelve.) There were stops at the city's finest restaurants. Lunch at Epicure. Cocktails at the Plaza Athénée. Dinner at Le Jules Verne. The prince had left the tenets of Islam in Saudi Arabia, along with his prayer rug.

And now the hotel bill totaling one hundred twenty-two thousand euros.

Which left approximately six hundred thousand for the taking.

"They're headed your way," said his contact.

Coluzzi came to attention. In the window's reflection,

he watched as bellmen streamed from the lobby, ferrying mountains of luggage to the automobiles. The bodyguards returned. Four formed a loose cordon to block pedestrian traffic. A fifth—who Coluzzi recognized as their leader—walked between them, eyes sweeping the street for threats. Seeing nothing, he retreated to the door and motioned that all was clear.

By now, passersby on both sides of the street had stopped to pay attention to the spectacle. The line of black sedans. The mountain of luggage. The bodyguards in their black suits. Turning around, Coluzzi allowed himself to gaze openly. It would be odd not to look.

The women and children filed from the hotel like prisoners on their way to jail, heads bowed, not a smile among them. For their return home, the mothers wore traditional black burkas, even their faces shielded from view. The younger girls pulled Hermès scarves over their heads. The boys slouched in ripped jeans and untucked shirts. Not one acknowledged the chauffeurs holding their doors.

The princess passed through the revolving doors and paused as the chief bodyguard ran ahead, looking this way and that. Finally, he waved her forward. The princess was not dressed in a burka like the others but in a navy blazer and tan pants, a large white purse slung over one arm.

"The prince and princess travel in the fifth car," the American had said, after Coluzzi had agreed to take the job. *"It's his lucky number. The money goes in the sixth, all by itself."*

The princess walked to the fourth car and spoke to the driver. Coluzzi felt a twinge of unease. Not the fourth car, he admonished her. The fifth.

She paid him no heed. She placed a foot inside the back and lowered her head. From the hotel, a man shouted a rebuke. The princess turned her head. Coluzzi saw the prince gesturing unhappily to his wife. Immediately, she retraced her steps and climbed into the fifth car.

Coluzzi relaxed.

And then it was the prince's turn. He exited the hotel in the company of the hotel's general manager, the two walking arm in arm across the sidewalk. The prince was a handsome man dressed in his country's traditional garb of a flowing white thobe and red-checked kaffiyeh secured with a black cord. As was his custom, he wore dark sunglasses. In his hand he carried a calfskin briefcase.

"All I want is the prince's briefcase. The rest is yours."

"Just the briefcase?"

"Tan calfskin. Leather handle." The American had offered no further explanation. *"Do we have a deal?"*

Coluzzi swore under his breath. For two days he'd seen nothing of the briefcase. He'd begun to worry that the prince did not have it with him on this trip. *Tan. Leather handle.* There it was, thank God. He was staring so hard at it that he almost didn't catch the bodyguard delivering the compact metal suitcase to the trunk of the sixth car.

The money goes in the sixth.

As the prince reached the car, his driver extended a hand to relieve him of the briefcase. The prince turned a shoulder to guard it, tensing like a rugby scrum half bracing for a hit. The driver retreated hastily.

The prince offered a last thank you to the hotel manager. There was a handshake. The manager bowed, slipping his gratuity into his pocket with a legerdemain

Coluzzi admired. A final wave goodbye and the prince disappeared inside the car.

Not a second later, the first BMW peeled away from the curb. Then the second. In a minute, they were all gone, heading south en route to Orly airfield.

The Avenue George V was quiet once again. The excitement had passed. It was just another lazy Sunday evening in August.

A white Renault pulled up alongside Coluzzi and he jumped into the front seat. He took a two-way radio from the center console as the car sped away.

"The pigeon has flown the coop," he said. "He's coming at you."

Prince Abdul Aziz bin Saud settled into his seat and exhaled. "Hurry up," he said to the driver. "I don't want to be late."

"It is our plane, darling," said his wife, covering his hand with her own. "We can leave when we choose."

The prince looked at her red nails, her mascara, and shook his hand free. "What do you know?"

The princess slid toward her door, saying nothing.

Prince Abdul Aziz stared out the window as the car crossed the Pont de l'Alma and slipped into the shadow of the Eiffel Tower. He knew he should be happier, rejoicing even. He'd pulled off the greatest coup of his career, yet it would mean nothing until the letter reached the proper hands. His only wish was to be gone from Paris as quickly as possible.

His eyes fell to the calfskin briefcase at his feet and his heart raced. He thought of the letter inside. A personal note from one man to another, handwritten in blue ink on the most exclusive of stationeries, in appearance as fresh as the day it was penned nearly thirty years ago.

And not just any note, but a note that would cause governments to collapse, alliances to realign, and death to many along the way.

Instinctively, he gripped the case between his ankles.

He leaned forward to squeeze the driver's shoulder. "Faster."

Tino Coluzzi followed the convoy across the city. The prince had chosen an unlikely route to the airport, using an August evening's wide-open boulevards and traffic-free surface streets to navigate through Montparnasse toward Porte d'Orléans at the southern edge of the city. It was a move that shaved ten minutes off the more oft-chosen route along the Périphérique, the eight-lane superhighway that circled Paris. The decreased transit time had a cost, however, and that cost was security. It was nearly impossible to stop a convoy of sixteen vehicles once it was on the highway. Coluzzi would have no such difficulty on surface streets.

The Renault hit a dip as it crossed through an intersection, and Coluzzi grasped the stock of his AK-47 assault rifle. The poplin blazer was gone, as were the Italian driving shoes. He wore the same assault gear as the other men in the car with him. Three blocks ahead, the traffic signal for Porte d'Orléans burned red. Once past it, the prince would join the highway. Coluzzi's chance would be gone.

"Tighten it up," he said, placing his right hand on the door handle.

With a burst of acceleration, the Renault came up on the last BMW in line.

Coluzzi put the radio to his mouth. "Take him."

A moment later, a car identical to his own darted into the street ahead of the first BMW. Red lights flared up and down the line of cars. Brakes squealed. The convoy stopped.

"Ram him."

Coluzzi braced as his vehicle struck the car at a speed of ten kilometers per hour.

The kill box was established.

Coluzzi pulled the balaclava over his face and stepped out of the car. As he ran up the line of BMWs, another white Renault approached from a side street.

Coluzzi's men poured from their vehicles. There were twelve including himself. All wore black commando gear, balaclavas pulled over their faces. Like him, all carried AK-47 assault rifles with an extra-long ammunition clip. The men fanned out to surround the convoy, weapons pointed at the idling automobiles. Coluzzi ran to the fifth vehicle and drove the butt of his rifle into the driver's window. A second blow showered glass over the asphalt.

"Unlock the car," he shouted. "Everyone out."

The driver got out, hands held high. Coluzzi forced him to the ground, landing a boot on his back for good measure.

"Out. Now."

A bodyguard emerged from one of the cars farther back. It was the leader, and his gun was drawn. He moved slowly, unsurely. It was a show of mad loyalty rather than an effort to stop the robbery. One of Coluzzi's men was on him before he cleared the car and clubbed him with the stock of his weapon. The bodyguard fell to the asphalt like a sack of rocks.

Coluzzi opened the back door. "Your Highness. If you please."

The prince stepped out, lending a hand for the

princess. The two stood, staring at each other, saying nothing.

Immediately, one of Coluzzi's men climbed behind the wheel and closed the door.

Coluzzi hurried to the next car in line. The sixth, carrying the money. "Out."

The driver climbed out.

"On the ground."

The driver lay down.

One of Coluzzi's men tossed his machine gun into the car and slid behind the wheel.

"My belongings," said the prince, his eyes shifting to the calfskin briefcase visible in the back seat. "Please."

Coluzzi returned to the prince. "Leave it."

"Papers for my work. They are of no value to you."

Already his men were running back to their vehicles.

Coluzzi shoved the prince away from the car, sunglasses falling to the ground, and the prince shoved back, fighting to go around him. The princess lunged at her husband in a vain effort to stop him. The prince knocked her away, then grabbed Coluzzi's tunic. "I will find you."

Coluzzi looked into the prince's eyes. He saw fire and resolve. They were the eyes of a man accustomed to cruelty and having his way. They were not the eyes of a playboy.

"Excuse me," he said, using the barrel of his rifle to free the prince's hands from his person. "I must be going."

The prince stepped away.

Coluzzi banged a fist on the roof of the prince's car. The engine revved, then pulled out of line and sped away. Coluzzi jogged to the rear of the convoy and jumped into the Renault. *"Allons-y."*

As the Renault accelerated, he looked over his

shoulder. The prince and princess stood staring at the space where the cars had been.

Coluzzi wondered if five was still the prince's lucky number.

Coluzzi threw the empty petrol can into the front seat of the burning BMW and watched the flames lick at the automobiles. His clothing, sunglasses, shoes, socks, even the false mustache he'd been wearing, were inside. Anything that could tie him or his men to the crime would be incinerated.

His phone rang. "Yes?"

"We counted it."

"And?"

"Six hundred twenty-two thousand."

"Not bad for a few days' work."

"Not bad at all."

"I'll be there in ten minutes."

Coluzzi returned to his car. The engine was running, and in a moment they were doing a hundred down the farm road. He looked down at the calfskin briefcase and recalled how the prince had so zealously guarded it. He thought of the sallow, fatigued-looking American with his rusty French offering him the job.

"All I want is the prince's briefcase," he'd said. *"The rest is yours."*

Just then his phone rang. It was the American. He let the phone ring and ring until the call rolled to his voice mail.

"Where to?" asked the driver.

Coluzzi put the satchel on his lap.

"Just drive," he said.

CHAPTER 2

Two hundred miles away as the crow flies, another man was contemplating theft.

Simon Riske strode across the lawn of Battersea Park, his fingers tingling with anticipation. Years had passed since he'd done a job of this nature. He wasn't frightened. He'd practiced for days and his skills remained sharp. If he was anxious, it was because he feared he might like it too much. He'd sworn never to go back.

"Tickets?" he asked the attractive blond woman accompanying him.

"Right here," said Lucy Brown, slipping them from her purse.

"Stay close once we're inside."

"Like I'm your girlfriend," she said, threading her arm through his.

"My assistant," Simon corrected her and gently freed himself.

He was a compact man, an American, markedly fit in a bespoke navy suit, white cotton shirt open at the collar. His hair was dark and thick, receding violently at the temples, and cut to the nub with a number two razor. He had his father's dark complexion and brooding good looks and his mother's beryl-green eyes. People mistook him for a European—Italian, Slavic, something Mediterranean. His nose was too bold, too chiseled. His chin, too strong. Take off the suit, add a day's stubble, and he'd fit in hooking bales of Egyptian cotton across a dock in Naples.

The night was warm and humid, the air alive with the scent of brine and exhaust. The first star winked from the violet canopy. Across the river, Big Ben and the spires of Whitehall cut a noble profile. Riske enjoyed a surge of contentment. He was thankful to be a free man.

His destination was a modern exhibition hall, all mirrored glass and shiny metal girders. Banners advertising fine French champagne and luxury Swiss watches lined the path. All around him, elegantly dressed men and women moved eagerly, drawn by a common excitement.

The event was Sotheby's annual classic car auction. In an hour, thirty of the world's most valuable automobiles were to be sold to the highest bidder. Ferrari, Lamborghini, Mercedes, Porsche. Estimates ranged from two hundred thousand dollars to twenty million.

But Simon Riske had not come to bid on an automobile.

"You ready?" he asked, pausing ten paces from the entry.

"All I have to do is show me bits and brass," said Lucy Brown. "Easy enough."

Simon appraised his companion. If memory served, she was twenty-three years of age. Far too young for him. She'd dressed in a white skirt and a navy blouse.

Though conservative, the garments did little to hide her toned legs and generous cleavage. No one would be watching him with her anywhere nearby.

"Don't really show them," he said. "Just…well, you know. Do as I told you."

"Of course, boss."

"And the glasses." He'd insisted she wear a pair of horn-rimmed spectacles to tone things down. It was a classy event, after all. To spite him, she'd tucked them into her shirt.

"Must I?"

Simon nodded.

Grudgingly, she put on the glasses. "Happy?"

"Thank you," he said. "Much better." He extended an arm. "After you."

Simon was given a sales catalogue at the door. Lucy led them inside. The hall was vast, dimmed lights making it impossible to gauge its true size. A stage occupied the right-hand side with a dozen rows of chairs set up in front of it. The automobiles to be auctioned were situated across the floor on raised platforms and bathed in flattering spotlights.

"See him?" asked Lucy.

"Just look for his bodyguards," said Simon. "He never goes anywhere with less than four. They're as big as Stalin skyscrapers."

"What skyscrapers?"

"The buildings in Moscow built by Joseph…Never mind. They're tall. You can't miss them."

Lucy wrinkled her nose. "What's he so frightened of?"

"He's Russian. He's a billionaire. And he's a gangster. Take your pick."

Simon flipped through the catalogue as he strolled. At one time all these people wandering the hall, laughing easily, holding their drinks with aplomb, had been his peers. Not long afterward, they were the enemy, adversaries to be shorn of their valuables—essentially prey. Today, they occupied a middle ground.

Simon was a man between classes. An outsider by choice and by circumstance. The tailored suit, the easygoing smile, the splash of Acqua di Parma. All of it was no more than a silk sheath over a razor.

"Ladies and gentlemen," announced a dignified voice on the public address system. "The auction will commence in fifteen minutes' time. Please make your way to your seats."

A waiter approached carrying a tray overloaded with flutes of champagne. "Madam, a drink prior to the bidding?"

"Why, thank you," said Lucy, reaching for a glass.

"But, no," cut in Simon, taking her by a shoulder and guiding her in the opposite direction. "This is work."

"It's free."

"I'll buy you a case of the stuff," said Simon. "After we're done."

"Promise?"

"Watch yourself. I'll put you on paint duty tomorrow."

"You wouldn't."

"Try me."

On the side, Simon was the owner of a small but well-regarded automotive shop in a quiet neighborhood not far from Wimbledon that specialized in European cars, namely Ferraris and Lamborghinis. He didn't just fix their engines, he rebuilt them from top to bottom, a process that could last two years and run to hundreds of thousands of dollars. In such cases, one of the first tasks was to strip the paint off the chassis. It was a tedious and exhausting job done with a heating gun and a scraper.

Lucy Brown worked in his shop as an apprentice mechanic. It was a long story.

"Let's find our man," he said. "He'll be bidding on the prized lot. That's as good a place as any to start."

Simon rolled up the catalogue and headed toward the center of the hall, where a crowd was gathered around a red sports car. The vehicle was a 1964 Ferrari 275, one of just twenty-three to roll out of the factory in Maranello, Italy. Of these, fewer than ten were in working order. LOT 31, as the Ferrari was labeled, was a prime example, and the first to come up for sale in a decade. Bidding began at fifteen million dollars.

Simon scanned the crowd surrounding the car. He didn't need a description to find Boris Blatt. The man was in the tabloids every other day. Blatt was in the process of building the largest house in London, a ninety-thousand-square-foot mansion atop Highgate Hill. Not a day passed without a neighbor, contractor, or city official having something ill to report. Simon couldn't buy a tin of Altoids at the corner kiosk without seeing Blatt's elfin features leering back at him.

"Excuse me." A security guard brushed past, nudging his shoulder. A second guard followed close behind.

"Go right ahead," said Simon, making way.

"What's that all about?" asked Lucy.

There was a commotion to his right. An emergency exit opened. The alarm sounded briefly, then died. Security guards formed a cordon to allow someone to enter. Simon spotted a large man with hulking shoulders and a crew cut leading the way. Another man identical to him followed behind. Simon's pulse quickened. Blatt's gorillas.

"He's here."

Cameras flashed. A murmur rippled through the crowd. He caught sight of a pale, fat man with close-cropped white hair. Boris Blatt was dressed in a black suit and open-collar shirt, his eyes focused on the ground ahead of him.

"Let's go, then." Simon took Lucy's hand and pushed through the crowd. He needed proximity to his target. Once everyone was seated, his window of opportunity would be gone.

"You can't be serious," protested Lucy, getting her first look at Blatt's bodyguards. "They're big as mountains."

"Don't think I can take care of myself?"

"They'll snap you like a twig."

"Probably right," he said. "I wouldn't stand a chance."

"Thank God," said Lucy, relaxing. "Can we go, then?"

"What about that case of bubbly?"

"I'm happy with a pint at the Dog and Duck."

"Really?"

"Really." Lucy nodded emphatically.

By now, Blatt was standing next to Lot 31, conversing with a slim blond man dressed immaculately in a dove-gray suit. The man was Alastair Quince, the evening's auctioneer and Sotheby's chief automotive expert.

"Let's take a closer look," said Simon.

"At Blatt?"

Simon smiled easily. "Forget Blatt. I mean the Ferrari. Might be the only chance we get to see one in person." It was a lie, but he needed Lucy relaxed. She had little experience in this line of work. It was essential she appear calm and at ease.

"Must we?" she asked, resisting the pull of his hand.

"We must," said Simon.

Blatt's arrival had drawn a crowd to the Ferrari, with more people arriving every moment. Simon maneuvered through the cluster of guests until he was standing behind Blatt's bodyguards. He formed a space for Lucy to join him, then tapped one on the shoulder. "Do you mind? The lady would like to take a closer look."

The bodyguard glared at Simon before catching a glance of Lucy. Simon squeezed her hand. As instructed, she smiled at him. The bodyguard's eyes widened and he rushed to clear a space for her. Simon followed close behind. Like that, he was standing next to Boris Blatt.

"But, Mr. Quince, we must fix your commission," Blatt was complaining heatedly to the auctioneer. "The seller is already paying you too much."

"Not if I do my job well," said Alastair Quince, shining and dapper and much too polished.

"Exactly my point," said Blatt. "To charge me another five percent on top…it is an insult."

Unconsciously, Simon tightened his fist into a ball and ran his thumb across the knuckles. In all manner of robbery, speed was essential. In pickpocketing, it was more than that. He had come to attempt something far more difficult than lifting a wallet.

"Alastair. Good to see you."

"Oh, Simon, hello. You here about this beauty?" Quince leaned forward to shake Simon's hand. The two knew each other in passing. A car restored by Simon's shop had sold for a handsome price. Still, it was apparent Quince wasn't pleased to be interrupted. "For a client, perhaps?"

"'Fraid not. Just wanted to take a closer look. I'll leave it for Mr. Blatt. Won't you introduce us?"

Quince forced a smile. "Boris Blatt. This is Simon Riske. He owns a small operation restoring Ferraris and Lamborghinis. Top quality workmanship."

Simon had his business card ready. "Not that this one needs any work," he said, then leaned closer to the car. "Though the paint on the hood appears a little spotty."

Ferraris in their original factory condition had a nasty reputation for shoddy paintwork. The men who'd designed and manufactured the cars in the 1960s had been concerned with speed and handling. Things like chassis fitting and paint had been of secondary importance.

"Really?" said Blatt, with more than a hint of outrage.

"Absolutely not," retorted Quince, his cheeks alarmingly flushed. "Mr. Blatt, I promise you…"

Blatt pushed past Simon to study the bodywork. For a second—less, even—shoulder brushed shoulder, arm brushed arm.

"No, no," said Simon, joining Blatt to look closely at the Ferrari. "I was mistaken. I apologize."

"You're certain?" asked Blatt. "Mr.—"

"Riske. And yes. I'm positive. A trick of the light." Simon threw the auctioneer a look. "Mr. Quince would never let a car get by with a run in the paint."

"I most certainly would not."

The public address announced that the auction would start in five minutes. The crowd around the Ferrari began to thin.

"Good luck, then," said Simon, leaning closer, putting his hand on Blatt's arm. "She's a beauty," he whispered, and Blatt leaned even closer. "But not a penny over twenty million."

Blatt stepped back and studied the business card. "American? Where from?"

"New York."

"I have friends there."

"Is that so?" Simon was quite sure he was acquainted with one or two.

"Maybe I call you," said Blatt, slipping the card into his jacket.

"Any time." Simon turned to leave and found himself staring at the chest of one of the bodyguards. *"Do you mind?"* he asked roughly, speaking a Muscovite's Russian.

Blatt uttered a command and the bodyguard moved aside.

Simon put his hand on the base of Lucy's spine. "Shall we?" he whispered, giving her a little shove.

"You speak Russian?" she asked.

"Just go."

Keeping the smile in his eyes, he steered Lucy away from Lot 31 and Boris Blatt. The light jazz piped in to foster a festive, sophisticated environment stopped playing. Guests headed toward the stage like a tide rushing back into the ocean. The mood shifted palpably. The time for small talk was past. A pall of nervous expectation filled the hall. Bidding on collectible automobiles was a serious business.

Simon carved a path toward the exit. It was a rule to put as much distance as possible between the mark and yourself. Should for any reason he be stopped and searched, he was in possession of stolen merchandise. Until he was clear of the building and had delivered the take to its rightful owner, he was a thief, and punishable as such.

Reaching the main doors, Simon stood aside as a last-minute rush of guests forced their way past. At that moment he saw Blatt take a seat in the front row, extend his left arm, and check the time.

"Leaving already? Mr. Riske, isn't it?" A hand touched his shoulder. Simon turned to see a member of the Sotheby's staff. Behind him stood a pair of security guards.

"We're not feeling well."

Lucy clutched her stomach. "Too much champagne, I'm afraid."

"I'm sorry," said the man from Sotheby's.

Simon had his eyes on Blatt, watching the Russian stand and gesture violently to a bodyguard, who rushed over. Words were exchanged.

"Dammit," whispered Simon, under his breath. "He noticed."

The bodyguard began to walk up the aisle. Toward Simon.

"What is it?" asked Lucy. "You've gone white as a sheet."

Simon didn't respond. The bodyguard was jogging now, his cheeks red. He raised a hand, signaling to him. Lucy turned and spotted the man approaching. "Simon," she said worriedly. "He's looking at you."

"Is he?"

The bodyguard came nearer, the crowd making room for him. He looked directly at Simon, then looked away and continued on another few steps, intercepting a server holding a tray of champagne. Hurriedly, he grabbed two flutes and returned to Blatt.

"Ready to go?" asked Simon as his heart recommenced beating. "I think we're done here."

A moment later, they were outside, cutting across the lawn to the parking lot.

"Did you get it?" asked Lucy.

"Keep walking," said Simon.

"But there were so many people."

"Exactly."

"But he didn't even—"

"Exactly."

"And you put the other one back on his wrist? How?"

"At one point in my life I had plenty of time on my hands and a very good teacher. That's enough about that."

They arrived at the car. Not a Ferrari. A Volkswagen Golf R model. It had more than enough power to get around London as fast as anyone was able. Maybe one day he'd buy himself a Ferrari. But not for a while. He had better uses for his money than a fancy automobile, no matter how much he loved them.

"Your chariot." He opened Lucy's door.

"A gentleman," she said, lingering a moment too long and a step too close.

"Lucy Brown, it's past your bedtime."

"What about my champagne?"

"Didn't you just say you've had too much?"

Simon stood aside. Lucy slid into her seat, slamming the door.

Simon rounded the car, pausing to slip the timepiece from his pocket. He held it so the moon glinted off the platinum case and illuminated its ivory-colored dial. The watch was a 1965 Patek Philippe perpetual calendar chronograph with moon phases. Value: three million dollars. A month earlier, a member of Boris Blatt's criminal organization had stolen it from a jeweler in the north of the city. Simon had been hired by the jeweler's insurance company to retrieve it.

Simon climbed behind the wheel and drove out of the parking lot. In moments, he was speeding beside the River Thames.

Three million for a watch.

Amazing what people would pay for things these days.

CHAPTER 3

Lloyd's of London, the world's preeminent insurance exchange, had its offices in a steel-and-glass skyscraper in the heart of the City, the one-square-mile district that was home to England's most powerful financial institutions. Late on a Sunday night, lights burned brightly on all floors. Insuring risk was a twenty-four-hours-a-day occupation.

Simon parked in the subterranean garage and showed his ID at the reception desk on the main floor. "Mr. Moore," he said, giving the name of his contact.

"Know the way, do you?" said the security guard.

Simon took an elevator to the eleventh floor. The door to the office was unlocked. He followed the scent of coffee and cigars to the end of the hall.

"Don't you sleep?"

D'Artagnan Moore sat at his desk, banging figures into his computer. "Did you get it?"

"And here I thought you were staying awake to make sure I got home all right."

"Well, did you?"

"You mean this?" Simon dropped the watch on the desk.

"Careful!" Moore scooped up the timepiece in his immense hands, appraising it before offering Simon a relieved look. "Of course I was worried about you. It's just that I was worried about this beauty more."

D'Artagnan Russell McKenzie Moore was a bear of a man, six and a half feet tall, three hundred pounds, with a mane of untamed hair and a black beard that had been neither groomed nor trimmed in years. As was his custom, Moore was dressed in a tweed hunting jacket over a cardigan vest. Simon had known him since the age of eight, when he'd lived with his father in the village of Royal Tunbridge Wells and the two boys had attended the same day school in Surrey. Simon's father, Anthony Riske, had come to London to set up a branch of his commodities-trading business. Moore, the son of minor nobility, went on to Harrow, Cambridge, and a stellar career in the insurance industry. Simon's path took him in a different direction.

"Still haven't told me where you learned the trade," said Moore, eyeing him from beneath a shaggy brow. "I don't imagine they taught you that at the LSE."

Simon smiled cryptically, then dropped into a chair across from the desk. "What are you going to tell your partners?"

"They know better than to ask. Discretion is the better part of profit." Moore slipped the watch into a beige jewel pouch and locked it in his desk. "Went well, did it?"

"To a point."

Moore's leonine head came to attention. "How so?"

"There was a second as I was leaving when I thought he might have noticed the switch. Not consciously, maybe, but by instinct. Guys like that have a sixth sense about this kind of thing."

"Takes one to know one."

"Are you saying I'm a thief?"

"Wouldn't dream of it," said Moore. "But he didn't… notice, I mean."

"No."

"Then none's the wiser. What's he going to do? Report it missing? By God, I've got friends at Scotland Yard who wish he would." Moore rose from his desk and poured two drinks from his sideboard. He handed a glass to Simon. "Health."

"Health." Simon swallowed the scotch in a single gulp.

"You Yanks," said Moore. "Think everything needs to be consumed at once. This isn't some cheap Tennessee sour mash. Sip it, lad."

"Laphroaig. Single malt."

"I'm impressed."

"You've told me a dozen times. And I'll take Jack any day."

"Cretin."

"And proud of it. How 'bout another?"

Moore brought the decanter to the desk and poured Simon another drink. "Talk. You're as nervous as a bull in a slaughterhouse."

"Just unsettled."

"Shop not doing well?"

"Pays for itself."

"And then some. We write insurance on automobiles, too, you know. The price of those Italian contraptions has gone through the roof of late."

"I restore them. I don't own them. There's overhead. Salaries. Parts are a fortune. I need to order a new dynamometer to test my engines. Thing costs fifty thousand pounds."

"Go back to private banking. I know a dozen shops would love to have you."

Simon looked around the office. He'd spent years toiling inside a plush coffin no different from this. In all, they were good years. Challenging, enriching, stimulating. He'd taken the job with an express purpose. He'd been tasked to find something. When he'd succeeded, he left.

He'd begun his career at twenty-seven, old for someone without an MBA. If anyone had been curious about the gap in his résumé between the ages of nineteen and twenty-three, they never said. They were too dazzled by his First from the London School of Economics and his medal for excellence in mathematics from the Sciences Po. And, anyway, by then they'd met him and that was enough.

Twelve-hour days had been common. Weekends, the norm. No one was more driven. But if Simon wore his ambition on his sleeve, he was the rare type whose motives were not in question. The bank's interests came first. His own, afterward.

His chosen field was private banking, catering to the investment needs of wealthy clients. His interest lay in helping people, building relationships, and instilling trust. It wasn't long before he was guiding clients in all aspects of their financial lives. He advised on art purchases, arranged for appraisals of jewelry, offered the bank's opinion on how much gold to keep in their vault and how much to keep at home.

And it was in these personal dealings that his special skills first became apparent. When a client suspected his son was falsifying his school's tuition bills and using the funds to purchase illicit drugs, Simon silently volunteered his help and within a week had the young man enrolled in a rehabilitation facility in Arizona and his dealer locked up in an interrogation room at Scotland Yard.

When another client suspected an employee was selling his company's proprietary technology to a rival, Simon asked (this time aloud) if he might look into the matter. A month later, the employee was arrested for industrial espionage while the business rival ponied up a generous settlement to avoid a lawsuit.

And when another let slip that his girlfriend had absconded with two million pounds sterling from his office vault and run away to Ibiza with a lover half his age, Simon took it upon himself to rectify the situation. In a short time, the money—or most of it—was back in his client's vault. Sadly, the girlfriend chose not to return.

Word of his uncanny ability to solve even the thorniest of problems spread rapidly. His mastery of language served him well. Besides his native English, he spoke French, Italian, Spanish, Russian, and a bit of Arabic. His clients often wondered if he'd spent time as a policeman or maybe a soldier or, pray tell, a spy—whatever that meant in this day and age. To which Simon had only laughed and said that their problems had not been as difficult to solve as they'd appeared and, really, anyone could have done it.

He had tendered his resignation without warning. Nothing the bank had offered could entice him to remain. He'd left them his private number and an offer to do what he could should a client have a special problem. That had been five years ago.

"Go back to the bank?" Simon downed the scotch and banged the glass onto Moore's desk. "Pass."

"Well, then, you have your investments," said D'Artagnan Moore. "Market's been doing nicely. You've always been a wiz."

"No complaints."

"What is it, then?"

Simon looked at Moore, at the dark eyes peering at him from beneath those impossibly tangled eyebrows. It was apparent Moore was sincere in his desire to help. Some things, however, Simon had learned were best kept to oneself. "Nothing," he said. "Just getting older."

"Aren't we all, lad? Aren't we all?" Moore produced an envelope from his top drawer and slid it across the table. "This should ease the pain. Go a ways toward buying that dyno…no—"

"Dynamometer."

"Gesundheit."

Simon slipped the envelope into his jacket pocket. "Nothing else on your desk that needs attention?"

"Not at the moment. Seems that all the cheats, crooks, and con men are away on holiday. Why not join them? Take a vacation. Spain. Portugal. Take a trip home."

"The States?"

"I hear Cape Cod is lovely. Take a lady friend. Man like you must have a string of them."

"Sure thing, D'Art," said Simon. "They're lined up in front of my flat." Three months had passed since his last relationship had ended. He was enjoying his status as a single male in a fast-paced, cosmopolitan city. He was in no hurry to change that. "Tell you what. I'll go if you go. Bachelors' road trip. Not Cape Cod. Ibiza. Saint-Tropez. You pick the spot."

Moore roared in delight. "Me in a bathing suit? God save us."

The two laughed a while longer. Moore stood and escorted him into the hall, a meaty arm laid across Simon's shoulder. "Relax, lad. I'm sure something will turn up. Until then, enjoy life."

Chapter 4

Tino Coluzzi drove rapidly through the forest, both hands on the wheel, face crowding the windscreen as he negotiated the single-lane road. It was crow-black. The canopy was so dense it denied the slightest light from the night sky. The track turned to the right and dropped. His stomach fell with it. Something large darted across his path. He braked. A shadow disappeared into the brush. A stag.

After leaving the highway at the village of Buchères, Coluzzi had cut his headlamps. The hills were filled with cabins belonging to hunters and those who'd simply withdrawn from society. He was anxious not to alert anyone about the Château Vaucluse's midnight visitor.

Another turn. The car shuddered as he crossed a barren stream. A dramatic incline and he was free of the forest. Stars appeared above a vista of rolling hills. He could see the château squatting on the hilltop a hundred meters ahead. It was a hulking structure with stone walls, narrow windows, and a slate roof. A local baron had built it as his hunting lodge two hun-

dred years earlier. For decades it had sat empty and
in disrepair. Coluzzi had picked it up at auction for a
song.

He crested the ridge and steered the car into the forecourt, breathing easier as the tires dug into the gravel
driveway. He continued through the archway and
parked in the garage, certain to immediately lower the
door behind him. Retrieving the case containing the
money and the prince's calfskin satchel, he crossed to
the main building. Before unlocking the servants' door,
he paused and closed his eyes to listen. All was still. Far
away an owl hooted. Then there was nothing but the
wind.

Inside, he carried the cases to the kitchen and, with
a grunt, threw them onto the island. The nearest house
was three kilometers away. Still, he moved from window to window, checking that the shutters were closed.
Only then did he turn on the lights.

He stared at the cases for a minute, then descended
to the cellar, picked out a decent Burgundy, and returned. He knew to a penny what was in one of the
cases. The contents of the second were a mystery.

He poured himself a glass of wine and drank it
slowly, pondering his dilemma. Stop now. Do as agreed.
Deliver the briefcase to the American, waiting for him
even now at a hotel in Fontainebleau. Don't ask any
questions and walk away. His cut was seventy percent.
Over four hundred thousand euros. For the next few
years, life would be easy.

The right course of action was plain to see.

And yet…why had he come to his château?

Coluzzi ran his hand over the smooth calfskin, tapping a manicured fingernail against the polished lock.
He was a thief. He could no sooner ignore the prince's

briefcase than he could leave an untended purse on a counter.

Setting down his wine, he went to work. Naturally, the case was locked and his set of picks nowhere at hand. With the help of a paper clip and a nail file, he freed the clasp, careful to leave the escutcheon unblemished. With the same care, he removed the case's contents. One Saudi diplomatic passport. Several files containing documents written in Arabic, and thus incomprehensible. A printout of an email from a "V. Borodin"—happily in English—with the header "Landing Instructions / Cyprus," giving the name of an airfield, coordinates, and radio frequencies. An envelope holding the bill from the hotel. Another overflowing with receipts cataloguing purchases made during the prince's stay. One copy of *The Economist*. One copy of *Paris Match*. One oversized business card on the finest stock in the name of "Madame Sophie," listing a phone number and an address in the 16th arrondissement, and redolent of costly perfume.

And, finally, another three packets of currency totaling thirty thousand euros. He thumbed the bills, considering whether to add them to the grand total to be split among his crew. The answer was a resounding "No." Finders keepers.

He studied the items on the table. Nothing appeared to be of value, though he was always pleased to learn the name of a high-class madame. There were no jewels, no bearer bonds, no plutonium, no secret formula for a nuclear bomb or for eternal youth. Nothing close to what his criminal mind had labored to imagine since taking the job.

Either the American was mistaken and something was missing or Coluzzi hadn't found it yet.

Certain it was the latter, he opened the briefcase and ran his fingers along its interior lining. No surgeon had a more delicate and perceptive touch. He found the hidden pouch without difficulty. He retrieved a flashlight from the pantry and shone it inside, running a thumbnail along the top seam. A spring mechanism opened an eight-inch pocket. He removed the manila envelope inside and withdrew the contents.

Five minutes later, he replaced them and returned the envelope to its hiding place.

Coluzzi had been right to recognize the cruelty in the prince's gaze. The papers he was carrying were correspondence between the FBI and the Saudi Arabian Mabahith, discussing the transfer of a prisoner from U.S. to Saudi detention.

The prince, it seemed, was the chief of his nation's secret police.

But surely the American knew this already. After all, he was some sort of spy himself. Such information did not warrant employing Coluzzi's services.

There had to be something else.

Coluzzi poured himself another glass of wine and waited for his heart to slow. There was nothing more hidden in the case's walls. He was sure of it. Therefore, it must be concealed in a false bottom. He pressed his fingertips around the perimeter, searching for a release. He picked up the case, studying it from each side, then from below. He decided the prince wasn't the sort to waste time searching for a hidden release mechanism. He set the briefcase back down on the counter and studied the lock. To open the case one had to first unlock it, then slide a circular nub to the left. He tried pushing the nub up, then down. Nothing happened.

Suddenly angry, he depressed the nub with his thumb. Harder still. He felt a catch. A tray slid from the base of the satchel.

Voilà!

Coluzzi pulled the tray all the way out. He viewed the contents and his heart sunk. A letter, he thought disappointedly as he took the envelope in his hands. It was small, square rather than rectangular, and unsealed. No name, but an address on the rear flap. Coluzzi was not an educated man in the traditional sense and it took him a moment to recognize the words embossed in blue ink.

"Really?" he whispered.

With care, he removed the paper inside and read the engraved header. Beneath it, in gold leaf, was a drawing of a structure he vaguely recognized.

"Dear Colonel," the note began.

The body of the letter was handwritten in neat, cursive script and ran to four sentences. On first reading, Coluzzi didn't grasp what might be so important as to warrant the chief of the Saudi Arabian secret police hiding it inside a briefcase or, for that matter, to induce a shadowy operator to offer a Corsican thief six hundred thousand euros to steal it. It was a thank-you note between two men. Nothing more.

Coluzzi read the note a second time, the names of both sender and recipient slowly registering. Anxiously, he picked up the envelope and studied the address inscribed on the rear flap to make sure he was getting all this correctly. His skin turned to gooseflesh.

No man should be in possession of this note, he told himself. Not the chief of the Saudi secret police. Not an

American spy who arranged meetings at luxury hotels. Most of all, not a lifelong bandit who'd been lying and stealing since he could say "Give me all of your money or else."

Seized by a sudden and irrational fear for his safety, Coluzzi slipped the letter back inside the envelope, replaced it in its hiding place, and dumped the rest of his wine in the sink. He was out the door seconds later.

Cases in hand, he returned to his car and, in minutes, was traveling at rapid speed through the forest. He was not a man who scared easily, but he was smart enough to know when he was in over his head. Experience had taught him that fear was the better part of self-preservation.

Yet even now he did not consider giving the American the briefcase.

Only when he reached the highway and joined the anonymity of his fellow late-night travelers did he breathe easier. He followed the signs south toward Beaune and Aix-en-Provence. He would not be safe in Paris. He was going where he could take sanctuary among his own kind. Corsicans. Thieves. Brigands. He was going home.

The drive calmed him, and before long, his natural, larcenous instincts asserted themselves. Others would come looking for the letter. This he knew. He had two choices. He could wait until they found him, in which case he would be a dead man, or he could find them first and make them a proposition.

Tino Coluzzi's fear vanished. In its place, he saw opportunity.

The letter was worth far more than six hundred thousand euros.

In the right hands, it was worth a million. Five million. Ten million euros, even.

And in the wrong hands?

Coluzzi smiled. In the wrong hands, it was invaluable.

CHAPTER 5

Nicosia, Cyprus

Another man was waiting to receive the letter Tino Coluzzi had found, but he was not American. He was Russian. Vassily Borodin stood like a sentry beside the landing strip, his face lifted to the sky. The plane was not due for another thirty minutes, but he preferred to stay out of doors, listening to the waves crash onto the rocky cliffs, enjoying the scent of the coastal scrub. Anything was better than remaining inside the waiting area with its wheezing air conditioner and ancient linoleum floor. The riches that his fellow Russians had brought to Cyprus had yet to make it to the northern side of the island. He allowed himself a look at his watch. It was nearly midnight. Four hours had passed since his last and only contact with the plane.

"There was a problem," the pilot had said. "A robbery."

"What do you mean 'a robbery'?"

"I don't know, sir."

"Let me speak to him."

"He doesn't want to talk to you."

After that, radio silence. By his own order.

A robbery. What the hell happened?

Borodin cursed his predicament, bloodless lips stretched taut across his teeth. It was unthinkable that in this day and age a man in his position could not communicate securely with whomever he pleased no matter his location. Yet such was the case. Technology had come full circle. There was no conversation he could conduct on his phone, his laptop, even his office computer in Moscow, that someone else—someone he did not know and might have reason to fear—might also be hearing. And he, Vassily Alexandrovich Borodin, director of the SVR—the Russian Foreign Intelligence Service—was as much responsible for it as anyone.

Tonight, of all nights, he could tolerate no risk.

"Sir! Come quickly! There's something you must see!" It was Kurtz, his deputy, standing outside the control shack, waving madly for him to return.

"All right," called Borodin, raising a hand to calm him down. Giving a look at the sky, he turned and walked toward the shack. He was a small man, barely five feet four inches tall, rail thin, with jet-black hair and a Mongol's high cheekbones and narrow eyes. Aware of his diminutive stature, he took pains to counter any impression of weakness. His posture was that of a ceremonial guard at Lenin's tomb. Spine rigid. Jaw raised to see over the horizon. When addressing a colleague, he looked him in the eye and gave him his complete attention, taking pains not to blink. He held his thoughts when others were eager to share their own. All these habits conspired to leave the impression of a secure, confident, and powerful man.

"The prince," shouted Kurtz. "A report about him is on television."

Borodin followed him inside. The control shed was small and squalid and reeked of burnt lamb. Kurtz and the others stood in a semicircle, gazing at an old television perched high on the wall while chattering incessantly. The television broadcast pictures of a line of black sedans he recognized to be somewhere in Paris.

"Silence," said Borodin.

The room quieted. With mounting despair, he listened to the reporter's account of the robbery targeting Prince Abdul Aziz of Saudi Arabia. At last he knew what the pilot had been referring to.

"Well," said Kurtz, when the report concluded. "What shall we do?"

Borodin offered his deputy an icy stare, then returned to his place alongside the runway.

In time, he spotted a pair of landing lights high in the sky. He followed them as they descended, and the prince's jet touched down, shooting past him to the end of the runway.

Minutes later, the jet parked. Stairs were wheeled to the fuselage. The door opened and the prince descended.

Borodin held his ground, making no effort to approach.

"It's gone," said the prince as he drew near.

"The news reported that it was your money that was stolen."

"They hijacked my car as well. My briefcase was inside."

"With the letter?"

"Yes."

Borodin considered this. For once, the prince was

not wearing his sunglasses, and Borodin noted that his eyes were red-rimmed and pouchy. The man looked as if he had been crying.

"I don't understand," he said with exaggerated care. "What do you mean they hijacked your car?"

"To get away."

"Didn't they arrive by car themselves?"

"My guess is that they didn't wish to move the money to save time. They were professionals."

"But the money was not in your car?"

"The car behind mine."

Borodin took this in. "And you had no indication they were interested in the letter?"

"None. It happened too quickly. One minute and they were gone."

"And you simply stood by and allowed them to take it?"

"Twelve men with machine guns. My men had pistols. What would you have done, my brave little friend?"

Borodin swallowed the insult as he'd swallowed a million like them before. He listened intently as the prince described the sequence of events. Afterward, he said, "It is apparent they observed you leaving the hotel. You said it was an ambush. But how did they know what route you would take to the airport?"

It was the prince's turn to remain quiet.

Borodin placed a hand on his shoulder and guided him onto the runway. The jet's engines whined softly as they spooled down. If anyone inquired, it was a refueling stop. No one had deplaned. No meeting between Prince Abdul Aziz bin Saud and Vassily Borodin ever took place.

They continued for a hundred meters, approaching the high cliffs that looked over the sea.

Borodin turned and faced the prince. "Who counseled you on which route to take to the airport?"

"I did not need any counsel. Paris is like a second home. I know the city like the back of my hand."

Borodin knew the city well, too. As a junior officer, he'd lived in the City of Light for three years. It was there that he was called upon to perform his first "wet work," assassinating an exiled oligarch with a loose tongue and opinions that cast an ill light on the government.

"Tell me," he asked. "Why did you decide to drive across the city instead of using the highway?"

"It is faster."

"Really?"

The prince nodded.

"And you told no one in advance about your chosen path?"

"My driver, of course."

"When?"

"Ten minutes prior to leaving the hotel."

Borodin considered this. In theory, there was just time for the chauffeur to have passed on the information to the thieves. It would have been close, but if everything went well, the thieves could have taken up position in time to intercept the prince.

He discarded the notion out of hand. It was evident the thieves were professionals. Whether the letter or the money was their priority, they would never have left something so crucial as the prince's route to the last minute.

The men continued their slow walk, stopping when the land fell away precipitously at their feet and the ocean crashed upon the rocks far below.

"There was someone else," added the prince.

Borodin turned to look at the handsome Saudi. *Of course there was someone else.*

"Delacroix. The hotel's chief of security. I discussed with him which route might be the quickest. I don't know if he suggested that we use surface streets or if it was me."

"When did this discussion take place?"

"Saturday."

"A day before you left."

"Delacroix is a friend," offered the prince with smug confidence. "I've known him for years. He is absolutely trustworthy."

Borodin nodded, as if in agreement. Never in his life had he met someone who was "absolutely trustworthy." He wondered what else the prince had discussed with Delacroix. There had long been rumors about the prince's sexuality. God knows what he might share with a lover, male or female. "The news says you left without speaking to anyone. Why didn't you stay and aid the police as best you could?"

"I am to see the king tomorrow morning. He does not tolerate cancellations."

"Of course." Borodin knew that there was more to it than that. Prince Abdul Aziz was afraid. Afraid that any time now the letter's theft would be discovered and he implicated in the crime. He put his hand on the prince's shoulder and drew him near. "You saw it?" he asked. "With your own eyes?"

Prince Abdul Aziz nodded and there was no mistaking the excitement in his eyes. "The paper stock matches a letter my grandfather received."

"You're certain?"

"Positive."

"And the handwriting?"

"Identical."

"I see." Borodin's voice betrayed no emotion, but behind his back he clenched his fingers into a triumphant fist. It was true, then. Everything he'd suspected for so long.

"I'll find whoever stole it," said the prince. "I have contacts with the French police."

"That won't be necessary."

"But you can't allow him to keep betraying your—"

"I will find it," said Borodin, more forcefully than he wished. "Or I won't. You've already done enough."

"What will you do?" asked Prince Abdul Aziz.

Borodin didn't reply. He turned and looked out over the cliff, over the dark, roiling mass that was the Mediterranean. For the first time that evening, he smiled, briefly, cryptically, and the prince smiled, too.

"Do you know," said Borodin, "that if you look very hard you can see the lights of Turkey."

The prince turned his gaze in the same direction, stepping nearer the precipice. "Not tonight."

"Ah yes." Borodin pointed to the north. "Just there."

"Really?" The prince narrowed his eyes, his neck craned as pebbles scattered from beneath his shoe and tumbled over the cliff. "I can't make them out."

"Sparkles, there and there. Surely you can see them."

The prince stared harder, shaking his head, patience waning.

"Perhaps you need to be a bit closer, my friend."

"Pardon me?"

Borodin put a hand in the lee of the prince's back and gave him a mighty shove. The prince lost his balance and put a foot forward. It found only air. He teetered, a hand reaching out for assistance. "Please…"

Borodin stepped back.

And then the prince was gone, his scream drowned by the wind and the tide.

Borodin retraced his steps down the runway, passing the jet without a sideways glance. His mind was on the letter and how he might get it back. He'd come too far to stop now. Wheels were turning. The intricate machinery he'd assembled these past months had been set in motion.

He threw open the door to the shack and signaled Kurtz to a corner. "I need to locate one of our agents. Top priority."

"Of course, General," said Kurtz. "Who?"

"Major Asanova."

Kurtz's sullen face took on an uneasy cast. "Major Asanova is no longer technically under our command. After the Dubai incident…"

"Where is she? I don't care if she's been reassigned. I require her services."

Kurtz frowned as if experiencing intestinal discomfort. "General, please. With all due respect. Let's not be hasty."

Borodin stood on his tiptoes and brought his face closer to Kurtz's. Close enough to see the beads of perspiration pooling on his lip. "I just asked the prince if he could see the lights of Turkey. Would you care to try?"

Kurtz looked out the open door toward the plane, which remained on the runway. Finally, he returned his gaze to Borodin and discerned in his expression what had happened. "No, sir," he replied with a violent shake of the head.

"Well, then."

"Berlin," said Kurtz. "H and I against the Americans."

"H and I" stood for "harass and intimidate," and

referred to provocative, often violent, measures taken to keep the American diplomats in a state of fear and apprehension, aware at all times that Russia was not a nation to be taken lightly.

"Call her at once," said Borodin. "Get her back to Moscow by the time we return."

"If I may remind the general, things did not turn out as neatly as planned the last time we engaged her services."

"Tell me, Ivan Ivanovich, did she fail to accomplish her objective?"

"No, sir. Not that. It's just that she…"

"What?"

"She tends to get a bit too…too…"

"Too…?"

"Involved," said Kurtz, spitting the word out as if it were a bone stuck in his gullet. "The woman doesn't know when to stop. She's reckless. I'm only thinking of you, General."

"Under our current circumstances, I'd prefer to use the word 'effective.'"

"'Effective,' then."

"That's precisely what I'm counting on." Borodin walked to the door and cast a backward glance at the foul room. "Berlin, eh? What the hell is she doing there?"

CHAPTER 6

The dark figure crept closer to the mansion, crawling expertly through the undergrowth. It was nearly eleven p.m., the sky cloudless, the moon overhead. From her position in the woods bordering the home, Valentina Asanova, a fifteen-year veteran of Directorate S, Department 9 of the SVR—currently on enforced segregation—surveyed the property. Am Grossen Wannsee 42 was an old imposing mansion built on the western shores of Lake Wannsee, an inlet of the Havel River twenty-five kilometers from central Berlin. A guardhouse stood at the entry to a long curving drive-way, manned twenty-four hours a day by plainclothes United States Marines. A mesh fence enclosed the grounds, topped by a double strand of razor-sharp concertina wire. At the back of the house a dock extended into the water, a handsome motorboat moored at its end. Here, too, an armed sentry stood guard, his silhouette visible as he paced back and forth. The home's current resident was the Honorable Thomas Pickering, the United States ambassador to the Federal Republic of Germany, and his wife, Barbara.

Valentina edged forward until her hands touched the lawn that ran to the forest's end and she enjoyed an unencumbered view of the home. She was thirty-eight years old, trim and athletic, clad only in tight shorts and a black tank top, a watch cap concealing her hair, and bootblack on her face. Few lights burned from the upper floors. The grounds were quiet, almost too still. At the moment, the ambassador was away, attending a ball at the Hotel Adlon at the foot of the Brandenburg Gate, celebrating the end of the G20 summit. It was the first time in twenty years Russia had not been invited to the meeting of the West's largest economic powers.

Valentina had been sent to give voice to her government's displeasure.

Crouching, she dashed to the fence, throwing a compact black bag over the top. Even before it landed she was loping down the slope to the lake. She waded into the water and swam out past the final fence post, her head barely above the waterline. The guard on the dock faced away from her, smoking a cigarette against regulations.

Valentina emerged from the lake, silently and with purpose, and skittered up the gentle grade to retrieve her bag. Lying flat, she pulled on black leggings and a skintight, long-sleeved tunic. On her feet, she wore crepe-soled shoes, soundless on any surface. She secured her tool belt around her waist. Two items remained in the bag: a Taser set to twenty thousand volts and a knife. Both were to be used only in emergencies.

Keeping low, she continued to the side of the house. The walls were built of rectangular stone blocks, deeply carved grooves separating them. Using her fingers, she scaled the wall to the first floor and vaulted onto a spacious balcony. She remained still long enough for her heart to slow, her eyes on the sentry, checking that he had not registered her presence.

French doors leading to the master bedroom were secured. She selected a pick and jimmied the lock. A minute later, she was standing inside the ambassador's home.

Valentina had not come to steal. Her mission was of another nature: to harass and intimidate.

She started in the bathroom. She dumped Madam Ambassador's perfume in the toilet and emptied her medications on the floor. She snapped a pearl hair comb in two. Finding an appropriately violent shade of lipstick, she wrote "Die Americans" on the mirror. Coarse, perhaps, but frightening enough.

She continued her work in the closet, slashing dresses with a pair of scissors and throwing them into a heap on the floor.

Returning to the bedroom, she spent fifteen minutes rearranging the furniture. She dragged a pair of Louis XV chairs from one corner of the room to another. She spilled books off their shelves onto the floor. She tore the comforter and sheets off the bed. She rehung the paintings upside down. She placed bedside water glasses in a towel, stomped on them, then spread the shards over the parquet floor.

Moving across the hall to the ambassador's study, she caught the wash of headlights that swept across the driveway and illuminated the grand foyer. She heard a car door slam. Footsteps crunching on the gravel drive. The front door opened. Voices echoed from the grand foyer.

She froze. Her heartbeat did not accelerate. Her blood pressure did not rise. If anything, she grew calmer, oddly excited by the slip-up in her briefing. It came to her that she might have a chance to do something more than deliver a minor fright.

"Did you hear what that Dutch prick Van der Miede said about the president?" A man's baritone voice. The ambassador. "The gall. Has he forgotten I'm a political appointee?"

"Oh, darling, I think he was rather drunk."

"Listen, I have to send State a summary of the dinner. I'll be ten minutes."

"I'll be waiting, dear. You got me started in the car."

"Why you," said the ambassador, laughing lustily. "Make that eight minutes."

Footsteps climbed the staircase.

Valentina retreated into the bedroom. She searched the room for a place to hide, a spot to guarantee complete surprise. Her eyes moved from the furniture to the narrow entry hall. Placing a foot on each wall, she stemmed to the ceiling, positioning herself flat against it, hands on one wall, feet on the other.

She listened as the ambassador's wife approached, hearing the rustle of her dress, a faint humming of a popular tune. The woman passed beneath her and Valentina dropped to the floor. Feeling the vibration, the woman turned. Her eyes opened in surprise. Before she could speak, Valentina slugged her in the jaw, an uppercut delivered with all her force, fracturing the mandible, breaking several teeth, and knocking the woman unconscious.

Valentina caught her before she collapsed and was careful to lay her down away from the broken glass. She slid the knife from its sheath and, kneeling closer, carved two words into the woman's forehead, the tip of the blade dragging against the skull. Six letters that would deliver her master's message more eloquently than any speech or discourse.

"Honey," called the ambassador from his study. "Don't go to sleep. I'll be right there."

Valentina walked to the French doors and lowered herself from the balcony, dropping to the lawn. The sentry remained with his back turned at his post on the dock, twenty meters distant. She slid into the cool water and, when she was fifty meters from shore, removed her belt and shoes and allowed them to sink to the muddy lake bed. She looked once more at the house before swimming across the lake to where a car awaited.

She did not hear the ambassador's anguished cry when he discovered his wife a few minutes later. It would only be when he cleaned her wounds that Valentina's message would be read and the purpose of her late-night visit communicated.

The six letters read *"Yeb vas."*

Fuck off.

CHAPTER 7

The sign read EUROPEAN AUTOMOTIVE REPAIR AND RESTORATION. It was past eleven and Kimber Road in southwest London was quiet. No lights burned in the reception as Simon continued past his shop and turned into an alley leading to the work entrance. He parked the VW in a lot surrounded by tall fencing and barbed wire. The fence wasn't for his car. It was for the Ferraris parked next to it—valued at over a million pounds each—waiting to begin restoration.

Inside, he turned on an overhead light and crossed the shop floor. There were six cars being restored at the moment. Five Ferraris and a Lamborghini Miura. He snaked his way through them, taking note where each stood in its renovation. One was nearing final inspection after eighteen months' labor, paint sparkling, tires gleaming, prettier than the day it had left the factory. Another was well along the way, a new interior installed, covered with protective plastic, its hood open, the engine compartment empty and awaiting its rebuilt motor. Another had only just begun its journey, its doors removed, interior yanked out, paint stripped. A husk of an automobile.

Simon's team did nearly all the work themselves. They rebuilt the engines, cleaning each and every component, discarding faulty pieces, and machining new parts as needed. They pounded out the chassis, installed new suspension and exhaust, bringing the automobiles up to the most demanding modern standards. Even the painting was done on the premises in a sealed-off workshop adjacent to the main floor. Only the leatherwork—seats, dash, ragtops—was subcontracted to a shop in Sussex. They were mechanics, not tailors.

Reaching the far side of the floor, he unlocked an unmarked door and ran up the stairs to his flat. A second door guarded entry, this one steel, bulletproof, and secured by twin deadbolt locks. He wasn't paranoid, just "properly security conscious," as the policeman who'd suggested the new setup termed it after arresting an unwanted midnight guest for attempted murder.

The flat was large and airy, sparsely furnished with sleek, modern pieces; no walls separated living spaces, except the bedroom. Vintage posters advertising the 24 Hours of Le Mans and the Grand Prix de Monaco decorated the walls. There was a picture of Steve McQueen, leaning against his famous Ford Mustang, and another of Carroll Shelby, the legendary American automaker going face-to-face with Enzo Ferrari, his even more legendary Italian counterpart. Lining the wall to his bedroom were seven large black-and-white photographs. Each showed a stone sculpture of a man set into the recess of a tall, formidable rock-and-mortar wall. Each figure was depicted in an uncomfortable, contorted position made to represent one of the seven deadly sins. Pride, envy, wrath, sloth, greed, lust, and gluttony, in no particular order. He wasn't a fan of the sculptures. In fact, he found them so ugly as to be hard to look at. The pictures were a reminder. Not of his weaknesses or any character defect, but of the grim landmark where the sculptures stood.

In the kitchen, he cracked open a bottle of mineral water and drank half of it down. It was late. He knew he should go to sleep, but the night's work was fresh in his mind. Time and again, he replayed his actions. The deft approach, shoulder brushing shoulder, one hand tapping the Russian's forearm, distracting him, the other slipping inside the shirtsleeve, unclasping the deployment buckle, guiding the watch off his wrist. And then—in a motion so fast the naked eye would have been challenged to see it—replacing it with the counterfeit. A dozen tactile sensations, each imprinted on his mind. A precisely choreographed motion completed in the blink of an eye while Boris Blatt himself felt nothing.

Three hours after the fact and two scotches for the better, Simon was still jacked up, dancing on broken glass. With a sigh, he collapsed onto his sofa and turned on the television. Sky News was showing highlights of the day's football matches. He watched for a few minutes, only half paying attention. He'd lived in London a long while but he'd yet to form an attachment to any particular team. His loyalty would forever lie with Olympique de Marseille, a team playing in the French premier league from the city where he'd gone to live after his father's death.

Marseille.

Heat. Dust. The scent of the sea. The mistral sweeping off the ocean, swirling through the alleys in the hills above the city where he'd lived. The perpetual buzz of a city on the make, a city where violence crouched hidden beneath the surface, ready to spring at any time. A city on edge.

"Once again, our top story. There has been a daring robbery in the streets of Paris this evening by a band of professional thieves wielding automatic weapons."

Simon reached for the remote and turned up the volume.

"Initial reports indicate that the team of twelve armed bandits hijacked a convoy of vehicles carrying a Saudi prince and his family to the airport and made off with over five hundred thousand euros."

Simon scooted to the edge of the couch, studying the images of the boulevard in Paris, listening to one of the livery drivers describe the incident.

"Ils avaient tous des mitrailleuses et portaient des masques. Nous avions tous peur."

They all carried machine guns and wore masks. We were all afraid.

The camera moved back to the reporter. "It appears the bandits blocked the street and surrounded the trapped vehicles, making off with their take in a short time. Amazingly, no shots were fired. No one was injured."

When the report ended, Simon realized he hadn't taken a breath the entire time. First the job at the Sotheby's auction, now this.

Agitated, he rose and walked to his bedroom. He took off his suit, hung it up with care, taking time to dust the shoulders and lapels with a mohair brush. Finished, he threw his shirt in the hamper and returned his shoes to the rack.

A pull-up bar was bolted to the ceiling at the back of his closet. With a grunt, he grabbed hold of it and did fifteen chin-ups, then hung for a few seconds, feeling his shoulders burn, his biceps strain under his weight, his stomach grow taut. And when he couldn't hang a second longer, when his fingers began slipping off the bar, he summoned the strength to grip it tighter and knock out five more.

"I can," he grunted with each repetition. And then: "I will."

Four words he'd adopted as his creed a lifetime ago.

He dropped, savoring the rush of blood to his arms, the hard-won lightheadedness, the victory, however fleeting, of mind over body.

I can.

I will.

Winded but still antsy, he pulled on a T-shirt and jeans and returned to the living room. He switched the channel to BBC 2, only to be confronted with another report about the robbery in Paris. He shook his head in frustration but listened nonetheless, like a child made to sit through a lecture he'd heard before. He turned off the television the moment it ended.

There would be no sleeping for a while.

He knew of only one salve for what ailed him. Work.

Back in the garage, he hit the lights. A dozen floods lit up the floor as if it were high noon. Already feeling better, he walked to his office. In its prior incarnation, the shop had been a posh nightclub managed by a hood who'd been skimming twenty percent off the top and cooking the books. Simon had been hired by the investors to obtain the real ledgers. He'd traded his success fee for the lease on the building, making sure the deal included the sound system, lock, stock, and barrel.

He opened the audio cabinet and punched in a playlist. The growl of an electric guitar reverberated across the floor. Marc Bolan and T. Rex. The seventies.

Rock 'n' roll at its wildest. Raw. Primal. He cranked the volume, then went onto the floor and surveyed his small Italian dukedom.

The latest arrival was a '74 Daytona Spider set for full restoration. His father had owned a car identical to this: *corsa* red, beige leather, wire-spoked rims. He'd called it his "stallion," after the rampant horse that decorated the badge on the hood.

Simon slid into the driver's seat and placed his hands on the wheel, fingertips brushing the polished wood. He'd done the same thing hundreds of times as a child when his father was away on business and he'd been left alone with Abigail, the bibulous housekeeper. He was eight or nine, the age when cars are objects of awe and worship, emblematic of all things sophisticated and mature. All things adult, and thus off-limits.

He remembered the scent of the old garage: damp hay, oiled leather, rotting rafters. They'd come to England from New York to open the European office of Riske Commodities Trading Corporation, a firm his father had started from an office in Lower Manhattan, and which at its peak included branches in Boston, Chicago, and San Francisco.

The divorce had been far in the past. All he'd known of his mother was that she lived in France and had a new family of her own. It had been just the two of them, Anthony Riske and his son. They'd lived in a rambling country house in Kent, forty miles outside London. Even now, Simon had little idea what his father had done for a living. He recalled talk of gold and silver and oil, and howls of protest about prices being too low or too high.

Sundays had been reserved for excursions into the city and surrounding countryside. Visits to the Natural

History Museum and Covent Garden, lunches at the Compleat Angler. Invariably, on the way home, his father would stop the car on a country road, drag Simon onto his lap, and teach him to drive, goosing the motor to make his son squeal with delight.

"Twelve cylinders with a dual six. That's not an engine. It's a force of nature. You can feel it in your bones."

And when Simon asked when he might drive by himself, his father would pat him on the head and answer in his rich, tobacco-cured voice, "In due time. In due time."

The downfall, when it came, was swift, brutal, and without warning.

One day all was fine. The next, Simon was pulled out of school, the house put up for sale, and the housekeeper, nannies, and gardener let go. The cars were loaded onto trailers and driven away by men in blue jackets with a half-dozen policemen watching. All the while, his father stalked the empty house promising that it was all a misunderstanding, a "temporary problem of liquidity," and that he was going to make it up to him.

"In due time. In due time."

It was Simon who discovered the body. His father had not come down to breakfast after failing to tuck him in the night before. Hungry and frightened, he'd searched the house, calling for his father, before venturing outside and padding barefooted through the damp rose garden. With every step, his worry grew. Something was wrong. Terribly wrong.

He found his father in the garage hanging from a rafter. Simon was twelve but small for his age. He rushed to his father, wrapping his arms around his legs, trying with all his might to lift him, hoping to relieve the pressure even a little so the rope would stop digging into his neck and maybe his father's eyes wouldn't bulge so horribly.

If there was a note, no one found it.

For years Simon was certain that it had just been overlooked. At night, lying in his bed in the cramped, unhappy home in the hills above Marseille, he imagined what his father had written to him. Something about Simon being strong enough to go on, and him being sorry, that there had been no other way out, and that surely Simon would understand.

"In due time."

Simon fought off the memories and climbed out of the car. He left the main floor and entered an adjacent studio, passing through a plastic curtain to reach the paint room. A black Dino, a '74 or '75, sat in the bay, waiting to be stripped.

Simon opened a locker and donned a paint-smeared coverall. Grabbing a heat gun and a scraper, he went to work, starting on the hood, holding the gun inches away until the paint began to curdle and he could scrape it off. He worked in columns, inch by inch, slowly, meticulously. The job demanded muscle and concentration. Soon his shoulders ached and sweat ran from his forehead.

They all carried machine guns and wore masks, the witness to the robbery in Paris had said.

The images from the news had stirred things up as surely as a stick prodding a hornet's nest. There were things he didn't want to remember. Events dangerous to recall for the emotions they provoked, the long-buried desires they stoked. The memories came to him all the same, as he knew they would ever since lifting the watch off Boris Blatt's wrist.

He imagined the report of his old AK-47, the reassuring kick of the machine gun pressed to his shoulder, the wonderful, bittersweet scent of spent cordite in the warm air. Mostly, though, he recalled the thrill of it all.

Twenty years later, he could still taste it.

"Damn!" Simon called out as the scraper slipped and nicked his thumb. He stepped away from the car, shaking his hand, wiping the blood on his pant leg. He found a plaster in the locker and bandaged the cut. His eye fell to his forearm and the artwork on it. Some tattoos faded over time. For some reason his appeared to have grown brighter.

The past isn't dead. It isn't even past.

Someone famous had said that. An American writer. He didn't remember the name. He only knew that it was true.

Monday

CHAPTER 8

It was nine the next morning when Lucy Brown parted the curtain and stepped into the painting studio. "Someone to see you."

With rapt attention, Simon guided the scraper in a vertical stripe down the automobile's hood, the shavings falling away in a curlicue. "Client?"

"Never seen him before."

"Did he bring his car?"

"Just an umbrella."

"There," said Simon, stepping back and surveying his progress. After ten hours, he'd managed to strip the entire hood. Another week and the car would be finished, though he had no intention of completing it himself. Sometimes he had to remind himself that he was the boss. He rolled his neck, wincing as his bones cracked. Only then did he look at Lucy. "Does he have a name?"

"Mr. Neill. He said he was a friend of a friend. Oh, and he's one of yours."

"Mine?"

"American."

"Where is he?"

"In the workshop. He seemed to know his way round."

"Is he touching any of the cars?"

"No. Hands in his pockets."

Simon considered this. "Tell him I'll be there in a minute. Give him some tea."

Lucy nodded. But instead of leaving, she stepped through the curtain and crossed the studio toward him. She was unrecognizable from the night before. The pencil skirt and fitted blouse had been replaced by a gray coverall with the name "Max" sewn on the breast and sensible work boots. Her blond hair was pulled into a ponytail and tucked into a baseball cap. Her only concession to makeup was the streak of grease decorating her cheek.

"What is it?" asked Simon, noting the look on her face.

"You're not going to see him like that?"

"Like what?"

Lucy pointed to a mirror. Simon turned and caught a glimpse of himself. His coverall was stained with sweat. His face was red from exertion and his hands were blackened by paint shavings. "Were you up all night again?" she asked.

"Me? No. Course not. I got up early. Wanted to get a start on the week."

Lucy cocked her head. "Is that right?"

Simon put his hands on Lucy's shoulders, turned her around, and walked her back to the curtain. He wasn't interested in sharing his losing battle against insomnia with Lucy or anyone else. "Tell Mr. Neill I'll be there in fifteen minutes."

Simon returned to his flat. He showered, cleaning

his hands and nails with a scrub brush and industrial soap, then dressed in his real work clothes. Navy suit, white open-collar shirt, and loafers shined within an inch of their lives. Exactly fifteen minutes later, he was at his desk. He spun in his chair to study the monitor that broadcast feeds from the security cameras. He quickly spotted his mechanics, but he couldn't find the visitor. This disturbed him. He'd supervised the placement of the cameras to ensure that every square foot of the shop was covered. A look at the agenda showed no mention of an appointment for an American named "Neill." It was rare to get walk-in visitors. A second look at the monitor failed once again to find him.

There was a knock at the door. "Come."

Lucy opened the door. "Mr. Neill to see you."

Simon rose and came around the desk as the impromptu visitor entered the room.

"Mr. Riske, my name's Barnaby Neill. I'm a friend of Bill Shea's."

The handshake was firm and forthright.

"Ambassador Shea?"

"We go back a long way."

Lucy remained at the door, studying Neill. At some point in the past few months she'd appointed herself his guardian.

"Thank you, Miss Brown," said Simon. And when she lingered: "Off you go."

The door closed. Simon appraised the visitor. Barnaby Neill was lanky, fifty or fifty-five, with receding hair and rings beneath his eyes as black as coal. A worn, reliable face with a nose that had been broken. Married. College ring. Blue blazer. Rep tie. Gray trousers. Scuffed penny loafers. Hamilton wristwatch on a leather strap.

Simon did the math.

East Coast establishment.

Old money.

Friend of the U.S. ambassador to Great Britain.

Spy.

"You're with?" asked Simon.

"Same family as Ambassador Shea. Different branch."

Simon nodded to show that he got the picture.

Neill motioned toward the door. "Mind if we take a walk?"

"It's raining."

"I prefer the outdoors."

Of course he did, thought Simon. "Suit yourself. Give me a minute."

"I'll be outside."

On the way to the front door, Simon grabbed an umbrella from the stand. Lucy was hovering nearby, eyes following Neill. "Who's he, then?"

"Just a guy that wants to talk to me. Why?"

"Reminds me of the undertaker who took care of my brother."

"You don't like him?"

"He's fine, I suppose. I just had a strange feeling when I saw him."

Simon opened the door. Rain fell in sheets ricocheting off the pavement. He had no desire to leave his office to speak with a spook named Neill. He looked at Lucy and remembered something. "Stay here." He doubled back to his desk and returned with a sealed envelope. "Your fee for last night."

Lucy opened the envelope. "A thousand quid," she said, a hand rising to catch her falling jaw.

"You did a good job. Kept your cool. It was a big help."

"It's too much."

Simon took her by the arms. "Put it in the bank. No spending it on anything you shouldn't. Promise?"

Lucy met his eyes. "Promise."

"And remember...not a word."

Lucy rose onto her toes and kissed him on the cheek. "Thank you, Simon."

"Get to work on the Dino. I got it started for you last night." Simon opened the umbrella and ventured into the rain. He looked to his right and left, but his visitor was nowhere to be seen. "Mr. Neill!" he called.

The sidewalk was empty.

Simon started up the road toward Singh's Café. Ten steps and rain was sluicing onto his shoulder and dribbling down the back of his neck. "Mr. Neill?"

And then, out of nowhere, Neill was at his side.

Simon tried not to appear startled. "Happy?" he asked, bunching his shoulders to fit under the umbrella.

"Necessary precautions."

The two walked west along Kimber Road. The few pedestrians foolish enough to be out in the rain hurried past them without a glance. Simon kept close to the storefronts as much for the protection any awning might offer as to avoid being inundated by passing vehicles.

"How did you get into the car business?" asked Neill pleasantly. "I understand you were in finance. Royal Bank of Albion, was it?"

"Something like that." Simon wasn't about to go into his history. "You mentioned Ambassador Shea."

"We served in the marines together. Afterward, he went to State. I took a job in a more interesting field."

"My work for the embassy is strictly of a commercial nature," said Simon. "Helping out U.S. multinationals, handling contract disputes, gathering evidence to assist in background checks."

"The word is that you're resourceful."

"I'm sure your colleagues have me beat hands down."

"Sometimes a certain distance is required."

Simon drew up. He didn't like the direction in which the conversation was headed. He was a man who dealt in realities, not suppositions. "I'm sorry you had to come all this way, but I think you've got the wrong man."

"I haven't mentioned the job yet."

"Let me be clear. I apologize in advance if I'm rude. I don't work for people like you."

"Like me? In what way?"

"I prefer clients whose names match what's on their birth certificates."

"You might want to restate that."

"Excuse me?"

"You've done work for at least two U.S. intelligence agencies in the past."

"You're misinformed."

"Maybe some of the clients the embassy referred to you weren't as honest as I am."

Simon's mood darkened. The keeping out of camera view in his workshop. The paranoia about conducting their discussion indoors. He was not a man who liked games. "Goodbye, Mr. Neill."

He turned around and headed back to the shop. The pallid American was at his side a moment later. "Catch the news last night? The heist in Paris? The Saudi prince who had half a million euros stolen from his motorcade."

Simon walked faster. "I don't recall."

"Witnesses said the thieves only needed a minute to get the job done. I wanted to ask you about it."

Simon stopped. His shoes felt like he'd been stomping in puddles and his jacket was soaked. But neither the rain nor the damp had anything to do with the sudden blast of cold that had taken him in its grip. "Like I said, I don't recall."

Neill fixed him with a damning look. "Is that so? Because I'm curious as to how you would have handled that job."

"Pardon?"

"In Marseille. Back in the day."

Neill grasped Simon's left arm and slid back the jacket. With a titanium grip, he twisted Simon's forearm so that his tattoo was in full view. It showed an anchor held by a grinning skeleton and surrounded by crashing waves. Intertwined were the words *"La Brise de Mer."* The ocean breeze. It was a tattoo given to members of the Corsican mafia that ruled the South of France.

"The thieves who did the job were from your old stomping ground. I know because I put them on to it. Problem is they didn't just take the money. They took something that belongs to us, and by us, I mean the United States government. Something important. I am asking you to get it back."

Chapter 9

"Here's how things stand," said Neill. "I want to be as straightforward as I can, but I can only go so far. Some elements I just can't reveal."

The two men sat across from each other at the kitchen table in Simon's flat. Simon sipped from a mug of tea. Neill had asked for a fernet to calm a "touchy tummy."

A call to Ambassador Shea had confirmed Neill's status as a high-ranking officer attached to an unnamed but well-regarded intelligence shop, some ultra-secret cousin of the CIA. Still, Simon was not entirely sure why he'd decided to hear Neill out when his every instinct screamed to run the other way. Was it Neill's mysterious knowledge of Simon's long-buried past? Or the flattery of being handpicked to carry out an important assignment on behalf of his nation's government? Or was it something else still?

"It's my experience that it's better to know everything up front," said Simon. "Even then, there's always something that pops up to surprise you."

"I'll tell you everything you need to do the job. Frankly, there's only so much you'll want to know."

"I'm glad you're looking out for me."

Simon wasn't simply bored, as he'd conveyed to D'Artagnan Moore. The affair with Boris Blatt had stirred up something lurking inside him. A desire for trouble he'd kept tamped down for too many years. Even now, he could feel his fingers slipping the watch off the Russian's wrist, the rush of superiority that came with breaking the law, the anarchic joy of breaking the rules.

And so, with his darker appetites whetted, his discipline flagging, along came Neill, offering a gold-plated, government-sponsored invitation to revisit his outlaw past.

"A week ago we became aware of a theft from CIA archives in Langley," Neill said. "Before we could apprehend the thief, he was able to pass what he'd stolen to parties unfriendly to the cause."

"In this case?"

"Prince Abdul Aziz bin Saud."

"The target of the heist in Paris?"

"One and the same. What you don't know is that Prince Abdul is chief of his country's domestic intelligence agency, the Mabahith. They're a tough group. Shoot first, ask questions later. Follow?"

Simon nodded and drank his tea. He decided to let Neill speak his piece and ask questions afterward.

"You're a smart guy," Neill went on. "I know you're thinking 'Saudi Arabia's our ally. What's a member of their royal family doing accepting stolen top secret materials, and by doing so, engaging in de facto espionage against the United States?' And you're right. But we're talking the Middle East. Everyone's got conflicted loyalties. Not a person over there who doesn't keep two masks in his dresser, if not three. Prince Abdul's been an America hater since way back. Don't ask me why. It doesn't matter. He probably doesn't remember himself. Anyway, he comes to Washington once a year, makes the rounds, shakes our hands, takes our intel, then goes home and dreams up ways of screwing us. I'm not saying he does a bad job for his own people. He's actually a crackerjack cop. He's broken up a dozen rings of extremists in Saudi. You can see how our hands are tied." Neill paused, drawing a world-weary breath. "But this time he went too far. He got ahold of something we can't allow him to pass on. Just the fact that he's become privy to this material is giving everyone back home a nervous tummy." Neill picked up his glass of fernet and drank down the last drops. "Present company included."

"Another?" Simon asked as he poured himself more tea.

"Tea's fine. I'm already feeling better." Neill smiled. "You don't have anything to eat, do you?"

Simon found a box of biscuits from Fortnum's in the cupboard, arranged them on a plate, and set them down in front of Neill along with a clean mug. He'd been in London too long. Proper manners and all that. To his credit, he made Neill pour his own tea.

"Which brings us to the heist," Neill continued, putting down the mug and leaning across the table. "We had to move fast and we had to cover our tracks. Sure we have plenty of resourceful men and women on payroll, but the nut of this is that we can't use them. Our position is that the missing item does not exist. Not only can we not admit that it was stolen from our archives, we can't be seen to make any effort to retrieve it. I have some contacts with French intelligence. I mentioned I had a hush-hush job I needed done—no unnecessary details—and they steered me to the Corsicans. Since your day they've moved north. Paris is their territory as much as Marseille. I met with one of their capos and let him know about the prince's habit of traveling with ungodly sums of cash. He didn't need more prodding. All I wanted in exchange were the prince's private belongings, especially a briefcase he carries all his confidential information in. We know about the case because we had it custom made to his specifications two years ago. Can't x-ray it. Secret compartments. Some other nifty stuff that makes him feel like James Bond. Anything for an ally. Follow?"

Simon nodded. If anything, he was following too closely and not liking what he was learning.

"Anyhow," said Neill, "the job went down perfectly. No one got hurt. Our guy got away scot-free. As far as anyone's concerned, it was all about the money."

"But?"

Neill smiled bitterly. "But our guy decided to get smart. The plan was for us to meet up last night. Hand over the case. Go our separate ways. Our guy never showed."

"And so you're here?"

"With open hands. We need your help."

Simon dipped his biscuit in his tea. He noted that the spy's skin had a translucent quality. A slight tic disturbed his right eye. "Quick decision. I mean, to contact me."

"Like I said, you'd come to our attention before."

"Apparently."

"Any questions?"

"Just one. What's in the case?"

"Something important to the ongoing security of the United States."

"That's not going to cut it."

"Fine," said Neill. "A letter."

"We're making progress. A letter stolen from the CIA's archives and passed on to a closet enemy of the United States. A letter that's crucial to the security of our country yet so secret we can't appear to want it back."

"That's right."

Simon finished his biscuit. "I'm going to need more than that."

"Best I can do."

Simon wiped his mouth and tossed the napkin on the table. So much for manners. "Tell me this: Prince Abdul Aziz...what did he plan on doing with this letter?"

"I'll let you figure that out."

"Turn it over to the enemy," said Simon. "The *real* enemy. That narrows it down to a few thousand choices."

"None of that matters," said Neill with a dismissive wave of his hand.

"Of course it matters," retorted Simon. "If this letter is all you say, you're not the only one who wants it. For starters, I imagine the prince is upset it was stolen. He'll be looking for it. And so is whomever he planned to give it to. They'll be looking for it, too. And we haven't even gotten to the Corsicans. There's a reason your man missed the meeting. He found the letter. He knows all of you guys want it back. He's going to wait a few days, let everyone get hot and bothered, then sell it to the highest bidder."

"I was told you were a quick study."

"I'd damn sure have something in mind if I were going to screw the United States government."

Simon slid his chair back from the table and stood. A weight had lifted from his shoulders. He no longer felt so eager to feed his personal demons. He might be "resourceful," as Neill had put it, but he was not interested in getting involved in a matter of this magnitude. He was no expert on espionage, but even a casual reader of the news knew that things often ended badly for all concerned. Stealing a watch was one thing; stealing national secrets was another.

"Excuse me," said Neill with concern. "I don't believe we've finished."

"I'm flattered you think I'm the man for this job. There are plenty of others who left La Brise. You don't need me."

"No Americans. Certainly no one we can even begin to trust."

"I'm sorry."

Neill stood and followed Simon into the den. "I'm authorized to offer you one hundred thousand dollars. Tax-free in an account of your choosing."

Simon buttoned his jacket. He frowned, noting that his sleeves were still uncomfortably damp. "Mr. Neill, the Corsicans aren't just going to give me the letter, provided I can track it down. It's going to get ugly. It always does with them. Pay what they ask. It's the easiest way."

Neill took the suggestion as an affront. "You think they'll stop there? What if they make a copy and sell that to the other side? No, Mr. Riske, we need the letter."

"I can't help you."

"We'll double your fee."

"My answer stands."

"Two hundred thousand dollars. More than enough to pay for that dynamometer you're looking at."

"Excuse me?"

Neill stared at him unapologetically. Simon laughed at himself. To think he'd actually considered working for him. He made a note to call Bill Shea and ask that he strike Simon from his list of investigators.

Simon opened the door and waited for Neill to precede him downstairs. Outside, the rain had stopped. "Need a cab?" he asked.

"I can give you the name of the man who engineered the heist," said Neill, coming to his side.

"Not interested."

"You should be."

"Nothing you can say is going to change my decision."

"You're wrong about that."

"Pardon me?"

"I said, you're wrong about that."

Simon took in the smug expression, the knowing cast to his head. Suddenly he had his hands on Neill's jacket and the American agent was on his toes pressed against the wall. "Didn't you hear me?" he said. "I said no. Now go. Just leave."

Neill didn't struggle. He continued to stare at Simon dispassionately, with a gaze that said he'd been right all along.

"The man's name is Coluzzi," he said. "Tino Coluzzi."

Chapter 10

It had been a hot day. Early September. Tourists gone. The mercury scraping eighty degrees Fahrenheit at dawn. And dry. The sirocco blowing across the Mediterranean, the "devil wind" from the Maghreb sending dust and grit and last week's garbage spiraling through the narrow streets of the 15ème in the hilly northern reaches of the city.

Simon left his house early and dipped down to the coast, taking La Gineste toward Cassis. They met at a café high on the hill with vineyards all around and a view of the sea. They had breakfast and coffee and made a toast with a shot of grappa for good luck.

This was the big one. The one they'd practiced for. A Garda armored truck carrying payroll for the navy, whose fleet was anchored down the coast in Toulon. Five million euros.

It was Simon's job. He was nineteen, six feet tall, hair tied in a ponytail that touched his back, the last vestiges of his American roots burnt away by the Marseille sun. It had been seven years since his unwelcome arrival. His mother was no longer Mary Riske but Marie Ledoux, mother to three children by Pierre Ledoux and stepmother to his two teenage sons. Pierre drank. He made no secret of his displeasure at Simon's arrival. The young American prince whose clothing was nicer than his children's. School was a violent mix of poor French and poorer Africans. He returned home with a split lip after his first day and a swollen jaw the second. He learned to fight. He grew taller. He made himself stronger. He discovered he was every bit as vicious as his classmates. And then he discovered he was more vicious. He took refuge on the streets. His home sat in the center of the city's worst neighborhood, an area so lawless police refused to patrol its streets. At fourteen, he became a lookout for a small-time hood who controlled a block of the tenements that grew like weeds in the wild northern suburbs. It wasn't long before he moved up to cars. No one could hot-wire a Renault faster. And from cars to real jobs. Breaking and entering. Smash and grab. Banks. Jewelry stores. The luxury mansions around Cannes and Antibes.

And then the big targets.

Simon didn't need the tumbler of grappa to get him going this morning. He'd started his day with a line of Bolivian coke and a hit of Thai stick. He was primed. Bristling. This was his sixth armored car. First time he was in charge. He was a name. The cops knew him. The other crews knew him. He was a man on the rise.

They left the café in two cars and traded them for two others stolen the night before, new plates, full tanks of gas. Simon rode with Léon and Marcel, both a year younger, both as crazy as he was, rock solid. Theo Bonfanti, Il Padrone's son, drove the other car, with Franco and Tino Coluzzi, a few years older, the veteran. Two years pulling jobs together and they'd never been caught. They were invincible.

They parked near the Port de Toulon and waited. Lookouts along the route reported as the Garda truck passed by, *until finally Simon spotted it in his rearview and flashed his high beams.*

Theo Bonfanti pulled into traffic ahead of the truck. Simon cut in behind it. The guns were out. AKs for every man, round chambered, safety off, two spare clips apiece. A thousand bullets between them.

They followed the truck for ten minutes through town. Their destination was the Crédit Lyonnais. The largest bank in the city. The government's bank.

They hit the truck as it stopped at the last light a hundred meters out, the bank in sight. Simon gave the signal. Theo and his guys jumped out, firing before their feet hit the ground, raking the front of the truck, flaming out the engine block, blowing the tires, fragging the windscreen to leave the driver blind.

Simon and his team took the rear, Léon keeping an eye for police who came too close. Simon emptied his clip, firing on full auto, mainlining adrenaline, juiced by the heat and the noise and the drugs. He placed a charge on the lock and blew the door, the guards jumping clear, deafened, hands raised. Simon met each with the butt of his AK, putting the two on the ground, bleeding, semiconscious. He jumped into the cargo bay and hurried to the sturdy twill bags bulging with cash.

Except there were none. The bay was empty.

It was then he heard the sirens. Flashing lights approached along the Avenue de la République. Not one car but three...no, four...too many to count. Simon leapt from the truck and slammed home a fresh magazine as the police cars skidded to a halt, blocking their retreat, doors opening, cops coming at them with shotguns and automatic weapons.

For a moment, there was calm. A last vehicle braked too hard. Somewhere a church bell tolled.

The police opened fire.

Léon went down right away. Marcel stood tall, rifle to his shoulder, blowing the hood off one of the cars, the windows out of another. And then he collapsed, knees buckling, falling to the ground like a rag doll.

Simon fired in disciplined bursts, adrenaline pumping, but something new with it. Fear. Over his shoulder, he saw Theo on the ground, dead. A head shot. Franco had dropped his AK and stood with his hands raised above his head. And Tino, already cuffed and standing out of the line of fire, the cops pretty much leaving him alone.

Simon gave no thought to giving up. He continued firing, spraying the police wildly, the bullets deafening him to his own war cry.

The first bullet hit his thigh and he dropped to a knee. Another struck his forearm. Another grazed his shoulder. Blood spurted from his leg like a blown well. He felt dizzy, spent. The machine gun fell from his hands. He propped himself against the rear tire as the police surrounded him.

Graziano, the city's commandant de police, kneeled beside him. "Nice to meet you, Mr. Ledoux," he said in English. "Our American."

"Who told you?" He desperately needed to know, but the words crumbled in his mouth.

The police formed a cordon around him, and when the ambulance arrived, they refused to let the attendant pass. They stared down at him, hating him. Through their ranks, he spotted Tino Coluzzi being led to a patrol car. He was smoking a cigarette.

It was Coluzzi, thought Simon as the world grew hazy.

Light faded.

The sirocco gusted.

CHAPTER 11

Tino Coluzzi walked down La Canebière toward the Vieux-Port de Marseille. It was a humid, windless afternoon, the sun relentless. He navigated his way through the sea of pedestrians, muttering about the endless parade of North African faces. If he had ten euros for every Algerian, Tunisian, or Libyan walking past, he'd never have to pull another job in his life. The *pieds-noir* were bad enough. But this…this was an outright invasion. There wasn't a real Frenchman to be seen.

Flushed, sweating, and anything but relaxed, Coluzzi looked nothing like the man watching the Hotel George V the day before. He'd cut his hair as short as a recruit in the Légion Étrangère. He'd traded his blazer and slacks for a T-shirt and jeans. A pair of scuffed-up sneakers completed the trick. Hands stuffed in his pockets, wraparound sunglasses shielding his eyes, he was indistinguishable from the other jobless wretches crowding the sidewalks of his country's poorest city. A day or two in the sun and he'd be as brown as a Somali.

He passed beneath a stand of Mediterranean pines and slowed to take advantage of the shade. There were others around him doing the same, and over the course of several minutes he picked up a gaggle of languages. Spanish, English, Arabic, Italian. A regular United Nations. The only language he was interested in, however, was Russian.

Coluzzi wiped the sweat from his forehead and continued down the hill. The problem of Russians—or, more precisely, how to contact one—had been first and foremost on his mind since opening the prince's briefcase. On the surface, it shouldn't present a challenge. The South of France was crawling with them, but most were thieves of one stripe or another. Even those he counted as friends he couldn't trust. What he needed was an honest Russian, if there were such a thing. And not just an honest Russian, but one with contacts at the highest levels of his country's government.

It was a tall order.

He'd come to the conclusion that there was only one place to start.

Jojo's.

That's where things got tough.

Reaching the bottom of the hill, he skirted the old opera house and cut down an alley toward the port. Ten years ago, the four square blocks adjacent to the waterfront had been the city's toughest. Even at four in the afternoon, he would've been watching his back. Times had changed. The only thing to be afraid of today was choking to death on the perfume drifting out of all the froufrou boutiques and clothing stores. At least there weren't so many Africans near the water.

He rounded the corner and saw the sign for Jojo's. Officially it was called Le Nightclub, and it was the last of the old clubs standing. He ducked into a doorway, checking the knife strapped to his calf and adjusting the pistol in his waistband. It wasn't his practice to carry when not working. Which brought him once again to Jojo.

A year back they'd pulled a job together in Cannes, a smash and grab at Harry Winston around the corner from the Carlton Hotel. The job went off like clockwork. Coluzzi drove a stolen van through the jewelry store's front window. Jojo and his boys piled in, smashed the displays with hammers, filled their bags with loot, and were gone before anyone knew what was happening. Coluzzi fenced the jewels in Monaco. Everyone made out like bandits. It was months later, when he was back in Paris, that he heard rumblings that Jojo was unhappy, carping about how Coluzzi had shorted him and his crew, vowing to get even. Nothing more had come of it and Coluzzi had forgotten the whole thing.

Until now.

The weapons were a precaution...*just in case*.

Steeling himself, Coluzzi crossed the street to the nightclub. The front door was locked and he remembered the place didn't open until six. He walked past the photos of the girls working, lowering his sunglasses to take a better look. No doubt about it. They'd gone upmarket along with everything else.

The alley door was unlocked. He stepped inside and waited for his eyes to adjust to the dark. Music was blaring from the bar. He made his way down the corridor, past the kitchen, and entered the main room. Jojo was sitting at the bar, smoking, head buried in the sports pages. On stage, a statuesque brunette was trying out some moves on the pole, throwing her head back while kicking up a leg. Beneath all her war paint, she was eighteen tops.

"You got teenagers working here now?" Coluzzi sat down on a stool and slapped his hands on the bar. "What next?"

Giovanni "Jojo" Matta looked up from his paper. He was sixty, deeply tanned, with wavy white hair and a gold chain hanging around his neck. "Thought we'd gotten rid of you for good," he said sternly. "Mr. Big Time."

Coluzzi felt the pistol digging into his back. He looked around the room. Apart from the dancer, there was only a busboy setting the tables. Even so, there was no way he wanted to shoot Jojo in front of a witness. "Me? Gone for good? Never. This is home."

Jojo looked at him a second longer, then a smile cracked his face and he stood, arms stretched wide. "Of course it's home. Good to see you," he said loud enough for everyone to hear. "What's it been? A year? Longer? Come here."

Coluzzi accepted the hug, putting his arms around the older man. Jojo had owned Le Nightclub for as long as Coluzzi could remember. He was a pimp, a drug dealer, a fence, and a decent chef. Nothing went on in the city without his knowing. "Good to see you again, too. Get any tanner and people are going to think you're one of them."

"Stop it," said Jojo. "How you been? We haven't heard from you in forever."

"I'm doing good. Real good."

"You look different."

"It's the hair."

"You're dressed like a kid."

The music stopped. Jojo clapped a few times and the

girl left the stage. "Be back at eight," he called to her. His smile disappeared the moment she left the room. He looked at Coluzzi. "When did you get back?"

"This morning."

"How are things up north?"

"Okay."

"Just okay?"

Coluzzi walked behind the bar and poured himself a Kronenbourg from the tap. "What do you mean?"

Jojo studied him out of the corner of his eye. "That you on the television?"

"On television? Where?"

"You're still a shitty liar."

"You talking about Paris?"

"You know what I'm talking about."

Coluzzi took a long pull and wiped his mouth. "You think I'd be back here if I pulled off a job like that? I'll tell you where I'd be. Out of the country. Some place like Ibiza. Get myself a casita in the hills. Go down to town every night for some sangria, a good piece of fish. Get laid."

Jojo shrugged. "Thought the M.O. looked familiar. Brought back memories."

"That was a long time ago. I gave up armored cars after I got out."

"That wasn't an armored car."

"Give it a rest. It wasn't me."

"Okay, okay. Just curious."

"You...you all right?"

"Sure. Why not?"

"Heard some things. I want everything to be good between us. We're family. I want to keep it that way."

"We're family, Tino. Don't know what you're talking about."

"Forget I brought it up." Coluzzi returned to his stool and took his time drinking his beer. After a while, he said, "I need your help on something."

"Oh?"

"Any Russians in here lately?"

"Russians?" said Jojo, as if he'd asked about aliens. "You mean, besides Svetlana and Olga?"

"Men. Clients. Maybe from the consulate. Remember, way back when, a few of them would come in here Saturday nights. We called them the Ivans. Joked around that they might be spies. Those shitty suits, smoking those lousy cigarettes. Seen anyone like that lately?"

"Couldn't tell you," said Jojo. "I'm in the kitchen."

"You mind if I check receipts?"

"Credit cards?"

"Yeah."

"Any Russians in here pay cash?"

"Not the ones I'm looking for."

Jojo considered this. "You're serious?"

Coluzzi nodded.

"And you're not going to tell me what for?"

"First I need to find 'em."

Jojo looked at him for another second, then folded the newspaper and led the way to his office. "We have a program that keeps track of all charges. You can check by date, name, transaction amount."

Coluzzi sat down in Jojo's chair and scooted close to the keyboard. "I'm good."

"All yours."

Jojo left the room and Coluzzi brought up all charges for the past six months, then looked at them by name, A to Z. There were quite a few customers with Russian last names. He concentrated on those who spent less than five hundred euros. Russian diplomats weren't any better paid than any other state employee.

In five minutes, he had two names. Andrei Gromov and Boris Stevcek. Both men often came together. Usually Fridays. Gromov consistently spent more, but not much. Neither charged more than two hundred euros, which meant they never took a girl to the VIP room for a blow job or bought them out for the night. Lookers, not touchers.

Still, Coluzzi had no proof either worked for the Russian government. They might as easily be with one of the tech companies sprouting up these days like mushrooms or a foreign airline or just about anyone. In fact, he didn't even know if they were really Russians and not just French citizens with Russian names.

He exited the program and logged on to the net. Earlier he'd looked at the website for the Russian Consulate. Names of employees weren't listed, not even the consul general. The question was who best to approach with the letter. He had no friends in the Russian spy service. Even if he had, he wasn't sure how to present the letter. Coluzzi assumed that the Saudi prince had planned on delivering it to someone at or above his own level. The printout of the email he'd found in the prince's briefcase had indicated there was to be a rendezvous on the island of Cyprus with a man named V. Borodin. A check on the Internet indicated that the current chief of the Russian spy service was a man named Vassily Borodin.

But how does one reach the head of the SVR? You might as well try to reach God.

Coluzzi typed each of the men's names into the search bar. Stevcek had a Facebook page and Coluzzi looked through the photos he'd posted. He could tell

Stevcek was Russian just by looking at him. Pale skin, high cheekbones, bony nose, and the real giveaway, those Asiatic eyes.

He was also a prolific uploader of pictures. Coluzzi made it through fifty before giving up. He saw nothing that indicated what Stevcek did for a living, or if he worked for the Russian Consulate.

He started reviewing the man's posts. All were written in Cyrillic, and thus incomprehensible. Still, he scanned down page after page. Gibberish and more gibberish.

And then he saw it. An anniversary page that denoted a special event. This was written in French. March 20—Started work at the Consulate in Marseille.

Immediately, Coluzzi looked up the number of the Russian consulate. "May I speak with Mr. Stevcek?"

"No one by that name works here."

"Of course he does. I met him last week and he asked that I call him here."

"There is no one here by that name. Is this in reference to a visa?"

Coluzzi cursed under his breath. Stevcek had probably been transferred to another posting. "It's a different matter." He took a breath and dove in. "I am in possession of information that may benefit your country."

"What kind of information?" The reply came matter-of-factly, as if they received offers of this kind on a daily basis.

Coluzzi fumbled for the right words. "Technical. Sophisticated industrial plans. I'm an engineer. I wish to help Russia."

"I'm sorry, sir. We cannot help."

"Very secret. Confidential, understand? Top secret."

The line went dead. Embarrassed by his amateurish performance, he put down the phone, erased his browsing history, and returned to the bar.

"Any luck?" asked Jojo. He'd changed into his chef's whites for the evening, but the cigarette was still dangling from his mouth.

"Dead end."

"In town for a while?"

"A few days."

"Stop by tonight for a drink. Better yet, I'll make you dinner."

"Steak-frites?"

"You got it."

"My favorite," said Coluzzi, pleased that Jojo didn't have a clue he'd ripped him off the year before. "And, Jojo, don't overcook it this time."

CHAPTER 12

Don't overcook it.

Jojo Matta felt his cheeks color as he watched Coluzzi go down the hall. He stamped out his cigarette and marched to the kitchen, angrier than he could remember. The nerve. As if he'd forgotten all about how Coluzzi had cheated him.

Jojo tied on his apron and began the evening prep. He had two specials planned, grilled swordfish with steamed vegetables and mussels with garlic sauce. He opened the refrigerator and removed the fish, dropping it on the chopping block. He found his filleting knife and set to work cutting the slab into steaks. He could have purchased his fish precut, or even prepackaged, but he preferred to do it himself. It was a question of respect. If he charged thirty euros for a meal, he wanted to give his customers their money's worth. It was how he did things. He wasn't a cheat like Coluzzi.

Jojo looked down and saw that his hand was shaking. He drew a calming breath and set to work chopping the potatoes and carrots, the razor-sharp blade moving in a blur. He liked to go to the farmers' market every morning and pick out the produce himself. It was another way he showed his customers respect. The best ingredients at a fair price.

The mere thought of fairness brought Coluzzi back to mind. How long had they known each other? Fifteen years? Twenty? Even if they weren't family, they were friends.

And friends didn't steal from friends.

The blade jumped. Jojo felt a nick and looked down to see a sliver of his thumb lying on the cutting board. The blood came a second later. He put his thumb under cold water for a minute, then rubbed it with a styptic pencil and bandaged it.

He'd been cooking since he was fourteen and was forced to take a class in meal preparation at a reform school near Perpignan. The school believed that learning the rudiments of French cooking offered their unruly charges a career path while channeling the anger and lack of discipline that had led them to commit crimes in the first place. The first part was true enough. Jojo had worked as a chef on and off for the past forty years. The second part less so. It wasn't always a good idea to put sociopathic teenagers in proximity to sharp knives and boiling water. Jojo had left school with his leg scarred by scalding water and missing half an index finger. The upside was that he knew how to prepare a world-class coq au vin.

And that, he decided, was Tino Coluzzi's problem. He didn't respect anyone. Not friends. Not family. No one.

It was at a party last year that Jojo had run into Massimo Forte, the biggest jewelry fence this side of the Italian border. After a few drinks, Forte had let slip what he'd paid Coluzzi for the take from Harry

Winston. The figure was double what Coluzzi had told them.

Not ten percent more.

Not twenty percent more.

Double.

One hundred percent more.

Jojo wasn't averse to a little padding here and there. It had been Tino who'd cased the boutique, rounded up the crew, and jacked the truck they'd used to drive through the window. Likewise, his planning and execution had been top-notch. Tino ran a tight ship. No question he deserved a fatter share.

But padding was one thing. Gouging, another.

Jojo went back to work. He dumped the bloodied vegetables in the garbage, washed off the chopping block, and started again. He'd tried to put Coluzzi's double-dealing out of his mind, but that was no longer possible.

The man was here.

In Marseille.

It was a question of pride.

Jojo had to make things right.

Dropping the knife, he went to his office and closed the door behind him. He wiped his hands before making the call.

"Hey," he said. "You'll never guess who just walked into the club? And he's coming back for dinner. I'm thinking we should give him a special welcome."

An hour later, Tino Coluzzi sat alone outdoors at the Café la Samaritaine, drinking an espresso and watching traffic trawl through the Vieux-Port. Skiffs bringing in the second catch of the day. Tourist boats returning from Les Calanques. Day sailors mooring motor yachts.

Coluzzi looked past them and out to sea. In the distance, the walls of the Château d'If sparkled as if laced with gold. Though he'd lived in and around Marseille for twenty years, he'd never visited the castle and one-time fortress where the Count of Monte Cristo had been imprisoned. Right now he was thinking that prison might be a safer alternative, all things considered.

He dipped a biscuit into his coffee and stirred it. He was dumb. There was no other explanation. Dipping his feet into water far too deep for him. Not for a second had he considered who he must contact to offer the Russians the letter. The lure of a quick fortune had blinded him to the impracticality of his situation. He'd made a fool of himself calling the consulate, pretending to have industrial secrets to peddle. Now what was he supposed to do? Call back the American and say it had all been a mistake? Hide the letter under a rock and run away?

Coluzzi shook his head. There was no going back. He'd compromised his life the moment he read the letter.

Nearby a car honked. Two policemen walked past, eyes scanning all those seated around him. Suddenly, he felt exposed and vulnerable. He finished his espresso and left a five-euro note on the table. It was foolish to show himself at such a public location, he thought as he crossed to the promenade. His recent haircut and change of attire lent him a superficial anonymity, but it only went so far. Were anyone to take a closer look, they'd recognize him in no time.

He felt his phone buzz in his pocket. He stopped near a fish stand and answered. "Yeah?"

"You called us."

"Who is this?" asked Coluzzi.

"Who is this?"

And then he placed the accent. It was the Russians.

"Stevcek? Is that you?"

"Yes, I am Boris." The voice was high-pitched and wavering. Stevcek sounded more nervous than he.

"When can we meet?" asked the Russian. "Please tell me. I'm happy to come to your home."

Coluzzi held the phone away from him. His home? He was proposing to hand over sensitive materials that he had more or less admitted to stealing and the Russian thought it prudent to come to his home.

"Hello?" said the Russian. "Are you there?"

At that moment, a ship's horn sounded. Coluzzi looked to the mouth of the harbor and spotted the bow of a very large luxury motor yacht nosing into the harbor. Two hundred feet. Three-story superstructure. Helicopter lashed to an aft landing platform.

A superyacht.

The boat was moving rapidly, and from its size, profile, and navy-blue hull, he recognized it as the *Solange,* the largest yacht moored in Marseille harbor. A tattered black-and-white flag fluttered from the mast. The skull and crossbones.

The yacht belonged to Alexei Ren, the fifty-year-old Russian billionaire and owner of the Olympique de Marseille football club.

Coluzzi realized then that he was making an error trying to barter the letter through a minor diplomat posted to a second-rate consulate who sounded as if he'd gone through puberty the week before. A man who couldn't even afford a blow job at Jojo's.

Boris Stevcek had as much chance of reaching Vassily Borodin as Coluzzi did the president of France.

"Hello? Sir? Sir?"

Disgusted with himself, Coluzzi ended the call and walked toward the imposing yacht. Music blared from the top deck, where a party was in full swing. He was not the only man on the docks staring at the bevy of topless women dancing energetically, champagne flutes in hand. The yacht drew closer and soon passed.

A lone figure sat in the shade of the aft deck, studying a laptop. He had dark hair and a thick beard—a pirate in appearance, too—his white linen shirt billowing in the wind.

Alexei Ren.

Coluzzi stared at the figure, transfixed.

He had his answer.

CHAPTER 13

It was raining when Borodin landed in Moscow. As he stepped from the plane, a biting wind snapped at his cheeks. He rode alone into the city, his mood as stormy as the sky.

"I'm running late," Borodin informed his driver. "Get me to Yasenevo by four."

The sedan surged ahead, and in moments he was traveling at one hundred fifty kilometers per hour in the private lane reserved for government officials and the wealthiest of the land. Next to him, traffic on the outer ring road was at a standstill. Three o'clock and rush hour was in full swing. In fact, Borodin had noted, traffic was always bad. The experts dismissed the problem as a side effect of the growing economy. One more lie. The economy was cratering and everyone knew it.

He arrived in Yasenevo fifty minutes later. Located in the southwestern suburbs of the city, the headquarters of the Foreign Intelligence Service comprised three towers grouped around a central lawn, as well as several single-story buildings spread over a grassy campus. The largest tower, and first to be built thirty years earlier, had suffered from shoddy construction and had begun sinking into the soft Muscovy earth months after it was occupied. During Borodin's first years as an agent, the building's frame had become so warped that the windows would not open. While the central heating worked like a dream, air-conditioning was sporadic at best. During the short but extremely hot and humid Russian summer, air inside the building would grow warm and ripe. Worse, it was an ingrained habit of Russians, many of whom who had grown up sharing apartments with two or even three families, to ration their showers. A good wash once a week was as much as one could expect. Recalling the ungodly stench on the hottest of summer days, Borodin winced. Because of the smell, the main building had garnered a nickname repeated to this day. "The Outhouse."

"Everything all right, sir?" asked the driver, noting his expression of disgust.

"As good as can be expected," said Borodin.

Only after Boris Yeltsin came to power—his protégé, an undistinguished KGB agent formerly exiled to the hinterlands of East Germany, at his side—were funds discovered to retrofit the building and replace the HVAC system.

"Three fifty-five," announced the driver as he pulled to a halt in front of the main building. He turned, his eager face beaming. "Five minutes early."

Borodin patted him on the shoulder. "Thank you. Now if you'll give me an umbrella."

The driver's face fell. "A what?"

Outside, the rain was falling heavier than before. Twenty meters separated the car from the entrance: Borodin maintained a dignified gait as he walked to the building. He refused to run or appear at all put out by the dismal conditions. He knew that subordinates were watching, eager as always for something to gossip about, even if it were only how the director had made a clumsy dash to the lobby, or, God forbid, slipped and fell. If anything, he walked more slowly than usual. To hell with them. Heavy rain and whipping winds were of no consequence to the director of the SVR.

Once inside, he took his private elevator to the tenth floor. His secretary took one look at him and flung herself from her desk, rushing to his side, helping him take off his sodden overcoat.

"Get me a towel and a change of clothing," he said politely. "Oh, and tea."

His secretary was older and rotund, and immune to fashion. "With a little something to lift your spirits?"

"Thank you, but no. Just hot. Very hot."

It was then that Borodin noticed the blond woman seated outside his office. He passed her without a word or a glance. At his desk, he busied himself reading messages and checking his favorite American websites for the requisite time. At some point his secretary entered with a change of clothing. Borodin's job often required him to stay at his desk for days at a time. Over the past few years his closet here had filled to overflowing while his closet at home had thinned to the bare essentials. He changed and combed his hair before taking his place at his desk, a slab of mahogany as big as an aircraft carrier. A new headline appeared on the *New York Times'* website. Any other day, it would have made his blood boil. Today, it was exactly what the doctor ordered.

"Send in Major Asanova," he said, speaking into his speakerphone—like the desk, a relic from a bygone era.

The door opened. The blond woman entered and

saluted. Even without heels, she was a head taller than he. He waved away the salute and rose from his desk, greeting her with a kiss to each cheek, and a third to show she was in good favor. "Sit, Major."

Valentina Asanova tucked her skirt beneath her legs as she sat down.

"I understand you were in Berlin."

"Yes." A nod. No further words. No smile. The psychologist inside every field man noted she displayed no visible wish to ingratiate.

"On assignment to Division Two," he continued, without prejudice. No one wished to be assigned to Division Two.

Another nod. The gaze unwavering.

Borodin returned to his desk. He had forgotten how striking the woman was. The blue eyes. The white-blond hair. She was undoubtedly beautiful, but it was her air of maturity and intelligence that elevated her allure to another level.

Valentina Borisovna Asanova was a child of the state, an orphan raised in government institutions. As a youth, she'd excelled at gymnastics and spent her teen years as a member of the national team. After an injury ended her sporting career, she'd studied electrical engineering at Moscow State University. Later still, she'd graduated at the top of her class from the Russian foreign intelligence academy.

Indeed, she possessed the entire package. Intellect, physical prowess, beauty, ambition.

There was, however, something else that had recommended her to Vassily Borodin. As a child, she had suffered abuse at the hands of a succession of counselors, teachers, and coaches. Sadly, such treatment was the norm for the cold, unregulated institutions run by the state. If a child complained, she—or he—was simply abused worse. As a caring human being and a father, Borodin abhorred such treatment and was ashamed to be part of any apparatus that had allowed it to go unchecked. As director of the country's spy service, however, he took a different view.

Valentina Asanova's years of trauma had left her a clinical sociopath with limited emotional capability and an abiding antipathy toward her fellow man. In short, she possessed no conscience. Her battered psyche's greatest need was recognition. In the greatest of Russian traditions, her sole ambition was to serve the state.

She was the ideal recruit.

"Harass and intimidate," he went on. "That's your mandate, isn't it?"

Again the nod. He noticed that she'd placed her hands under her thighs and that her features had settled into a resigned grimace.

"Correct me if I'm wrong, Major, but a hallmark of H and I is stealth, is it not? The job does not demand physical confrontation. On the contrary, it is to introduce an element of fear, an intimation of terror, of uncertainty; to frighten the target without actually doing any physical harm."

The muscles in the woman's jaw tightened. Her eyes narrowed, but she said nothing. Borodin noted a daub of color in her cheeks that had not been there a moment earlier. He spun his monitor so she might see it. "This story just hit the wires. 'Ambassador's wife attacked by assailant in Berlin.' At the ambassador's residence, no less." He paused to allow her to read a few lines. "Any comment? It was you, wasn't it? I can't imagine who else would wish to break into the American ambassador's house precisely when he was attending a meeting to which we were not invited."

A vein at the woman's temple had magically appeared. Even at a distance, he could see it pulsing with frightening intensity.

Borodin turned the monitor back toward him and adopted a less benign tone. "Well?" he demanded. "I suppose you think it was a success because you weren't caught. Don't you realize it doesn't matter if they can't prove anything? The Americans know who was behind it. Damned careless of you. But then that's something of your trademark, isn't it, Major?"

Still no answer, the grimace as tight as a death rictus.

"Just what the hell did you do to the woman? Answer me!"

Valentina Asanova slid forward in her chair. Her hands came free of her thighs. She began to stand, her very pretty lips opening. Borodin felt the force of the wrath, as if hit by the concussion of a grenade. But as quickly, she relaxed. With a schoolgirl's modesty, she adjusted her skirt, ran a hand across the gold chain at her neck, and offered a polite, subservient smile. "May I inquire why you requested my presence?"

Borodin sat back in his chair and expelled the breath he'd been holding. "I'm glad to see you don't let your emotions get the best of you all the time."

"No," she replied with good humor. "Not all the time."

They eyed each other, but neither laughed.

Borodin slid a dossier across the desk. "I have a job for you."

CHAPTER 14

Simon arrived at the Gare du Nord at four p.m. The station was hot and as crowded as a Moroccan bazaar. A new custom of placing pianos in train stations had spread across Europe. An elderly man with wild gray hair played a lively boogie to no one's apparent appreciation. Simon kept a tight grip on his bag as he negotiated his way to the taxi stand. Young North African males accosted him at every step, aggressively demanding to help with his bag, shouting offers of rides in their own cars or on the back of a motorcycle. He ignored them.

Once outside, he was discouraged to find that the line for taxis stretched around the block. He turned the corner and walked north to where cabs joined the queue. He raised a hand in the air. A moment later, a liveried sedan pulled over. Cabbies didn't like waiting any more than he.

"Quai des Orfèvres," said Simon, climbing into the back seat.

"*Oui, Monsieur.*"

Simon handed him a ten-euro note. "*Vite.*"

The driver nodded officiously and put the car into gear.

Simon settled in and enjoyed the sights. On the way, he called the workshop. He informed his floor boss, Harry Mason, that he would be gone for a few days and that he should order the dynamometer for the engine shop. "You sure? That's an expensive piece of kit."

"Do it," said Simon. "And pass me to Lucy."

"She's been working like a dervish on that Dino you started last night."

"Is that so?"

"Odd, if you ask me."

"Better keep a sharp eye, Harry. Maybe she's after your job."

"That'll be the day."

Simon waited as Harry Mason went to find Lucy. Traffic was only marginally awful. He gripped the armrest as the driver accelerated through the streets, then slowed dramatically to cross the Pont Neuf. He hated being driven by others, taxi drivers most of all.

"Where are you off to, then?" asked Lucy Brown by way of a hello.

"Paris. Business."

"Never been."

"One day I'll take you. School trip."

"For that guy who was in here this morning?"

Simon gritted his teeth as a work van zeroed in on them, only to veer away at the last moment. "Did you deposit the check?"

"Straightaway at lunch."

"You know what I do when I make a little money? I buy myself a gift. Nothing too big. Just something to congratulate myself."

"So what did you get, then?"

"A dynamometer for the shop. Just gave Harry the green light to order it."

"Sexy."

"Isn't it, though?"

"Funny you mention that, because I already got something."

"You did? What is it?"

"A watch."

"I thought no one was wearing watches these days."

"Oh, I'm not going to wear it. At least, not all the time."

"You're not?"

"Nope."

"Okay," said Simon. "I'll bite. Why did you buy it?"

"So you'll show me just how the hell you did what you did last night."

"Goodbye, Lucy."

The headquarters of the Paris police department, better known as the Police Judiciaire, or PJ, was located at 36 Quai des Orfèvres in a nineteenth-century stone building that ran the length of a city block along the Seine. Men and women hurried up and down the broad limestone stairs. New recruits in their royal-blue uniforms climbed aboard a bus to the academy. Police cars ferried in and out of the lot, beginning a shift or returning after a long day. The rest of Paris might have shut up shop and gone on vacation, but the police were afforded no such luxury. Certainly not after a high-profile robbery that had made headlines around the globe.

Simon presented himself at the reception and received his visitor's badge and instructions to Commissaire Marc Dumont's office on the fourth floor. He walked past the elevator and entered the interior stairwell, running up the three flights, partly to ease his anxiety, partly because he liked elevators even less than police stations.

Reaching the fourth-floor landing, he paused to straighten his jacket, then passed through a swinging door into the main hall. His timing was good and he spotted Marc Dumont heading toward him. "Marc."

Dumont saw him and frowned. "Don't you ever gain any weight?"

"English cooking."

"Still no woman?"

"What are you? A cop?"

"No ring," said Dumont, pointing at Simon's left hand. "Besides, you look too happy."

The two shook hands warmly and Dumont led the way into his private suite. Two secretaries sat at desks in an anteroom. "I'm expecting Detective Perez," he said to one. "Send her in as soon as she arrives."

The secretary's expression soured. "As if I could stop her."

Dumont continued into a large corner office overlooking the river. He dropped the dossiers he was carrying onto his desk and sat in a tall padded chair. "Coffee? Tea? I don't usually drink in the office, but I'll make an exception in your case."

"Tea's fine."

Simon remained standing, taking in the room, the view. Life had been good to Dumont in the years since he'd last seen him. The French policeman was a little grayer, a little heavier. His suit was nicer and he wore a better wristwatch, though nothing compared to the Patek Philippe. Simon was pleased to note that the bullets Dumont had taken on his behalf had not left him with a limp.

The two had forged a tenuous friendship years earlier when Simon had enlisted his help in tracking down the daughter of an English financial executive. They'd found her in the drug den of her Serbian boyfriend in Paris. She didn't come without a fight.

"So, Monsieur Riske, still chasing rich runaways?"

"Once was enough," said Simon. "I've moved on to bigger and better things. Looks like you have as well."

"I left anti-gang last year," said Dumont, referring to the division charged with handling important robberies and kidnappings. "Like you, I have moved up in the world. I'm part of l'État-Major these days. I'm officially a bureaucrat."

"Don't tell me the bad guys finally got to you."

"Twenty years was enough. I got sick of being shot at by stoned teenagers. And you, Riske, staying out of gunfights?"

"As best I can. I still owe you one."

"I thought it was the other way around."

"I didn't take the bullet."

Dumont laughed or grunted. With the French, it was hard to tell the difference.

Simon had phoned before leaving to provide Dumont with a few details about the man he was looking for. He'd purposely kept the description short and vague. A professional criminal active in Paris. Someone from the south. Bouches-du-Rhône. Côte d'Azur. Possibly a Corsican. His preferred targets were art, jewels, and historical artifacts. Worked with a team.

"Mind telling me what he did?" Dumont had asked.

"He stole something that belonged to a client. Something valuable."

"In Paris?"

"Yes. A few days ago. That's all I can give you for now."

A secretary arrived with tea. Dumont poured two cups. "Sugar?"

"Please," said Simon. "And milk." He accepted the cup and sat down. "I appreciate you seeing me. I know you have your hands full. Any luck?"

"Nothing yet," said Dumont as he arranged the papers on his desk into neat piles. "Slavs or Russians, I'm sure. These guys were trained. Burned the vehicles. Didn't leave a print. The prince was dropping a fortune around town. He might as well have painted a bull's-eye on his back."

"Well," said Simon, settling himself in his chair, "good luck."

"We'll find them sooner or later. Someone will brag about it…either here or in Zagreb or Moscow. Crooks can't keep their mouths shut."

"Lucky for us."

"Between you and me, I'm not sure why we should care," said Dumont quietly, as if passing along a secret. "The prince didn't stick around long enough to file a report. He was on his plane and out of the country forty minutes after it all went down."

"Maybe he didn't want to talk," said Simon in the same restrained tone. "You know who he is, don't you?"

"Yes," said Dumont. "But how do you?"

Simon shrugged. "Maybe he wasn't here just to shop."

"Oh?"

There was a knock on the door and Dumont's countenance went from dark to darker. He shouted, "Come in," but he was a beat late. A slim, energetic woman dressed in tattered jeans and a black T-shirt entered.

"*Commissaire,*" she said, taking up position directly in front of Dumont's desk. "Reporting as ordered."

Dumont pasted a smile onto his face. "Simon, may I present Detective Nicolette Perez."

Simon stood. "How do you do?"

The woman turned toward him and shook his hand, gripping it a little too hard, meeting his gaze long enough to make it clear she didn't want to be there. "Nikki. Nice to meet you."

"The pleasure's mine."

"Detective Perez came into anti-gang a few months after I left," said Dumont. "Since then she's taken the lead on several high-profile cases. I informed her about the inquiries you're making on behalf of your client."

"It would help if he actually told us what he knew," she said to Dumont.

"Mr. Riske is a friend of the PJ," said Dumont reprovingly. "You will extend him every courtesy."

"It's all right," said Simon. "I know I'm taking her away from her job."

"Do you?" said Nikki Perez. "How very understanding."

He looked at her closely. She had tousled brown hair that fell to her shoulders and a streak of blue thrown in toward the back to show that she made her own rules. Her brown eyes were large and unapologetic, and they went nicely with a wide, expressive mouth cast until now in a frown. She wore little or no makeup and Simon didn't think she needed any. No fingernail polish, but slender hands and nice nails. He had a thing about hands. He also had a thing about guns, and she was carrying a SIG Sauer with an extra-wide grip on her belt that said she was all business.

She dropped into the chair adjacent to Simon's and stretched a leg out in front of her. "Look," she said. "We have a half-dozen organized crime groups working the city today. Russians, Slavs, Africans, and a few others. The Corsicans are way down the list. Mostly they're into protection, gambling, prostitution. Once in a while they bring in a crew to take down a bank or a jewelry store. There hasn't been anything reported that even remotely fits what you're looking into. No stores knocked off. No paintings stolen from private collections. No thefts of expensive jewelry. Not much more I can add."

"I'm happy to give you some more details," said Simon. "My client doesn't want the theft made public."

"It's a crazy time. I'm sure you've seen the news. I've got a lot of work. Like I said, I haven't heard a thing." She stood and smiled woodenly. "Good luck, all the same."

"Detective Perez," said Dumont. "I'm certain you can offer Mr. Riske a few minutes of your time…no matter how valuable it may be."

"Sure," she said, moving to the door. "Maybe tomorrow…or the next day."

Dumont stood. "This afternoon."

"But, Commissaire, I told you…"

"Especially given your current status." Dumont stared at her for as long as it takes a spark to die, then returned his attention to Simon. "As I said, Nikki would be more than happy to speak with you."

Nikki Perez ran an exasperated hand through her hair, sighing for dramatic effect, before looking Simon's way. "All right, then, let's go."

Simon thanked Dumont all too quickly, hurrying to catch the detective at the elevator, sliding in as the doors closed.

"Still here?" she said.

"Like gum on your shoe."

"More like something else. Come on. I need a coffee."

She was first out of the elevator and made a beeline through the reception area and out the front doors. She took the stairs two at a time and turned right once she hit the sidewalk. Simon turned left.

"Hey," she called. "This way."

"I know a better place." He continued up the Quai des Orfèvres. After a moment, he heard her footsteps behind him.

"Fifteen minutes," she said. "That's all I have for a 'friend of the PJ.'"

"More than I need."

Simon turned onto a street lined with cafés and restaurants. Waiters wearing white aprons stood on the sidewalk next to chalkboards advertising daily specials. The Notre-Dame was a few blocks away and its towers loomed over the rooftops.

He cut into an alley and opened the back door of an unmarked building. A spiral staircase led to a coffee bar on the first floor. Locals sat at tables lining the wall. Simon walked to the counter. "One espresso and one…"

"*Café crème.*" Nikki took a tobacco tin from her pocket and opened it. Inside were rolling papers and a lighter. She began fashioning a cigarette. "I'm impressed," she said. "You know Julien's."

"I was at school here for a year."

"Sorbonne?"

"Sciences Po. I studied mathematics."

"That must have been a while ago."

"Ten years."

"That's all?" she asked with sarcasm.

"I started late."

Nikki flicked her tongue across the paper and sealed the cigarette. Simon plucked it out of her hand. "Hey," she protested, throwing out a hand to grab the cigarette back.

"Foul habit."

"You have some nerve!"

He looked at his watch. "Eight more minutes. I think you can wait that long."

The barman placed the demitasses of espresso and coffee on the counter. Simon sipped his slowly. He was remembering his year at the Sciences Po, the nation's elite business university. He'd come to earn a master's in mathematics after finishing his undergraduate degree in London. He'd lived in a fourth-floor walk-up in Montmartre and worked nights and weekends doing odd jobs to cover living expenses.

Education is not the filling of a pail, but the lighting of a fire.

It had all been part of the monsignor's plan for him. Yeats by way of a jail yard priest.

"Five minutes, Mr. Riske."

Simon finished his espresso. "I need everything you have on three people. Paul Modriani, Salvatore Brigantino, and Tino Coluzzi."

"You've narrowed down your list."

"I hope that helps."

Nikki set her elbows on the counter. "Modriani ran things five years ago, but he's retired. He has a restaurant in Lyon, where he spends his time. You can forget him. I haven't heard anything about Brigantino for years. His son manages a casino in the Bois de Boulogne. Gambling's not my jurisdiction. I heard Coluzzi's name a year ago in connection with a theft of a shipment of prescription medication—OxyContin, opioids, something like that. Nothing since. He's probably back down south. Now it's your turn."

"Like I told Commissaire Dumont, I'm looking for something valuable that was stolen from my client."

"And a little birdie whispered in your ear that it was stolen by one of these men."

"Exactly."

"What is it that you're looking for?"

"A letter."

"You're serious? What are you going after next?" she asked with a smirk. "A pen?"

"They didn't take the pen," said Simon.

"Very funny," said Nikki. "If you know so much already, why do you need me?"

"Reliability. Confirmation."

"You dragged me away from the biggest theft in the last six months to find a letter?" She looked at the ceiling, shaking her head. "I know what you are, coming here in your expensive suit and your expensive shoes, calling in a favor from the commissaire. You're a fixer. The guy that does somebody else's dirty work. The commissaire told me about your last job—finding the runaway heiress who'd fallen in love with her coke dealer. Classy. What is it this time? Tracking down an incriminating letter one of your rich friends dashed off to his much younger girlfriend? Well, then. Another worthy cause for the Paris police. At least I don't have to worry about being shot."

"Not by the bad guys," said Simon.

"Tough guy, eh?"

"Not especially."

Nikki stepped closer, her fingers tracing a path along his lapel. "Must be some letter."

He took her hand from his jacket and lowered it to her side. "Point me in the right direction. I'll take it from there."

Still, Nikki didn't move. She stared at him, not

bothering to disguise her contempt. Simon held her gaze. Her brown eyes had flecks of gold and he caught a hint of expensive perfume. He decided he liked the streak of blue. It was fading and he wondered when she'd put it in and why.

"Time's up," she said, before sliding down the counter and collecting her tobacco tin. "I'll ask around about your friends from down south."

He threw a ten-euro note on the bar. "Sooner rather than later."

"I have other cases that take precedent on a letter."

Simon buttoned his jacket and reached for the door, but she was there before him. She paused, halfway out the door. "Hey, Riske, my cigarette."

"I gave it back to you."

"Actually, you didn't."

"You sure?"

Nikki fished out the tobacco tin and opened it with a thumb. The cigarette lay inside. "How…?"

"Talk to you tomorrow," said Simon.

CHAPTER 15

The lobby of the Hotel George V was an oasis. Marble floors. High ceilings. A large spray of colorful flowers rested on a table placed between the reception desk on one side and the concierge on the other. The door closed behind him and Simon was in another world, a world governed by wealth, elegance, and the scent of blooming florals.

And paid for by Mr. Barnaby Neill and the United States government.

Simon checked in and was shown to his room by an efficient trainee. He tipped her generously, then unpacked, hanging up his suits, placing his shirts in drawers, and arranging his toiletries on a washcloth spread out next to the sink. His orderliness was a mystery. He'd been as messy as any teen. T-shirts belonged on the floor. Shoes were to be left where he'd kicked them off. At no time had he received lectures on cleanliness being next to godliness. His quest for order began the day of his release from prison. He was sure that someone somewhere had an explanation, probably something about a need to control his environment. He didn't care to hear it.

Maybe he had Tino Coluzzi to thank, thought Simon as he put on a clean shirt and notched his belt. He had a nice idea for a fitting gesture of gratitude. It did not involve a smile, a handshake, or a kind word.

Tino Coluzzi.

Now, there was a name he'd never expected to hear again.

For a moment a rash of near unimaginable anger passed through him.

He picked up his phone and scrolled through his contacts until he found the name of a man he knew in the city capable of getting him whatever he needed, quickly, discreetly, and without question. He thought of Detective Perez and the pistol she wore on her belt. A SIG Sauer identical to it would do nicely.

As quickly, he put the phone down. Nothing could change the past.

"The best revenge is to be unlike he who performed the injury."

Another of the monsignor's rules.

Simon had been hired to retrieve a letter. Nothing more.

As for Coluzzi?

If Simon recalled, his weapon of choice was a stiletto. He'd have the blade in his chest before Simon cleared the pistol from its holster.

He moved his attaché case to the desk and opened it. Inside, packed in foam, were the elements of his surveillance kit: bugs, transmitters, a parabolic microphone, high-def cameras disguised as screws or hidden in lapel pins. A separate, smaller case contained some new gear his technical advisor had sold him. Simon expected good things.

He finished dressing and took the elevator to the

ground floor. A gallery with sofas and chairs and tables ran alongside the atrium around which the hotel was built. He chose an empty seat with an unobstructed view of the lobby. Nearby tables were occupied by flamboyant Germans, taciturn Saudis, and a flock of giggly Asian women, who, by the volume of shopping bags on the floor and couches around them, appeared to have visited every store on the Avenue Montaigne.

A server arrived, and he ordered a mineral water and a croque monsieur. He relaxed and picked up a copy of the *New York Times Global Edition* lying on a table. From his position, he was able to observe the hotel staff and the comings and goings of guests. He was wondering how Coluzzi had known in which car the prince carried his money and, more importantly, the precise route he would take to the airport. He was wondering who had told him. Simon knew an inside job when he saw one.

The sound of a door closing loudly drew his attention to the reception desk, where a compact, officious man emerged from a room behind the counter and spoke to the night manager in a stern manner.

Hotel security, thought Simon, spotting the man's earpiece and lapel microphone. An important guest was due for arrival. The alarm had been sounded.

The server brought Simon's food. He had time to eat half his sandwich before the VIPs arrived. Doormen poured into the lobby. The night manager positioned himself at the entry. The hotel security man retired to a far corner, appearing to admire a showcase displaying sparkling gold watches.

A moment later, a Middle Eastern family filed into the lobby—six children, two wives, a sheikh—accompanied by a two-man contingent of private security. The night manager greeted the sheikh and led him to the reception as the bellmen began ferrying in trolleys overflowing with trunks and cases. But Simon's eyes instinctively stayed on the security man who had approached one of the bodyguards and discreetly led him aside for a more serious discussion.

The hotel's chief of security was fit, full of vim, maybe fifty, with a prizefighter's brow and thick hair gone prematurely gray. He wore a stiff blazer, pressed slacks, and polished leather shoes with thick soles that indicated he spent a good deal of time on his feet. His entire bearing screamed "military."

The bodyguard led the hotel security man to the sheikh. There was a handshake, a bow of the head, and a solemn exchange of words before the sheikh returned to his family.

Simon settled the bill and passed through the lobby onto the street. The sun had set a while earlier. The night was warm and breezy. He strolled to the Champs-Élysées and walked its length to the Place de la Concorde, admiring the obelisk, gazing up the grand boulevard to the Arc de Triomphe before heading back to the hotel.

As he strolled, he couldn't erase the unsavory image of the sheikh slipping a neatly folded wad of bills into the hands of the hotel's chief of security. He wondered if, like the prince, the sheikh also traveled with a million euros in cash.

Or if, perhaps, the payment was in exchange for helping chart the safest route to the airport.

Chapter 16

Jojo's was in full swing when Coluzzi entered just after ten p.m. All the tables in the main room were occupied, with the overflow leaning on the brass railing and crowding the bar. Music blared as the girls worked the room, most not bothering to cover themselves with anything more than a G-string. He moved through the crowd, ignoring their entreaties, caught up in the smells of sweat, perfume, and lust. He gave the bartender a wave and pointed toward the kitchen, then continued down the hall.

"You're back?" Dressed in chef's whites, Jojo looked up from the grill.

"Didn't expect me?"

"Already put aside my best steak for you."

"Appreciate it."

Jojo took out a steak from his prep drawer and threw it on the grill, dumped a handful of freshly cut fries into the basket, and dropped it into the fryer. Wiping his forehead with a towel, he returned his attention to Coluzzi. "Find your Russians?"

"Dead end."

"Want to tell me what it's about?"

"Actually, I have a question for you."

"Yeah, what?"

"Still have your season tickets?"

"Thirty years running."

"You ever see Alexei Ren?"

"Now and then. He likes to stand on the sidelines with his players."

While the public knew Alexei Ren as a glamorous businessman who attended fashion shows in Paris and threw lavish parties at his home in Saint-Tropez, as well as the owner of the Olympique de Marseille football club, Coluzzi was privy to a darker truth. At one time Alexei Ren had been the king of the Russian mafiya in the South of France.

"You two friends?"

"Me? I know him. He used to come in not long after he got out of the gulag in Siberia and was setting up shop. He was a different man then. Absolutely ruthless. On a mission to get back the years he'd lost. The girls were scared of him. He couldn't get enough."

"You ever work together?"

Jojo flipped the steak, flames shooting from the grill. "That's right," he said, testing the meat with his fork. "You wouldn't know. That was about the time you were doing your stretch for that armored car job."

"Know what?"

"We had a sweet deal running that summer. I had some boys working legit jobs at the spots up and down the Riviera. Sporting Club in Monaco. Hôtel du Cap. Byblos in Saint-Tropez. Moulin de Mougins. Only the best places. The kids were locals. They knew everyone, especially the movers and shakers. When they spotted one of the high and mighty coming into their establishment, they'd give me a call. I'd pass the word to Ren, shoot him their home address, and leave the rest to him. He had a slick crew. Very talented. Get in. Get out. Fast. Fast. Fast. They could smell jewels through three feet of concrete." Jojo rubbed his finger-tips together, grinning at the memory. "Rich pickings, my friend."

"I never read about it."

"Of course you didn't. People that rich don't want their names in the paper. They keep it all hush-hush. The insurance guys talk to the police. The police do a little looking. No one wants to give other thieves the idea there might be more. That was the summer I bought my boat. Good times."

Jojo plated the steak, cleared the basket from the fryer, and dumped the contents into a bowl, dusting the fries with a pinch of salt from on high. After a few crisp shakes, he spilled the golden fries onto the plate and slid it in front of Coluzzi. "Hey," he said in warning as Tino drew it nearer. Jojo spooned a dollop of garlic butter onto the steak, then gave his blessing. *"Bon app."*

Coluzzi took his time eating, careful not to betray his interest in Alexei Ren. He asked for more fries, dous-ing them with the melted garlic butter and warm juices. "You know how to cook, Jojo."

"Hope it's not overdone."

"Perfect." Coluzzi put down his knife and fork, then wiped his mouth. "Why didn't you keep working with Ren? I'd like to be in on a gig like that."

"He cleaned up his act. He's smarter than guys like us. He took that money and invested it. Pretty soon he bought that big computer company and he was off to the races. Now he's like a superhero. Big family. Lots of kids. Setting up foundations for the poor." Jojo laughed caustically. "Like everyone forgot what he looked like without his shirt."

"What do you mean?"

"The tats. He was *vor v zakone*. A criminal for life. He didn't come to France because he wanted to. He was kicked out."

"That right?"

"Hoods like that have their personal history tattooed on every inch of their bodies. He came out on my boat once. It's something you'll never forget. Anyway, that's why you never see him without a long-sleeved shirt and high collar. He doesn't want anyone remembering."

"I thought he was just being careful not to take too much sun."

"Thing I liked about him," said Jojo, "he was fair. The man never tried to short you. He thought about the future. Keeping your friends, friends."

Coluzzi pushed the dish away from him. "That right?"

"You ought to try it sometime."

"What's that supposed to mean?"

"It means you pay your partners what you promise."

"So it's true. You were talking behind my back."

"And now I'm saying it to your face."

The door of the kitchen swung open. Two men Coluzzi recognized entered.

"Or tell it to Bobby or Claude," Jojo went on.

"Yeah," said Bobby, who was squat and stocky with a neck like a tree trunk and hands as big as cleavers. "Tell us."

Claude nodded. He was a "hitter"—a killer for La Brise—slim and oily with long black hair and a yellowish cast to his skin. If he said ten words in a day, it was a lot.

"What is this?" said Coluzzi. "I asked you earlier if there was a problem. Come on, Jojo. You can't be serious."

"Knowing you, I'm pretty sure you've already spent what you owe us. We'll take payment in a different currency."

"I paid you your share."

"No," said Jojo. "You didn't."

Coluzzi saw there was no point in arguing. "So what are you going to do? Bust my legs? Grow up."

"For a start," said Jojo. "Then I'll let Bobby and Claude get creative on you. Unless, of course, you want to settle up."

"How much do you think I owe you?"

"A hundred grand."

"Not likely."

"Then it is what it is."

Coluzzi shrugged, giving Jojo one last chance. "Come on. It doesn't have to be like this."

"Yeah," said Bobby. "It does." He stepped toward Coluzzi, his fat hand going into his jacket for his gun, Claude casually picking up a carving knife, testing it for weight.

"Hey, hey," said Coluzzi, standing from his stool, eyes wide, trying to make them think he was pissing his pants, that his time in Paris had softened him up, turned him into a pussy who shied from a fight.

Bobby cleared his gun, a snub-nosed .38. "You greedy…"

Coluzzi drew his stiletto from his sheath and slashed it through the air, the tip slicing Bobby's fleshy neck, releasing a spray of arterial blood. Bobby fired a shot, even as he dropped the pistol and reached for his ruined neck. Claude lunged at him, the carving knife aimed at his belly. Coluzzi had always been the fastest guy around. He jumped to one side, the blade missing him by a long shot. In the same motion, he thrust the stiletto into Claude's chest, just below the sternum, giving the handle a vicious twist when he felt the blade tear through something heavy and fibrous, probably the lung or the liver. Claude opened his mouth and blood seeped out over his lousy teeth.

Coluzzi yanked the blade free and turned on Jojo, who just then launched a pounding hammer straight at his head. Coluzzi ducked, the hammer bouncing off the wall and clattering onto the floor. In his other hand, Jojo held his stubby chopping knife. Realizing it wasn't any kind of weapon, he searched the counter for something he could use, settling on a rolling pin. He came at Coluzzi like a barroom brawler, swinging the rolling pin and jabbing with the knife.

Coluzzi backed up as much as he could in the cramped area, hemmed in by counters and shelves and the ovens and stoves. He had to be careful. No one cared about Bobby or Claude. They were both Italians, not even real members of La Brise. But Jojo…he was royalty. Should Coluzzi lay a hand on him, do any real damage, there would be hell to pay.

Coluzzi ducked and dodged the wild blows, shouting for Jojo to calm down. But Jojo liked a fight and there was no doubting the blood in his eye.

Jojo lurched at him, the knife catching Coluzzi on the forearm—nothing serious, but a cut nonetheless. The rolling pin swooshed angrily at his head, barely missing.

"Enough," said Coluzzi, fed up with Jojo's nonsense. The man was sixty. Didn't he know when to throw in the towel? Coluzzi waited for his spot, then lunged at Jojo, knocking the knife to one side and slugging him in the jaw.

It was enough.

Jojo went down on his knees, half out of it.

As luck had it, Bobby's gun was right there, in arm's reach.

"Don't," said Coluzzi.

But Jojo was already going for it, probably not even thinking what he was going to do with it or how he might get a shot off. His fingers found the grip, his hand pulling it closer. Coluzzi dropped to a knee and drove his stiletto through the top of Jojo's hand, impaling it on the cracked linoleum floor.

Jojo was too stunned to shout. He sat there as if paralyzed, staring at the blade protruding from his hand, shaking with rage.

Coluzzi tossed a packet of ten thousand euros onto the floor. "There," he said. "We're even. Got it?"

Jojo looked at him, then at the money. "Sure," he said. "We're even."

"Swear it."

"I swear."

"And you'll never pull any kind of bullshit like this again."

Jojo nodded.

"Say it."

"I swear."

"Okay, then." Coluzzi pulled the stiletto out of Jojo's hand. "Jesus," he said, wiping the blade on a dishtowel. "What a mess."

Jojo stood up, shakily, and put his hand under a stream of cold water.

"And one more thing," said Coluzzi. "I need your ticket to the game tomorrow."

Tuesday

CHAPTER 17

Simon woke at seven. After a shower and a light break-fast ordered from room service (cost: one hundred euros—apologies to Mr. Neill), he walked to the Champs-Élysées and hailed a cab.

"Porte d'Orléans," he said.

Twenty minutes later, the taxi turned onto the Av-enue du Général Leclerc in the southern perimeter of Paris. It was a working-class area, the street lined with bakeries, laundries, hair salons, and corner grocery stores.

It was here thirty-six hours earlier that the prince and his entourage had been robbed.

Simon stepped out of the car, handing the driver a fifty-euro note and asking that he wait. Slowly, he made his way up the block. He envisioned the line of sedans advancing along the boulevard. Coluzzi would have needed to wait until the last one crossed through the intersection before blocking the lead car. Timing was crucial.

All over in sixty seconds.

Simon started the timer on his wristwatch, then

retraced his steps, stopping in the middle of the block, looking one way, then the other, playing out the scenario in his mind. The entry to the highway lay three hundred meters ahead, the green placards in sight. The drivers would have spotted them and relaxed. For all intents and purposes, they were home free. So much more the surprise when Coluzzi's men appeared from a side street to bar the route. The lead chauffeur would have had no time to warn his colleagues before they were blocked from the rear as well.

Fifty-eight...fifty-nine...sixty.

Simon stopped the chronograph. The Corsican had chosen his spot well. There was no question but that he'd known the route in advance. A day, if not more, to allow for him and his accomplices to rehearse.

"How would you have planned it?" Neill had asked him yesterday morning.

Simon had his answer. No differently than Coluzzi.

He made a second tour of the block, more briskly this time, looking for security cameras. Paris wasn't London. He couldn't find one.

He had a last impression before returning to the taxi. Tino Coluzzi had gotten smarter since he'd last seen him. Simon would be wise not to underestimate him. He'd done so once before and it hadn't turned out well.

"Back to the hotel," said Simon.

He rode the entire way in silence, lost in thought. He was not in Paris. He was in Marseille. In Les Baumettes. Reliving the worst moments of his life.

They came at him on his third day while he was in the yard. There was nothing hostile in their approach. Five prisoners casually walking his way. They knew his name. They knew what he was in for. They said they wanted nothing more than to introduce themselves. They were his "brothers." Simon knew better.

The yard, like the entire prison, was segregated by race and religion. The natives, "les blancs"—comprising French, Corsican, and any other Europeans with white skin who had run afoul of French law—had the southern side. The southern side had benches, a handball court, a bocce pit, and, most importantly, abundant shade from the coastal pine trees that grew on the steep hills surrounding the prison. The Muslims, referred to as "les barbus"—the bearded ones—and by far the largest group in the prison, had the east side of the yard, hardly more than a fifty-square-meter patch of concrete. The blacks had what was left, a patch of dirt as hard as rock during the blistering summer, damp and muddy in the winter.

At first they made small talk. "Everything okay?" "You get a room with a bed?" "Need any weed or anything else, for that matter?"

Simon replied that he was fine. He required no favors. He'd known what to expect coming in. In Les Baums, you found your own space. Cells stood open twenty-four hours a day. The assignment given on arrival didn't count for anything. Built in the 1930s to house a population of six hundred, the prison held three times that number. On the day he arrived, Simon became inmate 1801.

He'd fashioned a shank during his time in the city jail and concealed it the only way he could. He knew how to spot the weaker man. The fight, when it occurred, was brief and bloody. Simon had his bed.

Situated in the suburbs of Marseille, the prison anchored a leafy neighborhood of lower-middle-class homes and businesses, separated from its civilian neighbors by no more than a street and a twenty-foot stone-and-mortar wall. There were no watchtowers. No barbed-wire fences. Just the wall *with statues of the seven deadly sins built into its side and the towering steel door that served as the prison's sole entry and egress.*

Inside, conditions were hellish. Few renovations had been made since its construction. Even fewer repairs. The interior was bare concrete, same as the beds. There were no bars on the cells, just doors that closed no differently than ones in your home. Each cell had a bed and a hole in the ground and whatever furniture you could bribe a guard to allow you to smuggle in. Some even had windows. In the summer, temperatures inside the housing unit rose to over one hundred degrees Fahrenheit. The air, rank with the shit and piss and stench of nearly two thousand sweaty men, was insufferable.

Simon's sentence was six years with the opportunity to reduce his time with good behavior. It was a light penalty as far as armed robbery with aggravated circumstances (firing with deadly intent at police) went. The judge, a woman of forty and a new mother, had been weak. She had taken into account his age, his father's suicide, his difficult family environment. When Simon had addressed the court with his new haircut and pressed shirt, and said with a halting voice that his days as a criminal were behind him, she had believed him.

"Someone wants to meet you," one of the men said.

"I'm not hiding."

"Signor Bonfanti doesn't like it outside."

Simon followed the men without further protest. Bonfanti was "Il Padrone," the boss, and was the de facto ruler of La Brise de Mer. His son, Theo Bonfanti, had been killed in the course of the aborted robbery. Bonfanti's room was on the fourth floor and had windows that opened wide enough to crawl out of. The room had a real bed and a Moroccan carpet and every other amenity of civilized life, including an independent supply of electricity. In theory, he could have engineered his escape any time he chose. For the past five years, it had been safer for him inside.

"You're Ledoux?"

Simon nodded.

Bonfanti was a short, toad-like man with gray hair and an ample belly, his voice as rough as asphalt. "You got my son killed."

"The police killed him."

"It was your job."

"It was."

"And the police were waiting."

Simon nodded again.

"So who talked?"

Simon said nothing. From the corner of his eye, he noted the other men drawing closer. They were no longer either casual or friendly.

"Who talked?" Bonfanti asked a second time.

Simon maintained his silence. The men pressed against him, ready to kill him if given the word. He could smell their eager sweat. Simon suddenly felt his age, a nineteen-year-old in far over his head.

Bonfanti gestured at a wooden chair. "Sit."

Simon did as he was told.

"Here's how things stand between us. It was your crew. Your plan. You were in charge. Whatever happened that day, you're responsible. Agreed?"

Simon said yes.

"First, you owe me for my son's share, then you owe me for his life. Still with me?"

Simon met Bonfanti's eyes. The answer had already been made for him. To say no, to ask a question, was to sign his death warrant.

Bonfanti extended a callused hand. Simon shook it.

"There's a man here who wishes me harm," said

Bonfanti. "You don't need to know why. You only need to know his name. It is Nasser-Al-Faris. He's a barbu."

He explained that Al-Faris ran drugs inside for the barbus and the North Africans. Like Bonfanti, he was a powerful man. He was protected at all times. He never ventured into the yard without a bodyguard of five soldiers. He lived in the far corner of the housing unit, separated from les blancs. The only time he was unprotected was when he showered. Guards on his payroll cleared out the bathing unit. Every day at nine a.m. Al-Faris had fifteen minutes and all the hot water he desired for himself.

"Al-Faris has one weakness," Bonfanti said, leaning close. "He is homosexual. He prefers young partners. Like you."

"I'm not that way."

"You don't have to fuck him. You just have to kill him."

The plan was put into motion the next day.

Bonfanti's men set upon Simon in the yard as punishment for an unseen infraction. In plain sight of the population, Simon allowed himself to be beaten. He cowered. He ran. For the next week, he walked the yard alone, careful to keep his distance from everyone. He was a pariah, not welcomed by any group. He found a stretch of wall and made it his own. Each day, returning to his room, he passed les barbus. One day, he saw Al-Faris. He looked at him. He met his eyes. He allowed his gaze to linger. The next day, he did the same.

A week later, he received a note. A meeting was set. Nine a.m. The bathing unit.

Simon arrived at the designated time. He stripped naked. A guard checked his hands, felt beneath his balls, then looked away as Simon entered the shower.

Al-Faris was alone. He beckoned Simon forward. The bargain was made without words. In exchange for his body, Simon would receive protection. He would no longer be alone. He would be welcome among les barbus.

Al-Faris was Egyptian, a tall, muscular man with tattoos covering his back and his arms. He put his hand on Simon's chest. He rubbed his back. He came closer so their bodies touched.

Simon looked into his eyes, playing his part.

Al-Faris cupped Simon's buttock in his hand. He opened his mouth to kiss him.

Simon turned his head. In his mouth, he clenched a razor between his teeth. For the past ten days he had practiced the violent motion required to puncture a man's neck and sever his carotid artery. He must bring his jaw high, grasp the man by his shoulders, hold him tight, then propel the blade powerfully downward, entering the neck just below the ear, slicing diagonally, viciously, and without hesitation.

He did this now.

Al-Faris opened his mouth to cry out but could make no sound. Blood erupted from his ruined throat in a panoramic geyser, pulsing with the last powerful beats of his heart. He grasped madly at Simon, but Simon held him in his grip, looking into his eyes as the life dimmed. Al-Faris slid to the floor. In seconds, he was dead.

Simon spat out the razor.

The guard whisked him away. Today he was on the Corsican's payroll.

Minutes later, Simon stood before Bonfanti. He was given a hit of hashish and a thimbleful of cognac. He was informed that killing the Egyptian satisfied but half of his obligation. The murder of Al-Faris took care of the monetary debt. If Simon had not killed him, Bonfanti would have been required to pay another of his soldiers to do the job. That sum, in Bonfanti's mind, covered what was due his deceased son had there actually been money in the hold of the Garda armored truck. What remained of his obligation, said Bonfanti, was payment-in-kind for his son's death. Bonfanti was alone *in the world. Simon must also be alone. He would be placed in solitary confinement in a dank subterranean cell known to all as "the hole." For how long was Bonfanti's choice.*

A day.

A month.

A year.

There was, however, another alternative.

Should Simon tell him who betrayed the crew to the police he would not have to endure "the hole." Not for a minute. One name and Simon's debt would be discharged in full. Even more, he could move to the fourth floor to occupy a private room near Bonfanti's for the duration of his sentence. He would enjoy permanent protection while on the yard. It was his choice.

"And so," Bonfanti asked, "who betrayed you?"

Simon did not answer. He'd promised himself he would not say. He would keep the name for himself. Revenge would be his and his alone.

"He's mine," said Simon, with the vehemence of a wronged man.

The taxi driver looked over his shoulder, startled. "What is it, sir? You are all right?"

Simon shook himself from his haunted reverie. "I'm sorry. Yes, I'm fine."

The taxi drew to a halt in front of the hotel. "We have arrived. You are at your destination."

"Yes," said Simon, still shaky, fighting off the memories. "Thank you."

But inside him another voice answered. *No,* it said. *Not yet, I haven't. There's someplace I still need to go. Someone I need to find.*

CHAPTER 18

Nikki Perez entered headquarters and took the elevator to her office on the second floor. The lieutenant was loitering in the corridor. Before she could turn around, he spotted her.

"Perez, come here," he shouted, wagging a finger in her direction. "You finish taking statements from the drivers?"

"Three to go."

The lieutenant was short and chunky and wore white short-sleeved dress shirts all year round. No one called him by his name. "Clock's running. Get to it."

"We're thirteen for thirteen," said Nikki. "No one's offered anything useful. Twelve men with machine guns. All wearing black utilities. Combat boots. Faces covered. Plates off the cars. No one said a word except the leader and he spoke only to the prince."

"And so?"

"It's like listening to a broken record. I'd be better off spending my time working the streets, talking to my sources, the staff at the hotel. The bad guys had to have had a lookout there."

"Since when do you dole out assignments?"

"Just an idea, sir."

"Like the one that got you on administrative duty for ninety days?"

"Better than that."

"So you say." The lieutenant stepped close enough that his gut rubbed against her. "I want all the reports on my desk by noon. Including the last three."

Nikki turned to leave. "Prick," she said under her breath.

"What was that?" The lieutenant was in her face, eyes bulging.

"By noon. Yes, sir."

"That's what I thought you said."

Nikki continued to her desk. Ten years on the job and still the same nonsense. She'd joined the police a month after passing the "bac"—or baccalaureate—the nationwide examination that determined eligibility for entry into France's elite universities. With a score in the top two percent, she'd had her choice of the litter: the École Normale Supérieure, ParisTech, Sciences Po, or the Sorbonne. France was very much a hierarchical society. Graduation from any of these universities would have guaranteed her a place in the nation's ruling classes. But Nikki had never had an interest in joining the technocrats who governed the country from their stately offices on the Boulevard Haussmann, or the corporate warriors with their perfect hair and perfect suits charging across the esplanade of La Défense.

For as long as Nikki could remember, she'd wanted to be a cop. Maybe it was all the Clint Eastwood movies her father used to watch. *Dirty Harry, Magnum Force, The Gauntlet.* Or maybe it was because she'd always loved guns. Or maybe it was because she enjoyed breaking rules and being naughty just a little too much, and she knew that being a cop was her best shot at keeping that part of her in check. She'd stopped explaining her career choices long ago. It came down to this: She liked carrying a gun and a badge. She liked the feeling she got when she solved a crime. And she liked thinking of herself as someone who gave back more than she took. At the end of the day, she wanted to make a difference.

She sat and perused the statements she'd taken the day before. A stack of pages as thick as a phone book and as much help. Thirty-six hours after the crime, the task force had yet to come up with a single clue. She dropped her head to the desk. So far she'd served ten out of her ninety days on desk duty. She wouldn't make it through eighty more.

Her latest infraction took as its root an unwillingness to either "obey" or "respect" a statute in the police handbook regarding who was to receive official recognition for making an arrest. Or to put it in language anyone could understand: who got the collar for nabbing a perp.

The perp in question was Elias Zenström, an Estonian computer wiz who ran a phony credit card operation in the north of the city. Zenstrom and his gang would buy credit cards from Gypsy pickpockets, copy the data from the magnetic strips, and fabricate duplicates, which they would then sell or use themselves. Nikki had been assigned the case by her superior, a man whose name she refused to utter ever again.

For nine months she gathered evidence, interviewed dozens of victims, filed hundreds of requests for phone taps, spent countless nights in surveillance vans, and when the day came, she broke down the bad guy's door and, at risk of grave bodily harm, entered into an exchange of gunfire. Zenstrom was captured, as was his superior, who'd been visiting at the time. The gang was disbanded. Case closed.

Except for one thing.

Nikki made an error in her final report. When prompted to fill in the name of the officer in charge of the case, she typed her own: Nicolette Perez. Despite all her dogged work, she had not been—according to the police handbook—the officer in charge. The credit for the arrest of Zenstrom and his gang went to her superior, who had done precisely nothing other than assign her the case. And it was her superior who received a promotion. Nikki received a bottle of cheap champagne and, from her superior, a pinch on the ass and a drunken invitation to spend the night.

She was not pleased.

So she'd done what she'd done to earn her third ninety-day suspension.

Next time she nailed a perp she was going to make damn well sure she got the credit.

The phone rang. It was the reception informing her that one of the chauffeurs had arrived. "Send him up."

She leaned back in her chair, hands clasping her head. There was a disgruntled smile on her face. She was thinking about Simon Riske. She couldn't keep from wondering how he'd managed to slip the cigarette back into the tin. She'd kept the box closed during their conversation and was certain she'd seen him put the cigarette into his jacket pocket.

Then there was the scar on his forehead. Car accident, she decided, though she was sure any trained surgeon would have done a neater job stitching it. She'd been mistaken in her assessment of the man. He was hardly as polished a customer as he wanted people to think.

"Hey, what the hell are you doing?"

Nikki looked up to find Commissaire Dumont standing before her. Immediately, she sat up straighter, placing her hands on her desk. "Planning my day," she said.

"How did it go with Riske?" he asked.

"It went."

"Meaning?"

"He's an arrogant one. Coming into our office, asking of our time to help solve his client's problem. An English client, I'm sure."

"You might want to cut him some slack."

"I already have enough on my desk as it is. You know what he's looking for? A letter."

"Must be important."

"You're joking?"

Dumont sat on the edge of her desk. "Something I didn't tell you. The time we worked together tracking down that English girl…Riske had done his homework. He warned me that her boyfriend had connections to an Eastern European syndicate. He suggested that we go in heavy. Bring backup. I didn't believe him. I was like you. I thought he was a lightweight. We didn't have the kid anywhere on our radar. I thought he was just some punk. Simon didn't argue. We went in just the two of us. I was armed. He wasn't. We knock. The door opens and there's this guy standing there with a gun pointed right at me. He fired before I could draw my weapon."

"You took two bullets."

"In the hip and thigh because Riske shoved me out of the way…which left him standing unprotected not two feet from this coked-up maniac waving his gun around."

"You didn't say anything about Riske being shot."

"He wasn't. The guy's gun jammed. At least, I think it did. We never really talked about it afterward. All I can say is I've never seen anyone move so fast." Dumont snapped his fingers. "Like that, it was over. The guy was down, his arm broken so badly the bone was sticking clean through his sweater, and screaming like a stuck pig. Suddenly, I wasn't feeling so sorry for myself and my two lousy bullet wounds." Dumont leaned closer. "I guess I'm trying to say that Riske saved my life. So give him a hand. For me."

"I'm nailed to my desk for another eighty days. Lieutenant's orders."

"I'll talk to him. Get out of here."

"Really?"

"Move it."

Nikki grabbed her jacket off the back of her chair. "Oh," she said, scooting out the door. "And, Commissaire, there's a witness coming up. He's all yours."

CHAPTER 19

When Simon returned to the hotel, his seat in the gallery was available. He read a copy of the *New York Times Global Edition,* keeping one eye on the lobby. Fifteen minutes passed before he spotted the chief of security, bustling across the lobby in the company of another Middle Eastern guest. Their manner was serious yet intimate and bespoke a relationship as much personal as professional. The two men stopped at the concierge's desk. The head of security made his good-bye and headed Simon's way.

"Excuse me." Simon stood as the hotel security man passed. "Do you have a moment?"

The man stopped at once, giving him his full attention. "Of course," he said, trained smile at the ready. "How may I help?"

"My name is Riske. I'm a guest of the hotel. I was hoping we might speak." He offered his business card, which stated his affiliation with a firm called Special Protective Services and Investigations and listed addresses in London, Hong Kong, and New York. "Mr. . . . ?"

"Delacroix," he replied, coming to attention. "Jean-Jacques Delacroix."

"It's a matter of some importance. If you'll allow me to explain."

Delacroix studied the card, then looked Simon up and down. "Follow me."

Delacroix's office was located in a suite behind the reception. The room was small, windowless, and orderly. He studied the card before sitting, glancing at Simon as if deciding whether the man matched the profession. Finally, he gestured to a chair. "Please," he said. "I'm always happy to be of service to a fellow professional."

As Simon sat, he took in the photographs decorating the wall. There was Delacroix in combat gear, arms around fellow soldiers, looking weary and victorious. By the location, Simon guessed somewhere in Africa. There was a framed diploma from the military academy at Saint-Cyr. And a commendation from France's defense department with a medal attached nearby.

"You served?" he asked.

"Parachute brigade. Twenty years. And you?"

"In a different field," Simon answered, allowing Delacroix to imagine what he wished.

"Am I correct in guessing this has something to do with the prince?"

"Yes," said Simon, then in a bit of impromptu: "Did my office call ahead? They're a bit rattled about this one."

"No. They didn't blow your cover, if that's what you mean. I haven't stopped answering questions about the robbery since it happened."

"I'm sorry to make matters worse."

"That's why I'm here," said Delacroix. "Fire away."

Simon cleared his throat and assumed what he considered to be his professional voice, a little deeper, a little smoother. "First, I must ask that you treat our conversation as absolutely confidential."

"Of course."

"I'm sorry to be so blunt, but it's best to get these things out of the way."

The Frenchman made a show of spreading his hands. A man with nothing to hide.

Simon paused before continuing, studying Delacroix as if deciding whether he could trust him. "My firm has been retained by persons with close ties to Saudi Arabia. I don't need to tell you the position he holds in his country."

"Naturally."

"What you may not know is that at the time of the robbery, he was carrying sensitive government documents. Highly confidential. Were anyone unfriendly to our interests—and those include the interests of France—to get their hands on them, the damage would be incalculable."

Delacroix nodded, giving away nothing.

"He didn't mention anything about these to you?"

"No."

Simon considered this, nodding in a gesture of some relief, before assuming a new tack. "The prince is a frequent guest. Is that correct?"

"He stays with us from time to time."

"Once a year?"

"Twice, at least. Often four or five times."

"And it is his practice to travel with large sums of money?"

"As do many of our guests."

"So you're familiar with his security arrangements?"

"Intimately. It's my job to ensure his safety and that of his family and his possessions when he is a guest."

"I imagine he keeps the money in the hotel's safe."

"I can't comment on the prince's actions. We do, however, dispose of a strong room to keep our guests' valuables secure at all times. It's small but impregnable. Guests make use of it to store their jewelry and other items of particular value."

"And I understand he travels with his own staff when he leaves the hotel."

"Team of five. Four junior, who vary each trip. One senior, who's been with him forever. A Punjabi. Name of Vijay."

"Do you coordinate arrangements with this Vijay?"

"The prince prefers to work directly with me. He respects my expertise in these matters."

"Best to keep it between two professionals."

"It's the wise thing to do."

"I couldn't agree more. That's why I'm speaking with you. One professional to another." Simon scooted to the edge of his chair. "What other arrangements did you provide? Check his room for bugs? Counter-surveillance sweeps?"

"Again, I can't answer for the prince, but those are services that can be provided to any client upon request."

"And if you had provided those services," Simon went on, "*hypothetically* . . . did you have occasion to alert him of any unwanted attention?"

"If we had, the prince would have had nothing to worry about . . . *hypothetically*."

"No undue attention?"

"None that I'm aware of."

Simon stifled a smile. It was his way of thanking

Delacroix, before moving on to a more delicate topic. "What about transport to and from the airport?"

"Ensuring safe passage of our clients upon their arrival or departure is another service the hotel offers. Arrangements are made by the hotel concierge. We use the same livery service for all our clients."

"Based on your recommendations?"

Delacroix shrugged. "It's necessary to vet any firm the hotel employs on behalf of its clients."

"And you've been using this particular firm for how long?"

"Many years. We've never had a problem."

Simon rubbed a finger across his chin, eyes narrowed. Then he leaned closer and placed his arms on Delacroix's desk. "I have a question about the route the prince took to the airport Sunday night."

"Yes?"

"I lived in Paris years ago. I didn't have a car, but I got to know my way around. Me, personally, I never would have driven all the way across the city when the entrance to the highway is only a kilometer away. The route taken by the prince left him far more vulnerable to an attack than otherwise."

"Alas, I was not involved in planning the prince's route."

"Really? A moment ago you said you were intimately involved in all his security arrangements. Wouldn't such arrangements extend to finding the safest route possible to the airport?"

Delacroix sat straighter, shoulders stiff. A man accused. "The prince mapped his own route to the airport."

"Without consulting you?"

"No. As I said, the hotel provided for the livery, then it was up to him."

"So you have no idea why he decided to take this particular route?"

"None. My responsibility for him, his family, and his affairs stopped the moment he left the hotel."

Simon challenged his gaze. "Even after all these years?"

Delacroix stared back, a current of dislike flashing behind his eyes. He placed his hands on his desk and stood. "If there's anything else, Mr. Riske."

But Simon remained firmly seated. "A crime has taken place," he stated. "Documents relevant to the security of the West are missing. The time for discretion is past."

"What are you trying to say, Mr. Riske?"

"You and I both know that the criminals had advance knowledge of the prince's route."

"And I told the police as much," replied Delacroix. "Clearly, it was an inside job."

"So no one approached you?"

"No. And had they, I would have been the first to tell the police."

Simon waited, eyes fixed on Delacroix. Finally, he stood. "That's all I need. Thank you."

"Any time. I'm sorry I could not be of more assistance."

Simon waited for Delacroix to open the door, as he knew he would. As the Frenchman circled his desk and made his way to the door, Simon stepped forward a moment too soon and collided with him.

"Are you all right?" asked Delacroix, backing away.

"My mistake," said Simon, ruffled. "Good morning."

He did not look behind him as he walked down the corridor.

CHAPTER 20

Simon proceeded directly to the nearest men's room. Inside, he entered a stall—in this case a compartment unto itself with walls running from floor to ceiling—and closed and locked the door. If a commode had to serve as a workspace, at least he'd chosen a nice one.

Like most European models, Delacroix's phone ran on a SIM card that housed the phone's memory—calls, texts, emails, photos, and all apps—and could be transferred between devices, for instance, whenever one upgraded models. He popped the back of the phone and removed the micro SD card and the battery, revealing the SIM card, which was white and rectangular and no larger than his thumbnail. Using a spudger—nothing more than a miniature spatula—he pried the SIM card loose and snapped it into the card reader he held in the palm of his left hand.

Thirty seconds later, the contents of Delacroix's phone belonged to him.

Simon reassembled Delacroix's phone and left the men's room, returning to the lobby. At noon, the large, airy room was bustling, guests and staff moving purposefully in all directions. Delacroix was nowhere in sight. Simon stopped at the concierge's desk and asked for a table at Le Relais de l'Entrecôte, a few blocks away. As the concierge consulted his computer for the establishment's phone number and placed the call, Simon allowed Delacroix's phone to slip from his pant leg to the floor, then used his toe to scoot it close to the counter.

"Monsieur Riske, a table is booked under your name."

Simon slipped the concierge a ten-euro note. "On second thought, cancel it. Something's come up. Thank you."

Simon left the hotel and walked down the street toward the Pont de l'Alma. He had not lifted Delacroix's phone to learn about the Hotel George V head of security's activities, though he suspected he was in some way involved. Delacroix was too smart to have left any digital breadcrumbs on his phone—or anywhere else for that matter—that might tie him to Coluzzi.

Simon had borrowed Delacroix's phone for another reason entirely. He was certain that it contained a great deal of information about Prince Abdul Aziz bin Saud.

If Mr. Neill refused to tell him what exactly the prince had stolen, that was fine.

Simon intended to find out for himself.

Valentina Asanova stood across the street from the Hotel George V, staring into the window of an exclusive jewelry store. The display showcased a diamond necklace, emerald earrings, and a sapphire ring large enough to sink a ship. She was not a fan of what the French called *haute joaillerie*. It was just as well. Any one of the items cost more than her monthly salary.

Valentina turned from the store to study the hotel.

Since receiving the assignment, she'd read everything she could find about the robbery two days earlier and viewed every newsclip available on the Internet. Director Borodin had provided her a single lead: his belief that Jean-Jacques Delacroix, the hotel's chief of security, was somehow involved. Otherwise, he'd given her no specific instructions. How she found the man who'd robbed the prince was up to her.

She had dressed appropriately for the mission. No spandex shorts and watch cap today, but a dark skirt, a white blouse, a string of pearls around her neck, a Rolex on her wrist.

Valentina continued up the street, watching hotel guests come and go. She did not pay special attention to the man with close-cropped black hair and a tailored navy suit leaving the hotel, other than to remark on his purposeful gait and fine posture. She liked a man with a spring in his step.

After a moment, Valentina abandoned her casual surveillance and continued up the street toward the Champs-Élysées. Like the man in the blue suit, her stride was purposeful and her posture beyond reproach. She mapped out the afternoon ahead. Coffee, a short rest, additional surveillance, then time to go to work.

She'd done her homework. She had little doubt she could convince Monsieur Delacroix to tell her everything he knew.

Valentina put on her sunglasses and lifted her face to the sky.

Alone in a foreign country on a mission for her government and with a mandate to take any and all necessary measures, no questions asked. She'd never been happier.

Chapter 21

Nikki gunned her bike, a Ducati Monster, hugging the tank, eyes glued to the road as she weaved in and out of traffic. Aziz François still hadn't called back. This irked her. François was her best informant and one of the city's biggest drug dealers. He was in hot water.

Ahead, the light turned yellow. At the intersection, cars nosed forward. Nikki feathered the throttle, the bike's throaty engine urging her forward, daring her to make a move. The light turned red. She punched the gas and rocketed across the intersection, horns blaring to either side. She looked over her shoulder, thinking it was closer than she might have liked, but not caring. Inside her helmet, she smiled. It was the first jolt of excitement she'd had all day.

For as long as she could remember, Nikki had enjoyed going fast. Maybe "enjoyed" wasn't the right word. She enjoyed a nice quiche Lorraine or a crisp Sancerre. She loved going fast. She lived for the moment when the needle on her speedometer crossed two hundred kilometers an hour and the world got a little fuzzy around the edges and there was only the asphalt beneath her tires and the white line running down the center of the road.

Nikki turned onto the Boulevard Barbès. The neighborhood changed dramatically. There were no more banks and pharmacies and electronics stores. The streets were decorated with colorful awnings, vendors offering kebabs and plantains, stalls full of T-shirts and leather goods. The sidewalks coursed with a dark-hued humanity. This part of the 18th arrondissement was called the Goutte d'Or—the Drop of Gold—and it belonged to the immigrants who'd migrated to France since Napoleon III had begun colonizing West Africa in the nineteenth century. If she weren't looking at the dome of the Sacré-Coeur, sparkling at the top of the hill, she'd have thought herself in Dakar, not Paris.

She parked the bike two blocks from Aziz's and locked her helmet in the rear case along with her leather jacket. Taking care, she untucked her T-shirt to cover her firearm. Aziz did his business out of a clothing boutique called Fleur d'Afrique that offered dashikis, swatches of colorful fabrics imported from Senegal, Niger, and Guinea. She stopped across the street and spent a minute observing the noontime foot traffic. A few women dressed in native garb left the store. Nikki crossed the street and continued to the alley running behind the store. Halfway down, she saw a door open and a thin white man in a black leather jacket emerge from Aziz's back room and jump into the passenger seat of a waiting Mercedes. She grabbed the license and ran a check. The result came back in real time. Nikki shook her head. Aziz was being a bad boy. No wonder he wasn't answering his phone.

She checked the back door and found it locked, then walked around to the main entrance. She walked past the counter, through the racks of clothing, and passed through a bead curtain. A pall of pot smoke hung in the air. She opened a door marked PRIVATE and stepped into Aziz's office. A large muscular black man sat behind a desk piled high with folders and loose papers.

"Come on," she said, waving a hand in front of her face. "It's barely noon."

"Wake and bake, sergeant," said Aziz François, exhaling twin streams of smoke through his nose. "Help yourself."

"Put it out," she said.

Aziz gave her a sour look and stubbed it out in the ashtray.

"Thank you," she said.

Aziz François sat up straighter. "How can I help my favorite police officer this fine morning?"

As always, she was intimidated by his size, the notion that he could be across the desk with his hands around her neck before she could do a thing to stop him.

"Who was that guy I saw coming out the back?"

"Of my place? No one."

"Sure about that?"

"I've been alone all morning."

Nikki let it slide for now. "I'm looking for two men. Salvatore Brigantino and Tino Coluzzi."

"Why are you asking me? Do I look Italian?" Aziz threw his head back and laughed.

Aziz François was a native of Senegal. Head shaved, a gold hoop decorating one ear, and wearing his favorite mirrored Ray-Bans, he stood six four with the physique of a heavyweight boxer. He did not look Italian.

"They're Corsican," she said. "You know why I'm asking. It's the reason you're not sitting in a cell in La Santé doing twenty to life."

She'd busted Aziz two years earlier as he made a buy of a hundred kilos of Colombian marijuana—"*l'herbe,*" in the parlance. The volume of the buy guaranteed him a long stretch in prison. She had dropped the charges to a misdemeanor and made sure he was out in three months. Ever since, he'd been her eyes and ears on the street. The fact was, most criminals used drugs on a regular basis, be it marijuana, coke, meth, or, more commonly these days, opioids like OxyContin that mimicked heroin's narcotizing effect. Aziz carried them all.

"What did they do?" he asked.

"Let me worry about that." Nikki crossed her arms and gave him the look. She wasn't about to say they stole a letter. She preferred not to be laughed out of the place.

"Brigantino's dead. Long time now."

"I hadn't heard."

"Cancer. He was in Germany getting some experimental treatment. His son was in here last year looking for some painkillers for the dad."

"Last year?"

Aziz nodded.

"And Coluzzi?"

"Don't know the man."

"Sure you do. He took down a shipment of ten thousand OxyContin a year ago. There's no way he could have moved that amount without you hearing about it."

"Russians control that market."

"So if I needed a few pills for my back, you can't help me?"

"I can ask around, you really want. These days it's just weed, meth, and a little coke if it's good."

"But you had some painkillers for Brigantino?"

"I didn't say that."

"And that Mercedes that I saw leaving here about fifteen minutes ago, the one registered to Vladimir Kuznetsov…" Nikki waited a minute, letting Aziz know not to screw with her. "You don't know anything about that either?"

Aziz stubbornly shook his head.

"I bet if I look around I'll find something other than weed and 'a little coke…if it's good.'"

"Be my guest."

Nikki stood and slipped her folding knife from her back pocket. She left Aziz's office and made her way through a storeroom that was a maze of boxes and bales of fabric piled nearly to the ceiling. She chose a box at random and cut into it. Inside was bright orange cotton.

"Come on," said Aziz, who had left his desk and was standing at her shoulder. "You're ruining good merchandise."

Nikki disregarded him and continued through the storeroom. She rammed the blade into another box. More fabric.

"Tino Coluzzi," she said. "I'm waiting."

One of Aziz's men was standing by the back entrance, cradling a submachine gun, the barrel pointed at her.

"Watch it." Nikki walked past him, pushing the barrel toward the ground before turning into another row. It was darker here, the overhead lights too dim to reach the farthest recesses. She stopped, retreated a step, and thrust the knife into a box. The cardboard was newer, darker, and did not look as if it had been thrown around on an airport freight conveyor or packed tightly in a twenty-foot BEU. When she pulled the blade out, a drizzle of white powder fell to the floor. She looked at

Aziz, then ran her finger along the blade and tasted the residue.

"We had an agreement," she said, turning to face Aziz.

"First time. I swear. The deal was too good to pass up."

"You know how I feel about heroin."

"I know, Nikki. Your brother…"

"Don't talk about my brother," she said, standing on tiptoes, getting in Aziz François's face.

"It's only a couple keys," he said plaintively. "How'd you find it, anyway?"

"Must be my lucky day. Turn around. Hands behind your back. I can't let this one stand. I'm disappointed in you, Aziz."

Suddenly, the guard was standing in front of her, the barrel of the machine gun prodding her chest. "Let him go," he said.

The guard was young, maybe twenty years old, but hardened by his time on the streets. She had no doubt he'd hated the police since before he could walk. His finger was inside the trigger guard and he was sweating. Five pounds of pressure—barely more than you needed to tap a letter on a keyboard—was enough to fire a round. His unblinking gaze said he'd shoot her if given the chance.

"Tell him to fuck off," she said, unsnapping her cuffs from her belt.

Aziz sighed mightily and told the guard to leave them alone.

"But…" the guard protested.

"Leave us," said Aziz. "Go to my office. Shut the door."

Reluctantly, the guard lowered the machine gun and walked away.

"Okay," said Aziz when he heard the door close. "I can help you."

"Too late."

"I know this man Coluzzi."

"Sure you do," said Nikki. "His name just popped into your head."

"I bought some merch from him last year."

"Oxy?"

Aziz nodded. "Like you said."

"Go on."

"He was getting a crew together not too long ago."

"Last year?"

"Last week."

"He doesn't work with your people. How would you know?"

"Another guy like him was in, looking to score some weed. Just a key. We smoked a blunt and he mentioned that he was working for this dude. A real smooth operator."

"Coluzzi?"

"Yeah, that's the name. I remember now."

"Of course you do. What else do you remember?"

"That's it. Coluzzi was getting some of his guys together, used to be part of some gang in Marseille."

"What were they going to do?"

"No idea. I swear. The guy who told me was high. He probably knew he'd already said too much."

"So where can I find your friend?"

"I don't know. He just called me, came by."

"What's his number?"

"He uses a burner. I kill my log every day."

Nikki reached again for her cuffs.

"Wait, wait," said Aziz. "We hung out once. This bar in the Marais. Full of guys like him from down south. Names like Luca and Giovanni. Leather coats. Gold chains. Too much cologne."

"Give me your friend's name."

"I can't do that, Nikki. That's asking too much."

Nikki opened the cuffs. "Hands in front or in back?"

"Jack. Giacomo's his real name."

"Jack or Giacomo who hangs out at a bar in the Marais."

"Le Galleon Rouge."

Nikki considered this. It might be true or it might not. She'd never heard of the bar, but then again, she wasn't one to hang around the Marais. She put away the cuffs. "I'm going to need to take it."

"Cost me fifty grand."

"How much is your freedom worth?"

Aziz sat on a box, shoulders slumped, a hand contemplating his bald scalp. Nikki tapped him on the shoulder. Aziz glanced up.

"Which side?" she asked.

"Excuse me?"

"I've been back here with you too long. Can't have anyone thinking I'm your friend."

Aziz touched his right cheek. "Go easy."

Nikki made a fist and slugged him in the face. Aziz toppled off the box and onto the floor. To his credit, he didn't whimper.

"That was for my brother," said Nikki.

CHAPTER 22

The match between Olympique de Marseille and Paris Saint-Germain was a preseason encounter slated to begin at three p.m. Tino Coluzzi joined the throngs of fans streaming across the grounds toward the Stade Vélodrome. While most were attired in shorts and T-shirts, Coluzzi was dressed in a summer-weight tan suit, a white shirt open at the collar. He didn't plan on watching the game with the masses. It was his objective to watch alongside the richest man in the stadium: Alexei Ren.

Nearing the entry, he removed his jacket and slung it over his shoulder. The heat was oppressive, with only the faintest of breezes. He dug a handkerchief from his pocket and wiped his forehead. If he didn't get into the shade soon, he'd sweat through his shirt. It was not the kind of impression he wanted to make.

The heat wasn't the only thing making him sweat. He'd had no contact from the American in almost two days. Lying awake in his cramped, low-ceilinged bedroom, doors and windows battered shut, he'd wondered with concern bordering on fear who was coming after him. He didn't peg the American as someone who would walk away after being betrayed and leave things as they stood. He was coming for the letter.

And so were the Russians.

Coluzzi took this as fact because he would do the same. And he'd be coming with a vengeance.

There was a long line to gain entrance to the stadium. Besides the men and women taking tickets, a healthy contingent of police was standing at or near the turnstiles. Their presence didn't unsettle him. Crowds at Marseille football matches were known to get rowdy. What did unsettle him were the newly installed cameras perched atop the gates. He was no expert in technology but he knew that the facial-recognition systems implemented at high-profile venues around the country had resulted in several of his associates being arrested.

Coluzzi handed his ticket to the worker, doing his best to keep his head down, his face away from the cameras. The police paid him no mind and he proceeded into the stadium without incident, taking an escalator to the mezzanine concourse.

Years had passed since he'd attended a game. The old wooden benches were gone. Everything looked new and much too shiny. Beer came from polished taps behind neon-lit logos for Heineken and Kronenbourg and was sold by men and women in pressed uniforms. He missed the colorful vendors tossing out insults along with the cups of lukewarm brew.

The players were on the field warming up. He spotted Alexei Ren standing at midfield, kicking a ball back and forth with a few players. Despite the heat, he was wearing a long-sleeved shirt buttoned at the collar.

The scoreboard ticked down the time until kickoff. Ren retreated to the sideline. The game began and still he stood with his players. Coluzzi kept his eyes on the Russian, worried he'd remain on the field the entire game. At five minutes, the visiting team scored. Ren hung his head in dismay and walked into the stadium, Coluzzi assumed to the elevator that would take him to his luxury box.

Coluzzi looked to his right, where an escalator took ticket holders to the club level and to Ren's luxury box. Two security guards examined tickets and waved a metal detector over each guest's torso. A pair of Marseille policemen stood nearby, checking IDs. Jojo's ticket was good enough to get him into the stadium, but that was it.

Coluzzi continued down the concourse, stopping to buy a beer. Hand in his pocket, he sipped the beer, all the while examining the comings and goings of the stadium personnel. He'd spent his life studying an organization's security arrangements. Be it an armored car company, a bank, or a jewelry store, all had one thing in common. A schedule.

By now, the concourse was more or less empty. He was able to observe the stadium staff at work. Passing the next escalator he noted that with the game under way, security to the luxury level had slackened. Only one guard and one policeman remained in place. Still, that was enough. The escalator was out of the question.

Farther along, he dumped his beer and purchased a frozen piña colada. The drink was perfect cover, he decided. What kind of a man in his profession drank a sweet icy drink with a maraschino cherry on top? He prayed he didn't run into someone he knew. Some things you couldn't explain.

A team of two workers dressed in canary-yellow

shorts and shirts stopped at an elevator a few steps past the escalator. Sipping from his curlicue straw, he watched as they summoned the elevator, then used a key to unlock the door when it arrived. Coluzzi stayed in position. Ten minutes later, the two returned, carrying several trash bags. They crossed the concourse to an unmarked door, entered, deposited the trash, and returned to continue their rounds.

After the third pickup, he followed them to the trash room. He waited until they were inside, then opened the door and entered, stumbling purposely.

"Excuse me, sir," one of them said, dark-skinned, maybe twenty-five, Algerian or Libyan. "Can I help you?"

"I'm looking for the men's room," said Coluzzi, feigning drunkenness. "I can't wait another second."

The workers exchanged a look, then approached him. "This is not the men's room, sir."

"Isn't it?" Coluzzi threw the frozen drink into the dark-skinned worker's face, then turned and punched his colleague, two knuckles to the cheek with brio. The man fell to the ground, grabbing at his busted face. The Algerian recoiled, wiping the drink from his face. Coluzzi slugged him in the stomach. The man doubled over. Coluzzi delivered a blow to his exposed neck. Second man down.

The other man tried to get to his feet. Coluzzi took a length of hair in his fist and slammed his forehead against the concrete floor. Once. Twice. Again and again until the man went limp.

Standing, Coluzzi kicked the Algerian in the face and ribs until he was sure the man was incapacitated. Then he kicked him some more because he hated immigrants.

He found the key to the elevator and yanked it free from the fob.

A minute later he was standing at the work elevator below Alexei Ren's luxury box. And a minute after that he was alone in the box's service kitchen. He passed through a door and found himself in a large air-conditioned lounge with a serve-yourself bar, a counter piled high with sandwiches, a popcorn machine, and a lovely young blonde pouring champagne.

He asked for a flute, and when he received it, there was Alexei Ren, walking past him. A pretty Asian woman followed him, an iPad clutched in one hand.

The box was nearly empty and no one seemed to pay any attention to the new arrival. Coluzzi watched the game, speaking to no one. A few minutes later the Asian woman returned. He approached her, a smile on his face.

"Yes?"

"I'm an old friend of Mr. Ren's. Could you ask him if he has a minute?"

The woman regarded him askance. "Your name?"

"Jojo."

"Jojo what?"

"Just Jojo. He'll know me."

"Mr. Ren will see you now."

The Asian woman led the way to a private suite and showed Coluzzi in. The room was empty, a magnum of Dom Pérignon on ice next to a tureen of caviar.

Coluzzi paced the room, unsure of how to broach the reason for his urgent appointment. It would be the truth. There was simply no way around it.

Ten minutes passed. Finally, the door opened. Alexei Ren entered, followed by two bodyguards. Ren eyed him, then whispered something to the bodyguards. The men retreated to a far corner. Ren approached him. "You're not Jojo Matta. Actually, how the hell did you get in here?"

Coluzzi introduced himself, saying he was an old friend of Jojo's and that he'd grown up in the area. He didn't need to say more.

"I'm no longer in that line of work," said Ren.

Coluzzi said nothing, meeting his gaze, his expression calling bullshit on him.

Ren came closer. "Why shouldn't I have you thrown out?"

"That might be a mistake you'd come to regret."

"Is that a threat?"

"Absolutely not. Just a missed opportunity. It's not often a man is given the chance to make a difference to his country."

"And you're offering me such a chance?" Ren regarded the possibility as humorous. "I didn't realize I was in the company of a patriot."

"Or a chance to get even," said Coluzzi. "I understand your departure from Russia wasn't voluntary."

"I like to say I received the same treatment as Lenin…only in reverse. I was shipped out of my country like a plague bacillus."

Coluzzi smiled wanly. He had no idea what Ren was talking about. "You must miss home."

Ren checked his watch. "The second half is about to begin, Mr. Coluzzi."

"Before you said I was a patriot. Are you one as well?"

"I am a businessman."

"And if you were given the chance to rid your homeland of a traitor, would you take it?"

Ren came closer. All traces of a smile had vanished and Coluzzi noticed the faintly bloodshot eyes, the spidery veins in his cheeks, the sour breath smelling of vodka. "What do you want?" asked Ren.

"Look at this." Coluzzi held up his phone, displaying a series of pictures of the letter, the envelope, and the stationery found in the prince's briefcase. "Everything you see is authentic. I have it in my possession. It's my intention to give it to the man for whom it was intended."

"Who is that?"

"Vassily Borodin. Director of the SVR."

"I know who Vassily Borodin is." Ren snatched the phone from Coluzzi's hand and examined the pictures. "If this is authentic—and I have no reason to believe it is—how did you get your hands on it?" He handed Coluzzi back the phone. "Excuse me, but I must be going."

Coluzzi grabbed his arm. "Wait."

Ren stopped and faced him, eyes wide. The bodyguards, who had been keeping a distance, closed in.

Coluzzi released Ren's arm. "You saw what happened in Paris. I found this in the prince's briefcase along with an email indicating that he was working on behalf of Borodin."

Ren angled his head, a new appreciation in his eyes. "It was you who took down the convoy in Paris?"

Coluzzi nodded. He had no intention of mentioning the American spy who'd put him on to it. He'd already let slip too much information.

"*Chapeau,*" said Ren, meaning "well done." He ran a hand over his beard before asking to see the pictures once again. "I'll need to examine the letter."

"It doesn't look any different than in the picture."

"You don't trust me?"

Coluzzi offered no response.

"And you believe Borodin will pay you?"

"I believe he had plans to use the letter to his advantage."

Ren handed back the phone. "Not interested."

He walked out of the suite and into the lounge, Coluzzi following close behind. All heads followed their departure.

"Don't you want to get even with the man who threw you out of Russia?" asked Coluzzi.

Ren turned on him. "Don't ever presume to tell me what I do or do not wish to do. Now get lost."

He barked off a series of commands to his bodyguards, who immediately took Coluzzi by the arms and escorted him to the door.

"And don't come back," said Ren, heatedly enough to cause his guests to look. "Ever!"

Coluzzi didn't resist as the bodyguards escorted him physically from the box. Once outside, he tried to shake himself loose, to no avail. "You can let me go now."

"Those are not Mr. Ren's wishes."

"Where are you taking me?"

"The same place we take all people who upset Mr. Ren." The bodyguards exchanged a look. The grip on his arms tightened. Coluzzi considered struggling, then spotted several policemen twenty yards or so down the concourse.

The men descended the escalators to the entry level, then continued down farther to the second subterranean level. They passed through steel doors with armed sentries standing to either side. Neither gave Coluzzi a second look as the bodyguards led him into the players' parking lot. The doors closed behind them and he was guided to a silver Mercedes sedan.

"Get in."

"Really?" said Coluzzi. "Let's stop this here. I was only talking to Mr. Ren."

"That's the problem." The larger of the two fired a fist into Coluzzi's gut. He saw it coming and recoiled, weakening the blow. He fired a jab in return, catching the man's jaw, buckling his knees. The second man hit Coluzzi in the ribs, knuckles curled, and then again in the sternum, full force. That was that. A moment later, Coluzzi found himself in the back seat, doubled up, breath a hundred miles away. He was only mildly aware of the engine turning over and the car traveling out of a tunnel. When he sat up, he observed that they were traveling down the Avenue du Prado, heading into town, not out of it.

"Don't ask," said the driver, eyeing him in the rearview mirror.

Coluzzi coughed and was disheartened to see flecks of blood on his hand. He laid his head against the window, the stream of air-conditioning bringing him back to life. He remained silent as the car passed the old fort, then descended toward the water. They rounded a corner and the port came into view. The first vessel he saw was the *Solange,* its sharp navy bow closest to the entry. The car passed through a security gate, drove a short distance, and stopped in front of the gangway.

The smaller man opened the door. "Out."

Coluzzi dragged himself from the car, holding his ribs to the bemusement of the bodyguards.

"Mr. Ren asked that you wait in the main salon. Help yourself to the buffet and keep out of sight. He will see you after the match."

"Have a drink," said the larger man, grabbing Coluzzi by the collar and straightening him up.

"On us," said the other.

Coluzzi nodded his head weakly, then spun and kneed the larger man in the testicles, hands on his shoulders, pulling him into the blow. The other took a step toward him, one hand going for his gun, then hesitated, his eyes searching the dock. Coluzzi grabbed the gun hand and twisted the wrist, snapping it, then shoved the bodyguard off the dock and into the sea. The man came up sputtering a moment later, swearing oaths at Coluzzi.

The captain rushed down the gangway. "What's going on?"

Coluzzi straightened his jacket. "These gentlemen offered me a drink. I plan on making it a double."

CHAPTER 23

Simon found a table in the shade at the café Les Deux Magots on the Left Bank. A waiter arrived and he ordered a beer and a ham and cheese baguette. He set his laptop on the table, using a flash cable to attach the SIM card reader. Waiting for the files to transfer, he placed a call to the shop. After checking that everything was on schedule, he asked to speak with Lucy.

"She's not in," said Harry Mason.

"Sick?"

"Don't know. Didn't call. Just didn't show." His floor boss was a bluff Irishman who regarded speaking as an exquisite form of torture.

"Did you call to see if she's all right?"

"What am I...her daddy?"

"Give me her number."

"Don't have it."

"Jane at reception will give it to you."

"Yeah, all right."

While he waited, Simon thought how little he knew about Lucy. He'd found her at the bar of the Dorchester hotel. Not quite a pro, but getting ready to test the waters. Beneath the makeup and the overconfidence, she appeared a frightened, desperate girl nearing the end of her rope. He bought her a pint and she spilled her story. Broken home, dad left the country, mom remarried, the new husband hit on Lucy. When she told the husband to fuck off, he lied and said she'd come on to him. Her mother took the husband's side and that was that. Lucy was on her own at the age of fifteen. For a year she moved from one friend's to another. School became an afterthought. She worked at entry-level jobs at fast-food joints, hotels, and restaurants. As she grew older and she filled out into a curvy, attractive woman, she began working as a hostess or server at bars and clubs, even though she was years underage. She started to drink and do drugs. Men approached her to "work" for them. She turned them down, but it was getting harder to pass up the money. She'd finally decided to say yes when she met Simon.

He saw enough of himself in her to give a damn. He set her up in a flat, gave her a job that taught her a trade, and made her promise never to touch drugs again. That had been eighteen months ago.

Harry Mason came back on the line and gave Simon her number. "When are you back?"

"Next week. Anything you can't handle, give me a call."

"Won't be necessary." Mason hung up.

Lucy Brown didn't answer her phone and her mailbox was full. Simon didn't like the vibe he was getting. He sent a text requesting that she call him immediately. Ten minutes later his phone hadn't rung. He wondered if he'd erred in giving her such a large check for her help the other night. There were a lot of ways a twenty-three-year-old girl could go off the rails in London, especially a girl with a dark history like Lucy's.

Have faith, he told himself. *There are plenty of reasons why she might not be answering.* He made a mental note to try later in the afternoon.

Lunch arrived. Simon took a bite of the sandwich, then started looking at the contents of Delacroix's phone. He began with text messages, scrolling through the names of those with whom Delacroix had communicated over the last few days. The first ten were hotel staff, as indicated by the subjects they discussed. The eleventh name was someone named Pascal, who appeared to be his bookie. A perusal of the texts showed that Delacroix was a gambler and owed Pascal over ten thousand euros. Real money.

The twelfth name was "Prince AA."

Simon counted over fifty texts. The first exchange began upon the prince's arrival in Paris.

Prince AA: Landed. Confirm pick up.
Delacroix: Cars at airport. Terminal 1.

…and ended minutes before the prince left the hotel.

Prince AA: Coming down. Have cash ready.
Delacroix: Done.

In between was everything from A to Z.

Simon found nothing that indicated Delacroix's involvement in the robbery—no mention, for example, that it was he who had suggested that the prince alter his route—but plenty of background to hint at the close relationship between the two men. It was evident that Prince Abdul Aziz trusted Delacroix absolutely.

The phone rang. He checked the screen. "Hello there, young lady," Simon answered pleasantly. "How are things?"

"Fine," said Lucy Brown.

"Just called the shop. Harry said you were MIA."

"MIA...what's that?"

"Missing in action. You sick?"

"You checking up on me?"

"As a matter of fact, I am."

"Fuck off, then. I can take care of myself."

"You sound like you're fighting a pretty good hangover."

"Maybe I am."

Simon took a breath, wondering how to play this. Like Harry Mason had said, he wasn't her dad. He was her boss. A concerned boss, but that was as far as it went. "You coming in tomorrow?"

"Yeah."

"You're sure?"

"Look, Simon, it was my friend's birthday last night. We were out at the pub. It was the first time I've been able to buy a round in a long time. It felt good to show off a bit. Anything wrong with that?"

"No, Lucy. There's nothing wrong with that. But next time, do it over the weekend. And if you're going to miss work, call in. Harry was worried sick about you."

"Harry?" asked Lucy. "Bullocks!" And they both laughed. "How's Paris?"

"Paris is Paris."

"You promised to take me one day."

"Just show up for work tomorrow. Goodbye, Lucy."

Simon finished his sandwich and went back to the laptop. He concentrated on Delacroix's emails. Again, he found nothing about the robbery. Nowhere was there a mention of a connection to Coluzzi—no emails and no texts. But Simon hadn't expected to find anything. He figured Delacroix to be a smart operator. He knew better than to leave a digital trail of crumbs.

Simon continued on his hunt, nosing through Delacroix's apps. He found the treasure buried in one named "Notes," within a subfile with the prince's name. The breadth of the information confirmed his impression that Delacroix enjoyed the prince's full trust, and amplified his disgust at Delacroix's subsequent betrayal of it. Among the information listed was the prince's passport number, his date of birth, nine credit card numbers along with corresponding security codes, and multiple phone numbers with telecom companies.

"Something else for you?" asked the waiter.

Simon glanced up from the laptop. "Just the bill."

His phone rang again. He didn't recognize the number. "Hello?"

"I'll be at Julien's in fifteen minutes," said Nikki Perez. "I can't stay long."

"I'll be there."

Simon slipped his laptop into his shoulder bag and stood, leaving a fifty-euro note on the table.

It was the waiter's lucky day.

Chapter 24

"So here's the tough guy."

Alexei Ren stood in front of Coluzzi, staring down at him. An hour had passed since the match ended. Coluzzi had passed the time doing shots of vodka, hoping they'd kill the pain in his ribs. They hadn't, and now he was half in the bag. "Have a seat. Your boat."

"You owe me two security men."

"Is that what you call them?"

"One has a fractured wrist. The other won't be walking for a few days."

"Send me the bill."

Ren studied him. "You know," he said, unbuttoning his collar and rolling up his sleeves, "I'm actually glad to see you."

"Your boys let me know," said Coluzzi. "Thrilled."

"You remind me of how things used to be."

"That right?"

"When things were a little tougher and a man had to know how to look out for himself." Ren picked up the vodka. "Can I pour you another?"

"Better not," said Coluzzi. "Just in case you want to let me know how glad you are to see me again."

Ren poured himself a shot and Coluzzi saw that Jojo hadn't been lying. Ren's arms and chest were covered with a latticework of inked art.

"Nastrovje," said Ren, raising his glass and downing the vodka. "Did you see the game? Almost had them, but they were too strong in the end."

"You need a new fullback."

"We need two, but we can't afford them at the moment. It's a principle of mine that all my businesses pay for themselves."

"Good idea."

"Only way," said Ren, falling into a low-backed chair. "Otherwise you find yourself throwing good money after bad."

He poured them both another shot. "I admit it was a surprise hearing from a friend of Jojo's. We go back quite some time. If you'd been a bit more discreet, I wouldn't have had to make my boys teach you a lesson."

"Sure you would have."

Ren shrugged. "Old habits. I don't pal around with your type these days. Just the way it is."

"My mistake."

Ren looked at him for a long moment, the blue, emotionless eyes boring into him. Suddenly, he smiled and slapped Coluzzi on the knee. "And so, my friend. What's your guess? Just how badly does Mr. Borodin want that letter?"

"He flew to Cyprus to pick it up. You decide."

"No, you. Go on."

"I'm no expert on world affairs. To be honest, I've never left France. The only people I trust are my family. The people I work with. But Borodin...he didn't use his own people to bring him the letter. He wanted to keep it a secret. He can't trust his own guys."

"You're talking about Russia, my friend. A country built on distrust from the ground up. People are born with two sets of eyes—one to see ahead, the other behind to protect against being stabbed in the back."

"That may be," said Coluzzi. "But Borodin didn't obtain the letter to protect his boss. He got it to bring him down."

"One letter?" Ren scoffed. "Never!"

"What do you mean?"

"Anyone can deny one letter. He will claim it's a forgery. A plant by the CIA. Who knows? Maybe it is. Either way, one letter isn't enough. There's got to be more."

"Maybe," said Coluzzi. "But the letter is the capper. Borodin may have other information, but without the letter it doesn't mean much."

Ren poured another shot and swirled the vodka in his glass. "That part is true, my friend. You're smarter than a back-country peasant."

Coluzzi inclined his head politely, vowing to kill the arrogant Russian. He'd use his stiletto. Ren wouldn't feel it entering his rib cage until it was too late.

"I can reach Vassily Borodin," said Ren. "It will not be cheap, however."

Coluzzi remained impassive. Ren was a man who wore two hats. He'd seen the public version at the stadium. The polished, successful businessman who never missed his team's games. Now he was seeing the private version. Not hardly as polished, and every bit as ruthless as Jojo had warned him.

"How much?" he asked finally.

"How much did you steal from the prince?" asked Ren.

It was impossible to lie. A newsman had gotten to a

hotel cashier who had divulged the amount the prince kept in the safe. "Six hundred thousand and change."

"Exactly?"

"Six hundred twenty-two thousand."

"Think of it as your buy-in to the game. In return, you keep all that Borodin agrees to pay."

"I was thinking more of a shared arrangement."

"Oh?"

"You make contact with Borodin, help with the negotiations. We split what he pays."

"An interesting proposition, except for one fact." Ren put down his glass. "Without me, you have no chance of getting one ruble for your letter. Do you really think he will negotiate with you? A common hoodlum? He's the chief of the second most powerful intelligence agency in the world."

"I think he will talk to whoever has the letter. Me, you, or a hooker from Jojo's."

Ren threw his head back and laughed. "Maybe you are right after all, Tino. Maybe so. Anyhow, my offer stands. Take it or leave it. I don't want a kopek from the men who placed me in prison for five years, stole all that I had, then exiled me from my homeland. You, however, are a different story."

"I've had to pay my associates. There were expenses. There is nothing close to six hundred thousand euros left."

"Let's say five hundred thousand, then. That's a nice round number. I'm not a greedy man. I'll make the call as soon as you hand over the money."

"You'll get the money once the meeting is set. I'll do my own talking, if you don't mind."

"Fair enough," said Ren, as if he'd expected the demand all along. "And, Tino, I will need to look at the letter. I have no doubt that it's real, but face facts. You're a small-timer who steals a crumb here, a crumb there, and you're asking me—Alexei Ren—to use my contacts to reach out to the highest levels of a foreign government."

"I'll arrange it."

Ren extended a hand. His forearm was covered with grotesque drawings of skulls and snakes and onion domes and daggers dripping with blood. "Partners must trust each other," he said. "Believe me, I want this deal to happen far more than you."

Coluzzi doubted that, but he shook his hand nonetheless. "How much should we ask?"

"Ten million euros," said Ren. "Bastards at the SVR have deep pockets. Let's make Vassily Alexandrovich sweat a little."

Coluzzi suspected Ren had his own designs on the money. He would have to be like a Russian himself, with a set of eyes to look ahead and another to look behind. Like it or not, there was no other way of contacting Borodin.

"Twenty," said Coluzzi.

Ren squeezed his hand. "Even better...*partner*."

CHAPTER 25

Delacroix locked the door to his office at precisely five p.m. and left the hotel. It was not his practice to leave promptly at the end of the workday, but he was not feeling like himself. The past few days had been taxing. The hotel had welcomed a larger than usual number of obscenely wealthy clients, and from dusk to dawn he'd been called on to see to their needs. This meant everything from arranging bail for the Indonesian prime minister's fifteen-year-old daughter after her arrest for shoplifting at Galeries Lafayette to supervising daily surveillance sweeps of a German Internet tycoon's suite. And, of course, there was the presence of the police, questioning all the staff, and himself, in particular, after the robbery two days earlier.

On top of all this, at some point today he'd mislaid his cellphone and spent a tense hour after lunch combing the hotel for it. By the grace of God, the concierge found it lying on the lobby floor. What rattled him more was that no matter how hard he tried, Delacroix could not remember setting it down anywhere near the concierge.

Still, he knew that neither the phone nor his duties were the root cause of his unease. It was the visit from the American investigator that worried him.

They knew.

Once on the street, he lit a cigarette and threw his jacket over his shoulder. It was a breezy afternoon and the warm, frantic wind lessened his anxiety. He came to the Metro and halted. The thought of taking the subway home held no appeal. He had no desire to spend thirty minutes in a hot, cramped car with his fellow Parisians. He needed to keep moving.

Delacroix threw his cigarette into the gutter. "Riske, Riske, Riske," he repeated, running over the conversation with the American. The more he thought about it, the more certain he was that Riske hadn't believed him. He took the man's business card from his pocket and called the number. A woman answered and gave the name of the company.

"I'd like to speak with Simon Riske."

"He's away on assignment at the moment. May I have him call you or would you like to speak with another of our professionals?"

"No message. Thank you."

Delacroix hung up. The firm appeared to be legitimate. He'd accessed their website earlier, too, finding it professional but bland. He told himself he was getting worked up over nothing. There was no reason for Riske to suspect him of tipping off the bad guys. Delacroix cursed his luck. How was he to know Prince Abdul Aziz was carrying something of diplomatic value?

Of course Riske was correct. It was he who'd told Coluzzi about the prince's route to the airport. He'd never liked the Saudis or, in fact, anyone from the Middle East. It wasn't prejudice but experience. During the First Gulf War, he'd fought alongside the Saudis' vaunted Haj Brigade. The Saudi soldiers showed the courage of a mouse and half the heart. They were paper soldiers.

Delacroix lived on the fourth floor of an upscale building on the Rue de Grenelle a block away from Les Invalides. Two bedrooms, a living room, and a kitchen that needed upgrading. Not much, but he kept it neat and clean, and he had a view of the park nearby. He dropped his keys in the bowl and threw his jacket on the chair. There was a pleasant scent in the air and he imagined a beautiful woman walking beneath his window. The thought made him smile. He took a Heineken from the fridge and walked into the living room. There was a good match on television this evening. He needed a few hours to let his mind relax.

"Monsieur Delacroix?"

An attractive blond woman sat in his favorite leather chair. She wore a black T-shirt beneath a loose-fitting checked shirt, jeans, and men's work boots. His first thought was *What is this gorgeous dyke doing in my apartment?* Then he saw the pistol in her hand. A Glock fitted with a suppressor. His smile vanished.

They knew.

He threw the beer at her and bolted for the door.

The bullet struck his right knee. He crashed to the floor, writhing, grasping at his leg.

"Look at me," said the woman.

Delacroix rolled onto his back. He knew what this was about, why the woman was here.

"Who are you working with?" she asked.

"What are you talking about?"

She raised the pistol.

"Please," he cried, lifting a hand to shield his face. "I

already explained everything to your partner. It was the prince's idea to take an alternate route to the airport."

"I don't have a partner."

Delacroix grimaced. He was confused. Who was she if she was not the American's partner? "You don't work with Riske?"

"Riske? Who is this person?"

"An investigator with an English security firm. His name is Simon Riske."

"Riske…He is English?"

"American."

"Of course he is. And what did you tell him?"

"I told him that I had nothing to do with the robbery."

"Americans believe anything. We are not so gullible. *Ponyatno?*"

Delacroix closed his eyes tightly. Tonight there would be no escape. *"Ponyatno,"* he replied in Russian. "I understand."

The woman circled him, the pistol dangling from her hand. "Who paid you?"

"His name is Coluzzi. Tino Coluzzi. He approached me Friday. He'd been following the prince around the city. He knew the prince carried a great deal of cash. He asked for my help. I agreed to steer the prince his way."

"He's a friend?"

"No. I only met him then."

"Go on."

"That's all. I met Coluzzi twice. Friday and Saturday morning. I haven't seen him since."

"And this?" The woman had found the twenty thousand euros he'd hidden in the freezer.

"One of his men left it for me at a bar last night. Le Galleon Rouge."

"Who?"

"I forget...no, no." Delacroix searched feverishly for the name of the man with long sideburns and a peasant's mustache he'd met at the bar. "Jack. Giacomo Pizzaloto."

"Did you see Coluzzi there, too?"

"Coluzzi? No. He wasn't there. Please take it. Take the money."

The woman dropped the stack of bills onto the floor. "It's yours. You earned it. Use it to buy a new knee."

Delacroix swallowed hard and nodded. Maybe he would live to see another day.

The woman asked: "So you don't know where Mr. Coluzzi is or how I can reach him?"

"No."

"No phone? No email?"

"No."

"And the American who visited you earlier..."

"I didn't tell him about Coluzzi. I swear."

"I don't imagine he was interested in the money."

"He said the prince was carrying important documents. He wanted them back."

"Did he mention the letter?"

"What letter?" Delacroix knew at once that it must be what the prince had had in his possession.

"*The* letter. We are not interested in the money either."

Delacroix shook his head violently. "I know nothing about a letter," he insisted.

"Did you read it?"

"I told you! I've never heard about a letter."

The woman crossed the room with slow, deliberate steps until she stood above him. "I'd simply like to know if you have read it."

"How could I have read something I know nothing about?" he pleaded.

"Yes or no?"

"No."

"Really?"

"You must believe—"

The pistol coughed. A bullet shattered Delacroix's other knee. He gasped, pain robbing him of his breath. He looked down and saw blood spreading across the floor. An artery, he thought, memories of his time in combat flooding back. He needed to tie it off quickly.

"I never saw a letter," he managed. "I promise you."

"I believe you."

"You do? Thank God. It's the truth. I swear. A tourniquet. My leg. Please."

"That won't be necessary."

"But…"

The woman placed the pistol to Delacroix's forehead and shot him.

Valentina surveyed the room, the pool of blood, the corpse. She sucked in the scent of fear mixed with the acrid cordite. She opened a window, allowing in needed fresh air, then turned on the air conditioner. She didn't want the smell leaking into the hall.

Valentina left the apartment. After she'd walked a block, she placed a call to Moscow. "The thief's name is Tino Coluzzi," she said. "A professional."

"I'll see if we have anything on him."

"I believe I can find him."

"I'm counting on you."

"There's something else. Another man is looking for the letter."

There was a long silence and Valentina wondered if

somehow she'd been mistaken to relay the information. "How do you know?" Borodin asked.

"Delacroix talked. An American named Riske came to see him earlier today. Simon Riske. He presented himself as an investigator working for an English firm. I took a photo of his business card."

Borodin swore under his breath. "Send it over. I'll see if we have anything on him. No matter what… make sure this man Riske doesn't get what is ours. Do you understand?"

"Yes."

Borodin ended the call.

Valentina put on her sunglasses and walked faster. She had a rival. The thought neither pleased nor displeased her. It was simply another element she must factor into the equation.

For the first time she wondered about the contents of the letter. She decided it didn't matter. Knowing might only prove a distraction.

To her, the letter was a means to an end. Nothing more.

Find the letter and get her old life back.

She would stop at nothing.

Chapter 26

Nikki Perez was sitting at a table in the back of Julien's Café when Simon arrived.

"You're early," he said, checking his watch. The place was empty except for an old man reading *Le Figaro* and the barman.

"My father taught us that five minutes early is on time."

"I'll remember that," said Simon. "It's warm in here. Let's walk."

"Sure," said Nikki. "You're the boss."

Simon eyed her warily, not trusting the nice act.

They left Julien's and crossed the Pont Saint-Michel toward the Boulevard Saint-Germain. "My favorite part of the city," he said. "I lived near here when I was at school."

"In the nineties, right?"

"Very funny. I slipped a sous-chef at a restaurant around the corner a few euros to give me the food they were going to throw out."

"You mean the rotten food?"

"Almost rotten."

Nikki wrinkled her nose. "How was it?"

"If you're twenty-six, broke, and starving, it's delicious. Fry anything in butter, cover it with enough ketchup or mayonnaise, and it tastes okay. I only got sick twice. Oysters. Haven't had one since."

"Nice story," said Nikki, suddenly all business. "Is any of it true or just part of your general line of charming bullshit?"

"Pardon?" Simon smiled, hoping to keep things light, agreeable. "What happened to 'You're the boss'?"

"Save it for someone else. You knew Salvatore Brigantino was dead. He was in Germany last year having some kind of experimental treatment. The word's all over the street. Commissaire Dumont told me you were sharp, that you had good contacts. How did you miss that?"

"We can rule Brigantino out. Good."

"You still won't tell me about your little birdie?"

"And Coluzzi?"

"Yes, Coluzzi. He's a funny one to be on your list. Why would a lifelong bad guy who did time for bank robbery, attempted murder, and felonious assault want to steal a letter?"

"Good question. Once I find him, I'll ask him and get back to you."

"Sure you will."

"Look, Nikki, I don't know what's gotten you so upset."

"You did. You're wasting my time. You knew Coluzzi was the one all along. Why did you lie?"

"Did you find him?"

"Maybe. Maybe not. Let's make a deal. You tell me what's in this famous letter and I'll tell you if I found Coluzzi."

"Fair enough."

"Really? You'll tell me?" It was Nikki's turn to be surprised. She stood arms akimbo, ready to deliver her next stinging riposte.

"Promise."

"All right, then," she said. "Go ahead."

"I don't know," said Simon.

Nikki threw him a look to say she was done here, turned, and walked in the other direction.

Simon hurried to catch up with her. "Word of honor. I don't know what's in that letter. My client in this matter—a man who I have every reason to believe— refused to tell me. He did make it clear, however, that it was important."

"Sure it is. To save his marriage or his bank account."

"More than that. A lot of people might be in trouble if the wrong people get it."

"What kind of people?"

"You. Me. Everyone."

"That's rich. I'm scared now, Mr. Riske. Trembling in my boots. Can't you see?" Nikki narrowed her eyes and laughed sarcastically. "Pass it on to the next rube. I'm out of here."

Simon grabbed her arm before she could take a step. "I wouldn't be here if I didn't believe it," he said.

It was only then that he realized that Neill had gotten to him. That he really did believe he must find the letter and that he was committed to doing everything in his power to make it happen.

Nikki looked hard at him, suspicious as ever. "So tell me why a hood like Tino Coluzzi would ever want something like that."

"Maybe," Simon said, "he didn't mean to steal it."

"What's that supposed to mean?"

"It means maybe he got it accidentally. Look, that's as far as I can go." He waited for a moment, expecting another rebuke. Nikki remained silent, though her expression was far from convinced. He said, "Your turn."

"Don't get your hopes up." She began walking, her shoulder nearly touching his. "I didn't pick up anything new about Coluzzi," she said. "Other than to confirm that he was behind a large theft of pharmaceutical drugs last year. I was able, however, to find out the name of a place where his friends hang out. It's a bar in the Marais called Le Galleon Rouge."

"Never heard of it."

"A dive. I asked around. Apparently it's popular with that crowd. You want to ask for someone named Giacomo, or Jack. Long hair. Sideburns. Mustache."

"Jack or Giacomo at the Le Galleon Rouge. It's a start."

She looked Simon up and down. "Don't go dressed like that."

"Thanks for the tip."

"The commissaire told me about you saving his life. Thank him, not me."

"He's exaggerating, but thanks anyway."

Nikki began walking backward, away from him. "Anything for a friend of the PJ. Oh yeah…" She put a finger to her forehead. "One day you'll tell me about that."

"It's nothing."

"I'll be the judge of that," she said. "By the way, word has it that your friend was looking to get a crew together."

"Coluzzi?"

Nikki nodded. "Must have been some job, whatever they really wanted to steal."

CHAPTER 27

Vassily Borodin stared at the image of the business card Valentina Asanova had sent.

SIMON RISKE
SPECIAL PROTECTIVE SERVICES AND INVESTIGATIONS
9 NEW BOND STREET
LONDON, ENGLAND

The firm's name meant nothing to him. There were dozens of such firms in every major world capital. Spying was a fully privatized industry.

He put down his phone, ruing the interruption in his work. On his desk a fan of dossiers was scattered, all neatly numbered and labeled. The information inside constituted his proof. Old-fashioned, hard proof in the form of damning papers from banks, corporations, and government ministries.

He thought of the effort required to assemble it and a wave of fatigue overtook him. He leaned back in his chair and looked out the window. The rain had continued unabated since the day before. His view gave north to the center of the city. When the air was clear and the sun shining, he had a direct view of the new business district and could count the Stalin skyscrapers set in a ring around the city. Today, the rain made it impossible to see anything except the dirt caked on his window.

He looked once again at the business card and questioned his decision to send Valentina Asanova to Paris. Was he getting himself into more trouble or doing what any patriot would? He sat straighter. He had never been a man who shirked his duty. He would never have succeeded in the old regime, when devotion to the Communist Party demanded a uniform, unwavering, and often blithely ignorant obedience. He was a man of his time, doing what any smart, ambitious, and patriotic man of his time should do.

It had all begun with a rumor of a clandestine meeting that had taken place almost thirty years in the past. Borodin, a major at the time, had been quick to dismiss it. A man in his position trafficked in hearsay at his peril. Then, a year later, a second source, independent from the first, repeated it. This time with a crucial detail added. The meeting had taken place at a dacha north of Moscow in the month of September, days after the momentous visit. More importantly, the dacha belonged to General Ivan Truchin, one of the first high-ranking officers to denounce the old Soviet regime.

The smart response was to say "Nonsense" or "Rubbish" and slam the door on such dangerous talk. But Borodin was at heart distrustful. It was in his nature to ask "What if?" or, better, "Why not?" Where others sought out the good in people, he was inclined to seek the ill, or at least the duplicitous. He was nothing more than the product of his training.

Though barely a teenager when the alleged meeting

had taken place, he remembered the time well. It was the era of glasnost and perestroika. The West termed the words "opening" and "restructuring." Borodin preferred "capitulation" and "destruction."

The great Soviet ship launched amid blood and tumult in 1918 by Vladimir Ilyich Ulyanov Lenin and his band of Bolshevik revolutionaries was sinking. Chaos reigned. It was every man for himself. Even the rats were fleeing the ship.

Borodin searched for his phone and for the thousandth time—no, the ten thousandth—looked at the picture. There they were, the biggest threats Mother Russia had ever known, all standing within feet of one another. Gorbachev, Reagan, and the worst of the three.

And so a meeting of this nature was possible. Perhaps more so because no one would have had reason to suspect that anyone would show an interest in such an unimportant man.

Borodin had put out feelers to get a stronger sense of the rumor's veracity. Again, he had been careful not to betray an unhealthy interest. If anyone inquired, he could respond with a clear conscience that he was only doing his job. Anything more could quite literally be fatal.

He had reached out to veterans of the secret world long retired. He had couched his questions elliptically and with purposeful vagueness. Do you remember a time when something unexpectedly went wrong with one of your operations? Did you ever feel as if someone were thwarting your efforts? Perhaps the suspicion that an invisible hand was hindering progress? Or if not hindering it, doing too little to help?

The answers had trickled in over the course of a year. In no instance had any of the retired officers pointed a finger at who might have been responsible. Certainly, no names had been mentioned. They, too, knew how to be purposefully vague.

Still, it had been enough.

By then, Borodin had risen to the rank of colonel. His seniority granted him unfettered access to the SVR's archives. He needed no one's permission to examine the case files involved, nor was he required to leave something so damning as a signature that might later attest to his interest. Under no circumstance did he reveal his intentions to even his most trusted colleagues.

One by one, he had drawn the operational records. He was patient. He allowed time to pass between his inquiries. A month or two went by between trips to the archives. (The SVR was, and remained, hopelessly backlogged in transferring its paper files to digital.) One by one, he had corroborated the veterans' statements.

More importantly, he had been able to spot a common thread. Over and over, the same name had appeared in each file. Earlier, he had been a deputy case officer. Later, he had acted as the case officer in charge. And later still, as a divisional chief.

The conclusion was inescapable.

Still, he had lacked the incontrovertible evidence necessary to make such a monstrous accusation. He had only come upon it later, after learning that his newest agent in the U.S. capital had a brother who toiled as an archivist at the CIA's headquarters in Langley, Virginia. Again, he had chosen misdirection to guard against detection. There had been no stealing of classified case files. Instead, it had been Borodin's idea to have him search a little known corner of the archives: the CIA's commendation reports, many of which dealt with the awarding of medals to foreign agents in place. It was common practice for espionage agencies the world over to present their operatives, or "Joes," a medal along with a written commendation during clandestine meets with a case officer, if only to take back both afterward. Spies were by definition insecure and unbalanced. A medal, a commendation, a promotion in imaginary rank, boosted their morale immeasurably.

And so it was that the archivist had found the letter.

The buff-colored envelope had been sitting in a box three floors below ground (sector R, row 51) in the section dedicated to Russian Operations 1990–1995. From there, the letter had made its way to Borodin's agent and onward to Prince Abdul Aziz, only to be stolen during a random robbery.

Or had it been random after all?

Borodin looked at the photograph one last time.

Of course it was not random, he said to himself, barely suppressing the desire to slam a fist on the table.

With a calming breath, he brought his attention back to the business card. Swiveling in his chair, he turned toward his desktop computer and logged into the SVR's intranet. He did not use his own name but that of a fictitious agent he'd created when he'd begun his inquiries, Nikolai Beria. A sharp-eyed historian might recognize the family as that of the founder of the NKVD, Joseph Stalin's dreaded secret police and predecessor of the KGB.

Borodin accessed the service's international intelligence registry and entered the name Valentina Asanova had given him. The registry contained names, aliases, and, when possible, physical descriptions of all individuals known to work for a foreign intelligence agency. The names included both overt employees like contract staff for the Central Intelligence Agency or the British Foreign Office and covert operatives who had been identified but not exposed. Currently, the registry contained names from over seventy nations.

The name Simon Risk(e) brought up no hits.

There was a Simeon Rosak, age fifty-seven, former paratrooper with the Israeli Defense Forces, now listed as an analyst with the Mossad. There was a Simon Rhys-Davies, age twenty-seven, graduate of McGill University, currently a minor official in the Canadian foreign ministry. And a Simone Risen, age forty-four, employed by the DGSE, the French intelligence agency.

But no Simon Riske, with or without an *e*.

Borodin logged out of the registry. He hadn't expected a hit. If the man was an agent, he was using an alias, though with the installation of facial-recognition software at nearly all international transport hubs as well as the widespread adoption of biometric passports, it was becoming increasingly difficult for covert operatives to move about unnoticed. These systems relied on the precise mapping of an individual's physiognomy—the distance between a man's eyes, for example, or the width of their lips—which no disguise could alter. An agent could make his eyes green or blue. He might wear a mustache or shave his head. He might use makeup to appear seventy or forty. But once the topography of his face had been captured, his days of moving freely were over, no matter what he called himself.

To amuse himself, Borodin pulled up his open-source web browser and Googled the man's name. Several Facebook accounts showed up, a LinkedIn page, and a mention in a British automotive journal. He checked them in turn, finding little of interest. As Riske's business card listed him working for a

London-based investigative firm, he paid particular attention to the article discussing the sale at auction of a vintage Ferrari restored by a garage in London owned by a Simon Riske...*with an* e. There was no further mention of the man, nor was there a photograph. He moved the cursor to close the page, his finger poised to click. He looked at the article again, his eye spotting the words "American born." For a second, less even, a spark of suspicion fired in his brain, much like the shock one receives when walking across a carpet in socks. But like that shock, the spark was short-lived and he discounted it.

He closed the article, then phoned the agent in charge at the Russian embassy in London.

"Find out everything you can about a firm named Special Protective Services and Investigations," he said. "I want something by morning."

CHAPTER 28

Boris Blatt walked down the Bahnhofstrasse, the stress of the past days easing from his neck and shoulders. He adored Switzerland, and especially Zurich. The food was uniformly excellent, the weather better than either London or Moscow, and the police well trained and incorruptible. His enemies knew better than to come after him in Switzerland.

Blatt continued down the prosperous thoroughfare lined with the world's most famous boutiques, jewelers, and, of course, banks. At one point he'd held accounts at nearly all of them. Bank Leu, Zurich Gemeinschaftsbank, Schweizerische Bankgesellschaft. Just saying the names was enough to trigger memories of his rise to power: visions of blood, lucre, and fear.

Boris Abrahamovich Blatt had started his career as a businessman peddling smuggled American Levi's at Sunday flea markets along Moscow's outer ring road. With the profits from jeans he moved into sports shoes and Italian designer suits. His new contacts in Italy, namely the Camorra in Napoli, proposed he look into selling more lucrative merchandise. They sent cocaine his way and Blatt sent unrefined opium theirs. By 1994, he was doing over a hundred million dollars a year in turnover.

It had been a frightening time. Even at a distance of twenty years, Blatt's palms grew clammy at the memory. With the fall of the Soviet Union and the move to a free-market economy, Russia descended into a state of chaos. Business was conducted at the end of a gun barrel. A successful negotiation was one where you walked away alive. A day didn't pass without a businessman being assassinated on the streets of Moscow. Blatt made it through by being smarter, stronger, and tougher than the rest. He was loyal to a fault, but woe unto those who betrayed him. His favored punishment involved boiling an enemy to death in a giant vat of hot oil. He did this often enough to know that a man could last between three and four minutes.

Blatt's timing had been fortuitous. As Russia began to privatize its industries, he stood ready with money, contacts, and ambition. In a series of rigged auctions, he scooped up the gems of his country's corporate might. Aluminum in the Urals. Timber in Siberia. Oil in the Caucasus. He earned his first billion in 1998. He hadn't looked back since.

For years he'd traveled to Zurich to call on his bankers. There was no pressing need for the trips. He could have checked his balances from home or simply spoken with his portfolio manager on the phone. Still, he visited as often as six times a year just to ensure his money was where he had deposited it and that no one had stolen it while he wasn't looking.

Blatt had examined this behavior and decided that it was as inescapable as it was irrational. The fear bred from the centuries of persecution visited upon the Jews of Eastern Europe had embedded itself in his genes, his very DNA. His behavior was no different from that of a merchant living in a shtetl outside Kiev a hundred years ago who constantly checked beneath his straw mattress that his money was safe and sound. This tie to his ancestors pleased him. It reminded him that he came from a race of survivors.

Today, however, he had not come to Zurich to visit his money.

He'd come for a different reason altogether.

Blatt crossed the Paradeplatz and continued along the Bleicherweg to Stockerstrasse. The lake was a few blocks to his left, and on this warm, sunny day he could smell the clean, crisp water. He'd brought a two-man complement with him, both registered with the Swiss government and permitted to carry firearms. They walked a few paces behind him, dressed in casual clothing. Bianca, his blond German girlfriend—decidedly not a Jew—walked at his side. As always, she insisted on holding his hand.

After a few blocks, Blatt turned up a side street and stopped in front of a door marked simply J. GRUBER ET CIE. He rang a buzzer and raised his face to the hidden security camera. He heard the lock disengage and pushed open the door, shooing in Bianca ahead of him.

"Stay here," he said to the bodyguards. "I won't be more than an hour."

The men crossed the street and blended in with a trendy crowd gathered at an outdoor café.

The door closed behind Blatt. He and Bianca stood in a security cage and waited for the second door to open. Strangely, he felt more vulnerable inside the box of bulletproof glass than when he was exposed on the street. Several of his former colleagues had been killed in phone booths and restrooms, and he was wary of confined spaces.

A buzzer sounded and the door opened automatically. Bianca led the way into a large, nicely appointed showroom not dissimilar to what a customer might find at Beyer or Gübelin or any of the other luxury watch and jewelry boutiques lining the Bahnhofstrasse. Maroon carpeting, tasteful leather chairs, antique Louis XV desks, a grandfather clock. There were no display cases, however, no vitrines sparkling with gold watches and diamond rings. There was just Herr Gruber, Europe's most discreet dealer in stolen goods, a thin, spritely octogenarian wearing an olive sweater vest beneath a black suit, his hair whiter than the last time Blatt had seen him, but the glimmer in the blue eyes as sharp as ever.

"Herr Blatt," Gruber exclaimed, arms raised in welcome. "So nice to see you. A good trip, I hope."

"Uneventful," said Blatt. "That's the most one can hope for these days."

"And who is this?" Gruber took both of Bianca's hands in his.

"Be careful," said Blatt. "Bianca is not as tame as she looks."

Gruber made a catlike hissing sound and dropped her hands. "Welcome, Bianca. May I offer some coffee or tea?"

"No," said Blatt curtly. Niceties bored him. He hadn't flown five hundred miles for a cup of coffee and a piece of apfelkuchen. "I have something interesting for you."

"So you said on the phone. I'm brimming with curiosity. Such mystery. Such intrigue. Sit. Sit." Gruber held a chair for Bianca and waited for Blatt to seat himself before taking his place on the opposite side of the desk. From a drawer, he removed a green baize display tray and set it between them. "And so? What is it today? A ruby necklace perhaps? A Fabergé egg?"

"A watch," said Blatt. "Swiss, of course."

"Oh?" Gruber's shoulders slumped, visions of a wildly lucrative transaction dashed.

"Don't look so glum. I didn't fly here to sell you a Swatch." Blatt unclasped his wristwatch and set it on the tray. Gruber picked it up by its strap and brought it close to his eyes. His effervescent smile returned. "This is not a watch," he said, once again all alacrity and goodwill. "This is a rarity. A Patek Philippe day date perpetual calendar chronograph with phases of the moon. Also known as Reference 2499. Patek manufactured ten pieces per year beginning in 1951 and ending in 1986. A total of three hundred fifty units. But most were of gold or rose gold." He paused and shook the watch as if it were a child's bauble. "This is platinum."

"So it is."

"Of which only two were created," continued Gruber. "One of which was last sold at Christie's Geneva in 2012 for the sum of 3.6 million dollars. I hadn't realized it had come on the market again."

Blatt met the inquiring look head-on. "I obtained it from a private seller."

"No doubt you have the box, all papers, packing slips."

"Sadly, no."

"Aacchhh." Gruber grimaced, shoulders falling. "In this circumstance, I couldn't offer you near its value. I'm sure you understand. It would have to go to a discreet party, someone content to keep his purchase confidential."

Blatt tapped his foot impatiently. He hated this part.

The circling of rivals. The staking out of one's turf. "He can wear it. Isn't that enough? He doesn't have to go around advertising the fact."

"Alas," said Gruber, "when one spends so much money on an item, one often likes others to share in his victory. It's the odd man, indeed, who buys such a masterwork only for the pleasure it affords him."

Blatt shifted uncomfortably. He was certain Gruber had read about his having bought the Ferrari at Sotheby's two nights earlier. The tabloids in London had pasted his face on the cover with the headline FERRAR-$KI and indicated in no uncertain terms that he had overpaid for the automobile. The American he'd met at the auction—Riske—had cautioned him not to go above twenty million, but once bidding began, Blatt made the decision the car would be his no matter what the price. And so when the bidding reached twenty-five million dollars, there he was with his hand in the air.

He was still smarting from the deduction to his bank account.

Worse, only yesterday he'd been forced to settle an outstanding invoice from a persistent contractor who'd built the underground Olympic-sized swimming pool beneath his new home in Highgate. He was hemorrhaging money. The watch would cover the cost of the pool, with a bit left over to purchase Bianca a small bijou. There was nothing like a large rock to stoke a woman's performance in the bedroom.

"How much?"

"I can offer one million," said Gruber.

"Euros?"

"Dollars."

"Two million," said Blatt. "And euros."

"One and a half," countered Gruber. "Dollars. And that is final."

"That's robbery."

Gruber set the watch on the tray and pushed it toward Blatt. "If you say so."

The Russian shot from his chair, taking Bianca by the hand. "I'll be back in an hour. Have a cashier's check ready."

Outside, Blatt spent a moment taking deep breaths in an effort to calm himself. He felt as if he'd been physically violated, raped even. At any other time he would have snatched his watch off the tray and stormed out of the building.

One million five.

The nerve.

Should anyone discover he'd accepted forty cents on the dollar, his reputation would be in shreds. In Moscow, in his salad days, he might have shot the man then and there. At least he could trust Gruber to keep quiet on the matter. Or could he?

Blatt dined with Bianca at the Kronenhalle, allowing himself an extra glass of Dole and a helping of the restaurant's excellent chocolate mousse to salve his wounds. By the time they left, he'd almost convinced himself that he wasn't being taken advantage of.

He returned an hour later.

Gruber was waiting in the showroom. Two men sat in the corner, both young, steel-eyed, pistols bulging beneath their jackets.

"What's this, then?" asked Blatt.

"There is a problem," said Gruber.

"At the bank?"

"With your watch. It is a counterfeit."

Blatt regarded Gruber with bewilderment. His men

had stolen the watch from the most reputable jeweler in Golders Green, who had been selling it on behalf of a client. There was no question but that it was authentic. "Impossible," he blurted. "I got it from…" He closed his mouth.

Gruber brought out the baize tray and Blatt observed that the watch had been disassembled. "The case is platinum," said the Swiss. "That I will grant you, but it was not manufactured by Patek Philippe."

"By who, then?"

Gruber wedged a loupe in his eye and read the markings from the interior of the case. "The Ming Fung Watch Company, Hong Kong." He handed Blatt the loupe and the case.

"Holy hell," said Blatt.

"Quite good, granted, but hardly Swiss."

Blatt replaced the case on the tray. "I don't understand."

"All of it is fake. The dial, the hands, the clasp, the movement. Fake. Fake. Fake."

"But…"

Gruber offered a weak shrug as consolation. "Boris, you've been had."

Blatt left the building. An idea had come into his mind, and with every step he grew more convinced of it. At some point during the four weeks he'd been in possession of the watch, someone had stolen it and replaced it with a counterfeit.

Blatt's bewilderment hardened to anger.

He would find the thief.

And he would punish him.

CHAPTER 29

Simon took a cab back to his hotel. He undressed and put on a robe, then ordered a light dinner from room service, including an order of fresh sardines and toast. He had an idea he might be drinking more than he'd like later in the evening, and the fish and bread was a proven measure to lessen the effects of alcohol. Waiting for the meal to arrive, he reviewed the notes from Delacroix's phone. Once again, he was astounded as to the security man's access to the prince's most private data. The next step involved using that data—national identity number, credit card numbers, and more—to gain access to the prince's email and phone records.

Dinner arrived punctually. He ate quickly, putting aside the sardines for later. Afterward, he rested for an hour, dozing fitfully. He woke at nine and showered. Toweling dry, he regarded himself in the mirror. The scar on his hip from the policeman's bullet had hardened to a weal the size of a bottle cap. The bullet that had struck his shoulder had done more damage, shattering the clavicle and tearing the deltoid muscles, requiring two bouts on the operating table.

The result was an eight-inch incision that after all the years had gone white as bone. He had other scars, but these were from prison: a few puncture wounds in the abdomen, a nasty zigzag on his ribs courtesy of a serrated shank, and a patch on his thigh where he'd been scalded by boiling water. All these he viewed with bemusement. The other guy had gotten worse on every occasion.

Which brought him to the unsightly memento on his scalp.

He leaned closer to the mirror, running a finger along the jagged mark. Until a few years ago, his hairline had covered it entirely. But Father Time owed him no favors, nor did he expect any. He'd cheated death once too often. The scar on his forehead was a reminder that each day was a gift.

He closed his eyes, remembering the day long ago. He saw himself coming out of the shower, naked, unarmed, and wholly unawares. "Ledoux," shouted someone behind him. He turned and stepped into the blow, delivered with an enemy's worst intentions. The weapon was an iron bar fashioned from the leg of a prison cot, its leading edge sharpened like a hatchet. There had been no pain—not then, at least. There had been only a sickening crunch that exploded in the space between his ears and the leering face of the man who wanted him dead. He would forget neither as long as he lived.

Simon opened his eyes.

He still owed the other guy for that one.

Weak people avenge. Strong people forgive. Intelligent people ignore.

Another of the monsignor's gems.

The jury was still out as to which of these Simon was.

* * *

Life in a box.

The cell measured ten paces by six.

Concrete walls that bled with damp.

A steel cot. No mattress. No blanket.

A hole in the floor.

A spigot.

A weak incandescent bulb protected by a sturdy cage that burned all day and all night.

Two meals a day.

Breakfast: bread, coffee. Dinner: boiled potato, egg, and, once a week, a square of dark chocolate.

No books.

No music.

No television.

No clocks.

Each day an endless journey to the boundary of his sanity.

Who betrayed you?

Every Sunday he was taken from his cell, escorted up the long stairway and into a small yard, confined on all sides by a twenty-foot-high wall. He knew it was Sunday because of the church bells. On the other side of the wall, cars drove past, mothers walked with their children, groups of men shouted on their way to the football match. Life went on.

Summer ended.

Fall.

The brief Marseille winter.

Spring.

A year passed.

Who betrayed you?

Another Sunday.

Finally, one hour outside. Sun on his face. The smell of grass. Of exhaust. Of the world in which he'd once lived.

A man was standing in the yard. A prisoner. Pale as chalk. Wild hair going gray, falling past his shoulders. Once a strong man. Broad beamed. Rangy. A face carved from stone. A man who refused to yield his dignity.

"My name is Paul."

"Simon."

They looked at each other and Simon could see by his expression that they shared a wretched condition.

"How are you, my son?" said Paul.

"Better now," said Simon. And for a reason he did not know, nor could later explain, he approached the old man and hugged him, holding him close until his muscles weakened and he could hold him no longer. "Better," Simon repeated.

"Me, too," said Paul. "I thank you."

The men walked to a corner of the yard, as far from the guard as they could get.

"How long?" asked Paul.

"A year," said Simon. "I think. What month is it?"

"September." Paul smiled. "I think."

"And you? How long?"

Paul didn't answer. He merely shook his head. Too long.

The guard appeared and ordered Paul inside. "Listen for me," he said as he was led away.

That afternoon, as Simon lay on his cot, hands behind his head, staring at a monstrous centipede that had emerged from a crack in the ceiling, asking himself if he were hungry enough to eat it, he heard a tap, tap, tap *coming from the wall. It was a new sound, divorced from the pinging of the generator and the buzzing of the light bulb and the stomping of the guards' feet as they walked up and down the stairs.*

Tap, tap, tap.

Simon rolled off his cot and grabbed his spoon. He

tapped it against the wall, but it was fashioned of such flimsy metal, it made little sound.

The tapping stopped.

A week passed. And another. Two precious Sundays and no other man in the yard. And then, one more week later, Paul was there again. A miracle.

"Tell me about yourself."

Simon did. A life story delivered in one hour—less, even—a blitz of emotion, of hope, and of regret. Last, he told about his crime, about the day he was betrayed.

"What is his name?" asked Paul.

"I can't," said Simon.

"But you know?"

"Yes. I know."

"And so?"

"He's for me."

In parting, Paul said: "Two paces from the back wall. Five fingers above the floor. Dig."

And then he was gone.

Simon dug, using the handle of his spoon. He didn't fear being discovered. The guard came morning and night to pass his meal through a slat in the steel door. Never more. Once, a long time ago, the wall had been impenetrable. Time and damp had weakened it, had softened hardest concrete to malleable mush. His small metal pick made easy headway through the rotting concrete and plaster. In a few days, he had fashioned a hole the width of his fist that extended nearly to his shoulder. At times he could hear Paul digging, too, and his spirits soared. It was not a question of escape but of communication. Of human interaction. Of grasping on to his only chance of maintaining his sanity.

One day the two inconsequential tunnels met.

Simon was saved.

* * *

His name was Paul Deschutes. He had been educated in Belgium and taken the vows of priesthood. For a time, he was a servant of Christ, a soldier of Ignatius Loyola. A Jesuit. But no longer. More he would not say, except that he deserved his punishment.

It was his wish to help Simon. He proposed to give him the education he had chosen to forgo, if Simon was willing. He would be the Abbé Faria to Simon's Edmond Dantès. They were in Marseille, after all. Life would imitate fiction.

Simon had no idea who Faria was or, for that matter, Edmond Dantès. The only Dumas he knew was a goalie who'd played with Bordeaux ten years earlier. His knowledge of literature, math, and science was an eighth grader's. The last book he'd read was about Lucky Luke and Black Bart. It was a comic book.

He told Paul this. He said he had no use for book learning, that he knew how to hot-wire a car in thirty seconds and how to cover an armored car's vents with wet towels to force the guards to open the doors. He knew how to drive fast and to reload a pistol before the empty magazine hit the ground. He knew how to touch a woman so she'd never want to leave him and to kiss her like he loved her. That was enough.

To which Paul laughed. But then he grew serious and asked a simple question: "Do you want to come back to this place?"

Simon said no. He could not return. To come back would be to die.

"Well, then," said Paul.

And so they began.

Every morning after eating his breakfast and making his ablutions (a word he only learned in the course of that tumultuous year), Simon would lie on the floor and listen as

Paul lectured. For three hours in the morning and three hours in the afternoon, Paul would cover a dizzying range of subjects. He would speak about Picasso, the Second World War, and the works of Jean-Paul Sartre and Albert Camus. About Napoleon and Bauhaus and Max Planck and Albert Einstein. About the Meiji Restoration and Arthur Rubinstein. A wildly random survey course on the learnings of Paul Deschutes in his seventy-three years on planet Earth.

There was also instruction in language. Simon was already trilingual. While English was his mother tongue, he was also fluent in French and Italian. To which Paul added Spanish and Russian.

But the area where Simon shined brightest was mathematics, and his abilities were all the more impressive as he had no materials with which to write the multitude of equations and concepts Paul discussed. His mind possessed the rare ability to hold abstract figures and apply sophisticated numerical concepts to them. When Paul talked about "the x and y axis," Simon saw them effortlessly. When Paul recited the value of pi to the twentieth digit, Simon could repeat it instantly, and remember it the next day. And the next. When Paul explained the theory of prime numbers, Simon grasped it immediately and, without prompting, could list primes in order until you asked him to stop.

And so they worked. Day in, day out.

In time, Paul revealed more about himself. He'd lived all over the world. He'd taught at prestigious universities. He'd risen in the hierarchy of the Catholic Church. For five years he'd served as the monsignor of Lyon. And then came the fall. A love of alcohol that he could no longer keep hidden. A greater love for women that he could no longer suppress. An affair. A child out of wedlock. Separation from the Church. Worse, an estrangement from God.

An abandonment of principles. A descent into debauchery. Drugs. Crime. He gave details sparingly. His regrets were many. Over and over, he said he deserved his punishment. That he had sinned and fallen from God's grace.

But now, here, with Simon, he could begin his penance. He could try to atone. Teaching brought him closer to his God, even if his God chose to keep his distance.

Simon called him "Monsignor Paul."

A warm spring morning in the yard, the air buzzing with keen, fresh scents of awakening, the earth damp, sprigs of grass pushing through the mud. Beyond the walls, the chirping of happy children walking with their parents to church, the chatter of families on a sunny, promising Sunday morning. And inside the walls, an hour of respite from the damning isolation.

"Why are you here?" asked the monsignor.

"You know why," said Simon, and he began to explain about the morning so many months before when he and his crew had been betrayed.

"I don't mean that. I mean here. In the hole."

The question took Simon by surprise. Surely they had discussed the circumstances of their segregation at some point during the past months.

"I killed someone for Signor Bonfanti," he said. "Didn't I tell you?"

The monsignor continued and Simon knew he was after something. "So it was punishment?"

"Not exactly."

"Oh?"

For once, it was Simon's turn to perplex his mentor. "It was my choice."

"To come here? To spend your days in a bug-infested cell smaller than a shoe box?" The monsignor shook his

large, shaggy head, laughing dryly at this impossibility. Simon had never seen him smile so broadly. The priest's teeth
were straight and white, and he became ten years younger
on the spot.

"What's so funny?"

A wave of the hand. "Nothing. Please go on."

Simon explained about his agreement with Bonfanti and
explained that after killing the Egyptian, Al-Faris, he had
been given a choice. He could give up the name of the
man who'd betrayed his crew or he could serve an indefinite
sentence in the hole.

"And you refused?" said the monsignor.

Simon didn't reply. He was standing there, wasn't he?

"Why?"

"Why do you think?"

"Because you're a tough bastard who doesn't forget or
forgive."

"That's about right." The answer pleased Simon and he
couldn't ignore the surge of pride, the reflexive swelling of
his chest.

"Sure you made the right decision?"

"I've had eighteen months to think it over."

"And you don't know how much longer you'll be here?"

Simon shook his head and the monsignor looked away,
his face screwed up in the way it got when he was thinking.
After a minute, he returned his gaze to Simon.

"How do you know it's going to be worth it?" he asked.

"What do you mean?"

"Well, this fellow you're after may have died since then,"
the priest explained reasonably. "Or he may have moved
away. Maybe he found God."

"Coluzzi? No. He's alive. I can feel it. And he definitely
hasn't found God. I'll see him again."

"And when you do?"

"I'll do what I have to do."

"Take his life?"

"He's getting off easy dying. The way I see it, he killed four of my friends."

"And nothing you can do will bring them back," said the monsignor, adding force to his words for the first time that morning. "Do you think they would do the same for you? Pretty expensive ticket to punch."

Simon wanted to say yes, but in truth, he didn't know. He could only answer for himself.

"I guess, Simon, my question is, are you really here for them or are you here, suffering like this, for yourself?"

"I'm here because I have to be."

"That may be so, but it isn't you who made that decision."

"What does that mean? Who else made it for me?"

The priest shrugged and Simon knew that it was his way of saying that there were mysteries in the world and that any man who thought he knew all the answers was a fool. After a moment, he drew nearer.

"You're not here," he said, "because you blame this man, this Coluzzi. You're here because you blame yourself."

"I don't know what you're talking about."

" 'It is mine to avenge,' sayeth the Lord. 'I will repay. In due time, their foot will slip. Their day of disaster is near and their doom rushes upon them.' "

"Save the Bible for the next guy."

"I believe that's you. How many more do you think I will have the chance to help?"

"Plenty."

"Look at me."

"Don't talk like that."

Simon cast his gaze elsewhere. In the short time they'd known each other, the priest had grown visibly weaker, his skin grayer, his shoulders more stooped.

The monsignor put his hands on Simon's shoulders and looked into his eyes. " 'Do not repay evil with evil,' " he said slowly, meaningfully. " 'Repay evil with blessing, because to this you were called so you may inherit a blessing.' "

"You've got a lot of them up your sleeve this morning."

The monsignor put back his head and smelled the air. "I have hope, Simon, and my hope is you."

But the hours in the yard were not just for examining his soul. The monsignor had more practical advice to pass along, some of which surprised Simon, and at first even hurt him.

"Hit me."

Another Sunday. Cold and rain instead of the spring sunshine. An atmosphere of gloom inside the yard, and outside, where no voices could be heard, no joyous cries from passing children. Just quiet, and quiet was the enemy when you spent your days locked up alone in a cell underground.

"Did you say 'Hit me'?" *asked Simon.*

The monsignor nodded easily, as if this were the most normal request in the world. "In the face. Here. A jab to the cheek."

"I will not."

"Frightened you might hurt me?"

"You should be frightened, not me."

"All right. Suit yourself."

Simon enjoyed an uneasy laugh, when suddenly something slapped him in the face and his cheek smarted. "Hey!"

The monsignor had assumed a fighting stance, feet shoulder-width apart, hands raised.

"Did you just hit me?" *asked Simon.*

The priest nodded and motioned with his fingers for Simon to approach. "Do as I tell you. Don't worry."

Simon studied the priest, appraising him in a new and not entirely friendly manner. "You're sure?"

"Go for it."

Simon smiled at such juvenile words coming from the smartest man he'd ever met. He raised his fists and threw a tentative punch. The monsignor batted it away. Simon tried again, harder this time. Again the priest blocked it, redirecting the blow in a manner that caused Simon to lose his balance and stumble.

Retaking his position, Simon decided to let the priest have one, a real haymaker, the results be damned. He hadn't figured the monsignor to be a big mouth, but, hey, if he wanted to get punched, Simon was willing to oblige.

He shifted his weight onto the balls of his feet. He moved this way and that, shoulders bobbing, then threw a punch, restraint leaving him as he struck out, putting all his muscle behind it.

His wrist snapped and the punch hit nothing but air. This time the priest took hold of his fist and tossed him over his hip and onto the dirt, where he landed flat on his back.

Simon scrambled to his feet. "How?" he asked, winded. "What…"

"I wasn't always a man of the cloth," said the monsignor.

"Where did you learn that? I mean, whatever that is that you just did. Karate or kung fu or—"

"Not karate. Something I picked up in Mozambique."

"Where?"

"A country in Africa. Lots of jungle. Beautiful beaches. And the women…" The monsignor caught himself. "Anyway, it's Portuguese and Brazilian and a mix of some others. I don't know that it has a name. Would you like to learn?"

Simon answered in a heartbeat. "Absolutely."

* * *

Simon shook himself awake. He'd been dozing.

He rose from the bed and opened his laptop, typing in "Le Galleon Rouge." A map showed its location on a side street not far from the Place des Vosges. There was a picture of the bar, too. A sign above the door advertised its name. Otherwise, there was no indication what was inside. Le Galleon Rouge was not trawling for customers.

He closed the laptop and went to the closet. He didn't need Nikki Perez to tell him how to dress. Black V-neck T-shirt, jeans, and ankle boots with zippers. Crucifix and braided chain around the neck. Pinkie ring with amethyst. Pomade for his hair. He'd come prepared. But the clothing was only window dressing. His entry card to Le Galleon Rouge was inked on his forearm. The tattoo designating him as a member of La Brise de Mer.

Two tasks remained before he could go. First, he accessed an app on his laptop, checked that the wireless connection was robust, and set it to record. Then he opened his metal briefcase—or as he liked to think of it, his "bag of tricks"—and removed his newest addition. The StingRay was the size and shape of a fat pack of cigarettes, made of black metal. The only visible controls were an on/off switch and a tiny bulb that burned green to indicate the unit was activated. Originally, it had been designed to allow law enforcement authorities to locate and track cellular phones, and it worked by mimicking a wireless carrier's cell tower in order to force all nearby mobile phones to connect to it instead of the real tower. Simon had opted to purchase the latest version, code-named Hailstorm. Hailstorm attracted all calls in a given location, recorded their conversations, and, by a trick of wizardry, collected all data stored

on those phones. Emails, texts, call logs, photographs—
everything. It was an indiscriminate beast that cared as
much about an individual's privacy as a Peeping Tom.
At twenty thousand dollars a copy, it had better be.

Satisfied he was giving the enemy as little chance
as possible, Simon slipped the StingRay unit into his
jacket pocket and turned to his last bit of business. The
sardines.

He ate them with plenty of toast and butter and
didn't bother brushing his teeth when he'd finished.

When in Rome…

On the way out of the room, he passed a full-length
mirror. A low-class, street-smart hoodlum stared back.
He froze, shaken by the image. He was looking at the
man he'd almost become.

Somewhere—in heaven or in hell—Monsignor Paul
was smiling.

A fifteen-minute cab ride took Simon to the Marais.
He got out at the Église Saint-Paul-Saint-Louis and
walked a block to the Rue des Rosiers. Le Marais was
an historical district popular with tourists. The streets
were lined by old government buildings, *maisons de
villes,* and churches dating from the fourteenth century.
At night, when traffic quieted and the sidewalks grew
deserted, it was easy to lose one's place in time. Even
now, Simon could imagine the wheels of a tumbrel cart
clattering over the cobblestones, delivering its unfortu-
nate charge to the Place de la Concorde for his date
with the guillotine.

He spotted the sign for Le Galleon Rouge. In ten
steps, he was miles away from the quaint, clean streets.
Garbage bags lined the sidewalk. Pools of grease sullied
the road. Urban music blared from an open window.

The side street was like any other gritty alley in the wrong part of town.

Nearing the bar, Simon slipped the StingRay from his pocket and dropped it behind one of the garbage bags. A man stood near the entry, leaning unsteadily against the wall. He looked at Simon, then pushed open the door with one arm. *"Salut."*

"Salut." Simon stepped inside, pausing to allow his eyes to adjust to the low light. It was a small room, choked with cigarette smoke, tables to one side, video poker games on the wall, and a foosball table in the corner. At 10:30, the place was half full but lively, a few couples dancing to Italian disco music. He walked to the bar and propped his elbows on the counter, aware that all eyes were on him. He might look like one of them, but he was an outsider, and outsiders were not to be trusted.

He ordered a beer and remained standing, facing straight ahead. The bartender set the glass on the counter. "Visiting?"

"Quick trip."

"Know anyone in town?"

"I've been away for a while."

The bartender's eyes gave him the once-over. He saw the tattoo and the penny dropped. "This one's on the house."

Simon raised his glass.

The bartender left and Simon gave a look over his shoulder. The place was filling up, mostly men in their thirties and forties and their dates. The women ranged from brassy blondes showing too much flesh to dark-haired matrons who looked like they'd come straight from Mass. From the corner of his eye, he noticed the bartender speaking to an older man at the end of the counter. The man's eyes turned to Simon. He smiled faintly and made his way over. "Mind?" he asked, pointing at an empty stool.

"All yours."

"Luca Falconi," he said.

"Simon Ledoux." If he was visiting the old gang, he might as well use his old name.

Falconi offered a meaty hand. He was pushing sixty, wavy hair dyed black as oil, an extra thirty pounds hanging from his gut. "Laurent told me you'd been away. Where were you, on vacation?"

"Down south."

"Les Baums?"

Simon nodded and sipped his beer. "It was a while ago. I've been out of the country a few years."

"What brings you here?"

"Looking for a friend."

"Maybe I can help."

"His name is Tino Coluzzi. We go way back."

"Coluzzi, eh?" Falconi made a show of searching for the name, eyes moving here and there, mouth twisted in puzzlement. To Simon's eye, it was a poor performance. "Doesn't ring a bell."

"He's a little taller than me. Better looking. I heard he liked this place."

"Really? Where'd you hear that?"

"Nowhere special. In fact, we did some work together back in the day."

"Can't help you. Not a name to me."

"Too bad. I wanted to give him a message. You see, he has something I'm looking for. He might have found it by accident, but he needs to give it back. Otherwise, he could get into a lot of trouble. I wouldn't want anything to happen to him."

"Sounds serious."

"It is what it is."

Falconi considered this, his eyes never leaving Simon's. "What did you say your name was again?"

"Ledoux. Simon Ledoux."

"Well, Mr. Ledoux, like I said, I can't help you."

"Tell him there's still time. No hard feelings. Just in case you remember."

Falconi raised his glass. "Stay out of trouble."

"I'll try." Simon went back to minding his own business. Falconi disappeared into the back office. Simon had a good idea what he was up to. It looked like Nikki Perez was right about this being Coluzzi's hangout.

CHAPTER 30

Tino Coluzzi was asleep when the phone rang. He sat up and checked the number before answering.

"Yeah, Luca," he said. "What is it?"

"Something's up. A guy's in here asking about you."

"A cop?"

"It's not about Sunday. All the boys are keeping their mouths shut."

"Then why are you bothering me?"

"The guy's one of us."

"La Brise?"

"Yeah."

Coluzzi rubbed his eyes, still half-asleep. "Recognize him?"

"Never seen him before, but he says he knows you."

"Who is he, then?"

"Ledoux."

The name rocked him like a swift kick in the nuts. "Say again."

"Ledoux. Says he'd heard you liked to hang out here. And he wanted to give you a message."

"What's that?"

"He thinks that you might have something he wants. Something you found by accident but that you need to give back. You know what he's talking about?"

Coluzzi was fully awake now and on edge. Still, he needed time to put everything together. He rose and stalked through the small, low-ceilinged house, throwing open the doors to the terrace and stepping outside.

He called the place Le Coual, and it was situated far off the beaten path on a promontory overlooking the sea twenty kilometers outside Marseille. He'd built the place himself over the course of two summers not long after he'd gotten out of prison. He'd learned at a young age that he needed a place to lay up from time to time. A place where no one could find him, friend or foe. The line between the two could be razor thin, and subject to change without notice.

"You there?" asked Falconi.

"Yeah, I'm here." Coluzzi put a foot on the retaining wall and breathed in the sea air. A thousand feet below him the ocean crashed against the rocky shoreline. "I got no idea what he means. I don't have anything that belongs to him."

"He said there's still time. No hard feelings. Mean anything to you?"

"Nah. Nothing."

"You think he's talking about the other day?"

"Of course not. Anyway, it's impossible. It can't be Ledoux."

"You sure? He said you two did some work together a while back."

"What's he look like?"

"Black hair, not too big, green eyes. About forty. Just a regular guy. Oh yeah…and a scar on his forehead."

"A scar?"

"A nasty one. Like a fishhook."

Coluzzi remembered delivering the blow, swinging the sharpened stick of iron, putting all of his weight into it, all of his anger, all of his fear. "No, no," he said. "That can't be. No way."

"I almost forgot. His first name is Simon."

Coluzzi felt the wind against his scalp, heard the breakers crashing on the rocks far below. But in his mind, he was back in the prison yard, standing over Ledoux's unmoving body, the sun beating down, thinking he'd never seen so much blood in his life. "Listen to me, Luca. There's no way Simon Ledoux can be in Paris."

"So you do know him?" said Falconi with relief. "I thought something was up."

"Know him?" said Coluzzi. "I killed him."

Chapter 31

A voluptuous brunette with cunning dark eyes and ruby-red lipstick took Falconi's place next to Simon. She set her purse on the counter, then arranged her hair, giving him a look he was too experienced to misinterpret. Her name was Raquel. He bought her a few drinks and listened to her hard-luck story. She was just what he needed to keep an eye on the place.

Luca Falconi had installed himself at a table in the far corner. He was seated with a fidgety man with sideburns and a thick mustache, and a svelte blonde who looked too sophisticated for the place. Simon allowed his gaze to linger, letting the restless guy see him, guessing that this might be the Giacomo Nikki had mentioned.

Raquel was getting drunk quickly and laid a hand on Simon's thigh. "Hey," she said huskily. "Why don't you take me to someplace nice?"

"Any ideas?"

"I'll bet you live someplace nice."

Simon smiled. She smiled back. The woman's eyes were glazed and her mouth had a sloppy habit of hanging open at one side. He leaned closer. "You're right," he said invitingly. "I do. But you're not ever going to see it."

The woman quaffed the rest of her drink before grabbing her purse and walking toward the ladies' room. As Simon's eyes followed her, he observed that Falconi and his nervous friend had been joined by two men, both of whom looked like they came from the enforcement side of the business.

"Another beer?" asked the bartender.

"No, thanks. Just the bill."

"Didn't find your friend?"

"Must be at the wrong place." Simon paid the bill. When he turned to leave, Falconi and his cronies were blocking his path.

"Ledoux," said the one with the mustache.

"Do I know you?"

"My name's Jack," said the man, not offering a handshake. "You were asking about Tino Coluzzi?"

"Jack" for Giacomo. No doubt now. Nikki had steered him to the right place.

"He's an old friend," said Simon. "Like I said to Luca."

"Is that right?" said Jack. "Maybe we can talk about this outside."

"I'm fine here."

"It's confidential," said Falconi easily, buddy to buddy. "Just take a minute."

"Sure thing." Simon crossed the room in a leisurely manner, the four men close behind. He opened the door and stepped outside. At the end of the alley, a steady stream of pedestrians passed by on the well-lit street. Jack walked in the other direction, deeper into the shadows, before addressing Simon.

"So you are a friend of Tino?" he asked, more of an accusation than a question.

"I am."

"Because I know all of Tino's friends. I've never seen you or heard him mention you."

"We worked for Signor Bonfanti."

"Bonfanti," said Jack, rising up onto his toes. "He's done. No one cares about him anymore."

"Giacomo," said Falconi. "Show some respect." The older man directed his attention to Simon. "When did you work for Il Padrone?"

"A long time ago. Almost twenty years. Don't remember you."

"You wouldn't. I was away. In Italy. Cremona."

"Making violins." As well as the home of the finest violin manufacturers in Italy, Cremona housed one of Italy's largest maximum-security prisons.

"Something like that," said Falconi. "I need to ask you a couple of questions, then we can all get out of here. What do you say?"

"I'm listening."

"What exactly is it that you think Tino Coluzzi took?"

"I'll tell Tino when I see him."

"He'd prefer that you tell me."

"So you do know him?" Simon said. "You had me going back there. You're very good, you know. Usually I can tell straight off if someone's putting me on. But you? I was sure I'd come to the wrong place. The problem was that I was sure Jack had mentioned that he hung out here with Tino."

"The hell I did." Jack looked at Luca. "I've never seen this guy in my life."

"You also said that Tino was getting a crew together. Mostly guys from back home."

Luca Falconi gave Jack a withering glare, shaking his head. It was clearly not the first time Jack's big mouth had betrayed him.

"Answer the question," said Jack, growing more agitated.

"Tino knows what it is," said Simon. "I don't need to tell him. Where is he, by the way? Maybe we can meet up. It'd be good to see him again."

"He would like to know who you're working for," said Falconi.

"Like I said, I'll be more than happy to explain everything to him when I see him. If you want, give him a call. I'll tell him over the phone."

"I can't do that."

"Didn't you call him already? I mean, why else are we out here? Bet you surprised him. Not the kind of news I'd want to get in the middle of the night." Simon laughed. "How'd he take it?"

Luca Falconi said nothing,

"Don't listen to this guy," said Jack. "He's not one of us. He's a cop. Look at him. Why else does he show up now?"

"Shut up, Jack. Look at his arm."

"It's fake."

"I'll give you a chance to take that back," said Simon.

"Whoever you are, Tino doesn't like you asking questions," said Falconi.

Jack took a knife from his pocket and flicked open the blade. Black carbon steel. Serrated along one edge. A gutting knife.

Instantly, Simon was back in the yard at Les Baums. Instinct took over. Reflexes fired before reason could control them. He slugged Jack in the jaw, dropping him to the ground.

"Kill him," said Falconi.

The two enforcers moved in quickly, one from either side. Simon heard the click of a switchblade, caught a flash of steel. He threw out a foot and hooked the assailant's leg, landing him on his back, the man's head bouncing off the asphalt. The other threw a wild punch that struck Simon's neck, stunning him. He rolled with the impact, taking two steps, then spinning, anchoring a foot, and putting a fist into the charging man's sternum. The man stopped cold, mouth opened wide, all of his breath expelled. Simon finished him with an uppercut to the jaw, feeling a knuckle break, grabbing the man by his lapels and tossing him against the wall.

Two down.

Jack scrambled to his feet, knife in hand, coming at him, eyes crazed. He lunged at Simon, and Simon retreated. He lunged again, quick as a cat, and Simon felt the blade nick his ribs. He danced to his right, away from the hand brandishing the switchblade. He could feel the blood rolling down his torso. One more scar to brag about.

To his left, he was aware of Falconi digging into his jacket, but he knew better than to chance a look. He kept his eyes fixed on Jack, on the blade carving tight circles. Simon stumbled, catching his toe on a cobblestone. Jack jumped at once. Simon was ready, his ploy working as expected. He reached for the outstretched hand, finding the wrist, twisting it violently as he dropped to a knee, the bone cracking like a dry branch. The knife fell to the ground. Simon kept hold of the ruined joint, rising as fast as he could, wrenching the arm and forcing Jack to the pavement. Still, Simon didn't let go. He placed his boot on the man's shoulder and twisted the arm again. Spiral fracture of the humerus. Shearing of the rotator cuff. Jack screamed. Simon released him.

Falconi stood a few feet away, arm extended, a compact, nickel-plated pistol glimmering in the darkness.

He advanced on Simon, raising the weapon, thumb cocking the hammer.

"*Vaffanculo,*" he said. "You are no friend of Tino's, whoever you are. Simon Ledoux is dead."

Simon backed up a step, knowing that no matter how fast he might be, he couldn't outmaneuver a bullet. "Tell Tino to hit me harder next time."

"There won't be a next time," said Falconi. "Tino thinks Simon Ledoux is dead. I'm not going to tell him otherwise."

The arm extended. The grip on the pistol firmed.

"Hold on," said Simon. "Don't do it. There's a cop behind you."

"Really?" said Falconi, too old and too wise to fall for it.

"Really," said Simon, his eyes locked on the fast-moving figure behind Falconi.

There was a sudden motion. A raised voice. The scuff of a boot. The older man reacted too slowly, turning his head as Nikki Perez brought down the butt of her pistol on his skull.

Falconi collapsed to the ground, his gun clattering across the bricks.

Nikki picked up the pistol, then gave him a nudge with her boot. Falconi didn't move. "You okay?"

"I think so," said Simon. "How long have you been here?"

"Long enough."

A small group stood outside the bar, watching them. A man ran inside, sounding the alarm.

"Let's go," said Nikki. "Now."

She ran down the alley toward the Rue des Rosiers. Simon ran after her.

* * *

"What was that back there?"

Nikki was bent at the waist, hands on her thighs, catching her breath after the mad dash from Le Galleon Rouge.

"What?"

"Those moves. I thought you were going to kill him."

"Nothing," said Simon, eyes trained for pursuers. "Just some stuff I picked up a while back."

"Another story you'll have to tell me."

"Yeah," said Simon. "One day."

"This is how you dress when you hit the town?"

"You told me to ditch the suit."

"Gold chains. The shoes. You went all out." A concerned look clouded her face. "You're bleeding."

Simon followed her eyes to the droplets spattering the ground. He lifted his shirt to reveal a gash four inches long, laid to the bone. "Maybe I should have killed him."

"There's an emergency room across the river. You can tell me what's going on after you get fixed up."

Simon touched the wound and winced. Half an inch higher and the blade would have punctured the space between his ribs, most likely killing him. "Okay."

She raised a finger in warning. "The truth this time."

"Yeah," said Simon. "Fine." He followed her a few steps farther to an imposing motorcycle. "This yours?"

"What did you expect? A pink Vespa?" Nikki unlocked her case and handed Simon her helmet. "Put it on."

Simon touched her arm. "Thank you, Detective," he said. "That wasn't going the way I'd planned."

"Really? I hadn't noticed." Nikki threw a leg over the seat. "Keep pressure on the wound," she said, firing up the engine. "Any blood gets on my bike, you're cleaning it off."

Wednesday

CHAPTER 32

Cloaked in the shadows opposite Le Galleon Rouge, Valentina waited for Luca Falconi to emerge. She wasn't a smoker, but she lit a cigarette and tapped her foot like any other tramp waiting for her date.

She'd arrived earlier, looking for the man who'd paid off Delacroix on behalf of Tino Coluzzi. Gaining entry had been a matter of loitering out front and asking the first man heading into the place where a girl could get a drink. Her leather miniskirt and tight blouse did the rest. In minutes she'd been seated at Falconi's table, listening to a group of increasingly drunken criminals discuss their work. One made his living hijacking gasoline tankers. Another was a forger specializing in passports and identity cards for Middle Eastern refugees. All of them smelled as if they'd eaten garlic at every meal for the past month.

Valentina was careful not to ask any questions about Tino Coluzzi, or, in fact, about anything that might betray her intentions. She laughed when they laughed. She drank when they drank. And she had a hand on Jack's leg half the time and Falconi's the other.

Everything changed when the dark-haired man entered the bar and started asking questions about one of their friends. The drunken men were no longer so drunk. Even so, they hadn't guarded their conversation. She learned that the man at the bar was interested in Tino Coluzzi, too, and they didn't like it one bit. Valentina had a clear view of him. Even with the dim light and the pall of smoke, she recognized him at once. Blue suit. Purposeful gait. He was a man who left an impression. She'd seen him earlier in the day leaving the Hotel George V. He had to be the man Delacroix had mentioned. Simon Riske.

The door to Le Galleon Rouge swung open. Luca Falconi walked out, an ice pack held to the back of his head. She called his name. "Are you all right? Someone said there was a fight."

Of course, she knew there had been a fight, as did everyone in the place. Falconi had run inside afterward screaming about Eddie's head being knocked in and Jack having his arm ripped off. In the chaos, she'd hurried outside in time to see Riske in full flight turning the corner. It had been a difficult decision whether to follow him or to stay with Falconi.

"Guy that was here earlier," said Falconi. "Troublemaker. That's all."

"And your friends? Are they all right?"

"Let's not talk about them."

She put a hand on his arm. "I wanted to thank you for the drinks."

"Don't worry about it."

"No, really." She gave him a smile that was too warm by half.

Luca looked at her. "Tell you what, I could use a coffee. You?"

"It's late, but thanks anyway. Maybe next time."

"I make a mean espresso."

"I need to get home. I have work in the morning."

"You don't have to stay long. It's not far. I could use a hand getting home."

"That's three reasons. How can I say no?" Valentina smiled. "All right. But I can only stay for a minute."

Falconi put an arm around her shoulder. "Just a few blocks. And don't you worry. I'm a gentleman. Word of honor."

Valentina allowed herself to be pulled closer. When his hand fell to her rear and began to fondle her buttocks, she moaned and put an arm around his waist.

She didn't mind that he wasn't a gentleman.

She wasn't a lady.

Word of honor.

"Strip," commanded Valentina.

She stood near Luca Falconi in his bedroom on the top floor of a modern building a fifteen-minute walk from Le Galleon Rouge. She'd put up with his groping the entire way, allowing him to nuzzle her neck and whisper garlicky nothings in her ear. Once upstairs, he'd forgone his famous espresso in favor of generous snifters of grappa. He'd continued his seduction, playing French disco music from the 1970s and singing along as he put a hand up her skirt. After another grappa and an hour of being pawed, she decided it was time to go to work.

"Me?" Falconi smiled nervously. "My clothes? *Now?*"

Valentina ran a fingernail along the underside of his chin. "Yes, you. Yes, now. And, yes, all of them."

"But the espresso…"

"Forget the espresso." Valentina unbuttoned her

blouse and, when it was open, unclasped her brassiere and thrust her bare chest toward him. "Let me show you how."

Falconi fell upon her like a hungry wolf, kneading her breasts, putting a greedy mouth to her nipple. She gasped and threw back her head. "Luca," she moaned.

His reply was a pig-like grunt.

She counted to five then pushed him away gently. "Strip, I said."

Falconi stepped back, eyes wide with desire, nearly tripping over his own feet. *"La diavola!"* he said.

Growing impatient, Valentina helped with the last few buttons, then adroitly unbuckled his belt. By now Falconi was panting heavily enough that she feared he might drop dead of a heart attack before she could get any information out of him. Falling to her knees, she pulled his trousers to the floor, then yanked down his boxer shorts and told him to step clear.

Falconi obeyed. A moment later, he stood naked before her, his pale, flabby breasts lying flat on his chest, his belly cascading over his waist in waves of fat beribboned with stretch marks. Somewhere, she supposed, the man had a penis, but she could see only a nest of gray pubic hair peeking from the marble-colored lard.

"It takes time," he said ashamedly.

Valentina kissed him delicately. "We have all night, *chéri.*"

As he lumbered onto the mattress, she took off her blouse and brassiere and unzipped her skirt. She allowed him plenty of time to regard her, feeling her power over him grow.

"Come," he said, extending a hand.

Valentina smiled and put a foot onto the bed.

Falconi labored to sit up against the headboard, one

hand manipulating himself. His eyes opened wider as she climbed onto the bed and straddled him. She moved closer, lowering herself, grabbing a fistful of hair and guiding his face to her womanhood. She felt an inexpert tongue against her and cried out. He redoubled his efforts, hands cupping her buttocks. She moaned again.

She maintained this position for two minutes by her watch, enough time for his neck to cramp, then stepped back, still towering above him.

"My pill," he said, eyes shooting toward the bathroom.

"Go get it."

Falconi slid to the side of the bed and, after much exertion, put his feet onto the floor. His work had winded him and he sat hunkered over, unable to stand.

She saw her moment.

"Luca? Darling?"

"Yes?"

As Falconi turned his head, Valentina wrapped her left arm around his neck and locked it into place with her right. He struggled for thirty seconds, then went limp.

Not dead.

Unconscious.

When Falconi came to, his prospects for sexual gratification had dimmed considerably. He lay on the bed, ankles and wrists bound with duct tape, another length of tape stretched across his mouth.

Valentina brandished a steel box cutter before his eyes, its razor-sharp blade extended. Her handbag was too small to carry the pistol she'd used on Delacroix. There had been no place to hide it in her skirt. Besides, it was unwise to fire a pistol in an apartment building at this hour. Even with a noise suppressor, the sound might carry through the walls. She was a polite guest. She didn't want to wake the neighbors. The duct tape was Falconi's.

The box cutter fell to his testicles. The blade nicked the wrinkled, sagging flesh. Falconi jolted.

"Tell me," she said, "where I can find Tino Coluzzi."

CHAPTER 33

It was past three when Simon and Nikki emerged from the hospital. Around them, the city lay asleep. Traffic was so light as to be nonexistent. There was only the creaking of the barges moored nearby, rising and falling with the tide, and the whistling of a steady breeze.

Lights burned from a bakery nearby. Nikki found the door unlocked. A bell tinkled as she entered. "Wait here," she said.

Simon sat down on the curb and gingerly probed the bandage beneath the fresh shirt he'd been given by the emergency room nurses. He had twenty stitches to add to his inventory of battle scars, not that he was counting. Nikki had accompanied him into the treatment bay while the doctor sewed him up. She was a tough woman, hardened by dint of her job. Even so, she'd been unable to keep herself from wincing when she viewed his torso.

She returned a minute later, a bag of croissants in hand. She sat down next to him, offering him one. Simon devoured it in two bites, mess be damned. "Helluva lot better than sardines," he said between chews.

"Excuse me?"

"What? Oh, nothing." He took a second croissant and ate it more slowly. A ruminative mood had come over him. He looked at the empty sidewalks, searching for another person. They were alone. "So," he began, looking over at Nikki. "Why'd you come?"

"I'm a detective," she replied, as if the answer were obvious. "You weren't telling me the truth, at least not all of it. I didn't have any pressing engagements so I thought I'd stop by and see for myself what was going on. I didn't know about you, did I?"

Simon followed her eyes to the tattoo on his forearm. "Proudest day of my life when I got that."

"How old were you?"

"Eighteen."

"You started young."

"I thought I was grown up. A man. One thing's for sure. They didn't appreciate anyone asking about Tino Coluzzi."

"But you're one of them."

"Not anymore. Guess it showed." Just then Simon remembered the StingRay he'd cached prior to entering the bar. "Get up," he said. "I left something back there."

"We're not going back to that bar."

"Not there. Just down the street."

"What?"

"A StingRay. A surveillance device that—"

"I know what a StingRay is. What are you doing with one?"

"It comes in handy."

"So you didn't expect to find Coluzzi there?"

"Odds were against it. I thought I'd let them find him for me."

"By calling to warn him that someone's asking questions about him."

"That and something more."

"Oh?"

"That it was someone from the old neighborhood."

Nikki reacted a second late, her body lurching as if she'd received a body blow. "You know Tino Coluzzi?"

"I do."

Nikki dropped the rest of her croissant into the bag. "Strangely, I'm not surprised."

"This StingRay's the souped-up model," Simon went on, eager to get over the difficult spot. "It captures all calls made within the vicinity. It can also mirror the SIM cards, which gives us the key to extract all the data a phone holds."

"That's illegal."

"If you're caught," said Simon. "Are you going to tell on me?"

"Depends. I'm no friend of the men who tried to beat you up—"

"To kill me."

"But I don't like a stranger coming into my city and taking the law into his own hands. Frankly, it pisses me off. I want to know what's going on. All of it. Who are you and why are you really here?"

As Simon tried to stand, he felt the sutures pull. He extended a hand. Nikki eyed it warily before helping him to his feet.

"Let's get the StingRay," he said. "Maybe there's something on it that will help both of us."

CHAPTER 34

Five hundred miles to the south, in his cliff-top hideout, Tino Coluzzi couldn't sleep.

Rising from bed, he walked to the kitchen, made himself an espresso, and took it onto the terrace. A three-quarter moon hung low over the horizon, casting a pale stripe across the sea. He remembered that day in the yard. He'd gotten into another scrape, one he couldn't trade his way out of, and had drawn a sentence at Les Baums. There was Ledoux, waiting, giving him the look. *He knew*. What other choice did he have? It was a matter of self-preservation. If he'd waited a day longer, he would have been the one on a stretcher with a blanket covering his face. There would have been no lack of takers.

And now it turned out that Ledoux wasn't dead after all, and that somehow, someway, he knew about the letter. What else was Coluzzi supposed to think he meant by telling Falconi that Coluzzi had something that wasn't his? Something he still had time to return? Had Ledoux become a cop? Was that it? Coluzzi dismissed the idea out of hand. It wasn't possible. Not the Ledoux he'd known.

He picked up his phone, staring at the blank screen, wondering why Luca Falconi hadn't called back with news that Ledoux was dead and with a picture to prove it. He paced the length of the terrace, beside himself with worry. Something had gone wrong. He could feel it. He didn't want to betray his anxiety by calling Falconi, but finally he decided he had no choice. Swearing to make Falconi pay, he placed the call.

The phone rang and rang while Coluzzi urged him to pick up.

And then he did. "Luca, that you?" Coluzzi waited for a reply. "Luca?" He could feel the other party's presence on the line. "Who's there?" he asked, fearing the worst. "Ledoux, is that you?"

"No," said a female voice. "It isn't Mr. Ledoux. I'm his competitor."

"What do you mean?"

"You need to give us back what is ours."

"Let me talk to Luca."

"That won't be possible."

"What did you do to him?"

"The same thing I did to Monsieur Delacroix. It's getting dangerous to be a friend of yours."

"Delacroix wasn't a friend. Let me talk to your boss."

"That is not an option."

"Do as I say!"

"I know where you are, Mr. Coluzzi. Your friend was very talkative. He told me about your hideout on top of the cliff. In fact, I feel like I know you already. All we need to do is set a time and place for the exchange. I can be there in a few hours. Be reasonable. This doesn't have to end badly."

"I'll take my chances, darling. Tell your boss I'll be in touch. Ciao."

Coluzzi ended the call. Immediately, he opened the back of his phone and ripped out the SIM card, dumping it down the neck of an empty bottle of wine. He found a container of ammonia, added a few fingers to the bottle, and shook it all up. He waited a minute, letting the solvent go to work on the card, then flung the bottle off the terrace, along with the phone. He had five more burners inside just like it.

Shaken, Coluzzi returned to his bedroom and retrieved the suitcase holding the prince's money from the floor safe under his bed. He laid out the money on the dining room table. Six stacks, ten packets each.

He had a rule. Never give out the take too soon. You needed a cooling-off period after a big job. There was always some guy who was unable to contain his excitement, to keep his game face on, who went out and got sloppy drunk and proceeded to brag about his accomplishments. Over time, Coluzzi had weeded out the loudmouths. He trusted his crew with his life. Still, a rule was a rule.

Which brought him to the dilemma at hand. What to do with the six hundred thousand euros on the table? Divide it up among the boys or do something a little different. A little riskier.

He knew what Luca Falconi would say. "Go for it, kid."

He balled his fist, swearing to get his revenge. The Russians would pay, one way or another.

He kept staring at the money. After a while, he decided that six hundred thousand euros didn't look like much.

He wondered what twenty million looked like.

Bigger.

Much bigger.

CHAPTER 35

The lobby of the George V was eerily deserted, a ballroom after the ball, the fragrance from the enormous spray of flowers intoxicating in the still air. A hotelier rose from behind the reception, offering Simon a discreet nod as they entered.

"I don't suppose it's a coincidence you're staying here," Nikki said as they headed to the elevator.

Simon regarded her without answering.

They rode to the fourth floor, neither speaking. Nikki stood next to him, closer than he would have liked. Her shoulder touched his and he guarded against the flurry of intimacy it roused. It had been an eventful night. Too much adrenaline. Too much pain. Too many heightened emotions. He warned himself that his attraction was merely the aftereffect of a shared danger.

He glanced at her and found her eyes closed. He noted that she had smooth, flawless skin. Her upper lip was full and he studied its boundary, the sharp border where pink turned to cream. Despite himself, he couldn't look away. He was counting her lashes, laughing at the adolescent streak of blue in her hair. He had an urge to put his arm around her, draw her toward him. He wanted very badly to kiss her.

The elevator stopped. The doors opened. Nikki jolted, eyes fluttering open, and he realized she'd been asleep on her feet.

"Here we are," he said. "Four twenty-one. To the right."

He led the way to his room, feeling more tired with each step. He put the keycard in the door, waited for the lock to disengage, and pushed it open with his shoulder. "Come in."

Nikki slid past him into the room. "So this is how the other half lives."

"Expense account."

"Nice client," she said.

"Deep pockets."

She turned to look at him. "We'll come to that."

The bed was turned down from the night before. She took the chocolate truffle off the pillow and popped it into her mouth, then toured the room, taking off her leather jacket and tossing it onto a chair. She stopped at the window and peeled back the velvet drapes. "Morning already," she said.

Simon looked at her thinking she suddenly looked soft and vulnerable. He fought back his desire. "Time to go to work."

He placed the StingRay monitor on the desk, inserted a power cord, then attached a USB cable to his laptop. "It takes a minute," he said, "for the program to open and transfer the data."

"Give you time to tell me what's what."

"I'll let you start. You're the detective."

"Always playing a game, aren't you?" Nikki was kneeling by the minibar. "Want anything?"

"Orange juice."

She grabbed a bottle for him and two minis of Grey Goose. She cracked the orange juice and handed him the bottle before pouring the vodka into a highball glass.

"Little early for a drink," he said.

"Nightcap," she said, downing the contents.

"Now who's playing the game?"

Nikki made a coy face and put down the glass. "All right, then, Mr. Riske. Here's what I think. You come waltzing into Paris the day after the most publicized robbery in ten years, claiming to be after a secret letter with magical powers. You waste my time asking about three criminals when, in fact, you're only interested in one, Tino Coluzzi, a childhood friend, no less, who only last week was getting a crew together. Now it turns out you're staying at the same hotel as the man who was robbed, Prince Abdul Aziz bin Saud. Finally, you're based out of London, which as far as I know is second home to half the Middle East." She'd recited her argument matter-of-factly and without rancor, her eyes never leaving him. "So what do I think? I think Prince Abdul Aziz hired you to get his money back and you believe Tino Coluzzi has it."

Simon turned his chair so it faced her. "Not bad. I'd have come to the same conclusion."

"But?"

"You're mistaken."

"Stop lying. There is no letter. You're here for the money. Fess up."

"Okay," said Simon, admiring her restraint, knowing he'd be going through the roof if someone had yanked his chain as badly as he'd yanked hers. "Enough bullshit. You saved my life. You earned the truth. But it stays between you and me."

"What's that supposed to mean?"

"You don't tell Marc Dumont."

"But he has to—"

"Hear me out." Simon stood, hands lifted in conciliation. "I am here about the robbery, and, yes, that's why I'm staying at the hotel. I needed to see how things work around here. But I'm not here for the money. I don't work for Prince Abdul Aziz. There really is a letter. I can only tell you the rest if you promise not to go to your bosses."

"I can't do that. Just because I broke some of the rules doesn't mean I'm disloyal or a bad cop."

"I'm not asking you to be disloyal and I think you're a great cop. I'm asking you to be patient."

Nikki sat down on the bed. "I'm listening."

"Tino Coluzzi is the man you're after. The man everyone is after. He's the one who hijacked the prince's motorcade."

"How do you know that?"

Simon sat down beside her. "It's like this," he said, and for ten minutes gave her the identical briefing Neill had given him two days before, leaving nothing out. "So that's it. Neill believes that Coluzzi found the letter, realized its significance, and is sitting on it until he can decide how to use it. It's my job to get it back before he does."

"Must be some letter."

"Must be."

Nikki considered this. She reclined on the bed, resting on an elbow. "What about you? How did you ever join La Brise when you were just eighteen? Are you American or are you French? And what the hell happened to you? I can't tell if you got hit by a hand grenade, fell into a tree shredder, or took a swim with a school of piranhas."

Simon shifted, looking at her directly. "I'm American. My parents divorced early. When my father died, I was sent to live with my mother in Marseille. I wasn't a welcome addition. I made my way on the streets. I jacked cars for a few years, then moved up the ladder to taking down banks and armored cars. Coluzzi was part of my crew. I did not fall into a tree shredder or swim with a bunch of piranhas. I got caught. I took a couple of bullets because I was too high and too dumb to give up. I did four years in Les Baumettes. And this scar up here, the one you were asking about"—Simon touched his forehead, feeling his blood boil, his vision narrow— "courtesy of Tino Coluzzi."

Simon drew a breath, shutting out the memories, letting the fury go. "Sorry," he said. "I didn't mean to get worked up."

"It's okay." Nikki put her hand on his arm, rubbing it soothingly. She pointed to the laptop. "That thing done yet?"

"Still downloading."

"Your expense account cover breakfast?"

"Go ahead. Order me oatmeal with sliced bananas and another orange juice."

"Freshly squeezed, I imagine."

"Better be for what they're charging."

Nikki called room service as Simon studied the monitor. The StingRay was programmed to extract a maximum amount of information from the intercepted calls: the caller's and responder's names, addresses, and other personal information associated with the handset, as well as everything stored on each phone's SIM card—emails, texts, apps, photos, and, finally, a list of the phone's GPS locations at the time the past thousand calls were made or received.

"What time did you get to the bar last night?" he asked over his shoulder.

"I watched you go in at ten thirty. You came out with your buddies after midnight."

"You were there at ten thirty?"

"Surprised you didn't spot me?" she asked with more than a hint of pride.

"Embarrassed. I try to keep a sharp eye."

Simon turned back to the laptop. According to the StingRay, six calls had been placed between midnight and three from within twenty meters of the bar. Nikki pulled up a chair in order to look. A list of phone numbers belonging to callers along with the handset owners' names filled one box. The same information for the numbers they called filled an adjacent box.

Simon scrolled down the first list. "Got it," he said, pointing to the screen. "Twelve sixteen. Outgoing call from a handset registered to Luca J. Falconi to an unregistered phone lasting two minutes."

"You think it's Coluzzi?"

"I don't think he was calling his mother." Simon plugged the GPS coordinates of the recipient's phone into Google Maps. A circle the size of a pencil eraser appeared near the city of Marseille. "Darn."

"What's wrong?"

"Whoever Falconi was calling was using a burner."

"How can you tell?"

"The handset only gives its location to within ten kilometers. Typical of cheap throwaways. The better the chip, the more accurate it is. Even so, that's him. That's Coluzzi."

"How do you know?"

"It's where we grew up," said Simon. "He's gone home to hide out."

"Can we listen to the call?"

"Depends. If you don't set it to pick up a specific number, the StingRay only records three calls at a time. Falconi's was the fifth call it picked up. If it was still recording the others, we're out of luck."

Nikki scooted closer to the desk, closer to Simon, her eyes glued to the computer.

He double-clicked on Falconi's number. All information pertaining to his handset appeared: date of manufacture and last software update, along with his name, home address, credit card number, and more.

"Well?" she asked.

Simon pointed to an icon of a musical quarter note in the final column next to Falconi's number. The note meant the call had been recorded. "We got him."

He hit PLAY. Nikki reached over and paused the recording before it began.

"What's the matter?" he asked.

"This is an invasion of Luca Falconi's privacy. No warrant from a judge. We haven't even opened up a case against him."

"He tried to kill me. Isn't that good enough?"

"No. It's not," she said, then after further consideration: "None of this is admissible in a court of law, anyway."

"No, it isn't."

"We're the good guys, right?"

"Last I looked."

Nikki shrugged. "Screw him. He doesn't deserve to have his rights respected."

Simon hit PLAY.

"Yeah, Luca," said Tino Coluzzi. *"What is it?"*

"Something's up. A guy's in here asking about you."

"Recognize him?" asked Coluzzi.

"Never seen him before, but he says he knows you."

It was Coluzzi after all these years. The smooth, assured voice, the clip to his accent. The words unleashed an avalanche of memories, none good. They listened without comment.

"Know him?" said Tino Coluzzi. *"I killed him."*

"Well, whoever this Simon Ledoux is, he's alive. What do you want me to do about it?"

"Finish it."

The call ended.

"So this isn't just about the letter," said Nikki. "I mean, why you're here."

"No. It isn't." Simon went back to studying the call log. "Doesn't look like Falconi placed any other calls."

"Anyone else call him after the fight?"

"Lots, but I don't recognize any names. Nothing to Marseille. Hold it."

"What?"

An interesting number caught his eye. A country code he recognized but could find no reason for it being there: 7 for Russia; 495 for Moscow. "Someone called Moscow at twelve fifteen."

"From the bar?"

"Yeah."

"Who does the phone belong to?"

"No name. No billing address. All registration information is a blank. All I can say is that Russphon is the service provider."

Nikki bit her lip. It was odd, if not impossible, for a phone to be issued without some data about its owner. "Who did they call?"

Simon double-clicked on the number. "Nothing there either. All we know is that both phones come from Moscow." He checked the respondent's GPS on

Google Maps. The coordinates corresponded to a place in the southwestern suburbs of the Russian capital. "Some place called Yasenevo."

"Can we listen?"

Simon spotted the quarter note, indicating that a recording of the call had been made. "StingRay nabbed that one, too." He hit PLAY. A high-pitched screeching tone shot from the computer. He stopped the recording.

"What was that?" asked Nikki.

"The phone is encrypted. Whoever it belongs to made sure no one could listen in."

"Is that uncommon?"

"Depends on who the phone belongs to."

"What do you mean?"

"It's not uncommon if you're a spy."

"Is that who else wants the letter?"

Simon recalled telling Neill his belief that the other side—regardless of who they were—would be coming for the letter, too. He input the Russian caller's number into StingRay, requesting a log of calls the phone had made in the last twenty-four hours. He was not prepared for what appeared next.

"Whoever called Moscow from Le Galleon Rouge placed another call to the same number ten minutes ago." His eyes danced across the screen. "Oh no," he said.

"What is it?"

Simon pointed to the column indicating the location of the caller. "This call was made from Luca Falconi's home."

CHAPTER 36

Valentina Asanova greeted the dawn in an anxious frame of mind. Standing naked in Luca Falconi's kitchen, she stared out the window over a sea of mansard rooftops, drinking the espresso of which he was so proud. Though the beverage had long since grown cold, she couldn't deny its sharp, zesty flavor. He was right. He did make a mean espresso.

Falconi would not be joining her. He was no longer in any condition to drink an espresso with her or anyone else.

Valentina finished the coffee, then washed the cup with soap and hot water, using a dish towel to ensure no fingerprints were left behind. Afterward, she spent a quarter hour passing through the apartment, wiping down any surface she might have touched. She paid particular care to the bedroom. Finally, she gathered Falconi's clothing, folded it neatly, and set it on top of his dresser.

Finished, she observed the mutilated body. There were cuts on his belly and his feet, and one finger was missing. Falconi had talked freely and volubly. He

admitted to his roles in the robbery and to having recruited the gang on behalf of Tino Coluzzi, who he
named as its ringleader. He was less forthcoming about
Coluzzi's present location.

Death when it came was painless, relatively speaking. She'd nicked his carotid artery and watched him
bleed out, studying his eyes as pain was replaced by fear,
then acceptance, and, finally, nothing at all.

She returned to Falconi's bedroom and rummaged
in his closet for suitable clothing. She'd done her best
to shield her face from the security camera when she'd
entered the building. She had no intention of giving
the authorities anything more than necessary. She came
away with a loose-fitting leather jacket, a driving cap,
and a pair of wraparound sunglasses. Hardly ideal but
they would do in a pinch. Trousers were a problem,
given Falconi's girth. She settled on a pair of corduroys
only ten sizes too large, rolled up the cuffs, then made a
new notch in one of Falconi's belts, to keep them from
falling to the floor.

Before dressing, she placed a call to Vassily Borodin.

"Coluzzi's in Marseille," she said. "Holed up at a
place called Le Coual."

"What's that?"

"A rat hole he built for himself outside the city. Even
his closest friends don't know its exact location."

"You're sure."

She looked at Falconi's body. "Positive."

"Do you have a phone number? Anything we can
track?"

"Falconi may have called him last night, but I'm not
sure."

"Give me the number. I'll see if I can get a fix on it."

Valentina read off the number.

"That's a start. How quickly can you get down there?"

"Trains run every hour."

"Call me when you know. Get some sleep on the ride. You've been going at it a long time. Hopefully, I'll have something on his whereabouts by the time you arrive."

"Another thing: I saw the man who's looking for Coluzzi."

"Riske? We drew a blank on that name. You're certain?"

"Try 'Simon Ledoux.' Apparently he worked with Coluzzi years ago."

"First he's an investigator for a British firm. Now he's a criminal. You're certain it's the same man?"

"Absolutely. He was at the hotel yesterday."

"If you see him again, you know what to do."

"Yes, sir."

"And you?" asked Borodin. "How are you holding up?"

"I am fine."

"You're certain?"

Valentina took a last look at Falconi and closed the bedroom door. "Positive."

CHAPTER 37

Simon stood at the entry of 41 Rue Charlot, reading the directory of tenants. "Falconi, L." was third from the bottom, a buzzer next to it. "He's not hiding."

"Go ahead," said Nikki. "Ring it."

Simon pressed the button. He looked at Nikki as he waited for Falconi to ask who was there. No one answered. He pressed the button again. "Must be out for an early walk."

"Or maybe a workout at his gym," said Nikki. "He looked like a CrossFitter." She stepped back and gazed up at the building. "Did the StingRay tell you what floor he's on, too?"

"One through six. Can't be too hard to find." He looked through the glass door at a dark, deserted lobby. Either he could wait for someone to leave the building or he could take matters into his own hands. He eyed the lock, an old Kwikset. "Come here," he said, motioning her closer.

Nikki stepped nearer.

"Closer. Like you're giving me a hug."

Nikki held her ground. "What for?"

"Please," he said as politely as possible.

Nikki approached so that she was brushing against his chest. He pulled her closer still, and for a moment, they were face-to-face. Content that no passersby could see what he was up to, he removed his pick kit from his pocket, selecting a slim rake and one slightly fatter. He slid both into the lock, sawing back and forth until the tumblers released. "Open it," he said.

Nikki pushed down on the handle and the door opened inward. "First illegal eavesdropping, now breaking and entering. I can't wait to see what laws we'll break by lunchtime."

"After you," said Simon, slipping his kit back into his pocket.

Falconi lived in a modern apartment building, which in Paris meant it had been built sometime after the Second World War. There was a small elevator with a door that opened outward and a stone stairway that wound around a central court. Two apartments shared each floor. Nameplates beside the doors indicated the occupants. They found the one with Falconi's name on the top floor.

"I'm not thinking this was a friendly visit," said Simon as they took up positions on either side of the door.

Nikki had her pistol drawn. "Me neither."

He rang the doorbell. Kneeling, he pressed his ear to the door. He heard nothing. No voices. No footsteps. Unlike the downstairs entry, Falconi's door was guarded with a double bolt up top and a standard single below.

"Be careful," he said. "Last time I did this it didn't turn out so good."

Simon needed ten seconds to get the single bolt and twice as long for the double. He stepped back as Nikki opened the door and entered the apartment, pistol at the ready.

"Mr. Falconi," she called. "Luca Falconi. Police. Come out with your hands above your head."

There was no response.

"Mr. Falconi," she repeated. "Are you all right?"

Simon entered the apartment and closed the door behind them. He stood in a bright modern alcove, travertine floors, lacquered entry table, a crystal chandelier hanging overhead. To the right was a tastefully decorated living area. There was a corridor to the left. Simon could see two doors and at the end, the kitchen. All the lights were on.

"Stay here," said Nikki.

Simon watched as she checked the first room, then the second. She reappeared a moment later, her gun hanging at her side. "In here," she said, much too quietly.

When he entered the room, Nikki was standing at the foot of the bed, staring down at Falconi's lifeless body. His torso was a latticework of gashes, blood running in great daubs across his pale flesh onto the bed and floor.

"I've never seen that," she said with disgust.

"You okay?"

"Of course I'm okay," she retorted. And as if to prove it, she stepped closer to the body and bent nearer still to study the wounds. "It took a while," she said. "Some of the wounds had begun to coagulate before he died."

"He was a tough guy."

"Or your Russian friend enjoyed it."

Simon averted his eyes from the mess on the bed and began searching the room, opening drawers, looking in the closet. He caught Nikki staring at him. "I'm looking for his phone," he said.

A pile of Falconi's clothing was folded neatly on the dresser. Simon rummaged through the pockets, finding a few breath mints, a lottery scratch off, and a cigar. "Well?" Nikki asked.

"No luck."

She left the bedroom and he followed her to the front door. They made a tour of the apartment, both commenting that there was no sign of a struggle. In the living room, they found the stereo on, a vintage turntable still spinning. "Claude François," said Nikki, reading the record label. "Know him?"

"My stepfather loved him. I preferred Pearl Jam."

There was a small office off the living room. Simon sat at the desk and looked through the drawers. It was apparent Falconi ran his business from here. A bound notebook held names and numbers that indicated a betting enterprise. Next, Simon turned to an agenda but was disappointed to find few notations, certainly nothing to do with Tino Coluzzi. He yanked the top drawer all the way out and dug through a hodgepodge of pens and rubber bands and boxes of staples and business cards. At the rear was an envelope from a photo developer dated March 2012. Inside were pictures from a trip Falconi had taken in the South of France. "Nikki," he called. "Come here."

She entered the office.

"Here's our guy," he said, holding up a photograph.

The picture showed two smiling men raising bottles of beer as if offering a toast and standing in front of a beach bar, the ocean visible in the background. "Falconi and Coluzzi. It was taken a few years back."

Nikki studied the photograph. "So that's your buddy?"

"That's him, all right."

Coluzzi had lost some hair and put on a few pounds

but otherwise looked as Simon remembered him. The smirking mouth, the shifty gaze. He was a man who followed no code, obeyed no rules, and demonstrated loyalty only to himself. In short, a scoundrel.

"Any idea where the picture was taken?" Nikki asked.

"Les Calanques. The bar looks familiar."

Les Calanques was an area along the coast east of Marseille composed of numerous narrow inlets with craggy vertical walls rising a thousand feet or more out of the sea.

"Your old stomping ground."

"Something like that."

Simon put the picture in his pocket. As he rose, he eyed a blank notepad with a pencil lying next to it. He picked up the notepad and turned it this way and that, studying the surface.

"What is it?" asked Nikki.

"Just checking something." Simon ripped off the top sheet and set it on the desk, then activated his cellphone's light and directed it at a low angle toward the paper.

"See anything?"

"Not sure," said Simon, but in fact he'd spotted several indentations made by a pen and a firm hand. Opening the top drawer, he found a pencil, and placing his index finger above the lead, brushed it vigorously across the page. A number appeared. Then another. Soon the page was colored over in lead…except for six phone numbers all beginning with the Paris city code. Above them, clearest of all, were the initials "T.C."

"Nice," said Nikki, looking over his shoulder.

Simon picked up the sheet. "The first number is the one Falconi called from Le Galleon Rouge."

"To Coluzzi?"

Simon nodded. "I'm guessing the other numbers are his, too."

"Burners he can use and throw away. We can't get taps on them without a warrant."

"You can't, maybe. I'm going to give them to my friend, Mr. Neill. If he wants that letter, he'll pass them along to his pals at the National Security Agency. They'll do whatever they do, and when Coluzzi uses these numbers, we'll be listening in."

"Didn't you say Neill didn't want to be involved?"

"I said he didn't want to be seen to be involved," said Simon. "You can't see who's listening in on your calls."

"Are you done here?"

"Think so."

"Okay, then. Follow me." In the kitchen, Nikki pointed to two snifters in the sink. She picked one up. "Still warm. Whoever did this cleaned up after himself."

"Not him. Her."

"How do you know?"

"I don't see Falconi asking a buddy to come over at one in the morning to listen to old disco music and have a drink."

"Maybe he's gay."

"Doubtful. Besides, I think I saw her at the bar last night."

Simon related his suspicions about the attractive blond woman he'd seen seated next to Falconi at Le Galleon Rouge. At the time, he'd thought her out of place, not only for the establishment but for chumming up with Falconi.

"She's the one who called Moscow?" asked Nikki.

"That's my guess."

"There's a camera on the front door downstairs."

"I noticed."

"We'll need to contact the building manager."

"Not necessarily."

"There's been a murder. We're calling in a homicide."

"Not a good idea."

"I already told you, Riske, I'm not a bad cop. I bend the rules. I don't break them."

"Think it through, Nikki. You'll have to explain why we're here and how we got in. You can forget about nailing Coluzzi. Once your superiors learn you were acting on information you got from a StingRay—*my StingRay*—you can forget about ever getting off administrative duty."

"Don't tell me how to handle my career. I don't need an ex-con passing himself off as a gentleman to give me advice."

"It's nothing you don't already know. I'm just laying it out for you."

"I suppose I should thank you. Do you want me to curtsy, too?"

"Just help me find Coluzzi. He's your 'Get Out of Jail' card."

Nikki stormed out of the kitchen. A moment later, Simon heard the front door open. "Shut the door on your way out," she called. "And lock it."

The building's surveillance and security apparatus was located in a cramped suite of rooms on the ground floor. Again, the lock proved no obstacle. A black-and-white multiplex broadcast feeds from two cameras. One showed the lobby. The other was trained on a rear entrance in the alley behind the building. The recording system was at least twenty years old, with video from each stored on a rewritable CD.

Simon rewound the machine recording images from the lobby until the time stamp read 12:30. A fast play mode allowed him to speed up images.

"Stop," said Nikki. "There he is."

It was not easy to miss Falconi entering the building at 1:15.

Simon hit PLAY, and they viewed Falconi and his female companion enter the lobby and cross to the elevator. The camera was situated high in a corner and did not offer a clear frontal view of either. But it was enough.

"That's her," he said.

Nikki looked more closely at the monitor. "The picture is a mess. Can we clean it up?"

"Not here." Simon froze the picture as Falconi and the woman entered the elevator. For an instant, the woman's face could be seen in a mirror at the back of the elevator. Simon snapped a photo of the monitor with his phone. "We got her."

"Not much help."

"Not now, maybe. With Photoshop we can enhance it enough to get a better idea of what she looks like."

"And then?"

"For a start, we'll know who else is looking for Tino Coluzzi. I don't want that woman sneaking up on me."

"What time did she leave?"

Simon forwarded the playback to 5:30, when the elevator door opened and a short man in a driving cap and heavy coat emerged, walked briskly—head down— across the lobby, and left the building. "Look at the rolled up cuffs," said Simon. "She's wearing Falconi's clothes."

"Where do you think she's going?"

"If we know Coluzzi's in Marseille, so does she."

Simon returned the recording equipment to its pre-set values and announced that he was finished. "Let's get out of here."

Nikki left the room. He turned off the lights behind her, casually slipping the CD with the woman's image, as well as his and Nikki's, into his pocket.

As they walked to her motorcycle, he checked the schedule for the next TGV to Marseille. "Think we can make the nine sixteen?"

"We?"

"You want to miss out on all the fun?"

"I'm on duty at eight."

"Call in sick."

"Out of the question."

"I thought you wanted to get him."

"I wouldn't have come this far if I didn't. Marseille is another *département.* An entirely different jurisdiction."

"A crime's a crime no matter where it's committed."

Nikki gave him a tired look. "This isn't bending the rules, it's nuking them. I like my job. I'm not going to throw it away for you."

"They can't fire you if you bring in Coluzzi."

"Goodbye, Mr. Riske. If you need some help from the police in Marseille, ask your friend, the commissaire. I'm sure he'll be able to recommend someone."

"And what are you going to do?"

"I'm going to do what I should have done all along. I'm going to call in the homicide, tell the lieutenant everything I know about who killed Falconi, and pass along the information that Tino Coluzzi was responsible for the robbery. I'm sorry if that puts a crimp in your plan to retrieve this all-important letter."

"I understand," said Simon.

"No, you don't, but that's the way it is." Nikki walked to her motorcycle and climbed on.

"You're sure?"

"My shift started five minutes ago. I'm late. *Bon voyage.*"

Simon stepped back as Nikki fired up her bike and disappeared into morning traffic.

CHAPTER 38

Valentina was not at Orly Airport. Nor was she aboard one of her country's aircraft en route to Marseille. Though she could not know it, Vassily Borodin, despite a budget of over ten billion dollars and a multitude of resources at his disposal, was unable to provide one of the SVR's jets to transport her to Marseille. Chartering a plane meant paperwork, and paperwork required opening a case file, and a case file required providing the name of a case officer. As Valentina's work for Borodin was a private matter, and she had not yet been officially reassigned to his complement of covert operatives, her activities were strictly off the record.

There was no case. Thus, there could be no jet.

If Valentina suspected she had embarked on a mission sub rosa or was undertaking a wildly dangerous lark, she put the notion out of her mind. She was aware that Borodin himself had booked her flight to Paris and that prior to her departure from Moscow he'd wired her ten thousand euros from his personal account. Neither fell under normal operating procedure. Borodin's explanation was that she was undertaking an important mission on his behalf upon whose successful conclusion she would be returned to active service. Like all spies, she knew when to ask questions and when not to.

So it was that at 7:49 a.m. she stood at the ticket window in the Gare de Lyon, hoping to buy a seat on the next TGV, or Train à Grande Vitesse, the high-speed train, to Marseille.

"Good morning," she began, smiling shyly. "I was wondering if a seat has become available on the 8:37 to Marseille."

The clerk tapped at his computer. "Sold out."

"Are you certain that there are no last-minute cancellations? It's a family emergency."

The clerk regarded her impassively. "Nothing is available, *madame*. I'm sorry."

"My son," she said. "He's ill. I'm happy with any seat."

Still the clerk did not double-check. "If you'd like, I will put your name on the waiting list. This is one of our busiest lines. There are already four people on the waiting list ahead of you."

Valentina checked her watch. She thought of the man who was also looking for Coluzzi. Was he already on his way to Marseille? Over the clerk's shoulder, she could see passengers filing through the checkpoint to board the train. Normally, she would simply board and purchase a ticket once the train had left the station. However, new security measures made it impossible to board a TGV without a ticket. She could only be thankful there was no baggage screening.

"When is the next train?" she asked.

"Nine sixteen."

"One ticket."

"First or second class?"

CHAPTER 39

Simon was out of his league. At some point in the last twelve hours his profession had changed. He was no longer a consultant for a corporation worried about industrial espionage or an investigator for a bank concerned about a larcenous trader or a recovery specialist for an insurance company tasked with retrieving a stolen watch. None of those involved having a gun aimed squarely at your chest or discovering the body of a man who'd been tortured to death with a sharp instrument. He had moved on to shakier ground. Soon, the choice of whether or not violence was required to complete his assignment might no longer be his. The list of professions that required a man to maim or kill for his country was short. He was neither a soldier nor a spy. He most certainly wasn't an assassin. To his mind, that left one thing. He was a secret agent.

He did not like the sound of it.

Entering his hotel room, he threw off his jacket and, with haste, gathered his clothes and packed his bags. In a stroke of good fortune, he'd nabbed the last seat on the 9:16 to Marseille. Once finished packing, he called Neill.

"Mr. Riske," said Neill. "It feels too early for you to have good news for me."

"You're right about that," Simon said. "I take it you haven't been contacted?"

"Not a peep."

"You still think he has it?"

"Why else would he risk getting us riled up? We have no choice but to continue working on this assumption. I gather this isn't a social call."

"We've got company."

"Oh?"

Simon brought Neill up to date on his efforts to track down Coluzzi, including his belief that Falconi was killed by a Russian assassin. He left out the part about hurting Falconi's friends and being saved by Nikki Perez.

"Seems they're more desperate than we are," replied Neill.

"The person she called was in Yasenevo. I wasn't familiar with the name, so I looked it up."

"Now you know who we're up against."

"The SVR." There he'd said it.

"Sounds about right."

Simon exhaled loudly as he walked to the window. The sky was cloudless. The Arc de Triomphe was a few blocks in one direction. The River Seine in the other. All he had to do was say "I quit," wire Neill back his money, and the job would be over. He could spend the rest of the day visiting the Louvre, strolling through the Jardin du Luxembourg, or even take the elevator to the top of the Eiffel Tower. He could be a tourist like everyone else in town at this time of year.

And then what?

He looked at his overnight bag and his case of electronic gear sitting by the door.

And then he'd have failed. He'd have failed Ambassador Shea at the London embassy. He'd have failed Barnaby Neill, and he'd have failed his country. Of course, there was more to it than that. It was no longer just about the letter. Maybe, as he'd admitted to Nikki, it never had been. Should he quit, he'd no longer have the ticket he needed to go after Tino Coluzzi, and by "ticket" he meant the official permission. The monsignor would not approve of revenge for revenge's sake.

"I have a picture of her," he said. "It's blurry. I need you to clean it up."

"Send it over and I'll do my best," replied Neill.

"Just do it *fast*. If she's anywhere near me, I'd like to think I have a chance."

"Does she have any idea that you've seen her?"

"Not that I'm aware of."

"And did she see you?"

"There's a chance she got a look at me in the bar. We have to assume that Falconi told her I was asking about Coluzzi, too."

"How long did you speak with him?"

"A couple of minutes. Five tops."

"She'd have to be awfully perceptive to put two and two together."

Simon thought back on the past night. While she might not have noticed Falconi speaking with him earlier, she wouldn't have missed Falconi, Jack, and the other two thugs escorting him outside for their little tête-à-tête. She might even have been standing in the crowd that had witnessed the fight. But that was Simon's problem. "You're right about that," he said.

"Keep at it. Try and be as quiet as possible."

"Things may get noisier when I hit Marseille." Simon made it a point not to mention Nikki Perez. Neill had been clear in his instructions not to involve a foreign law enforcement agency. Simon justified asking for Marc Dumont's help by not having revealed who his employer was or the true reason for his visit. He was certain Neill would object to his enlisting Nikki in his efforts. It was a rule never to disobey a client. He still needed her help, even if not entirely for the right reasons.

"There's more. I found several phone numbers in Falconi's apartment. My guess is that they belong to Coluzzi. Falconi was his man in Paris. He'd have to know how to reach his boss. If Coluzzi uses any of the numbers, I want to know what he's saying and where he is."

"That's a tall order."

"A man like you should need one call to see it done."

"It's not that simple."

"Are you saying the NSA doesn't have the capabilities?"

"I'm saying that the NSA has a backlog of requests a mile high."

"Then I'm guessing what's in that envelope isn't as important as you thought," said Simon.

"You might want to take that up with the person who dispatched Mr. Falconi."

"It's time you told me what I'm going after."

"You know who's involved. You've seen what they are capable of. I'll let you use your imagination."

"Mr. Neill—"

"Mr. Riske." The voice was curt and commanding. "Listen to me. Once you know it, you can't un-know it. There are people who wouldn't be happy that you have that knowledge in your head."

"Are you one of them?"

"I trust you implicitly or you wouldn't have been offered the job."

"You sure about that?"

"I'll see what I can do about the phone numbers."

"Thank you."

"When are you off to Marseille?"

"Nine. Arrive at one."

"Keep in touch."

CHAPTER 40

Nikki lived alone in a fourth-floor duplex on an unloved street a few blocks from the Montparnasse Tower. The apartment was barely three hundred square feet—a bit bigger than two shoe boxes stacked on top of each other, but not much. The bottom floor had a kitchen on one side and a living area on the other. A very steep, very narrow spiral staircase led to her bedroom on the second floor. To make efficient use of the space, she'd built a loft on which she slept. It had taken her a few weeks and several bumps on the head to learn not to sit up in the middle of the night. Below the loft she'd put a desk, a dresser, and a cabinet for her wardrobe. It was all a thirty-year-old detective earning twenty-five hundred euros a month could afford if she wanted to live in Paris, and she was proud of every square inch of it.

Arriving a little after eight, Nikki slammed the door behind her and threw her keys on the kitchen table. The elevator was on the fritz and she was out of breath from running up three flights. She made her daily vow to quit smoking, and to prove it, dashed up the stairs to her bedroom. Panting, she undressed sloppily, leaving her clothes in a pile, and made the five-step journey to turn on the shower. The bathroom was the size of a toilet stall. There was no bathtub, just a shower so confining she had to hold her breath to turn around, and a vanity with a washbasin atop it.

Waiting for the water to warm up, she went back to the closet and dug out her overnight bag. She threw in underwear, socks, a few T-shirts, and a clean pair of jeans. She found her favorite dress still wrapped in plastic, fresh from the dry cleaner. She smiled, thinking that at least she'd have one thing she looked nice in. She glanced up and caught herself in the mirror holding the dress close, almost hugging it, an expression of dreamy bliss pasted on her face.

It was at that moment that she stopped.

What exactly did she think she was doing?

Since meeting Simon Riske, she'd done nothing but labor on his behalf. Commissaire Dumont had asked her to assist him, not be his slave. At first, she'd viewed the assignment as a welcome opportunity to escape her administrative punishment. The fact that she'd confiscated a kilo of heroin from Aziz François had earned her a few bonus points with the lieutenant but had also prompted a tongue-lashing for not having arrested him on the spot. It was only through Dumont's intercession that she'd escaped an additional month's desk duty. And now here she was, rushing to pack in order to once again aid Riske, this time at even further risk to her career.

Nikki hung the dress back in her armoire and banished her dreamy expression to never-never land, where it belonged. She walked to the bathroom and tested the shower. The water was lukewarm. Suddenly reminiscent, she found herself dredging up memories of the last time she'd worn the dress. It was at Restaurant Guy Savoy when things had still been good between her and David. David Renard, the ace squash player she'd met on the courts, who happened to be the forty-year-old wunderkind of Lazard Frères. David, who—as her mother never ceased to remind her—was too good for her and "from another world entirely," as if they still lived in the nineteenth century and there was no mixing between classes. She'd gone home with him that night. They'd made love in his *maison de ville* overlooking the Champs de Mars, the culmination of a six-week courtship defined more by the dates she'd cancelled due to the job than by the time they'd spent together.

Lying in his bed, she'd decided that he could be "the one." He was smart, tender, and witty, and he treated her like a lady. If he wasn't the greatest lover she'd had, he'd shown promise. Of course, she'd gotten a call from the lieutenant the next morning at six a.m., ordering her to a crime scene. She'd been dressed and out the door before David could complain.

He called later that day to break things off. She made the mistake of asking why.

"I like a woman who cooks me breakfast," he'd said in all earnestness.

Even now, the words stung. Her heart had been only partly broken and had mended quickly. It was her sense of self that had been shattered. How could she have been such a fool to fall in love with him? Only then did she realize that desperation, not affection, had governed her choice.

Six months had passed since that day.

Nikki climbed beneath the showerhead, turning

sideways to close the folding door. Running a bar of soap over her body, she forced herself to take a more hard-eyed view of her feelings. The fact was, she knew nothing about Riske. He lied easily out of both sides of his mouth. She had no doubt that he was using her— with or without Dumont's consent—and that he would continue to do so until he found Tino Coluzzi and retrieved that damned letter. She had no way of knowing if he would keep his word and help her to capture him afterward. Most likely, it was a smoke screen. Nikki reminded herself that she was a detective. The first rule of the job demanded that she not believe people.

And the rest of it? The immediate attraction she'd felt toward him. The desire he stirred in her when standing close. The fear he could conjure with a look of his eyes. She imagined running her hand across his muscled chest, then lower. Her breath left her and she needed a hand to steady herself.

And what was that? she thought, stunned at the sudden rushed beating of her heart, the near giddy flood of emotion.

"No," she said aloud, standing taller. Emotions lied. Emotions deceived. Like people, they were not to be trusted. Her loyalty was to the PJ, not Riske. Her first order of business was to call the lieutenant and tell him everything she knew about Coluzzi, so he might alert their counterparts in Marseille. Consequences be damned. She would atone for her sins and finish her punishment with equanimity and grace.

And then? Sooner or later someone would bring in Coluzzi. The thought of another benefiting from her efforts made her sick to her stomach.

"No," she said again, louder this time. "This one is mine."

The answer had been there all along. She would use Riske as he was using her. Next time there would be no question whose name would be listed at the top of the arrest report.

Happier now that she'd decided on a course of action, Nikki climbed out of the shower, dried her hair, and dressed for the day. She glanced at her un-smiling, un-dreamy reflection in the mirror. She liked what she saw. A cold, calculating professional.

Reaching for her pistol, she looked once more at the half-filled overnight bag sitting on the floor.

And Riske?

Nikki grabbed her dress from the armoire and threw it in her overnight bag, along with her pistol and ammunition.

Que será, será.

She had fifteen minutes to get to the Gare de Lyon.

CHAPTER 41

"Did you get the numbers?" Barnaby Neill asked a technician seated at an electronics console in the mobile surveillance center. "Send them to NSA lickety-split."

"Already done, sir. Confirmed receipt. Substation Five. Western Europe."

"Make sure the duty officer patches us into their feed in real time. If these phone numbers really are Coluzzi's, I don't want to wait to find out about it. I want to hear every word he says, as he says it."

Neill stood up to stretch, careful not to hit his head against the roof. The van was a Mercedes Sprinter with blacked-out windows and fitted with a standard surveillance package. There was a StingRay, similar to Simon's, if many times more powerful, a directional microphone hidden beneath the van's opaque turret, high-def cameras linked to facial-recognition software, and much, much more. All with direct access to the new combined intelligence database code-named "Beast," which linked together the combined resources of the CIA, the Pentagon, the FBI, and a dozen other three-letter agencies, including the DEA, ICE, NGA, and IRS. It had taken 9/11, fifteen years of haggling, dozens of false starts, and twenty billion dollars, but the United States intelligence and law enforcement communities were finally functionally integrated.

Ten years earlier, he'd needed a month to shepherd a request for information from one agency to another. Today, he could do it in a few seconds from an automobile traveling at eighty miles per hour along a highway three thousand miles from Washington, DC. That, concluded Neill, was progress.

"What can you do with the picture?" he asked a second tech seated on the opposite side of the van.

The technician brought up the photograph of the Russian woman taken in the lobby of Falconi's apartment building. He cropped the photo close to her face, then applied a variety of filters and sharpeners, serving to amplify and clarify the pixel count. When he'd finished, he had a near-perfect, full-frontal portrait. "That's as good as we're going to get."

"Pretty little thing, isn't she?"

"Better than the girls I was at the Farm with."

The Farm being the CIA's training compound in rural Virginia.

"Hush," said Neill. "That's unpatriotic. Let's see if she shows up in any of our registries."

"May take a minute."

The van hit a bump and Neill put out a hand to steady himself. He walked forward to the driving cabin. "Everything ready for our departure."

"The bird is on the tarmac. Flight crew aboard and waiting."

"Outstanding."

"Sir," called the photo tech. "We have a hit."

"I'm listening."

"Valentina Asanova. Ph.D. candidate in electrical

engineering at Moscow State University. Graduate of
the foreign intelligence school. Assigned to Directorate
S, Department 9. First spotted in Dubai 2008, as part
of the team believed to have assassinated a key fund-
raiser for Hezbollah. Suspected of taking part in that
car bombing in Sana'a in 2016."

"That mess?" An extremist group backed by the
Russians had detonated a car bomb in the center of
a large religious gathering near the Yemeni capital,
killing over two hundred people. The problem had
been that the gathering was a wedding when the
intended target was attending a funeral.

"Last known assignment to be in Mumbai. Officially
retired from duty last year. Reputation as being reckless
with no regard for collateral damage."

Neill wrung his hands. *Oh, Vassily,* he thought. *We've
got you hook, line, and sinker.* "Looks like she's back,
though I'm betting it's unofficially. Did Mr. Riske
provide her number as well?"

"He did."

"Let's see where she's hiding."

The technician input Valentina Asanova's phone
number into his computer. The number was sent to the
National Security Agency at Fort Meade, Maryland,
where it was surreptitiously uploaded to a satellite operated by Russphon, the handset's service provider. The
satellite "pinged" the number. Less than a second later,
the GPS coordinates of the handset appeared on the
screen, along with an address. "She's presently at the
Gare de Lyon."

"Isn't that a coincidence?" The van came to a halt
and Neill gazed out the window at a large nineteenth-
century terminus building with a clock tower similar in
style to Big Ben. It was the Gare de Lyon.

"Shall we contact Riske and tell him about the Russian?" the technician asked.

Neill didn't respond. He'd had eyes and ears on Riske since he'd left London. He'd had a man in the lobby of the George V when Riske checked in and another at police headquarters when he'd met Commissaire Dumont. One of his men had followed Riske to Le Galleon Rouge and witnessed the fight outside the bar and, later, Riske's visit to the ER.

So it was that Neill knew Riske was working closely with Detective Perez. He was more than a little peeved that Riske hadn't told him, but he wasn't surprised. Everyone had his own agenda. Nothing was ever just business. It was always personal. But then he'd bet on that all along.

"Sir?"

Neill looked away, mulling his options. He had an agenda as well, and he was no longer sure if it was compatible with Simon Riske's.

"Can we at least send him the picture of her?"

"Quiet," said Neill. "Unless you want the man to hear you."

"Sir?"

Across the street a taxi had pulled up and disgorged a single passenger. He was a trim, dark-haired man dressed in a tailored blazer and slacks. Neill watched as Simon Riske paid the driver and set off at a determined clip toward the terminus.

Riske was his bird dog, not his retriever. His job was to flush the adversary out of the undergrowth, nothing more. So far, he was doing an admirable job. If the phone numbers found at Falconi's house did, in fact, belong to Coluzzi, Neill wouldn't need Riske much longer. He'd catch Coluzzi himself.

Neill saw no reason to offer help when help wasn't needed.

"Mr. Riske is fine on his own," he said.

"Yes, sir."

Neill put a hand on the driver's shoulder. "Let's get to the airport. The plane's waiting."

Neill arrived at Orly Airport thirty minutes later.

The van passed through a special security gate and drove across the tarmac to the Gulfstream jet parked anonymously at the far corner of the airfield. Unlike Valentina Asanova, Neill did have a plane at his disposal.

He'd be in Marseille in a little more than ninety minutes. Well ahead of his bird dog.

CHAPTER 42

Nervous, flighty, and fatigued from a poor night's sleep, Tino Coluzzi parked his car and walked the three blocks downhill to the port. The sky was a flawless blue. A light breeze scalloped the sea's surface. Gulls wheeled and turned overhead, crying lustily. The beautiful morning failed to lift the mantle of dread. A Russian assassin had killed Luca Falconi, his best friend. Worse, Falconi had seemingly told her everything he knew about him and about Le Coual. And in case that wasn't enough, Simon Ledoux, a man he'd thought dead and buried these long years, was not only alive but on his way to find him.

It had come to this.

One call.

Coluzzi crossed the Place aux Huiles and soon came in sight of the harbor. His heart sank. Panicked, he looked left and right. Nowhere did he see the *Solange*'s proud navy-blue hull, the sharp bow, the skull and crossbones fluttering from the fantail.

Ren had lied to him. He had not tried to reach Borodin after all.

In a daze, Coluzzi crossed to the quai and ran to the *Solange*'s mooring. In place of the two-hundred-foot superyacht was an eighteen-foot tender, bobbing at the dock. A lone crewman in white shorts and striped sailor's tunic busied himself wiping down the seats. Coluzzi lowered his head, feeling as if he were the brunt of some cruel practical joke. He thought of the briefcase cached at Le Coual and the letter returned to its hiding place inside it.

Now what?

"Mr. Coluzzi?"

Coluzzi looked up to see the young crewman waving. "What do you want?"

"Mr. Ren departed at dawn for Entre les Îles."

"I can see that."

"Come aboard. He asked that I bring you."

"To Entre les Îles?"

"He's expecting you."

"He is? …I mean, of course he is." Coluzzi hurried to the mooring. With a new spirit, he jumped into the boat. The sailor cast off and started the engines, maneuvering the boat past a line of incoming trawlers. When they'd cleared the breakwater, Fort Saint-Nicolas above their shoulder, he pushed down on the throttle. The bow rose, the wind picked up, and in seconds they were making twenty knots over a shallow chop.

The boat turned east and skirted the coast, leaving Marseille behind and traversing Les Calanques. After a minute, Coluzzi spotted Le Bilboquet, the beach bar where he'd spent so much time when he'd first arrived from Corsica. His eye moved up the craggy vertical face behind it to the bluff. He looked a few hundred meters to the right, trying hard to find Le Coual among the red rocks. He could not, and this made him feel safer, proud of how well he'd camouflaged his hideout. If he couldn't see it, no one could.

The boat turned away from the coast, heading out to sea on a course of south by southeast. The wind picked up. The sea grew rougher. The small boat began to rise and fall dramatically, the bow slapping the water with force. Coluzzi kept a death grip on the handrail. He was a landlubber, pure and simple. His family was from the mountains. Pig farmers, who even at the height of summer rarely visited the beach. The violent bounce, the subtle pitch and roll, provoked the first uneasy stirrings of nausea.

"Are you okay?" asked the skipper. "You look a little green."

"I'm fine," said Coluzzi, giving a tepid smile and a thumbs-up.

A smudge of brown appeared on the horizon and, soon after, a collection of white specks.

"Five minutes," said the skipper.

The specks grew into yachts, but the smudge of brown remained flat, barely rising above the horizon. The boat rounded the eastern tip of land and pulled into a broad channel, passing between two long, similarly low islands. The boat slowed. The wind abated. The water was calm and the color of aquamarine, the sandy seafloor visible below. No fewer than a dozen yachts were anchored here and there. The largest among them, occupying pride of place nearest the white sand beach, was the *Solange*.

The skipper continued past the motor yacht and pulled alongside a dock extending fifty meters from land. Directly behind the dock, situated on a low bluff overlooking the beach, was a restaurant with thatched roofs and billowing white canopies. The smell of smoked seafood filled the air.

"Mr. Ren asks that you join him."

Coluzzi negotiated his way onto the dock, pausing to steady himself and straighten his jacket before continuing to the beach and climbing the steep flight of steps to the restaurant.

A bodyguard waited at the top of the stairs. "Phone, please."

"I may need it."

"Mr. Ren doesn't allow phones."

Coluzzi handed over the burner phone he'd been using since midnight.

The bodyguard patted him down. He found nothing. *"Bon appétit,"* he said pleasantly.

"Merci." Coluzzi had known well enough to leave his stiletto at home.

The restaurant's charm came from its casual, near slapdash ambiance. Four long wooden tables were set end to end, each with ten to twelve rattan chairs along it. A liberal amount of sand had been spread over a poured concrete floor. Canopies overhead snapped like a ship's sails. Bouquets of flowers decorated the interior pylons.

Only one table was occupied. Alexei Ren sat at its head, one leg draped over the arm of his chair, a glass of champagne dangling from his hand. His guests numbered eleven or twelve: men, women, and a few children, dressed in linen shirts, shorts, and bathing attire. Sadly, Coluzzi spotted none of the lovelies he'd spent time with the day before. These guests had pale skin, high cheekbones, and dark eyes. Ren's Russian compatriots, no doubt.

Coluzzi counted ten empty bottles of Dom Pérignon

on the table and at least as many chilling in ice buckets nearby. "Tino!" Ren raised an arm in welcome. "Come. Sit."

Coluzzi grabbed a chair from the next table and brought it close. "Hello, Alexei."

"What'll you have? Some DP? Stoli? A beer?"

"Mineral water is fine."

"Come on," said Ren. "Join us. Today's your day."

"A beer," Coluzzi said to the waiter, "1664."

"There you go," said Ren. He was smiling much too broadly. No matter how he tried, Coluzzi couldn't smile back.

He knew all about Entre les Îles, even if he'd never been. There was a time when the place had been a local hangout, a sleepy lunch spot off the coast where you parked your boat, took a swim, then feasted on langoustines and beer for a decent price. All that had changed twenty years back when the Russians invaded the Riviera. Saint-Tropez had long been a chic destination ruined by rich tourists, but one by one even the most unprepossessing out-of-the-way spots were gobbled up by the surfeit of wealth and greed flooding the South of France. Why charge ten euros for a plate of ten langoustines when you could charge a hundred for just five?

The waiter brought the beer on a tray. Coluzzi had time to take a sip before Ren was on his feet. "Walk with me."

Ren lit a cigar and put an arm around Coluzzi's shoulder. "I don't see the money," he said.

"We said after you'd arranged the meeting."

"You said 'after.' I never agreed."

"Is there going to be a problem?"

Ren exhaled a cloud of blue smoke and hugged Coluzzi closer. "I know you're good for it."

"Of course."

The Russian led the way out of the restaurant to a shaded area overlooking the windward side of the island. Coluzzi noted that a bodyguard followed and stood ten steps away, his back turned to fend off unwelcome visitors. Ren busied himself relighting his cigar. Coluzzi remained quiet. Nothing betrayed nerves or weakness more than idle chatter.

"This man...Borodin," Ren began, assiduously lighting and pulling on his cigar. "He's damned tough to reach. I mean, how do you go about contacting the head of the Russian spy service?"

"If I knew," said Coluzzi, "we wouldn't be here."

"First," said Ren, "you must know someone close to him. Someone who you trust...and who he trusts." He opened his eyes wide and shrugged as if this were requesting the impossible. "I've been gone from Russia for years. My contacts are no longer what they once were. There was a time when if you asked me to call the head of the SVR, I would reply 'On his home phone or his cell?' Alas, those days are gone."

Coluzzi nodded, but he felt himself getting nervous. Yesterday Ren had practically boasted he could make the call then and there. Now he sounded as if he were hedging his bets.

"I'll ask again, is there going to be a problem?"

"Look at you," said Ren. "So worried." He clenched the cigar between his teeth and pulled a folded piece of paper from his pocket. "I didn't say I had no contacts at all. When you are a billionaire, there are always people eager to be your friend." He extended the paper toward Coluzzi, only to yank it back when Coluzzi reached for it. "Still," Ren continued, "it was expensive."

Only then did he hand Coluzzi the paper.

"He's expecting your call at noon. We have an hour. Hungry?"

Coluzzi put the paper in his pocket. "I could eat something."

Chapter 43

Car three, seat eighty-four," said the agent at the security checkpoint. "At the far end of the quai, just behind the locomotive. Have a pleasant journey."

Simon picked up his bags and started down the platform. Despite the rise of terrorist incidents in Europe, and in France in particular, there were no x-ray machines to scan luggage or carry-on bags. A half-dozen soldiers patrolled the platform, machine guns strapped to their chests. Two plainclothes policemen with German shepherds moved among the passengers as they boarded. Drug dogs, Simon guessed, as Marseille was the country's largest port on the Mediterranean and the primary conduit for illegal contraband to and from North Africa.

The TGV was a sleek, low-bodied train, the cars painted a warm silvery tone with blue accents. A few stragglers walked ahead of him, hurrying to board the carriages. Through the windows, he noted that the train appeared to be full. For a moment he stopped and looked behind him, checking for an athletic woman with tousled brown hair. As quickly, he turned and continued to the head of the train. He had no right to expect Nikki to join him. She'd done enough already. There was no money in continuing on a wild-goose chase that was potentially dangerous to her career, and quite possibly her health. She'd made the right choice.

Simon picked up his pace, taking a look at his phone. The forecast for Marseille called for sun during the day, with wind picking up in the evening and the possibility of a storm. He remembered the tang in the air when the mistral kicked up, the flecks of flume whirling about, wetting his cheeks—the swirling, unpredictable wind carrying the sea inland. After too many years, he was going home, back to the place that had done its best to destroy him and, when it had failed, had tried even harder to give him a second life.

"Wait!" A woman's voice echoed off the high ceiling. "Don't close the gate."

Simon turned to see Nikki Perez passing through the checkpoint, a carryall in one hand. He put his bags down and raised a hand, signaling to her.

"Traffic," she said when she reached him.

"What about work?"

"We can talk about that later."

The two walked briskly up the line of cars. Halfway there, a conductor asked them to climb aboard and continue to their seats once inside the train. Simon opened the door and Nikki climbed the steps. Almost immediately, the train began to move.

"Where's your seat?" he asked.

"Car fifteen. Seat seventy-one," said Nikki, checking her ticket. "Second class is the other direction. You?"

"Car three. Seat eighty-four."

"First class, of course."

Simon pulled his ticket from a pocket. "And eighty-five," he said.

"Excuse me?"

"I bought two just in case."

"You knew I'd come?"

"I hoped."

Nikki snatched the ticket out of his fingers and led the way, passing through car after car, all packed to capacity, luggage stored overhead or in the compartments between trains. Finally, they reached car 3 and identified the last two empty seats as their own. They threw their bags onto the overhead rack and sat down facing each other, a table in between them.

"I didn't know I was so predictable," said Nikki, settling into her seat.

"I know you want to get Coluzzi as badly as I do."

"Is that the only reason?"

"You're sick of desk duty."

"Also true."

"Hard to sit around pushing papers knowing that I might be closing in on him."

"No other reason?"

Simon thought hard. "Am I missing something?"

"No," said Nikki, gazing forthrightly at him. "That about covers it."

"Well?" said Simon.

"Well what?"

"Did you call in Falconi's murder? Did you tell Marc Dumont that we're after Coluzzi?"

"You're the know-it-all. You tell me."

"Since you're here, I'll take that as a no."

Nikki offered a dismissive smile. "Like you said, I want to get Coluzzi as badly as you. Well, then at least we have a few hours off."

"Actually," said Simon, taking out his phone, "work starts now." He found his earpiece and microphone and plugged them in, then attached a power cord so he wouldn't drain his battery before arriving.

"What are you doing?"

"Research."

"About Coluzzi?"

"About the prince."

Simon looked out the window. The train was passing through the city suburbs, tall concrete housing complexes that even in the cheery morning sun looked grim and unwelcoming. He remembered the rows of government-built apartments up the hill from his mother's house. The buildings had been nicer than these, at least to look at. Many apartments had had window boxes decorated with colorful flowers year-round. There had been decent playgrounds and a football field, upkeep paid for by the drug lords who governed the turf. Inside, however, the buildings had been decrepit and stank of overflowing sewage, the hallways narrow and dark, the stairwells a no-man's-land that reeked of urine, vomit, and the ever-present scent of pot. Elevators seldom functioned. He couldn't get from an apartment to the street without passing a drug deal in progress or a hooker bringing a john to her place or a group of bored, belligerent kids looking for trouble. Police made it a habit to stop a block away. It was as close as they dared to come.

"I grew up out here," said Nikki.

"Tough neighborhood."

"There are tougher."

"You got out. Good on you."

"And you? How'd you get out? From Les Baums to the Sciences Po. That's like from Earth to the moon."

"Long story."

"We've got four hours."

"Another time."

"Promise?" she asked, and he could see she was trying to be his friend.

"Maybe one day." Simon returned to his phone. He was studying the information he'd gotten from Delacroix's phone detailing Prince Abdul Aziz's personal data. His email address, credit card numbers, Saudi national identity number, and more. He felt a presence next to him and looked up to find Nikki perched on his armrest.

"What's that?" she asked, a hand on his shoulder.

Simon told her about his visit with Delacroix and how he'd lifted his phone and swiped the information from his SIM card.

"And so?" she asked. "How do you plan on using it?"

"With any luck I can get the password for his email account. After that, who knows?"

"Do you have any regard for the law whatsoever?"

"I sleep just fine."

"I'm sure you do."

"You want to listen in or would you like me to do this somewhere else?"

"I'm off duty. Please continue. One day when I'm a private investigator I may find it useful."

Simon found the number for the prince's Internet provider, a prominent Saudi Arabian telecom company. "Here we go," he said. "Quiet."

Nikki zipped her mouth closed.

"Good morning," he said when the customer service representative answered. His Arabic was slow and formal. His vocabulary was limited, but his accent was spot-on. "I have a small problem. I've forgotten the password for my account."

"I'm sorry to hear that, sir. I'm sure we can help

you find it without too much trouble. If you go to the sign-in page of your account and click on the 'Forgot password' link, you'll find instructions directing you how to retrieve or reset your password."

"I'm not at my computer. I'm on a phone and I don't have Wi-Fi access. I'd like to take care of this as quickly as possible, so when I do have Wi-Fi I can get to my messages."

"Of course, sir. I will have to ask you a few questions."

"Fire away."

"What is your email address?"

Simon read it off.

"Thank you. And what is the name of the account holder?"

Simon gave the prince's full name.

"Am I speaking with the prince?"

"This is Prince Abdul Aziz."

The representative began speaking Arabic excitedly. Simon did his best to understand but much escaped him. The gist, however, was clear. The telecom rep was honored, thrilled, gratified, to be helping the prince. Simon laid even odds that the representative knew what the prince's real job was.

"Please," said Simon. "I am with some American colleagues. I prefer to speak English."

"Of course, Your Highness. Please excuse me. I apologize. I—"

"May we continue?"

"Yes, Your Highness. I must still ask you these questions to verify your identity. No disrespect."

"I understand. You are just doing your job. And may I say you are doing it well."

"Thank you. Now, may I ask your date of birth?"

"November twelfth, nineteen sixty-seven."

"And when did you create this account?"

Simon gave a throaty harrumph. "Years ago. If I could remember that, surely I could remember my password."

"No problem, sir. In that case, do you have your national identity number?"

"Now, that I remember." Simon consulted the sheet listing the prince's information and read off the number.

"Thank you, sir. We are almost finished."

"I certainly hope so." He was tempted to add *And if you care about your family, you'll make sure we are soon.*

"What is the billing address on this account?"

Simon ran his eyes over the sheet. Nowhere did he find an address for the prince. "Shit."

"Excuse me, sir?"

"I sneezed. Pardon me. I have several residences. I don't usually handle my own billing."

"If you don't have that, I can ask you one of your personally chosen security questions."

"That might be easier."

"What city were you born in?"

"Now, that one I know." Simon mumbled a word as he typed the prince's name into his search engine.

"I didn't get that."

"One moment. We're going through a tunnel. I may cut out." Simon mumbled something that resembled Jeddah mixed with Riyadh, Saudi Arabia's two biggest cities, figuring that the odds were good he was born in one. The prince's Wikipedia page came onto the screen. And the odds were wrong. "Are you there?"

"Yes, sir, I am hearing you perfectly."

"London, England."

"One more question, sir."

"Goddammit," he said, switching back to Arabic. "Stop wasting my time and give me the goddamn password."

"Right away, sir," said the clerk meekly. "Everything has been taken care of. I've reset your password. Please log on and use the temporary password I am giving you to reset your account."

Simon wrote down the password and hung up before the clerk could start up again.

"Well?" asked Nikki.

Simon looked up at her. "We're in."

CHAPTER 44

Valentina Asanova rolled a black fountain pen in her fingers, staring out the window at the passing countryside. She was thinking that it looked very much like the countryside outside Novosibirsk, where she had grown up. Green meadows. Fields of golden wheat. Dark, wooded hollows. And villages on every hilltop, a church ever visible, though in her case there were onion domes, not steeples. The other difference was that by late August, temperatures in Siberia had already dropped precipitously and the skies were most often gray. By October, snow blanketed the ground. By January, a shelf of hard, unbreakable rime covered the snow, and the sun rose and set during the hours she had spent inside the schoolhouse.

Valentina preferred France. She preferred working for Vassily Borodin and traveling the world in the service of her country. And so it was that she knew she must kill the man who called himself Simon Riske, or Simon Ledoux, and who had passed within an inch of her, his thigh grazing her arm, only minutes before as he walked down the aisle on the way to his seat.

Valentina slipped the fountain pen into her pocket and discreetly peered over her shoulder. The aisle was clear. She rose and made her way to the head of the train, stopping at the entrance to each car, taking time to look through the glass door and study the passengers before entering. The problem was that she could see only those facing her. Among them, many were hidden behind newspapers or obscured by others. Of those facing forward, she had only the backs of their heads to go by. Half had dark hair, and it was difficult to tell if they were male or female until she was upon them. She could discount only those who were balding, blond, or of African origin.

She had more clues to help her: Riske was traveling with a woman. Though Valentina had only seen her from the back, she had nonetheless spotted a playful streak of blue in her hair.

Valentina moved briskly through each car, never slowing, never looking anyone in the eye. She was aware that Riske had seen her the night before. If he was a trained operative like herself—and she had no reason to think otherwise—he would likely recognize her if given the chance. She had dressed modestly for the trip: jeans, a loose blouse, her hair pulled back in a ponytail. She looked nothing like the dolled-up tart sitting at Falconi's table in Le Galleon Rouge.

She passed through four carriages before reaching the dining car. The interior was crowded with groups of travelers clustered around high tables. At the far end, she noted a line of people waiting to order at the counter. There was no way to move quickly and unobtrusively through them. If Riske was standing in the line, she would pass him face-to-face. Any chance of surprise would be lost. From her vantage point,

she was unable to get a good look at any of those in
line.

She considered returning to her seat.

And then? Wait till they arrived in Marseille and
take him in the station? Follow him to his hotel?
Neither option pleased her. Both were full of unknowns.

Riske was on the train. To an extent, he was already
her captive. She could dictate the terms of their encounter. She'd never have a better chance to eliminate
him.

It came down to her following orders.

Kill Riske at the first opportunity.

Her hand dipped into her pocket, feeling for the
fountain pen inside. It was more than a pen. A twist of
the cap filled its sharpened nib with a dose of cyanide
and strychnine, fatal within sixty seconds. The device
was standard issue, the natural descendant of the umbrella used to poison the Bulgarian journalist Georgi
Markov on Waterloo Bridge in London in 1978. One
jab, hardly more than a pinprick, and Riske would be
dead by the time she was back in her seat.

Valentina put on her sunglasses and entered the car.
Head lowered, she made her way through the crowded
dining car. He was not among those standing at the
snack tables. She slid past the order line, the corridor
narrower here, room for two abreast. She caught a
patch of trimmed dark hair, a navy blazer. The man
turned toward her. Glasses. Mustache. It wasn't Riske.

She reached the end of the car and looked behind
her, double-checking. It was only then that she realized she was holding her breath. She gathered herself
and continued across the connecting area. To her left,
the door to the restroom opened and a woman stepped
out, nearly bumping into her.

"Excuse me," she said. "Go ahead."

"After you," said Valentina.

The woman turned and opened the door to the next car.

It was then that Valentina saw the streak of blue in her hair.

CHAPTER 45

Simon had exchanged his phone for his laptop.

"We only get one shot at this," he said. "Next time the prince logs in, he'll know he's been hacked. He'll change the password back, or shut down the account. I'll copy anything interesting, but we need to move fast."

Nikki crowded next to him, eyes on the screen as he pulled up the Saudi Arabian website. As instructed, he used the temporary password to log into the prince's email.

"Here we go."

The prince's mailbox appeared on the screen. A notation indicated that there were two hundred seventy new messages. Simon began scanning the headers. Nearly all were written in Arabic.

"Can you read it?" he asked.

"Can't you?" said Nikki. "You were speaking Arabic a minute ago."

"The operative word is 'speaking.' I picked it up when I was doing my time."

"Let me," said Nikki, pulling the laptop closer. "Half the families in my neighborhood were Libyans."

"I'm thinking the stuff we're looking for will be in English."

Nikki scrolled through the new messages as Simon looked on. Most appeared to be from the prince's family: brothers, sisters, cousins. Lots of names ending in "bin Saud." He saw nothing related to the prince's government job. That, Simon figured, would be in a different mailbox.

"What are we looking for?" Nikki asked.

"Anything that can help us learn what's in the envelope."

"Why do you care so much? Isn't it enough that your client told you to get it?"

"If I'm going to lose even one drop of blood for something, I want to know what it is."

"Any ideas?"

Simon shrugged. "Whatever it is, it has people in Washington and Moscow worried."

Nikki scrolled down the list, going back one day, then another. A few messages in French popped up. There was one from the manager of the George V thanking him for his visit and offering his sympathy about the robbery. And a similar note from the manager of Cartier.

"Something's wrong," said Simon. "Two hundred seventy *unread* messages."

Nikki looked up. "So?"

"How often do you check your email?"

"If I'm busy, a few times a day. If I'm not, every other minute."

"Exactly. The last message the prince opened was from Jean-Jacques Delacroix on Sunday night."

"Two hours after the robbery," said Nikki, noting the time stamp.

Simon read the message aloud. "'Dear Prince Abdul

Aziz, I've just heard about the terrible affairs of this evening and wanted to inquire as to your and the princess's well-being, as well as that of your children. Please let me know soonest if there is anything I or the hotel can do on your behalf to be of assistance in this difficult time.'"

"Did he respond?" asked Nikki.

Simon opened the Sent Mail box. "He did." He read the missive aloud. "We are fine, Jean-Jacques. No one important was harmed. Thank you, my friend."

"'No one important,'" said Nikki. "Just the body-guard. Nice. And then? Anything more?"

"That's it. Nothing was sent since Sunday night."

"And no more messages were opened since then either."

"That's a long break."

"Too long." Nikki looked at Simon. "What do you think?"

"I'm thinking it's not good for your health to come in contact with that letter."

Simon worked his way through the messages in re-verse chronological order. The prince received nearly one hundred emails a day. Besides the correspondence from his family, there was junk mail from bookstores and department stores, newspapers and magazines, and one from his bank with a receipt for his with-drawal of ten thousand euros from the Bois de Boulogne branch.

Then he saw a name that increased his unease ten-fold. The sender was Borodin.V@Russcom.net. The header read, Handover details. The message, Kala-matos Airfield, Cyprus. Designation: KMTS. Radio frequency: 560 Hz. Sunday. 2300.

"Borodin," said Simon. "Ring a bell?"

"Something with music?"

"That was Alexander Borodin. Nineteenth-century Russian composer. This is Borodin, V." He typed the name into his Google search bar. "'Borodin, Vassily,'" he read aloud from a Wikipedia entry. "'Director Russian Foreign Intelligence Service.'"

"Now we know who's angry at us."

"Cyprus," said Simon. "A nice neutral location to hand over the letter...after which the prince fell off the map."

"You think something happened to him?"

Simon considered this. There was no question that something had happened to the prince that prevented him from checking his email. The question was what. "Maybe it wasn't so neutral after all."

He typed Borodin's email address into the search bar to bring up all past correspondence. A dozen messages appeared dating back over a year. The most recent was a message sent by the prince to Borodin dated the previous Wednesday. "'Prize in hand,'" Simon read aloud. "'Will transport to Paris. Advise handover.'"

"Is the 'prize' the letter?" Nikki asked.

"Must be," said Simon. "What everyone's dying to get their hands on."

"Next."

"Last Monday. There's a note instructing the prince to call a number with regard to 'picking up a certain package.'" Simon opened a new window and typed the ten-digit number into the search engine. "Alexandria, Virginia, area code," he said, waiting for the reverse listing to pop up. "That's across the river from the capital."

"How accurate is that?"

"Not very. I need to run the number past my contacts to get a name and address. It will take time."

"Who do you think it is?"

"Easiest guess is whoever stole the letter from the CIA, or who was in possession of it at that time. But, like I said, that's a guess."

"Keep going."

The next few messages between the men provided a clearer picture of their relationship and the events leading to Borodin requesting the prince's assistance with "a matter of utmost delicacy." It was in one of these messages that Borodin had attached a photograph captioned "Red Square 1988."

"Take a look."

"Who is it?" asked Nikki.

"You don't know?"

"That's, um…the Russian guy with the port-wine birthmark on his forehead."

"Mikhail Gorbachev."

"Yeah, Gorbachev."

"And the other guy?"

"The one shaking the kid's hand?"

"Yes, the man shaking the boy's hand."

"He's an American. He was president. Um…"

"Ronald Reagan."

"Yes, Reagan. The cowboy. It's your country. Why should I know?"

The photograph showed Reagan and Gorbachev along with a coterie of aides taking a stroll through Red Square. It was an informal "action" shot taken as Reagan extended his arm to shake the hand of a young Russian boy, a tourist by the look of him, about ten years of age.

"Okay," said Nikki. "Reagan and Gorbachev from a million years ago. What's the big deal?"

"Not sure." Simon studied the picture more closely and it hit him. "You see anything funny?"

"No," said Nikki, without interest.

"What about that guy?" Simon pointed to a slim man standing directly behind the boy, a person he took to be the boy's father. "Look familiar?"

"No."

"Sure about that?"

The father appeared to be in his midthirties, with high cheekbones and an Asiatic cast to the eyes. His blond hair was already thinning. He wore a short-sleeved shirt with a camera around his neck. The picture had been taken thirty years earlier, but Simon recognized him at once. Unlike many Russians, this one did not drink alcohol and was famed for his physical pursuits. He had aged well.

"It can't be," Nikki gasped.

"Why not?" Simon zoomed in on the blond man. To his eye, there was no doubt. The "father" of the boy was Vladimir Putin, leader of the Russian Federation. "It says the picture was taken in 1988. If I'm not mistaken, Putin was assigned to East Germany at the time. They must have brought him in for the job. Makes sense. Do you think Gorbachev would let just anyone into Red Square when the president of the United States was visiting? He couldn't take a chance there might be some dissident eager to voice his discontent. The loss of face would have been incalculable. Every last person in Red Square that day must have been KGB."

"And the boy?"

"Future KGB." Simon smiled, but only for a moment. His eye had shifted to a man standing directly behind Ronald Reagan's shoulder, an American in a khaki suit standing with a hangdog look about him. "No," he murmured.

"What is it?"

"Nothing," said Simon. "Just surprised." But for a few seconds longer he continued to study the pallid man in the khaki suit. If he wasn't mistaken, the man was Barnaby Neill, and he and Vladimir Putin were looking directly at each other.

"And so?" Nikki asked when Simon closed the photograph. "What does it mean?"

"Another piece of the puzzle."

Continuing to scroll through the messages, Simon spotted a receipt from the Four Seasons Hotel, Washington, DC, for the prince's stay in the U.S. capital the week before.

And he picked up the letter in DC.

Thirty minutes later, after digging through the prince's emails and finding nothing further of interest, Simon closed the laptop. He gazed outside. Everything looked so pretty on the surface. Clean. Well ordered. Idyllic. Only when you looked closer did you notice the cracks.

"Well?" Nikki asked. "Satisfied?"

"Not the word I'd use." He checked his phone to see if Neill had sent a message about the Russian assassin's whereabouts. He wondered if it really was Neill with Reagan all those years ago and, moreover, if there was anything to the look between him and Vladimir Putin. The fact that Putin and Reagan— and Reagan's handlers, presumably some of whom were CIA—were together had to mean something. Why else would Borodin send the picture to Prince Abdul Aziz?

"What's bothering you?" Nikki asked.

"Nothing. Just anxious to get to Marseille."

"Don't lie. We're a team now, right?"

"I'm wondering why Neill hasn't let us know if he's been able to track down the Russian who killed Falconi."

"Should he have?"

"My guess is yes. If we could track the number with a device anyone can buy over the counter, I'm fairly certain that a man with his resources could do a damn sight better."

"You don't trust him?"

"Let me put it this way: I don't distrust him," said Simon, "yet."

"How did he find you?"

"I'd done some work for people in his line of work before. Background checks. Industrial espionage. Nothing like this. They must have looked into my past. A deep dive. That's what they do, you know."

"I have a question," said Nikki. "If this guy is smart enough to find exactly the right person to go after this letter, how come he put a guy like Coluzzi onto the job to steal it?"

"What do you mean?"

"You don't think he looked into Coluzzi's past as deeply as he looked into yours? Did he really expect a career criminal to keep his end of the bargain?" Nikki looked at Simon, eyes mocking him. "He must not be as smart as you think."

Simon said nothing. He looked out the window again, seeking refuge in the passing countryside. Neill wasn't one to misjudge a person. If anything, he was smarter than Simon had thought. He looked back at Nikki, meeting her gaze, disliking her for having given voice to his deepest concerns. More and more, he felt like a puppet on a string.

He stood and started down the car.

"Hey," said Nikki, rising and touching his arm. "What's wrong? You mad?"

"Good guess," said Simon. "You must be a detective."

"Simon, what is it?"

"Look," he said. "I haven't put all the pieces together. I'm sorry if I don't have all the answers yet."

"I'm only trying to help."

"I need to stretch my legs," said Simon, hearing the apology in her voice, realizing he'd been rash. "I'm going to hit the dining car."

"Wait," said Nikki, picking up her handbag. "I'll come with you."

CHAPTER 46

From her vantage point in the rest area outside Riske's car—the two-meter-long no-man's-land between carriages—Valentina watched the American rise from his seat and head her way, followed by the woman she'd guessed to be his companion. Valentina retreated a step, seeking refuge in the bathroom. She tried the handle and found it locked. A brusque male voice registered his protest. In her fatigued state, she nearly shouted for him to hurry up and get out.

The American was ten steps away, four rows from the door. Turning, she rushed to the adjoining car and traversed its length. The next bathroom was vacant. She entered and locked the door, counting to sixty to allow Riske to pass. In that time, she removed the pen from her pocket, loosened the cap, and cocked its pocket clasp to ninety degrees, charging the nib with poison.

After a minute, she opened the door cautiously. Her eyes reconnoitered the rest area. The American was gone.

She walked to the next car in time to observe the

woman nearing the far exit. The American opened the door and let her pass in front of him. When they were both out of view, Valentina entered the carriage, moving slower now, aware that the dining car was immediately ahead.

A steward came through the door, pushing a beverage cart. His colleague held the door for him, offering Valentina a clear view of Riske, back to her, and the woman standing in line in the dining car.

"Excuse me, *madame*."

Valentina stepped aside as the steward passed. She advanced to the end of the carriage, peeking through the glass, her view blocked by a knot of passengers leaving the dining car. The element of surprise was vital. She couldn't allow Riske to see her approach, not even for a second. It was imperative no one witness her stabbing him with the pen.

The onslaught of the poison's effects was rapid and dramatic. Within seconds, the victim realized that something was horribly wrong. The heartbeat accelerated. Muscles tightened. Eyesight blurred. A terrific pounding pressed on the temple. Body temperature rose three to five degrees. The skin flushed. Perspiration increased. Taken together, the reactions made the victim feel as if his head were about to explode.

As the poison attacked the central nervous system, the victim became paralyzed. His muscles began to spasm. He could no longer speak. Pain became unbearable. He frothed at the mouth. Often, he vomited copiously.

In the final stages, the nervous system stopped functioning altogether. The person collapsed. His lungs no longer worked. In the last seconds before death, he suffered the sensation of asphyxiating, his mouth open but unable to draw a breath.

There was nothing subtle about it.

Valentina slipped the pen from her pocket, concealing it in her palm as she advanced. She caught a glimpse of Riske's dark blazer, his neatly trimmed hair, the sharp profile of his nose and jaw. The woman was still at his side, the two deep in conversation. The dining car was more crowded than when she'd passed through earlier. A number of passengers waited near the service counter, and she guessed that the dining steward was behind in filling orders.

Valentina stepped away from the window. Reluctantly, she decided that it might be necessary to reconsider her course of action. It would do no one any good were she to kill Riske and herself be captured. Her primary goal was Coluzzi, not Riske. She looked at her watch. Two hours remained until they reached Marseille. She needed to act wisely and bide her time. The odds were in her favor that she'd have another chance at Riske.

Resigned that she must wait, she glanced back into the dining car as a group of five left a table and made their way to the opposite exit. Riske's companion moved rapidly to the vacant spot, placing her handbag on the table. A moment later, another group of three or four left by the same exit. In seconds, the dining car had gone from packed to empty.

Valentina gripped the pen in her fingers, eagerly reappraising the situation.

Two women stood behind Riske, but the passage beside him was free of traffic, providing an open conduit. The American's back was to her, his face raised to the menu posted behind the counter. His companion was at the far end of the car speaking on the phone, gazing out the window.

There would never be a better moment.

Valentina dropped her hand to her side, the pen extended, nib up. Confident that she had made the right decision—*the only decision*—she pushed open the door and entered the dining car.

CHAPTER 47

Simon leaned closer to Nikki as they stood in line. "What do you want? Coffee? A croissant?"

"Coffee. Black."

"Nothing to eat? We didn't hang around to get our room service." He studied the menu posted on the wall. "I'm thinking a ham and cheese baguette and a Coke."

"You're a real gourmet."

"I haven't eaten much since leaving the emergency room. I don't care what I have as long as it's filling."

"Thank you, but I'll wait for a bouillabaisse in the Vieux-Port. Cheese toast. A glass of wine."

"What happened to Paris's toughest cop?"

"I'm tough, not a cretin. I've waited this long. It might as well be something good."

"You may be waiting a lot longer. We're hitting the ground running. You haven't forgotten that we're not the only ones looking for Coluzzi."

"I haven't forgotten," said Nikki. "Any ideas where he's at?"

"A few. We need to poke around here and there, ask some questions."

"That didn't turn out so good the last time."

"I'll be more careful. Besides, I have you to look after me."

"So I'm your bodyguard now, is that it?"

"You're one for one so far. That's a pretty good track record in my book."

"I'm here for my own reasons. Remember that."

"I noticed you're not wearing your gun."

"I'm off duty. Don't worry. It's in my bag."

"Good to know."

"A table's opening up. I'm going to grab us a place."

"Sure you don't want anything?"

"Fine," said Nikki, giving up. "Get me whatever you're having. I'll put my lunch plans on hold."

She left the line and took a seat at the vacant table. She looked at Riske. He was dressed once again in business mode. Blazer, white shirt, tan trousers. The vulnerability she'd glimpsed the night before, sitting outside the urgent care clinic, was gone, all intimations of mortality along with it. He'd pushed his brush with death out of his mind. Not once had he mentioned Falconi either. It wasn't an act. He'd seen a lot in his life, certainly more than she. The difference, of course, was that he'd lived it firsthand, while more often than not she was a witness after the fact.

Her phone rang. She checked the screen and answered at once. "Hello, Commissaire?"

"Hello, Nikki. How are things going? Did Riske find his man?"

"Not yet, but I think he's on the right track."

"Good. I hope he didn't put you out too much."

"He can be demanding, but nothing out of the ordinary."

"All the same, I owe you one. How are things over there? I heard it was a nasty one."

"Pardon me?"

"Delacroix. I heard it was messy."

"*Delacroix*...from the hotel?"

"Who else?" There was a pause, and Nikki realized she'd blundered. "Aren't you at the crime scene?" continued Dumont. "I know the lieutenant had you on administrative detention, but given the circumstances, I thought he might need you. Word was you had Delacroix pegged as an accomplice."

"Actually, I'm feeling sick. I took the day."

"Delacroix's dead. He was found in his apartment an hour ago, killed execution style."

"I see," said Nikki. It was the Russian. Evidently, the PJ wasn't the only one to mark Delacroix as a suspect. She signaled Riske to come join her. "When?"

"Last night sometime. When he didn't show up for work, his colleagues sent someone to his place."

"Any leads?"

"None, but you might want to call the lieutenant."

Nikki waved again, but Riske was looking at the dining attendant. "Thank you, Commissaire."

"Nikki?"

"Yes?"

"Riske is staying at the hotel where Delacroix worked, isn't he?"

Nikki began to answer when she saw a blond woman enter the car and advance along the corridor. Something about her manner captured her attention. There was a tautness to her body, a purpose that seemed out of place. She studied the face. It was her.

"Behind you!" Nikki shouted.

***

Simon heard Nikki's voice, met her eyes, saw the fear in them, the desperation. He spun to his left, his gaze fixed on the woman approaching, passing the queue of customers. He knew her at once, not only because he recognized her from Le Galleon Rouge. He could feel the tension emanating from her, her commitment, her blind will, and though she had yet to look at him, he was certain that he was her target.

All this he processed in less than a second.

In that time, she began her attack. He saw the right arm rise from her leg, a slim, black instrument clutched in her hand. He caught the sparkle of gold as she lunged at him. It was a fountain pen, yet she held it as if it were a weapon.

He stepped back, hugging the wall, and with his left hand arrested her forward motion, fingers curling around her wrist, crushing it. The woman grunted and leaned into him, the hand defying his grip, rising toward his chest, her eyes fixed on him.

Next to him, a man cried out in alarm, shrinking from the attack.

Simon turned his shoulder into her and, with his weight behind him, thrust her hand against the wall. She responded with a knee to the groin, missing its mark by an inch. He buckled at the waist and lost his grip on her hand. He felt no real pain, no fear. He was aware only of the fierce pumping of his heart and the adrenaline raging through his veins. In the same motion, he drove a fist into her solar plexus, feeling cartilage give but little more. The woman recoiled, eyes watering, but otherwise was unbowed.

Simon pushed himself off the wall and stood taller. The two faced each other at a distance of prizefighters. The passengers had scattered any way they could. He heard Nikki's voice behind him, telling him to run, but he had never run from a fight in his life. He was the fool who ran toward it. Somewhere buried in his psyche he knew he was merely answering the voice that had been calling to him with increasing frequency, telling him that this was his real self. That he couldn't hide any longer and that everything he'd become was a lie.

That he belonged on the wrong side of right.

In that instant all caution left him.

The woman lunged at him, her motion a blur. He darted to the side, angling his body, catching the outstretched arm and turning the wrist inward, his free hand locking her elbow. The woman struck him in the face repeatedly, knuckles curled, battering his cheek. He maintained his grip, holding her other hand high, then raised his leg and drove his heel into her kneecap, holding nothing back, collapsing the knee on itself, shearing the ligaments, dislocating the joint.

She screamed and fell to the floor, helpless.

Simon stood above her. "What's in the letter?" he asked.

The woman pushed herself away, eyes blinking, breath firing in ragged bursts. The door behind her opened. A security officer burst into the carriage, weapon drawn. She looked over her shoulder at him, then back at Simon.

"Tell me," he said.

The woman's eyes went to her hand, to the fountain pen clutched there.

"Don't!"

The woman plunged the pen into her neck, then dropped it onto the floor.

Nikki approached, bending down to see if she could help.

"It's too late," said Simon, pulling her away.

The Russian woman's back arched. Her eyes widened, and widened more. Her mouth opened in a paroxysm of terror. Spittle flowed freely down her chin. A horrible cry came from deep inside her.

And then all life fled.

Her body went limp and she collapsed, dead.

CHAPTER 48

Tino Coluzzi tossed two more langoustines onto his plate and sat back in his chair. He wasn't in the least hungry, yet he forced himself to eat, checking his watch every five minutes. Alexei Ren sat at the head of the table, holding court. The others present were his executives and their families. From what Coluzzi could gather, business was good. He turned his eyes toward the sea. A few more yachts had anchored since his arrival. None were as grand as the *Solange,* but they were impressive nevertheless, none shorter than a hundred feet, with sleek bows and shaded afterdecks. A few Jet Skis zipped in and out between them. The good life. It was so close he could taste it.

He caught Ren signaling to him from the head of the table, a nod toward the far end of the restaurant. Coluzzi rose and followed the Russian to a patio overlooking the windward side of the island and the open ocean.

"Go ahead," said Ren, giving him his phone. "He's expecting you."

"Now?"

Ren checked his watch. "It's nearly one in Moscow. If that's where he is."

"Did you already speak to—"

"This is your deal. I'm not involved. My friend alerted Borodin that you wished to speak with him about a serious matter. Apparently, he was expecting you."

Coluzzi looked at the numbers, then dialed without hesitation. All night he'd rehearsed what he would say to Borodin. Now his mouth was dry and he could no longer remember what he'd decided on.

The phone rang.

Ren stood facing him, cigar firmly in the corner of his mouth, arms crossed over his chest. His smile was gone. His eyes stared at him as if he were his worst enemy.

"Good luck," he said.

"*Allô.*"

"Borodin?"

"Director Borodin, if you don't mind. Am I speaking with Mr. Tino Coluzzi?"

The voice was calm, measured, not unfriendly, pitched higher than he'd expected, the man's French nearly perfect.

"My name isn't important."

"There are no strangers in this business. We've been looking for you since yesterday. Now you turn up with Alexei Ren. You are an opportunistic man."

"I do what's necessary."

"So it seems."

"I have your letter. I guess I don't need to tell you that."

"No, you don't. Mr. Delacroix was helpful in that regard, as was your friend Mr. Falconi. Or did you think we'd sit back and wait for you to come to us?"

Coluzzi swallowed, biting back his anger. He didn't care about Delacroix, other than to be angry he'd paid him up front, but Luca Falconi had been like an uncle. "I didn't think that."

Borodin paused long enough for Coluzzi to digest the information. "What do you wish to do with your prize?"

"I have a few ideas."

"May I ask you a question first?"

"Go ahead."

"How did you come to find it? The news says the robbery was only about the money."

"That's my business."

"So it wasn't a coincidence?"

"Let's say that there are others who want the letter as badly as you."

"Have you spoken with them?" Borodin's voice was suddenly too relaxed, almost nonchalant. Coluzzi realized that he was the more nervous of them.

"I thought you'd want it, seeing as how the prince was flying to Cyprus to personally deliver it to you."

"My, my. You never cease to impress me."

"The prince writes too much down. You might want to mention it to him next time you get together."

"Mr. Coluzzi, I'm a busy man. You are correct that we would like to take possession of the letter. Sooner rather than later. I'm prepared to offer you fifty thousand euros."

"I was thinking of a different number."

"Of course you were."

"How does twenty million sound?"

Borodin's laugh sounded like a seal's bark. "Did Ren give you that number?"

"All mine."

"Impossible. We have a budget like any other organization. It's not my decision alone."

"I don't think your budget applies in this matter."

"Why not?"

"This is your play. I know what's in the letter. I know why you want it. The number is twenty million."

"Never."

"Then I apologize for wasting your time. I'm a busy man, too. Now, if you'll excuse me, I have another call to make."

"Wait!"

"I'm listening."

"Two million euros. Cash. You'll have it in twelve hours."

"Twenty million. Also in cash. And have it here by six."

"Five million is the best I can do."

"The sun is coming up in Washington, DC. I know just the person to call. He's probably mad at me for not having given him the letter in the first place, but I suppose he'll soften up. I've kept the Americans waiting long enough."

"Ten million and that's final."

"What did you do to Luca Falconi?"

"Ten million, Mr. Coluzzi. Or you'll find out yourself what we did to your friend."

Coluzzi's eyes met Ren's. The Russian nodded.

"Deal," said Coluzzi.

"Call this number back in an hour and I'll give you the details."

Borodin hung up before Coluzzi could protest.

Ren slipped the phone into his pocket. He held a fresh cigar in his free hand. "Come on," he said. "Let's celebrate."

CHAPTER 49

Boris Blatt required four hours to determine where his watch had been stolen. He was not sure if he would ever discover how, or by whom.

He'd set to work upon his return from Zurich earlier that morning. His plane had landed punctually at nine at City Airport, his car waiting on the tarmac to take him home. The twelve-mile drive to Highgate in the north of London took nearly as long as the five-hundred-mile flight from Switzerland. It wasn't until ten that he pulled through the iron gates into Parkfield's grand forecourt. It was the first time Blatt had purchased a property with a name. Frankly, he thought "Parkfield" rather bland and lacking in grandiosity, especially for a ninety-thousand-square-foot Georgian revival set on five acres of grassland that counted as the second-largest private residence in the city. He preferred the name given to the largest private residence. Buckingham Palace.

Once inside, he took the elevator to the third floor and proceeded to his private office, locking the door behind him. A priori, it was a simple enough matter.

The watch had been either taken from his closet, where he kept it in a climate-controlled cherrywood case equipped with a "watch winder" that turned the time-piece this way and that every hour to keep the mechanism charged, or, more improbably, stolen while he was wearing it. Blatt had heard of thieves capable of lifting a watch from a man's wrist without him noticing. But he'd never heard of a thief so talented he could replace it with another watch—in this case, an exact replica—without him noticing.

A mathematician by training, Blatt focused his efforts on the first, infinitely more probable possibility. The watch had been stolen and a replica put in its place at his home.

Blatt's first order of business was to call his wife and ask if she'd looked at the watch. Her response was a somewhat distracted "No." He believed her. She had her own collection of watches, and they were worth far more than his. Moreover, she hadn't set foot in his bedroom either here in London or in any of their other homes—in Bermuda, Manhattan, Bel-Air, Saint-Tropez, or Moscow—in years. He ruled out his wife.

Next, Blatt summoned his chief houseman, Roderick, who was the only person—besides Blatt himself—allowed free entry into Blatt's bedroom. On the surface, Roderick was beyond reproach. He was well paid. He had no debts. He didn't drink, gamble, or keep a mistress on the side. All this Blatt had made it his business to know. It was this record of untarnished integrity that had landed him the job.

Even so, Blatt made sure his bodyguards were present, and at their most intimidating, when he inquired about the watch, and if they hit the old Englishman a few times, Blatt didn't notice. No matter how often he was asked, Roderick's answer remained an earnest, stammering "No." The same was true when asked if he'd let someone else into the bedroom.

Blatt thanked him and let him know he believed him entirely. By the look of the sweat running off the older man's forehead and the sad, defeated manner in which he limped out of the room, the acquittal was none too soon.

Of course, there was a more reliable way to determine if anyone had ventured inside Blatt's bedroom.

Leaving his office, Blatt retraced his steps down the corridor and took the elevator to the second underground floor. Using a special key, he unlocked a steel door and entered Parkfield's operational headquarters. It was from this warren of offices that all work done on the house was scheduled and supervised. Painting, carpentry, plumbing—all of it. Also housed on the second underground floor was Parkfield's security.

A door stood open at the end of the hall. Approaching, Blatt caught sight of the multiplex of eighty monitors showing live feeds from all cameras placed around the property. A dark, gnomish man sat at the console. Seeing Blatt, he shot to his feet.

"Good morning, sir."

"Anton, have you finished checking my request?"

"Just now, sir."

Blatt perched on the corner of the desk. He'd called Anton the night before, requesting he check the feed from his bedroom to see if anyone, besides himself and Roderick, had trespassed.

"Well?"

"No one, sir."

"You're certain?"

"The computer uses an algorithm to detect activity and stops the recording at those spots. While you were away, it was only Roderick who entered. There's been no one else."

Blatt slapped his hand against his thigh. He was livid. He wanted to shout "Impossible!" but he knew he could not impeach the camera's record. Without another word, he stormed out of the room and returned upstairs, making a beeline for his desk. Sitting, he pulled out his agenda and pored over the pages. A man of no small importance, Blatt led an active social life and dined out nearly every night. Reviewing his activities, he pinned down the two occasions when he'd worn the Patek Philippe. The first was to a dinner at the Russian embassy, the second to the Sotheby's auction in Battersea Park.

He could rule out the dinner with the Russian ambassador. It had been an official gathering, and by official, he meant secret. He alone had attended and had met with the ambassador and the resident chief of the SVR for just under an hour. No one else had been present. He didn't figure either of the men as world-class thieves.

It had to be Sotheby's, then.

He called up Alastair Quince at once. "Boris Blatt speaking. I have a problem."

"If it's about the car," said Quince, in his infuriatingly polite voice, "I'm pleased to tell you we'll have it delivered to your home tomorrow. And if I may say, it is looking more beautiful than—"

"No, it's fucking well not about the car," Blatt shouted, forgetting himself. He paused, feeling distinctly ill at ease at the prospect of telling Quince anything about the watch. "It appears I may have misplaced something the other night at the auction."

"What is it? I can put you in touch with Lost and Found immediately. I'm sure they can be of help."

"That won't be necessary. It's something valuable. If they'd found it already, you would know. I need to see your security cameras from the event."

"I'm sorry, but that's out of the question. Only the police are allowed to view footage from the security cameras, and even then they must have a warrant. The law, I'm afraid."

"This is a delicate matter that I chose not to report to the police."

"Again, I'm sorry, Mr. Blatt. Unless you file a report, there's nothing I can do."

"Twenty thousand."

"Excuse me?" said Quince, beyond offended.

"I'll give you twenty thousand pounds. Cash."

"Are you trying to bribe me?"

"Twenty thousand to see the tapes or you will regret the day you were ever born. Call it what you will."

"Twenty-five thousand and I'll have the tape ready for you in an hour."

Blatt hung up, enraged. He didn't know whether to have Quince killed or to hire him.

CHAPTER 50

I thought you said she was on a plane at Orly," said Nikki.

"Apparently, she didn't like to fly."

Simon stared out the window. The sun was still shining. The countryside every bit as picturesque as it had been before the attack. It was he who'd changed, or rather his place in the world. Instead of the hunter, he'd become the hunted.

"We need to get off the train," he said.

"We stop at Avignon," said Nikki.

"How long?"

"Thirty minutes from now. But the police are waiting to speak to you in Marseille. You need to give them a statement."

"It's not the police I'm worried about."

"You think there's someone else?" demanded Nikki. "Another one like her?"

"I don't see why not. We're working as a team."

"But she was the only one who came out of Falconi's apartment."

Simon leaned forward and took Nikki's hand. "Right now we need to consider every possibility. We're getting off this train as soon as possible."

Twenty minutes had passed since the attack. Escorted by the rail marshal, Simon and Nikki had returned to their seats, only to be accosted by nervous travelers inquiring what had happened. He told them the same thing he'd told the marshal. He didn't know the woman who'd attacked him. The assault had come as a complete and terrible surprise. And over and over again, no, he didn't think it was terrorism. As far as he was concerned, it was a random act of violence perpetrated by a crazed individual.

All of this the marshal accepted without question. He was not a policeman but a newly trained security officer, one of thousands who had recently been stationed aboard France's trains in response to the increase in terrorist activity within the country's borders. His lack of experience was apparent.

"And you?" the rail marshal had asked, after examining Simon's passport. "You are a cop in America? A soldier, perhaps?"

"No," Simon had replied, with a lucky survivor's shaken resolve. He was a businessman. The kick to the woman's knee was a reflex. Instinct, really. He was lucky to be alive. The rail marshal hadn't been convinced, but the answer had sufficed for the moment.

As for the very special pen, Simon had concealed it in his luggage, if only to delay the police in discovering that she was some kind of spy or assassin. He could explain away being an innocent victim. It would be harder if the police discovered the peculiar item she'd used to kill herself. Suicide by jabbing a poison-tipped pen into your neck was not an everyday occurrence.

Simon lifted a bag of ice from his cheek. "How does it look?"

Nikki gingerly probed the swollen flesh. "Red but not too bad. You have a hard head."

Simon winced. "Not hard enough."

"And your stitches?" Nikki asked. "Any tearing?"

"Seem okay."

Her fingers remained on his cheek. "You've taken quite a beating this last while."

Simon sat back, enjoying her touch more than he cared to admit. "The other guys got worse."

"Yes, they did, I suppose. And otherwise? How are you holding up?"

"Fine," said Simon. "No worries." He wanted to give her a smile, a little something to let her know he was okay, but all he could muster was a nod of the head. He looked out the window in case his unease showed. He wasn't fine at all. His mind was a mess of warring ideas far more bothersome than his bruised cheek. He wasn't sure who were his friends and who were his enemies, or if he even had any friends in this matter to begin with.

As he'd discussed with Nikki, he had to assume that Neill knew the Russian woman's location. If Simon's store-bought StingRay could track the woman's phone and link it to her masters in Yasenevo, then Neill—with his access to the world's most sophisticated surveillance system—should have been able not only to alert him to her presence on the train but also to give him the precise location of her carriage and her seat number.

The question then was, why had he chosen not to warn him?

Had Neill wanted Simon killed? Or was it something else? Something subtler. Had he, despite his statements to the contrary, wanted Vassily Borodin and his ilk to know that the Americans were giving chase?

The answer was moot. Simon must base his decisions solely upon Neill's actions, and that meant assuming Neill viewed his play in the game as complete. Simon had fulfilled his role. As desired, he'd forced the Russians to give chase. Moreover, he'd provided Neill with a list of phone numbers that likely belonged to Tino Coluzzi, allowing Neill, with help from the NSA, to find Coluzzi himself.

All of which left one question: What game was Neill playing at?

Simon was a card player. There was a saying that went round the poker table. If you couldn't spot the sucker, you were it. Well, he told himself, he was done being Mr. Neill's sucker.

"There's something else," said Nikki. "I had a call from Commissaire Dumont right before the whole thing happened."

"Oh?"

"It was about Delacroix. The police found him dead in his apartment this morning. He'd been murdered execution style."

"So he was the inside man. That explains how she got on to Falconi."

Nikki nodded. "It would be good if you told Marc what you know, if only to save him some time."

"I can't. Not yet."

"This thing is bigger than us. We could use their help."

"It's the same size that it's always been. Besides, what happens to you if we bring Dumont up to date?"

"Don't worry about me. That's twice someone's tried to kill you in the last twelve hours. Want to try your luck a third time?"

The train slowed as it approached Avignon. Fields of saffron as bright as the sun gave way to low-slung warehouses and a barren industrial zone, then the weathered yellow brick of Provence. Simon looked to the head of the carriage, checking if the security officer was anywhere near. "Give me your phone," he said.

"Why?"

Simon beckoned with his fingers.

"Absolutely not," said Nikki.

"I'm not asking."

"Simon, I need it."

"We'll get you a new one."

Nikki slid the phone from her jeans but still would not hand it over. "You think they're tracking us?"

"I wouldn't doubt it if they were listening to every word we're saying."

Simon plucked the phone from her hand and tucked it, along with his own, deep into the crease between the seats. He stood and took down her bag from the overhead bin. "Gun?"

Nikki set the bag on her seat and, using her body as a shield, discreetly removed her pistol and holster. At the same time, she took out a lightweight jacket and wrapped the pistol inside.

"Leave the rest here," said Simon. "You'll be able to retrieve it later."

"From the evidence locker?"

"I was thinking Lost and Found."

The train pulled into the station, a modern, daring work of architecture with vaulting ribs of white steel enclosing the terminal. A dozen police officers were gathered near the front of the train, anxious to board. "I thought they wanted to talk to me in Marseille," said Simon.

Nikki studied the uniformed men. "It's just a precaution," she said unconvincingly.

"So they don't want to talk to me?"

Nikki didn't answer.

"That's what I thought." Simon grabbed his bags from the overhead rack and led the way to the rear of the train, joining a group of ten passengers waiting to alight. He set his bags down in a compartment holding other large bags, ripping off his name tags and stuffing them into his pocket. It was an expensive decision but necessary. The police would have a field day if they tied him to his "bag of tricks." Innocent bystanders didn't travel with a StingRay, a parabolic microphone, and wireless cameras disguised to look like wall screws.

He was sorrier to leave behind his laptop. Though password protected and programmed to wipe the hard drive should a false password be entered twice, the laptop held plenty of sensitive information from past cases, not to mention the contents from Delacroix's phone downloaded a day earlier.

The train halted. The doors opened and he held on to Nikki's arm, allowing the other passengers to exit first. The tracks ran parallel to the terminal building. They needed to cross a wide expanse of open space to get inside. "Head down. Get inside as quickly as you can."

"And then? I'm used to chasing people, not running away from them."

"Same thing. Either way you have to run faster than the other guy."

The passengers near them stepped off the train.

It was their turn.

"Stay close." Simon descended from the train and headed across the platform. The air was hot and dry, smelling of pine and rosemary. It was the scent of the south. Le Midi. Earthy, welcoming, alive with promise.

At the other end, the police were boarding, pushing their way past alighting passengers. No one was looking in their direction. Relieved, he drew in a breath.

"Monsieur Riske!" A man's voice carried across the platform.

"Keep walking," he said to Nikki.

"Monsieur Riske. Please!"

Behind them, the rail marshal jumped from the train. A policeman was behind him, and both hurried in their direction. The policeman called to a cop behind him, and then it seemed like every policeman who had just boarded the train was getting off it.

"Monsieur Riske, please. We must speak with you."

Simon did not look in their direction. He had ten steps to the terminal. "Ready?"

"For what?" asked Nikki, looking more angry than scared.

"Run."

Simon took off toward the door, pushing it open, allowing Nikki to run past him. An escalator carried passengers to the terminal's main floor, a broad travertine plaza fifty meters long and equally wide filled with shops and kiosks. Timing was with them. At midday, the terminal was a hive of activity, hundreds of men and women crisscrossing the floor.

"The stairs," he said, heading down a staircase parallel to the escalator. Nikki followed close behind. He reached the main floor and slowed long enough to see the rail marshal appear at the top of the stairs. Simon circled behind the staircase and ran to the far side of the terminal, past a bookstore, a café, an electronics store. He came to a supermarket chock-full of shoppers and ran inside.

"Go to the back," he said, pausing to peer behind

him, catching a slew of uniforms spreading across the terminal, looking this way and that. He watched long enough to know the police had not seen them, then hurried to the back of the store. Nikki waited by the door to a storeroom.

"Let's get out of here." He opened the door and went inside. He looked to his right, then left, then zigzagged his way through crates of produce, soft drinks, and paper products, finally spotting the delivery entrance.

They were outside seconds later, standing in a loading zone at the rear of the station.

"Over there," she said, pointing to a group of warehouses across from a grass field. "You good?"

"I better be." Simon took a last look behind him. The door to the storeroom remained closed. He led the way across the parking lot, over a dirt berm, and through the field. A minute later, they had reached the warehouses and were effectively out of sight.

"Now what?" asked Nikki, bent over, hands on her thighs.

Simon peered around the corner as the door to the loading zone burst open, a half-dozen policemen pouring outside. A few looked in their direction. One of the men raised a hand and pointed at Simon. It was the rail marshal.

"Hold on."

The rail marshal jumped off the platform and began jogging across the field toward them.

"We've got company." Simon ducked back behind the wall and checked his surroundings. All the warehouse's doors were lowered. There were no vehicles nearby. No visible place to conceal themselves. A few steps away stood a stack of wooden pallets a head taller than him. He grabbed Nikki's hand and led her to the pallets.

"Get behind there."

Nikki tried to slip into the gap between the warehouse and the pallets. "Too tight."

Simon squatted and slid his hands beneath the bottommost pallet. With a grunt, he lifted the stack and moved it a few inches to one side. He repeated the motion on the opposite side, creating a narrow space between wall and pallet. Nikki squeezed into the opening and Simon pushed the pallets as close to the wall as he could. "Stay here."

"What about you?"

"I'll figure something out." He ran to the far corner of the warehouse. It was twenty meters across the road to the next building. Even if he made it before the marshal arrived, he had no place to hide. He searched for a door, a window to break, anything. Close by, the marshal's radio crackled.

Simon saw a drainpipe and began climbing, praying it remained anchored to the wall.

The marshal reached the warehouse before Simon had made it to the roof. The marshal pulled up directly beneath him, hands on his hips, gathering his breath. Simon froze. Twenty-five feet below him, the marshal turned in a slow circle, reconnoitering the area. For a moment, he looked directly at the pallets, directly at Nikki, then looked away.

Still, he didn't move on, but kept in his place as if nailed to the spot, his head scanning the area, nose raised like a cat scenting his prey.

Simon's fingers grew tired. Between the day's heat, his nerves, and the run from the terminal, his hands were moist with perspiration. He dropped one hand to his trousers and dried his palm, then did the same with the other.

Below, the marshal's radio crackled again. A man said, "Jacques? Anything?"

"Still checking."

Simon had wedged the toe of his shoe between the pipe and wall, the tip of his sole resting on a bracket securing the drainpipe. Now he felt the shoe slipping. He increased his pressure, wedging the shoe more tightly. Suddenly, his foot came free of his loafer. He slipped. His hands clutched the pipe with all his might. Miraculously, the shoe remained in place. He dug his other foot into the space, his ankle turned, his calf screaming. Hugging himself to the pipe, he guided his unshod foot back to the loafer. His toes touched leather. Slowly, he worked his foot into the shoe until he could put pressure on it and stand easier.

By now, it was not only his hands that were sweaty. His entire face was beaded with perspiration. He felt the drops rolling off his forehead, down his cheeks. As he stared at the top of the marshal's head, he counted the drops falling from his chin and watched powerless as they fell to the ground.

"Well?" asked the voice on the radio.

A hand touched his hair. The marshal gazed upward, but not at Simon.

"Nothing," he said finally. "They didn't come this way."

Simon let go a breath.

The marshal returned the radio to his belt. Instead of returning to the station, he took a pack of cigarettes from his jacket and lit up, leaning against the pallets, his shoulders inches from Nikki.

Simon held his position, hands burning with fatigue, growing stiff, unresponsive. He caught Nikki staring at him and he knew she was urging him to hold on. His hands began to slip. He dried them again but to less effect. His shirt was wet on his back, his legs quivering.

The marshal smoked contentedly and then, without warning, threw the butt to the ground with only half the cigarette finished and walked back to the terminal.

Simon slid down the pipe, his legs giving out when he hit the ground, his rear landing firmly on the concrete. After a moment, he stood and freed Nikki, who appeared as wrung out as he felt.

"Well," she said. "I guess it's official."

"What's that?" He was out of breath, too exhausted to pay much attention.

"I'm a fugitive, too."

The idea made him laugh. "How does it feel?"

"Not good."

"You'll get used to it."

"And so?"

Simon straightened his back, some semblance of his normal self returning. "Wheels."

"You mean a car?"

"Yes, a car."

"There must be a rental car office near the station."

"We're not going anywhere near the station."

"Sorry," she said. "I'm just getting used to this. I'm sure we can find one downtown. It's not far."

"You're still not getting it, are you?" said Simon. "You need a driver's license and a credit card to rent a car."

"What do you suggest? A taxi? It's a hundred kilometers to Marseille. It will cost a fortune."

"I wasn't thinking of that either."

Nikki stood taller, reading the look in his eye. "You want to steal a car?"

"Borrow it."

"That's where I draw the line."

"You crossed the line in Paris when you didn't report Falconi's murder. You crossed it a second time when we ran away from the police. My guess is one of those officers got a look at you. Dumont knows you're with me. It won't be long before you're made. You said it yourself. You're a fugitive. Welcome to the dark side, Detective Perez."

Nikki ran a hand through her hair, looking away, screwing up her face in anger or bewilderment. "I am a police officer. I can't do this."

"You're doing this because you are a police officer. Helping me is the best way we can take down Coluzzi."

"I sincerely doubt that."

"What do you mean?"

"Don't you get it, Riske? I'm helping you because I like you." She stepped forward and kissed him on the lips, placing a hand on his buttocks. "Just don't go thinking so much of yourself."

"Too late for that."

Simon grabbed her by the waist and looked into her eyes, seeing the flecks of gold he'd noticed when they'd first met in Marc Dumont's office. He kissed her softly, enjoying the feel of her lips on his, the warmth of her open mouth. She pushed harder into him and he kept his body rigid, responding to her pressure.

"That was nice," he said.

Nikki needed a moment to open her eyes fully and come back to herself. "Yes," she said. "It was."

They left the warehouse and headed into town. Ten minutes' walk took them to a leafy residential area with cars parked cheek by jowl on both sides of the street. Simon spotted a black Porsche 911. He slowed, seeing that the door was locked—naturally.

"Don't even think of it," said Nikki. "This is what we want."

She was standing next to an old white Peugeot—four doors, two-liter engine, decent tires, and gravely in need of a wash. In other words, as close to an anonymous vehicle as they were likely to find.

Simon looked around. A few kids were walking down the block a ways in front of them; otherwise, no one else was in sight.

"Gun," he said.

She slipped her pistol from its holster. He took the muzzle in his hand and touched the butt to the sweet spot on the driver's side window.

"Wait!" said Nikki.

Simon lowered the pistol to his side. Nikki opened the passenger door. "Unlocked."

She slid in, leaned over, and unlocked Simon's door. He climbed in and found the seat adjusted perfectly for his height. He reached below the wheel and yanked out the ignition cables. It had been years since he'd hot-wired a car, but it was like riding a bicycle or kissing a girl. He found the correct wires, peeled off the plastic coatings with his thumbnail, and crossed them.

The engine rattled to life. He touched the gas, and the car shook as if racked by a tubercular fit. "There's still time to get the Porsche."

"Drive," said Nikki.

Five minutes later, they joined the highway. Their train would arrive in Marseille in twenty minutes' time.

He wondered who would be waiting to greet them.

CHAPTER 51

It was the moment of truth.

In every operation, there comes a time when one must decide whether to pull the trigger, in metaphorical, and often real, terms. It is the moment after which there is no retreat and the only direction is forward.

Ending the call with the rascal Coluzzi, Vassily Borodin surveyed the bound dossiers arrayed across his desk. Each represented a documented instance of high treason.

The first sheaf bore the title "Kremlin Decree No. 1, 12/31/99." He opened the cover to read the text as set forth the day the traitor took office. "No corruption charges shall be allowed against outgoing presidents," it began, before listing in detail all such acts that might qualify as "corruption."

The decree was also known as the "grand bargain," the brilliant piece of political chicanery that secured the president his job by granting his predecessor immunity, and then protected himself against all financial misdeeds he might undertake during his own tenure.

For perhaps the thousandth time, Borodin marveled

at the man's audacity. Was there ever a more telling way to begin a regime?

The second dossier, dated 2002, was titled "Nord-Ost."

The third, dated 2007, discussed the Ivanchuk affair.

The fourth, the invasion of Crimea.

There was nothing damning about the events taken alone. In fact, it was possible to argue that the president's decisions in each case were made for the benefit of the country. It was impossible, however, to ignore payments to a series of shell corporations—set up in the name of the president's closest friends and housed in places like Liechtenstein, Panama, and the Cayman Islands—that corresponded precisely to the dates of these events.

The largest of the payments dated to October 2014, one week after the invasion of Crimea, totaled two billion dollars. The recipient was one Platinum Holdings of Curaçao, a shell company set up in favor of one Oleg Kharkov, aged eighty-seven, retired judo instructor and, by odd coincidence, the man who had taught the president during his youth.

Good luck explaining that, mused Borodin, to a group of generals living on a pension of twenty thousand dollars a year.

"But why would anyone pay me to invade Crimea?" the president would surely demand. *"Or Ukraine?"*

To which Borodin would pass out the documents his men had obtained detailing secret NATO meetings in which top U.S. generals had argued for a substantial increase in military spending to counter the "rising threat in the East."

"Because," Borodin planned to explain, *"without a threat, the West has no excuse to re-arm itself."*

Some traitors came cheap. Some even betrayed their country for free, so eager were they to do their homeland harm. Not this one. For him, every action was for sale. Every decision carried a price tag. The man viewed the country as his own candy store, which he could sell off piecemeal. Timber for two billion. Aluminum for six. Oil for ten. The highest price was for the store itself, the Rodina, Mother Russia.

Borodin slammed a fist onto his desk. *His Russia.*

The sum total of these payments came to sixty-one billion dollars. Not bad for a lieutenant colonel passed over three times for promotion and stationed in Dresden of the former German Democratic Republic, a backwater so unimportant its offices had been equipped with computers nearly twenty years old. No wonder the man hated his country.

One day soon he, Vassily Borodin, would present all this information to a group of senior government ministers and high-ranking members of the military. It was imperative his case was airtight. For that, he needed the letter. It was the detonator that would ignite the explosives he'd labored years to gather. With a sweep of his arm, he gathered the folders and replaced them in his private safe.

The moment of truth had arrived.

First a call. "Kurtz. Bring the car around in five minutes."

"Where are we—"

"Just bring it."

Springing from his chair, he dashed past his secretary with a speed she'd never before witnessed. He eschewed the elevator and ran down the stairs to the ground floor, reining himself in to a brisk but officious walk as he exited the building. Decorum.

It was a crisp, sunny day, a tinge of burning wood in the air, distinctly fall-like, though the autumnal equinox was three weeks hence. He crossed Andropov Plaza and made his way toward a modern single-story building constructed a year earlier. The building housed the SVR's administration and banking section.

He slowed to a suitable pace as he nodded to the two armed security guards situated on either side of the door. He continued past a reception area and down a long corridor. He stopped at a steel door, again guarded by two armed sentries.

"Open," he said.

A guard pressed a buzzer. A voice asked who was there. He answered, "Director Borodin." A loud, pleasing click as the lock disengaged. Borodin opened the door and entered the SVR's private bank.

"Good morning, sir," said the bank manager, a portly, pink-cheeked man with ginger hair, rushing to greet him. "This is a surprise."

Borodin had never set foot in the building. It was not the director's job to gather cash for an operation. In this instance, however, he could trust no one but himself. He dismissed the manager with a sideways glance and walked directly to the teller's window. On a withdrawal slip, he filled in the boxes with a ten and six zeroes. There was a space at the bottom for two signatures, one for the case officer and one for the director. He scrawled his signature on both lines and handed it to the teller.

"Ten million euros?"

"That's correct."

"Needed?"

"Immediately."

"Any particular denominations?"

"An even split of hundreds, two hundreds, and five hundreds. Vacuum sealed and placed in the smallest bag possible. I believe it should fit into a standard-sized suitcase."

"Yes, sir."

"And, Mr. Voroshin," said Borodin. "Not a word."

Voroshin flushed a violent shade of crimson and shook his head.

"You have fifteen minutes."

Voroshin spun on his heel and double-timed it down the hall, punching a code into a security system before disappearing into the vault room where the SVR kept a permanently stocked selection of the world's major currencies totaling over one hundred million dollars. The money was Borodin's and Borodin's alone to allocate, though it was by no means a private slush fund. He must account for every euro, yen, or pound at quarterly reviews led by the president's much too diligent anticorruption squad.

Borodin paced the room, hands clasped behind his back.

The moment of truth, indeed.

So far all actions taken over the past years to further his private investigation could be ascribed to his official responsibilities. The meticulous, time-consuming assembly of dossiers listing suspicious activities, the interviews with retired agents, the prolonged interest in the pirated legal emails. All were natural activities to be performed by the director of the Foreign Intelligence Service.

This was different.

To take government money of your own volition with the intent to bring down the president constituted an act of high treason, nothing less, and if discovered would be punishable by death, the sentence carried out immediately, a bullet to the back of the head delivered most probably by the president himself.

A sobering thought. Yet such was Borodin's confidence that he did not for a moment waver in the certainty of his actions.

He checked his watch, preparing to upbraid Voroshin for his lassitude, when the bank teller appeared, lugging a suitcase at his side.

"Ten million euros," said Voroshin.

Borodin took the suitcase from his hand and left without thanking him.

Kurtz, his deputy, had pulled the car to the rear entrance as commanded. He stood by the open trunk. "Sir," he said, "there is something you should see."

"What is it this time? We need to get the money to the airport and transported to France. I don't have time for anything else."

"Major Asanova."

"What about her?"

Kurtz handed Borodin his smartphone. A report from a French news channel was queued up. Borodin shot Kurtz a damning glance, then pressed PLAY. With horror, he listened to a reporter from France 2 describe the mysterious death of a female Russian passenger aboard a TGV from Paris to Marseille following a physical altercation with another passenger. A witness appeared on screen telling of the fight that took place in the dining car between a beautiful blond woman and an unidentified man, acting out how the woman had plunged a pen into her neck and then died gruesomely. The reporter ended by adding that the unidentified passenger with whom the Russian woman had quarreled had disappeared and could not be found.

Borodin returned the phone to his assistant. The unidentified man was an American, of course. Most probably, the one named Riske with an *e*. Oh, how they must want the letter back to engage in such theatrics aboard a train.

Instead of anger, he felt a sudden lightness of being, the fleeting beatific joy that came from knowing that one was right. The letter was genuine. Absolutely, incontrovertibly genuine.

"Well?" asked Kurtz.

"Take me to the airport."

"But, sir—"

"I'm going to get that damned thing myself."

"Out of the question. It was already too much of a risk going to Cyprus."

"Nonsense."

Kurtz stepped closer. "People are asking questions."

Borodin turned on Kurtz. "And I am going to bring them back answers."

"Not alone. Major Asanova was a formidable asset. Whoever did this—"

"I'll need a team of five. We have twenty men from Directorate S within three hours of Marseille. Find me the best. And make sure one of them is a decent shot. If Mr. Coluzzi thinks he can toy with me, he is sorely mistaken."

CHAPTER 52

It was a drive through the most beautiful landscape on Earth. They made their way south along two-lane roads that rose and fell with the hills and valleys, past vineyards and wheat fields and grand country estates, through towns and hamlets, the air rich with the warm, fertile scent of the earth, the colors a palette of russet tones.

Driving was one of the few activities that relaxed Simon. Often, the faster he drove, the calmer he grew. Today, he made sure to check those instincts. He kept to the speed limit and obeyed every light and stop sign. They were off the radar. He wanted to keep it that way.

Nikki asked him again about his past. This time he told her, joking he had better take the opportunity while he still had it. He told her the real story as he knew it, not the sanitized version he'd grown used to recounting even to those he was close to. It was the truth with the emotions exposed; he was surprised at how raw some still were all these years later.

He told her about the fear and abandonment he'd felt after his father's suicide, the bottomless well of anger at his not having left a note, the lingering notion that Simon was in some way responsible no matter how much he knew it wasn't the case. The move to Marseille, the beatings he'd endured at his stepfather's hand, until one day he'd decided enough was enough and he hit back. The decision to quit school. His first days on the street—*un petit voyou*—a little thug working the block. His distaste for the drug users he shepherded in and out of the dealers' lairs, until he started using drugs himself. His move up the food chain to stealing cars, the unbeatable rush of leading a dozen police cars on a two-hour chase through Marseille and the surrounding countryside. No one knew the area as well as he—every street, every alley, every shortcut. No one.

All the while, Nikki nodded and said she understood or asked him a question about how he'd felt or why he hadn't done something differently. Simon heard no judgment in her voice, just curiosity and empathy. And so he went on.

And then, the bigger move up to knocking off armored cars. The first time as part of a crew, surrounding the vehicle on all sides, one team charged with getting the cash, the other with fending off the police. The wild firefights in broad daylight, bullets whizzing everywhere, none by the grace of God hitting him. To this day, he admitted, he loved blowing off a clip of ammo on full auto with his AK. Yes, he owned one, but he kept it at his shooting club in London. He had lots of guns there. One day he'd show her.

He told her about the day he was arrested, what it felt like to be shot—it hadn't hurt until later; at the time, he'd been too pumped with adrenaline to feel anything. He knew who had betrayed them but told no one.

"Why?" Nikki asked.

But Simon had moved on. The answer was coming. He didn't want to get ahead of himself. He was back in Les Baums, and for the first time he told another person about killing Nasser-Al-Faris, how he felt nothing looking down on his dead body, not remorse, not guilt, not relief. Nothing. He was dead inside.

And then, his punishment in "the hole." His certainty each and every day that he was losing his sanity. The endless hours made worse by not knowing how long he must endure. A month. A year. Longer. And all of it avoidable if he gave up one man's name.

"Why didn't you?" Nikki asked in disbelief. "You knew who betrayed you. He was responsible for the death of Bonfanti's son. Not you."

"We were all responsible," Simon replied. "The second we decided to rob that truck, we'd given up any right to justice. Still, I should have known he was a rat."

"I don't understand. You could have walked out after a day."

"Looking back, the decision's easy. Then, things were different. I was different. I wanted to be the one who gave it to him. Face-to-face."

"How long were you in solitary confinement?"

"The hole? Two years, give or take."

"You were only nineteen. A boy."

"I was old enough."

Simon went on to tell Nikki how the worst experience in his life had turned into the best, all because of one man.

The monsignor.

He related the miracle Paul Deschutes, SJ, had wrought, a lifetime of education in one year, days that were too long, suddenly not long enough. The new and ineffable joy of learning. The wonderment of knowledge for knowledge's sake and the power that came with it. Eureka. Simon had found his purpose.

"What happened to him?" Nikki asked, her eyes lit with Simon's enthusiasm. "Did you stay in touch after he got out?"

"He didn't get out. He was sick. He knew he was dying. I never saw him after I was let out."

Simon slowed as he drove through the commune of Rognac. To their right, an inland lake, the Étang de Berre, spread to the horizon. They crested a hill, and he could see the Mediterranean, twenty miles in the distance.

"Then Coluzzi showed up. I can't remember what he'd done. All that time I'd dreamed how I was going to kill him. It was the thought of revenge that had kept me alive until I met the monsignor. But when I saw him, I couldn't do it. The monsignor wouldn't have allowed it. The last day we were together in the yard, one of those Sundays, he told me he had no one else in the world. His daughter had died ten years earlier. He hadn't seen her mother since long before that. He said I was the only one he had left. I remember him looking at me…looking into me with his blue eyes…he told me he had only one thing of value to give anyone. It was in a safe deposit box in a bank in London. He didn't have the key. He couldn't remember the box number, just the name and branch of the bank. He told me that it was very valuable, that it would, in effect, leave me rich for life. Before we went back inside to our cells, he made me promise that I would find a way to open the box and take possession of what belonged to me."

"Did you?"

"Yes, I did."

"How?"

"There was really only one way. I went to college. I earned my degree in economics. I applied for a job at the bank. I made sure I was assigned to the private banking department. Even then, I had to work for years before I could gain access to the files that showed which box was his and to convince someone to break the rules and open it for me."

"But you managed it? You opened the box."

"I did."

Simon narrowed his eyes, remembering the moment, standing alone in the small, cramped room deep in the ground beneath the bank. *From one cell to another,* he'd thought. For a while he sat on the hard metal chair, staring at the box, afraid to open it. Afraid of being disappointed. Afraid of discovering something that would change his life just when it was the way he liked it. Mostly, he realized he was afraid of all that the box represented. It was, after all, the end of his journey with the monsignor.

And then, remembering that his colleague was waiting for him, and that he was due back at his desk in a few minutes' time, and he must prepare for a client arriving just after lunch, he inserted the key, gave a crisp turn to the right, and opened it.

"Well?" asked Nikki. "What was inside?"

"Nothing. The box was empty."

"Empty? There was nothing in it?"

"I didn't say that."

"But he lied to you. He said it would leave you rich for life."

"It did."

For a moment Nikki didn't answer. Simon looked at

her and saw the disappointment in her eyes. Like everyone, she had expected a different ending.

"Don't you see?" he continued. "The box held my future. Its contents had given me purpose, a goal to strive for. I had an education. I had a job with unlimited prospects. A career on the *right side* of the law. That empty deposit box made me richer than I ever could have imagined."

"I think I see now."

"It was like the book by Dumas. I had found my treasure. The rest was up to me."

"So here you are."

Simon nodded. He kept his eyes straight ahead, offering a prayer to whoever or whatever was listening, thanking them for putting the monsignor in his life. The road dipped and began the long descent into Marseille. Already he could see the tips of the apartment buildings on the northern edge of the city.

After fourteen years, he was coming home.

He looked at Nikki and took her hand. "Let's go get that letter."

CHAPTER 53

Neill sat on a bench at the head of the platform reading a copy of the *Nice-Matin,* watching with dismay as the last of the train's passengers filed past without any sign of Simon Riske. He was dressed in shorts and sandals, checked short-sleeved shirt, a cap on his head, looking as Gallic as a native of Athens, Georgia, could hope.

The train had arrived ten minutes earlier and was met by a dozen police officers. The passengers had been made to wait to disembark while the police supervised the unloading of the Russian agent. From his vantage point, Neill watched as the body was removed on a stretcher, placed on a gurney, and wheeled past him.

"Where is he?"

"I checked the train. He's not here." The voice on the comm link belonged to Dobbs, a Paris-based field agent who'd shared the train with Riske.

"How is that so?"

"He must have gotten off in Avignon."

"Your brief was to keep an eye on him."

"I saw him return to his seat after the Russian killed

herself. The rail marshal was with him. It was impossible to keep eyes on him without drawing attention to myself. I just assumed—"

"So you didn't actually see him get off the train in Avignon?"

"At least thirty people disembarked. It was crowded."

"That's not my question."

"No, sir, I did not see Riske or Detective Perez with them."

"Stay in place." Neill called Riske's phone and, when it rolled to voice mail, hung up and dialed the team in the surveillance van. "Get me a location on Riske."

"One minute, sir. He's in Marseille…at the station… actually, he's about twenty meters away from you."

Neill hung up and addressed Dobbs on the comm link. "Get back on the train. See if you can find Riske's phone."

Neill continued to the café, where he ordered an espresso and a lemon tart. He dropped two cubes of sugar into the coffee and drank it before starting on the pastry. During his time in the air, the boys in the van had run a check on the phone numbers Riske had found in Luca Falconi's apartment. All five SIM cards had been purchased at a kiosk on the Rue Saint-Martin, a block away from the apartment. The first of the numbers had been activated several hours earlier, shortly after the number Riske had reported as belonging to Coluzzi had stopped functioning. At present, whoever was carrying a phone with that SIM card was on or near Entre les Îles, a pair of islands lying east of Marseille.

The men in the surveillance van had also followed Riske's calls to the Saudi telecom service. With dismay, Neill had listened to the tapes of Riske obtaining the prince's email password. The evidence led to an unpleasant and unimpeachable conclusion. The man knew too much.

"He ditched us," said Dobbs.

"Come again?"

"I found their phones stuffed between their seat cushions."

"Bring them to me."

With care, Neill carved off a piece of the lemon tart, only for it to crumble before he could place it on his fork. The French, he had come to decide, possessed a mastery of cutlery beyond his ability. He chewed on the creamy filling, pondering his next move. Riske, it had turned out, was that rarest of all birds. He was even better than advertised.

Neill finished his tart and dumped the paper plate into the trash. Walking toward the exit, he placed a call to a home in the hills above Antibes. A man answered. "Jacob." *Zha-cobe*.

"Is this Martin Jacob?"

"No, I am Gilles Jacob. I'm afraid you have the wrong number."

But the call did not go dead. There were several clicks as Neill was switched over to the secure line of the CIA substation located in the basement of Monsieur Jacob's house.

"Hello, Barnaby," said Larry Tanner, the agent who ran the place. "Didn't know you were in the neighborhood. How can we help?"

"I have a situation that's developing a bit too quickly. I need to borrow one of your men."

"Not a good time. We're stretched thin these days. What do you have in mind?"

"A shooter. I need him on-site within three hours. Should have him back to you by tomorrow."

"Let me check."

Neill left the station and walked up the hill a block to where he'd parked his car, a silver Audi sedan. Just then, Tanner came back on the line. "You're in luck. I have just the guy. Put in twenty years as a sniper with your old outfit."

"The Corps?"

"MARSOC." Marines Special Operations Command. The successor to Force Recon and the United States Marine Corps' most elite unit. "Spent a bunch of time in Afghanistan. He was a night soldier. In between he stopped off in Iraq. There's a note here says he held the record for the longest kill in his battalion. Took out a bad guy at twelve hundred yards."

Neill whistled long and low. "Quite some distance."

"Been with us since '11. He's solid. I'll task him out to your shop, but make sure you sign off on an inter-agency chit within thirty days. We're watching every penny these days."

"You got it. What's his name?"

"You're gonna love this. Jack Makepeace."

"You're right. I love it," said Neill, sharing Tanner's jocularity like any good fraternity brother.

"You'll have his records in a second," said Tanner. "Where am I sending him?"

"Marseille."

CHAPTER 54

Coluzzi's phone rang as he stepped onto the dock in the old port. The screen showed no number, only the word "Unknown." Unknown to others perhaps, he mused, placing the phone to his ear. "Yes," he said.

"I will be arriving this evening at eight p.m. at the aerodrome in Aix-en-Provence. I do not wish to stay long. Please have my property ready."

"Just bring the money. There won't be any problems."

"You'll have your money," said Vassily Borodin. "Eight p.m."

"One last thing," said Coluzzi, needling the Russian. "How will I find you?"

"If there are other Gulfstream jets there, look for the one with the Russian flag on the tail."

The line went dead. Coluzzi left the dock and walked up the hill toward the Basilique Notre-Dame de la Garde. The Aerodrome d'Aix-en-Provence was a modest airfield ten kilometers outside the city with a single runway long enough to accommodate only mid-sized jets. No commercial air service was offered. In fact, if Coluzzi recalled correctly, it wasn't licensed to welcome international flights. There was a reason he knew so much about the aerodrome. Years back, when he'd brought in planes from Morocco packed to the gills with hashish, the aerodrome had been his port of choice. Apparently, he wasn't the only one able to buy off the ground personnel.

Coluzzi arrived at the top of the hill. He was hot and sweaty and on edge at the prospect of making the transfer at the aerodrome. He didn't relish the idea of walking by himself across a wide-open runway to Borodin's plane. He'd be a sitting duck. Any of Borodin's men could take him out with an easy shot. How could he have agreed to such a thing?

He clutched his phone, weighing whether he ought to demand that Borodin meet him elsewhere. After all, he had what the Russian wanted. Why shouldn't he be the one to decide? Then an idea came to him. *Oh yes,* he thought. *That might work.* He relaxed, if only for an instant. Sometimes the best ways were the oldest.

If Borodin wanted to make the exchange at the aerodrome, so be it. Tino Coluzzi was one step ahead of him.

Buoyed by the clarity and cleverness of his thoughts, he stepped into a patch of shade beneath a grove of pines. From where he stood, he looked down on the old port. One slip was markedly vacant. He placed a call to the only other Russian he knew.

"I was beginning to wonder if something happened to you," said Alexei Ren.

"The meeting's set."

"When?"

"None of your business."

"I'm happy to offer my services in the form of any protection you might need."

"I'm fine on my own."

"You don't trust me?"

"On the contrary. I trust you to act entirely in your own best interests."

Ren laughed richly. "Perhaps you are correct. There's just the matter of my finder's fee."

"I don't suppose you'd care to wait until tomorrow."

"I don't suppose I would."

"You don't trust me?"

"As you said, I trust you to act entirely in accordance with your own interests."

"Do you think I might run before I give you your money?"

"On the contrary, Mr. Coluzzi. I think you might be dead."

Coluzzi sighed. He realized there was no way out of paying Ren. "Have your men pick it up at the main station after three. I'll leave it at the kiosk. Give them my name. They'll be expecting you."

Easy come. Easy go.

CHAPTER 55

Home.

Simon eased the Peugeot off the highway, taking the first exit into the city. The road narrowed to a single lane and led down a long, gradual hill, dumping them out at the western edge of the new port, a kilometers-long maritime freight depot with towering cranes, freight elevators, and gleaming steel warehouses. Traffic was sparse, and he sped along the coast past the tankers and freighters, a steady wind scalloping the sea's surface, filling the cabin with tangy sea air.

"How long since you've been back?" Nikki asked.

"A while. I got out when I was twenty-three. That makes it—"

"Ages ago. Eons."

"Glaciers have come and gone."

Nikki dodged the invitation to make light of his extended absence. "You never visited?"

"Smarter not to."

"Your mom? Stepbrothers?"

"Like I said."

Simon considered this, turning his head and gazing

out the window toward the expanse of blue running
to the horizon. It was a view as familiar as any he'd
known.

He'd promised himself never to come back. Yet here
he was.

Business, he told himself. It's different.

He'd imagined this moment too many times to
count, unsure what memories might surface that he'd
kept hidden, what recollections would sway him most.
The truth was, there had been plenty of good times to
go with the bad. He was honest enough to admit that
he'd enjoyed his days on the wrong side of the law. He
did not regret them. The peril and opportunity they
brought, the betrayal that followed, had forged his independent nature and solidified his will to dictate life
according to his own terms.

He also knew that despite his time in prison, the
years in solitary confinement, the acts he'd committed,
and those committed against him—all the events he
wished most to expunge from his past—part of him
would forever be an outlaw. He needed no more proof
of this than the quicksilver flash of desire and regret
he'd felt walking the scene of the hijacking and con-
juring images of Coluzzi and his crew taking down
the prince. For a few moments there, the longing for
his old life had won him over. False visions of ill-
begotten glory and bloody lucre had swum before him,
beckoning him with a harlot's wanton smile.

It's all still here, Simon. Ripe and ready for the taking.
Up to you...

But like a long-recovering alcoholic who one
evening smells his favorite whiskey and asks "Why
not?," Simon had quashed any misguided notions
about his past or what might be gained from returning

to it. Seeing the Château d'If sparkling beneath the midday sun and the twin forts guarding the entry to the old port, he felt solid and at ease, satisfied of what he'd made of himself and eager to continue in the same vein. He'd left Marseille as a prisoner and returned a free man.

The American author was wrong. The past might not be dead. But it was definitely past.

A modern commercial development had sprung up adjacent to the new port. There were boutiques and wine merchants and a slew of small restaurants with tables and chairs set out front. A parking space opened and he grabbed it.

"Hey," said Nikki. "Why are we stopping?"

Simon pointed to a chalkboard advertising the day's specials. "Bouillabaisse, fifteen euros."

"We have time?"

Simon opened the door. "Eat quickly."

Back in the car, Nikki said, "So where do we start?"

"City of a million. Should be easy." Simon eased into traffic, driving through the tunnel that ran beneath the port, then up the hill into the center of the city. "How are your contacts at Marseille PD? Any old pals that owe you a favor?"

"One or two."

"Anyone you can trust?"

"One," said Nikki. "Maybe."

"I need anything you can find on Coluzzi. If there's a piece of paper with his name on it, I want to see it."

The headquarters of the Marseille police department was located in a block of white concrete across the street from the Cathédrale la Major. Simon pulled to the curb a block away. Nikki jumped out and ran to a nearby kiosk. She returned five minutes later carrying two cellphones in their packaging. After activating both, Simon called her phone so that both had the other's number.

"Where are you going?" she asked.

"The old neighborhood."

Nikki looked both ways, then slipped him her pistol. "Just in case they don't like you any better than Falconi and his friends."

He looked at it, immediately thinking of where to stash it. "No," he said, catching himself falling into old habits. "I don't work that way."

"Sure?"

"I'll try and be more careful this time."

"Do that."

"How much time do you need?"

"Depends on how much I'm going to find."

"If you don't find a lot, you're not looking hard enough."

"How can you be so sure?"

"Someone high up recommended Coluzzi to Neill. We're talking cooperation between intelligence agencies at an international level. They didn't pick Coluzzi's name out of a hat."

"Meaning?"

"He's been doing this for a while."

"You think he started with you?"

"September 1999. Look me up while you're at it."

"Count on it."

"Call me when you're done."

Nikki nodded, then leaned into the car and kissed him. "Be careful."

CHAPTER 56

Simon shifted the car into gear and punched the gas, heading down the hill into the city. He rolled up the window and spun the AC to full. The engine coughed and a stream of lukewarm air trickled from the vents. He banged his hand on the dash. If anything, the flow of air diminished.

He headed into the Prado district, an upscale residential area with broad, leafy streets bordered by modern apartment buildings. Two hours had passed since he'd boosted the car in Avignon. It was prudent to assume the owner had reported it as stolen. In and of itself, such a report was no cause for worry. It could be hours before the police put out word to look for the car. Interest in recovering a stolen vehicle demonstrated a positive correlation with the car's value, meaning the better the car, the greater the desire to find it. Few resources would be expended looking for a twenty-year-old Peugeot with a crapped out air conditioner.

Simon wiped a bead of perspiration from his forehead, then opened the window, only to be met by a blast of hot, humid air, redolent of gasoline fumes and garlic.

Safety, he decided, was one thing. Comfort another.

He turned the corner and grabbed the first parking space he could find. Five minutes later, he was walking down the ramp to an underground garage beneath the nicest building he could find. He was done with twenty-year-old Peugeots.

The garage was deserted and poorly lit, half the spaces empty. He walked down one row, passing an Audi, an Alfa Romeo, and a very attractive Renault convertible. All were late-model vehicles with electronic ignitions. Without a key or a set of advanced tools, he would be unable to start them. The last car in the row was a canary-yellow Simca work van at least thirty years old. Getting it started wasn't the problem. He was willing to bet the air-conditioning was even worse than the Peugeot he'd just abandoned. He came closer and noted that the van had a flat rear tire. End of discussion.

A door to the garage opened and he ducked behind the van. Footsteps echoed across the parking lot. A moment later, an engine started. Tires squealed as the car climbed the exit ramp. Silence returned.

It was then that Simon realized he'd been wrong. The Simca wasn't the last car in the row. Another vehicle was parked behind it, covered by a weathered tarpaulin. By its height and profile, he knew it was a sports car. A Porsche, he guessed, or a Jaguar. With care, he peeled the tarpaulin off the hood. The first thing he saw was a rectangular yellow nameplate with the word "Dino" written on it. The car was a 1972 Ferrari Dino, nearly identical to the vehicle Lucy Brown was—hopefully—working on at that very moment. Color: *corsa* red. There was no missing this machine when it was on the street.

Kneeling, he checked the tire pressure. Low, but

drivable. Even with the tarpaulin, a layer of dust coated the hood. The car had not been driven in at least a year, maybe longer. He put his face to the window. The odometer read 88,000 miles. Doors locked.

Sometimes, he decided, one blended in by standing out. No one would be looking for him in a vintage Italian sports car worth a million dollars. And if they were, too bad. He'd outdrive them.

Simon looked around the garage. He saw no one. He stepped toward the van and snapped off the antenna, dropping it onto the floor and stepping on it, until round became flat, and flat became flatter. He picked up the antenna and deftly fit it between the door and window, closing his eyes, allowing his touch to find the lock and disengage it. He tried the door handle, waiting for the wail of an alarm.

Nothing.

Time was of the essence. He yanked the tarpaulin off the car and dropped it to the ground, then climbed behind the wheel. His hands found the ignition wires. Again, he stripped the wires and wrapped the copper filaments together. The engine sparked. The motor turned over, roaring magnificently, and for the first time in his life, he questioned why Ferraris always had to be so goddamned loud.

The fuel gauge read half full. He had a hundred kilometers before tanking up.

Again, an eye to the door. No one.

He shifted the Dino into first gear and guided it up the ramp and into the sunlight.

A minute later, he was doing eighty down the Avenue du Prado.

CHAPTER 57

Nikki's contact at the Marseille police department was named Frank Mazot, a grizzled fifty-year-old detective who headed up the city's major crimes division, the same team to which she was attached in Paris. Over the years, they'd worked a dozen cases together, ranging from tracking down the Pink Panthers, the Balkan crew that specialized in spectacular heists from *haute joaillerie* boutiques in Paris and Cannes, to the "Dream Team," four Marseille-based gangsters best known for robbing a passenger jet of twenty million euros before it took off from the Provence airport.

Mazot was strictly old school. He wore a white shirt and dark suit. He carried his gun in a shoulder holster—a .38 snub-nosed revolver, no less. ("If you need more than five shots to put a man down, you need to learn to shoot better.") And he always had an unfiltered Gitanes cigarette dangling from the corner of his mouth.

Nikki bounded upstairs to the third floor, stopping at a break room for two coffees before continuing to his office.

"Surprise," she said as she elbowed his door open. "Look who's here."

"Nikki, what in the world?" Mazot jumped to his feet from behind a desk piled high with unruly folders.

"The place is messier than last time I was here." She set down the coffees as Mazot came around the desk and greeted her with a kiss on each cheek. "Hello, Frank. How are you?"

"You know how it goes. Clear one case, two more pop up." He picked up a coffee, viewing her from over the top of a pair of smudged bifocals. "Four sugars?"

"How could I forget? I'm surprised you have any teeth left."

"Good genes," said Mazot, smiling to reveal shoddy dental work stained a grubby yellow by decades of nicotine and coffee. "What are you doing here, kiddo?"

"Last-minute deal. I'm working the big robbery in town. The Saudi thing. I need your help."

Mazot lit a cigarette. "So you came all the way down here?"

"You want something done right you have to do it yourself."

"I do have a phone."

Nikki smiled. "Maybe I wanted to see you."

"Bullshit," said Mazot, harshly enough to make them both laugh. He sat and offered Nikki a seat. The time for pleasantries had ended. "Any leads?"

"I need to poke my nose into your archives."

"Who's the lucky fellow?"

"Tino Coluzzi."

"That's a name I haven't heard in a while. Word was he'd skipped town. Some kind of dispute about a job." Mazot put two and two together. "Coluzzi's behind this?"

Nikki shrugged. "Call it a hunch."

"Or a wild hair?"

"Maybe a little of both."

"Which is why I haven't heard from the lieutenant."

Nikki leaned forward, her arms resting on the desk. She met Mazot's gaze head-on. "You do what you gotta do."

Mazot sucked down half the cigarette, stubbing out the butt in an ashtray filled to overflowing. Pushing his bifocals into place, he hunt-and-pecked Coluzzi's name into the computer. "Write this down."

Nikki scrambled for a pen and paper, jotting down the file reference. "So you're not digitized?" she asked, forgetting to hide her frustration. Digging through the archives could take hours.

"We don't have enough money to pay our detectives on time," said Mazot. "You think we're going to waste it scanning old files? You know what we say around here: 'If you really need to find something, get off your ass and go look for it.'"

"Sounds about right," said Nikki.

Mazot stood. A favor had been called in, the ledgers evened out. "That it?"

"One more thing," said Nikki. "It's personal."

"Oh?"

Nikki gave Mazot a second name, one that he claimed never to have heard before. He found it easily enough. She wrote down the file reference before following Mazot to the archives in the basement beneath police headquarters.

They found Coluzzi's files high on a shelf in the far corner of the basement. Mazot stood on his tiptoes to retrieve the storage box and handed it to Nikki. "You're stronger than I am. You carry it."

He led the way to a small reading room near the elevator. "All yours," he said. "Give me a ring when you're done. I'm at extension forty-nine."

"Sure thing."

"And Nikki? If Coluzzi is the one behind the Paris job, don't forget me. I could use a raise before I retire."

After Frank Mazot left, Nikki opened the box and began sorting through the files inside. Alphabetizing was not the archivist's strong suit. It took her fifteen minutes to locate Coluzzi's file, tucked between "Cranmont" and "Czell." The file was thick as a phonebook, a compendious mess of arrest sheets, interviews, court records, and sentencing documents, all mixed up haphazardly. She required a further thirty minutes to put them in something resembling chronological order before she could begin her research.

Coluzzi's first arrest was at the age of sixteen for burglary with a sentence of six months' probation. The second arrest was three months later, for which he served a year at a reform school near the Spanish border. A note from the school director called Coluzzi "willing to cooperate and a model student." Nikki wrinkled her nose. A handwritten note to Coluzzi's parole officer stated that the young man had come to the director with the name of a student who had been pilfering from the kitchen and selling canned goods to a local vendor.

The die was cast at an early age.

From there, Coluzzi's record grew at a blistering pace. Extortion. Assault. Grand theft. And then at the age of twenty-one, attempted murder. The trial lasted one day. Coluzzi was convicted and sentenced to five years at Les Baumettes.

Nikki paused, studying the paper. Something was missing. Normally, there should be a prisoner transfer sheet attached, documenting his remanding to the national prison system. In its place was a pink-hued form she knew all too well. She'd filed a similar one a dozen times, if not more, including one with Aziz François's name on it when she'd recruited him as a confidential informant.

At once, Nikki took a photo of the form with her phone.

Reports from Coluzzi's case officer followed, providing a comprehensive list of criminals with whom he regularly worked, as well as crimes they'd committed and crimes they planned to commit. There on the third page was "Simon Ledoux."

With mounting fury, she read Coluzzi's detailed, almost joyous recounting of the plan to rob the Garda armored car on September 2, 1999. The following page was a copy of the arrest record, including a brief description of the attempted robbery. Four men killed, names given. Simon Ledoux shot three times, taken to hospital, condition unknown.

Coluzzi stood trial to preserve his anonymity as an informant and received a cursory sentence of six months, of which he was released after two.

And like Aziz François, Coluzzi did not allow his work as a police informant to interfere with his career as a criminal. A few years after the Garda job, he was arrested for robbery and assault, and sentenced to a five-year stretch at Les Baumettes. This time, no amount of snitching could shorten his term. The prisoner transfer sheet showed the date of his arrival as shortly after Simon would have ended his time in solitary.

But nowhere was there mention of an attack on an inmate.

And then, as if a magician had snapped his fingers

and said "Abracadabra," the file ended. No mention of Tino Coluzzi for the past fifteen years. Even if he'd never committed another crime in his life, there ought to be more here—the mandatory reports from his parole officer, to begin with.

Something was wrong.

Nikki put down the last sheet and closed the file.

An administrative request form was stapled to the back of the folder. It was dated January 2003 and came from a Colonel M. Duvivier of the DGSE for an interagency transfer.

The Direction Générale de la Sécurité Extérieure was France's foreign security service, the equivalent of the CIA.

The request read: "All further information kept at 141 Boulevard Mortier, Paris."

It was the headquarters of the DGSE.

Nikki closed the file and slid it back in the box.

Now she knew who had given Tino Coluzzi's name to Mr. Neill.

Nikki returned the box to its place on the shelf, then forwarded pictures of all the pertinent documents regarding Coluzzi's work as a confidential informant to Simon. Satisfied she'd completed the first request, she consulted the notes she'd made in Mazot's office and ventured to the opposite corner of the archives. The light was dimmer in this part of the basement, the air mustier, and she felt as if she were walking deeper and deeper into a forgotten grotto. The box holding the information she sought was easy enough to find, located on a shelf she could reach without difficulty. Thankfully, the files were alphabetized correctly and she found the name quickly. The file itself was surprisingly thin, containing a single arrest report and a court declaration noting that the defendant had pleaded guilty and waived his right to a trial.

She leafed through the pages that followed, her eye trained to spot one piece of information. She found it on the last page. An addendum to a prisoner's death notice written in longhand at the bottom of the sheet, practically an afterthought. One sentence, but it was enough.

She replaced the box, then hurried upstairs. Frank Mazot was waiting in his office. With him were four men, all of them his superiors if dress and age were any indication.

"How did it go?" Mazot asked.

"Fine," said Nikki, aware that all eyes were on her.

"Get everything you need?"

"I did, actually. Thank you." She looked from man to man, meeting their gazes, and realizing with a sinking feeling that they were here for her. "Am I interrupting?"

"We received a call from Paris. From your lieutenant. He was curious as to what you were doing here when you'd been posted to desk duty on administrative assignment."

"I thought I explained."

"Detective Perez," interjected one of the men in a no-nonsense voice, "Frank told us why you're here. While we applaud your eagerness to help bring the investigation in Paris to a successful conclusion, our colleagues are concerned about your methods. They feel you may be assisting someone who isn't working within the purview of French law enforcement."

Nikki looked at the man. Sixty, gray hair, fit, with a fighter's jaw and cold blue eyes. Suit far above a policeman's pay grade. "You are?"

"Martin Duvivier. Office of Defense Intelligence."

Colonel M. Duvivier, formerly of the DGSE.

"I see," said Nikki.

"If you don't mind, Detective Perez," said Duvivier, with far too much deference, "we would like you to stay here until you can talk with one of our colleagues."

"If you don't mind," Nikki replied, in an equally unctuous tone, "I can come back as soon as he arrives."

"But he's on his way over right now," said Duvivier.

Nikki looked from face to face, meeting one stone gaze after another. She landed on Mazot. "Are you preventing me from leaving?"

"Please, Nikki," said Mazot. "Do as they say."

Nikki looked back at Duvivier. "Who is it that we're waiting on?"

"A friend of French law enforcement."

Nikki stared at the floor, concealing a bitter smile. That's exactly what Dumont had called Simon Riske. "A friend?" she asked.

"Yes."

"I want a name."

"Mr. Neill. An American. He's with the CIA."

Chapter 58

Alexei Ren climbed the fantail stairs to the landing pad and gazed north. Two hours after the *Solange* had raised anchor and left Entre les Îles, she was making twenty knots on a course due east, cruising past the Port de Toulon. Numerous warships crowded the harbor. Several destroyers were anchored nearby, sailors moving purposefully about the deck. He'd given the *Solange* over to his top executives for the week. Tonight's port of call was Saint-Tropez, with a gala dinner arranged at the Hôtel Byblos. The voyage would continue onward to Villefranche-sur-Mer, Monaco, and San Remo, across the Italian frontier. Ren, however, would not be joining them. A pressing matter demanded his attention.

Ren lifted a hand to shield his eyes from the sun and searched the sky. He'd exchanged his linen shorts and long-sleeved shirt for a pair of dark work pants and a black T-shirt. For once, he didn't care if his body art was on full view. In fact, he preferred it. Today he was no longer Alexei Ren, business tycoon, philanthropist, and owner of the Olympique de Marseille football club.

He was prisoner 887776, an unfairly convicted political refugee seeking his long-overdue revenge.

He heard the helicopter before he spotted it. He narrowed his eyes, and there it was, flying low over the water, nose dipped, an Aérospatiale Écureuil, built to carry five passengers and pilot with a top speed of two hundred knots.

What better symbol of his success than this sleek aircraft descending out of the sky like Apollo's chariot. Twenty years had passed since he'd arrived in France, a savagely ambitious man without a kopek in his pockets, the wounds from his last prison yard fight yet to heal. For the first while, he relied on his criminal skills to earn a living, but his time in the gulag had reformed him. He was determined to seek another, less fraught path. Once a profligate drinker and spender, he reined in his baser appetites and saved his ill-gotten gains. It was his goal to become a businessman, and if not a pillar of the community, then at least a law-abiding one. He kept his eyes open for the right opportunity, and when it came along, he acted. In this case, it was an investment of one hundred thousand euros in a fledgling software company operated by the son of his bookkeeper. The company flourished. Ren took his profit, bided his time, and when another promising venture presented itself, he acted once again.

In five years, his net worth reached ten million euros. Five years after that, it was one hundred million.

In time, he found a woman to marry. He raised a family. He purchased a mansion on the coast, vacation properties in exotic destinations, and of course the *Solange,* helicopter included. In short, he had it all. Success, the admiration of his peers, a healthy, loving family, and a level of wealth he'd never dreamed of. And all of it—or nearly all—earned from old-fashioned, honest labor. If he'd known that a life on the right side of the law could be so profitable, he would never have picked up a gun all those years ago.

The chopper came in to land, the rotor wash forcing him to step back, the wind playing havoc with his long hair. Ren waved in greeting. The pilot was another Russian who had escaped the frosty, unwelcoming climes of Moscow for the unfettered opportunities and sunshine to be had in the South of France.

The skids touched down. The boat swayed ever so gently.

Yet there, at that very moment, standing on the deck of his one-hundred-million-euro yacht, waiting to board his very own helicopter, the sun on his face, his prospects bright, his future secure by any reasonable definition, Ren was determined to embark on a course of action that risked it all.

But why? demanded a sober, somewhat incredulous voice from his newly polished soul.

Ren's phone buzzed in his pocket, saving him from answering. "Yes?" he said.

"The boys will be at your office in an hour," said a man speaking his mother tongue.

"Are they ready?"

"Ready for what? To take on the entire fucking Russian army?"

"Not the entire army," said Ren. "Just one man."

With that, he ended the call and climbed into the helicopter. Any lingering doubts about what he should or should not do vanished as the helicopter rose into the air and its nose turned toward land.

It was all very simple, he thought, enjoying the

sweep of ocean below him, the exhilarating pulse of rushing into the breach, of once more saying "What the hell?"

A man cannot escape his past.

The best he can hope for is to outrun it for a while.

Chapter 59

Simon turned the corner onto a narrow street and pulled the car to the curb. Drawing a breath, he stared at the row of three-story villas, all of them painted a curdled shade of yellow, all of them in the same miserable condition. A satellite dish was mounted on every roof. Wires ran here and there, telephone wires, electricity wires, who knew what all. Refuse littered the gutter, mostly spent cans of beer, crushed packets of cigarettes, candy wrappers. It was the laziness that had always angered him most, the communal lassitude, as if no one cared about their own neighborhood's general state of decrepitude. Not once had he ever seen someone stoop to pick up a piece of trash, himself included.

His eyes landed on a villa halfway down the street. To look at, it was no different from the other buildings around it. All the same, he wished that the door had a fresh coat of paint and that the second-floor window was not cracked and that bedding was not hung out to dry from the floor above it.

He wasn't sure why a sense of responsibility clung to

him after so long. His mother had died years ago. He'd lost track of his stepbrothers before that. His memories of the place were uniformly bleak. Maybe people were indebted to those who'd done them harm, as well as good.

Just then, the door to the villa opened and a woman, perhaps thirty, stepped out. She was petite and bent at the waist, dressed in the fashion of the Maghreb: headscarf, billowing dress, sandals. Three children followed in short order, none older than five or six. The family walked in his direction, the woman staring openly at Simon and the fancy sports car, as out of place here as a cow on Mars.

Simon started the car and drove away, past his old home. In his mind, he was processing the documents Nikki had sent him from the police archives. He'd known all along that Coluzzi was the informant. Still, there was knowing and there was *knowing*. Seeing Tino Coluzzi's name typed on the official police forms had taken him back to the day in prison when he'd spurned Il Padrone's offer of a safe cell in favor of solitary confinement and the dark, savory opportunity to gain revenge himself.

Memories of those days overtook him. A reckless spirit seized him. He punched the accelerator and raced down the hill, propelled by the untamed, violent zest of his youth. It came to him that he'd felt this way before, here on these same streets. Then, as now, he was on his way to doing something improper, something to benefit himself at the expense of others, something that might hurt others.

It was September and the sirocco was blowing.

It was the day he was going to rob an armored car with Tino Coluzzi.

* * *

The door to Le Nightclub was locked. Simon banged his fist several times against it. Finally he heard the lock turn and a man ask in a raspy, choked voice, "Who the hell's there?"

"An old friend," said Simon.

The door opened. Jojo Matta, dark as a chestnut, a little less hair, and a lot more wrinkles, looked at him. "Yeah?"

Simon stared back, saying nothing. Then a light came on in Jojo's eyes and he rushed to slam the door. Simon stopped it with his foot and threw his shoulder against it, sending Jojo toppling onto the floor. "Hello, Jojo."

"You're dead."

Simon closed the door and locked it. "Who told you that?"

"You ratted out our crew. Tino took care of you back in prison."

"He told you that?"

"Not just him. Everyone in the yard saw you."

"Yeah, well, guess he messed up."

Simon put out a hand and hauled Jojo to his feet. Simon told him to turn around, and when he did, Simon frisked him, finding a Walther nine millimeter in his ankle holster. "Mind if I hold this while we talk?"

"Be my guest."

"Let's have a seat."

Jojo led the way into the main lounge. Simon walked behind the bar and turned on the music. He couldn't count the number of nights he'd tended bar in the place and, when necessary, kept the peace. "I see things haven't changed much."

"Customers don't come here for the décor."

"That's for damned sure." Simon made himself an espresso. "What happened to your hand?"

Jojo held up his bandaged mitt. "This? Cooking injury. Knife slipped."

"You? You're a pro. Must have been some knife."

Jojo shrugged, not even trying to hide the fact that he was lying. "Simon Ledoux. In the flesh after all these years. What are you here for?"

"Where's Tino?"

"How should I know?"

"You know everything," said Simon. "Coluzzi's in town. I figure this is the first stop he'd make."

"'Cause you did?"

"Something like that."

Jojo perked up. "Where you been all these years?"

"Here and there. I'm not in the game anymore."

Jojo gave him a dubious look. "Then why do you want Tino?"

"He has something that belongs to me."

"Sounds like him."

"You know that thing in Paris? That was him."

"Oh?" Jojo didn't look surprised. Clearly, he'd considered the possibility himself. "You a cop?"

Simon shook his head. "Coluzzi stole something besides the money that I need to get back."

"That sonuvabitch. I asked him if he was behind that. That was our M.O. all over again. He said I was crazy."

"What did he want?"

"Came in here asking if I knew any Russians."

"Russians? That's odd. Do you?"

"One. Alexei Ren."

"And?"

"He wanted my seats to the game so he could meet him."

"Did he?"

"Don't know. We didn't part on the best of terms. We had an argument about some things in the past. That job in Paris wasn't all that he was bullshitting me about."

"Your hand?"

Jojo frowned. "He's always been good with a blade."

"Know where he is?"

"If he's not at his place, he's probably shacked up in that rat hole of his down the coast."

"You ever been?"

Jojo shook his head. "Luca Falconi helped him build it. He said he liked the place because it was near his favorite bar. That one on the beach. Le Bilboquet."

Simon remembered the picture of Coluzzi and Falconi in front of the beach bar. He'd left it in his briefcase. "Thanks, Jojo. And by the way, it wasn't me who ratted out our guys. It was Tino."

"How do you know?"

"Who's the one took three bullets that day? Who's the one got sentenced to six years at Les Baums?"

"Tino went to Perpignan."

"For two months."

"So you say."

Simon smiled to himself. No one liked to admit they'd been betrayed or taken advantage of, for fear it made them look stupid or somehow deserving of it. This went double for crooks. He took out his cellphone and brought up the photos of the documents showing that Coluzzi was a confidential informant for the Marseille police.

"These for real?"

"Do they look real?" Simon took back the phone. "Where's Tino been living these last few years?"

"Last place he had was over in Aubagne."

Simon finished his espresso and stood. "Looking good, Jojo."

"You too, Ledoux. Decide to get back into the game, let me know. Plenty of work."

"Sure thing, Jojo."

Simon started for the back door.

"Hey, what about my piece?" called Jojo.

Simon answered without turning. "I'm going to hang on to it for a while. You mind?"

Chapter 60

The door to the interrogation room closed, and Nikki listened as a key turned and the tumbler slammed home. The room was a three-meter-by-three-meter square with a linoleum floor, a table decorated with cigarette burns, and two plastic chairs. This was not voluntary. She was not doing Frank Mazot or any of his colleagues a favor. She was being held against her will. Upon entering, Mazot had politely confiscated her phone and not so politely relieved her of her weapon. The only thing separating her from official status as a prisoner was an arrest report similar to those she'd spent the last hour studying.

She sat down, clasped her hands on the table, and gazed out the windows at the squad room where a dozen cops sat at their desks trying hard not to pay attention to her. Mazot and Duvivier stood near the hall, deep in conversation, venturing a glance in her direction every once in a while. She stayed where she was, smiling vaguely, wondering if Simon was on his way to pick her up.

Her career was officially over. She wouldn't be fired,

at least not right away. Short of committing capital murder or joining the ranks of ISIS, it was nearly impossible to be fired from a government job in France. But there were worse fates. A transfer from anti-gang to traffic enforcement with a demotion and decrease in pay thrown in. Or a move to the drug brigade, her days spent patrolling the grim housing estates on the outskirts of the city, harassing pimps and dealers. Or worst, a two-year suspension to be served in the "crazy room," where you sat nine hours a day doing nothing but reading the newspaper and watching television.

Any way she looked at it, her fish was fried.

Contemplating her future, Nikki fidgeted in her chair, her nail digging into the palm of her hand. Simon had been right. Neill had been keeping track of them all along. She didn't know what Neill was playing at, but whatever it was, she didn't like it. She was on Simon's side. Her only chance at salvaging her career lay in bringing in Tino Coluzzi along with evidence proving that he was behind the hijacking in Paris. To make that happen, she needed to get out of here.

After a while she stood and walked casually to the door. She knew it was locked, but she tried it all the same. She continued her circuit, aware of the eyes on her. There were several avenues of escape. She could launch a chair through the window, hop the sill into the squad room, and make a run for it. Or she could use one of the chairs to break off the door handle and similarly try her luck dodging through the desks to the hall, then down the stairs. Or...

Nikki cut short her foolish plotting and returned to her seat.

It was over.

Fini.

Strangely, she felt worst for letting down Riske.

Just then, a detective signaled to Frank Mazot, holding up a phone, an old-fashioned landline. Nikki watched as Mazot took the call, his eyes shifting toward her. He put down the phone and came over to the interrogation room.

"Call for you," he said, poking his head inside the door. "Commissaire Dumont. Warning: he's pissed."

Nikki left the interrogation room and picked up the phone. "You found me."

"I never lost you," said Simon Riske. "Just nod and say yes, and make sure you wipe any silly look off your face right now."

"Yes," said Nikki.

"I called your phone fifteen minutes ago. Some guy answered, wouldn't give his name. I thought you might be in trouble. Am I right?"

"Yes, Commissaire, you are. Frank Mazot and his friend Colonel Duvivier, formerly of the DGSE, have me under lock and key until their friend arrives. Mr. Neill from the CIA."

"Neill's down here already? You've got to get out."

"I was thinking the same thing," she said. Then quietly, "Hey, I'm sorry."

"Don't be. The information you gave me came in handy. Coluzzi's in town. I've got the address of his place over in Aubagne. There's more. I'll tell you when I see you."

"It might be a while."

"I'm parked out front. I'm in the red car. Can't miss me."

"Red, seriously? What kind?"

"Don't ask."

"Oh Christ. You didn't?"

"Can you get out?"

"That's a tough one."

"They really got you under lock and key?"

Nikki said yes. Mazot was shooting the breeze with another detective, keeping one eye on her. Across the room, Duvivier guarded the door like a watchdog, arms crossed, staring at her as if she'd murdered his wife and children.

"Where are you? First floor? Squad room?"

"Yep. You know it?"

"Know it? I was practically raised there. Tell me one thing. Is there still a broken window in one corner, just above the water pipes? Big crack going right down the middle shaped like a lightning bolt."

"It's been almost twenty years," said Nikki dismissively, surveying the room all the same. "No way it's still—"

"Well?"

She'd spotted the window and the lightning-bolt-shaped crack. It wasn't easy. The glass was so thick with grime no sunlight had penetrated it for … "It's there."

"Then we're safe to assume not much else has changed."

Mazot had stopped talking and was giving her the evil eye. She gave him a weak smile and mouthed, "Coffee? Please." He considered this, then approached, grabbing the phone out of her hands.

"Hello, Dumont? Frank Mazot. Your girl's gotten herself into a heap of trouble. I'm looking out for her the best I can, but there's only so much I can do."

Nikki couldn't hear what Simon was saying. Mazot's features grew darker. His eyes studied Nikki more closely. He nodded, then shook his head, then laughed, then looked back at Nikki, as if he knew something really bad that she didn't. Finally, he said, "Will do. Thanks." He handed the phone back to Nikki. "Coffee, right?"

"No sugar." Nikki put the phone to her ear as Mazot headed to the break room. "What was that about?"

"Tell you later. Is he gone?"

"Getting me coffee."

"Okay, then. There's another way out of the squad room. There's a door at the opposite corner from the cracked window. It looks like a closet. It's not. It connects to a back stairway that was used by workers to deliver coal way back when."

"What if it's locked?"

"There's no lock on the door. Just give it a good pull."

Nikki looked over her shoulder at the door. Two desks were placed in front of it, but there was plenty of room to scoot through. One of the desks was manned, the other empty.

"I'll be waiting by the exit," said Simon. "What do you think?"

Frank Mazot returned and set her coffee on the table. He smiled to show they were still buddies, then sat down. Duvivier and his two colleagues were still at the main door, looking none too pleased she was using the phone.

"I think I don't have much of a choice."

As she was speaking, Frank Mazot's cellphone rang. The detective answered, his eyes immediately turning to Nikki. "Put down the phone," he said.

"Excuse me?"

"Put…it…down."

"I'm still talking to Dumont."

"No, you're not," said Mazot. "Now, do as I say, Nikki."

"What do you mean?"

"You can't be talking to Marc Dumont," continued Mazot. "Because I am."

Nikki glanced over her shoulder. A clutch of detectives were blocking the door Simon had mentioned. She looked back to the main entrance. Duvivier and his crew had his eyes on her, but there were only three of them. Once past them, it was a straight shot into the hall, then down the stairs.

"Keep the engine running," she said to Simon. "I'm coming out the front. Screw it."

She dropped the phone, picked up Mazot's coffee off the desk, and flung it at his chest.

"What the—?" Mazot cried out in pain and alarm, recoiling from her, wiping the hot liquid from his shirt.

The other cops in the room were either busy on their own calls or hadn't put together what exactly was going on. Only Martin Duvivier took action, moving quickly and decisively in her direction.

Nikki took off toward the door, making straight for the gray-haired man, dropping her shoulder and striking him squarely in the chest. Duvivier flailed at her with open arms as he fell backward onto his rear. His two colleagues were too stunned to do anything.

Nikki jumped over him, then bolted into the hall, running to her left toward the stairs. A glance over her shoulder confirmed that Mazot was in pursuit. She bounded down the stairs two at a time as Mazot hollered for her to stop. "Dammit, Nikki, are you out of your mind?," his raspy voice echoing in the stairwell.

The ground floor was an oasis of calm. Nikki landed on the polished stone floor, her feet slipping from under her. She threw out her hand and wrenched her wrist to keep from falling. Suddenly Mazot was on her, hands taking her by the shoulders. She knocked them off, bristling with violence.

"Give me ten seconds," she said. "Please."

Mazot lifted his hands to grab her, then dropped them. He glanced over his shoulder toward the stair-well. No one was following. He looked back at her. She said nothing. "Okay," he said. "But only ten. Go."

"I owe you."

Nikki ran through the grand doors and down the broad stairs to the street. The afternoon sun was punishing and she threw a hand to her eyes, shielding them, looking everywhere for Simon.

Across the street stood the Cathédrale la Major. Its bells began to toll the four o'clock hour. The pavement was crowded with tourists and cops, cars whipping past in both directions. She hurried to the curb. She looked left and spotted a flash of red. An arm was thrust out of the driver's window and held high. Simon's head appeared. He waved, shouting something she couldn't quite hear.

Nikki ran to the car. The passenger door was open. Simon accelerated as she hit the seat. She pulled the door closed and spun to look out the rear window.

"Anyone?" he asked.

"Clear," she said.

It was then that Nikki looked around her and took in the dashboard and the steering wheel and the bucket leather seats. "Really?" she said. "What happened to hiding out?"

"That part of the story is over."

Simon slammed the car into third and drove down the hill.

* * *

Behind them, not fifty meters away, a silver Audi sedan was stopped in traffic opposite the entrance to the police headquarters.

"Still want to go in?" asked the driver, a compact, muscled man with a pockmarked face and sandy hair. His name was Makepeace.

Seated next to him, Barnaby Neill had witnessed Nikki Perez's flight down the stairs and into a red sports car idling just ahead. Sometimes the gods sent you messages that you were following the proper course, thought Neill. The messages could be subtle or they could be obvious. Coming upon Simon Riske, the very man he was looking for, at the very time he needed to find him, qualified as the latter.

"No," said Neill. "I want you to follow that red car."

"The Dino?"

"That's the one."

Makepeace put the car into gear. "No problemo."

CHAPTER 61

Tino Coluzzi had no illusions. He was distrustful by nature, suspicious by profession, and one backward glance from being paranoid. When shaking a man's hand, he made a practice of checking afterward that he still had all five fingers. And so it was that he dismissed as preposterous the notion that Vassily Borodin would politely hand over ten million euros in exchange for the letter and go on his merry way. Coluzzi had only to remember the first thought that had crossed his mind when he'd grasped the letter's import.

No man should be in possession of this letter.

He was in a precarious position.

Equally troubling was the involvement of Alexei Ren. Though Coluzzi knew next to nothing about Ren's past, there was no mistaking the fire in his eye whenever Borodin's name was mentioned, the tactile enmity that juiced him up like a live current. Then, of course, there was the matter of Ren's tattoos. Coluzzi was no expert on Russian prison art, but he'd been in the company of enough *vory v zakone* to know that each symbol represented a past act and that most of them had to do with robbery, murder, and other accomplishments even he didn't want to imagine.

For a man like Ren, revenge wasn't a question of choice. It was a moral imperative. When he'd casually asked where and when Coluzzi would hand over the letter to Vassily Borodin, it was more than idle curiosity.

If that weren't enough, there was the lurking and unexplained presence of Simon Ledoux to consider. No question, Coluzzi had his hands fuller than he might have liked.

All of which explained why at 4:30 in the afternoon he was driving through an industrial district in the hills west of the city searching for a dented blue iron gate. Behind the gate was a parking depot used to house broken-down municipal buses, dump trucks and cement mixers idled by a stagnant economy, discarded postal vans, and lastly—and of primary interest to him—a host of armored cars either out of service or in need of repair.

Turning onto the Rue Gambon, he spotted the entry gate, a battered piece of iron one story high and ten meters long. A concrete wall topped by barbed wire ran to either side and circled the block. Coluzzi left the car running and pressed the entry button. A screen lit up, showing his face. "Open up," he said.

A buzzer sounded. The gate rolled back on its track, rattling loud enough to wake the dead. Coluzzi punched the gas and entered the yard, parking adjacent to the office. An unshaven man in dark coveralls was waiting outside, hands in his pockets. With a nod, he motioned Coluzzi inside.

"Didn't give me much time," he said, dropping into a chair on the business side of the desk.

"Well?"

The man opened a drawer and tossed a set of keys across the desk. "Brink's. Brought in yesterday for an oil change, new brake pads."

"Gas?"

"Full."

Coluzzi placed a neatly folded wad of bills on the desk. "One thousand."

"I need it back by midnight. All the armored cars have beacons so the head office can keep track of where they are at all times. There's an electronic inventory check performed automatically at shift change."

"At midnight?"

The man nodded.

"I'll have it back to you by ten."

The man stood, coming around the desk. "Need any help? Someone to ride point?"

"I'm good."

"You're sure? No one drives an armored car alone. What are you after, anyway?"

Coluzzi took the man's face in his hands, fingers clamping his jaw and cheeks. "I'm fine by myself, thank you very much," he said, holding him in his grip for a while longer, then shoving the man away.

"Just asking. I wasn't trying to upset you."

"You didn't," said Coluzzi. "If you'd upset me, you wouldn't still be standing."

The man gathered himself. "Still have your uniform? After what happened in Nice, police are checking drivers."

"Thanks for the info. I'll keep it in mind." Coluzzi patted the man's cheek. "I'll be back to get the truck at seven."

Leaving the lot, Tino Coluzzi skirted the northern boundaries of the city in an effort to avoid the worst of the traffic before joining the highway and continuing to his home in Aubagne. So far he'd managed to keep away from his local haunts—Jojo's notwithstanding. He'd known that sooner or later he would have to stop by the old place. It wasn't just the uniform he needed. If he wasn't going to take a crew with him, he was at least going to make sure that he himself was well protected. His pistol and stiletto weren't going to cut it in case anything went south. He was going in heavy. Just like the old days.

He reached Aubagne a little past five. He drove leisurely through the town, eyes darting here and there, looking for anything out of place. He'd bought the home ten years earlier. Tile roof, two bedrooms, two baths, a quiet garden with a birdbath that attracted every bird in the area. He knew his neighbors. He knew which cars belonged and which didn't.

Coluzzi's home was on a small, leafy road a ways outside town. He turned down the lane and slowed, windows lowered, eyes and ears open. A year had passed since his last visit. He was pleased to see the Clercs' motorboat in their driveway, as much dirt covering the tarpaulin as ever. Their cat, a very large tabby, sat nearby. The Guillo family had not taken in their trash barrels yet. One day late. Shame, shame. The Guillos were Basque and loved their wine. He recognized their Simca parked in the drive.

He dropped the speed further as his home came into view. The shades were down. The driveway was clear of leaves and pine needles, and the lawn was neatly mowed. He paid a gardener to come twice a month to keep things neat and tidy. A check in the rearview revealed nothing of interest, other than the Clercs' tabby, which was following him down the street. He wished he'd had men as brave on some of the jobs he'd pulled.

Coluzzi opened the electric garage door and parked his car, closing the door behind him immediately. The last thing he needed was a chat with his neighbors. He went to the window cut high in the door and peered out. You could never be too safe.

Satisfied that he had not been followed and that he had no reason for concern, he unlocked the door and entered his home. He went immediately to the bathroom and turned on the shower. The tank was old and needed five minutes to get lukewarm. He took off his jacket and shirt and laid them on the bed, along with his pistol and stiletto. He left the master bedroom and went down the hall to the guest room. Inside was a single bed and an imposing chestnut armoire that had belonged to his grandfather. He opened the armoire and rummaged through the clothing hung inside until he found what he was looking for. Pale gray short-sleeved shirt. Black trousers with an officer's stripe running down the outer leg. His Brink's uniform. He tried on the trousers and shirt and was pleased that they both still fit.

He needed one more thing. Something every bit as important as the uniform. He opened a door to a small closet at the back corner of the room. Inside was a large black safe, half the size of a refrigerator. It was his gun safe. He spun the combination—right, left, then right again—and the door eased open. He didn't intend on meeting Vassily Borodin empty-handed. He had a Russian friend of his own to bring to the party. His cherished Kalashnikov, which he'd owned for as long as he could remember.

He kneeled and looked inside.

His stomach turned, worry overcoming him.

The safe was empty.

He activated his phone's flashlight and peered inside. Nothing.

And then he knew.

Coluzzi stood, turning around slowly, raising his hands in the air. "Ledoux," he said. "You really are alive."

CHAPTER 62

You never changed the combination."

"You remembered it," said Coluzzi.

"One, twenty-three, forty-five." Simon recited the digits one at a time. "And put your hands down. Or I will shoot you."

"You were always the smart one," said Coluzzi.

"Not smart enough. I didn't figure you to be a snitch."

Simon studied his old friend. What else to call him? *Traitor? Murderer?* Since taking the assignment, he'd imagined this moment countless times. All the scenarios involved a spate of heated recriminations followed by some form of violent retribution and lots and lots of blood—Coluzzi's, not his. Now here he was looking at Tino Coluzzi, face-to-face with the man who'd done his best to kill him...and had, in fact, to his own mind, succeeded. Yet somehow he couldn't summon those long-simmering reserves of anger. It would be easy enough to shoot him and be done with it. And then? What would be solved? He wouldn't even have retrieved the letter.

In the end, he always came back to how it was between them before everything went south.

"I can't believe I'm looking at you," said Coluzzi.

"Not bad for a dead man."

"A little less hair, a few more pounds, but otherwise…" Coluzzi craned his neck to have a look at the scar on Simon's forehead. "I knew I was holding back. Just a little harder." He made a motion as if he were hitting Simon again, bringing down the iron bar, putting his weight into it. "Bam."

Simon smiled. It was the old Tino, always trying to impress, to explain away his failures. "Hard to kill a man face-to-face. Or, in your case, from behind."

"Is that what you think? I was scared?" Coluzzi considered this. "Maybe. Maybe not. Word was you didn't have much problem doing it. Killing Al-Faris, I mean. The Egyptian. Word was that you were his shower boy. You were a pretty kid back then. Long hair, ponytail, those elephant hair bracelets you thought were so cool. Guess he liked them, too. I heard all about it after you were dead. Or *whatever*. Easy to kill someone when they're on their knees—"

"Enough," said Simon. It was dumb of him, he knew, to be baited. *We're all still boys, aren't we?* He waited for the monsignor to offer some pithy saying to calm him, an old maxim about it being up to him to decide what or who got to him, but nothing came to mind.

It was then, standing feet from Tino Coluzzi, with the means to kill the man he detested more than any other at his disposal, carte blanche to do as he pleased, that Simon realized he didn't need the monsignor anymore. His lessons were learned. He was his own man.

"Something I say bother you?"

"No," said Simon. "Nothing you say or do could bother me."

"I wouldn't bet on that." Coluzzi laughed. "So how did you find me?"

"Jojo. He hadn't figured you for a snitch either. I'd be careful going back to his place. He's already mad enough about the hand."

"I appreciate you looking out for me."

"That's what we were supposed to do."

"I take it this is about the letter."

"Correct."

"Who are you working for? The American? He never gave me his name."

Simon didn't answer.

"If it isn't the Russians," said Coluzzi, "it must be the other side."

Simon shrugged. It never paid to give men like Coluzzi too much information. "Who are you planning on selling it to? Alexei Ren?"

"Jojo does have a big mouth."

"I'm trying to figure out why you're wearing that uniform. Or is it just for old times' sake?"

"Doesn't matter now. You've found me."

"I'm still curious."

Coluzzi ignored the question. "There was a woman. She killed Luca Falconi. You might want to watch out for her."

Simon made out a sliver of hope in Coluzzi's voice and he knew Coluzzi'd made a deal with the Russians— be it Ren or someone else, Borodin, even—and he was holding out for the chance it might still come to pass. "She's no longer in the equation."

"So it's just you?"

"Not exactly." Simon motioned for Coluzzi to move down the hall. Nikki waited in the living room, where they'd hidden when Coluzzi arrived. "This is Detective

Perez from the Paris police. She's going to arrest you for robbing the prince once you give me the letter."

Coluzzi looked her up and down with contempt. "And if I don't?"

"I'll shoot you," said Nikki. "No difference to me if I bring you in dead or alive."

"You?" Coluzzi laughed at her. "I know you, Detective. Aziz François is your bitch. He's been feeding you a line of crap for years."

"He told me about you and your friends at Le Galleon Rouge. I owe him that much."

Coluzzi's face dropped. "Go ahead then, Detective," he responded in a burst of false bravado. "Shoot."

"All right." Nikki glanced at Simon, then raised the pistol—the Walther he'd taken off Jojo—and fired a round into the wall, an inch above his head. The noise was deafening.

"Are you crazy?" Coluzzi asked, cowering as bits of plaster and wallpaper rained down on him.

"Ask Aziz François." Nikki trained the pistol on him. "I imagine one of your neighbors may have heard that. They might be calling the police even now. And then?" She shrugged.

"Your play," said Simon.

Coluzzi straightened up, drawing a breath to gather his composure. He studied them both for a moment. "I don't have the letter here."

"Of course you don't," said Nikki, already fed up.

But Simon was more optimistic. "It's at your place outside of town. Your rat hole."

For once, Coluzzi couldn't hide his surprise. "That's right," he said.

"Let's go, then," said Simon. "Time's a-wasting."

CHAPTER 63

"Yes, Victor, only men you can trust…He will put up a fight…Of that you can be sure…We will take him at his residence…Our time has come. Yes, my friend, I couldn't agree more. It is a new day for the Rodina."

Vassily Borodin ended the call to Moscow and stared out the window at the French countryside. Usually a master of self-control, he was finding it increasingly difficult to keep still. He felt like a schoolboy in church. Too many years had passed thinking of this moment. Too much effort expended. He grabbed the armrests with his hands, his knuckles white with tension.

So close.

Since leaving, he'd taken the final steps to put his plan into effect. He'd placed calls to like-minded men in positions of authority. At the National Police. The Army. The Air Force. And, of course, the Duma. He'd emailed all of them his last and most complete dossier containing the entirety of the evidence he had collected. He'd reached out to friendly members of the press. He'd even spoken to the few foreign government officials he considered friends.

The last and most important call was to his friends at the FSB, the Federal Security Service, the country's most powerful institution.

The die was cast.

Tomorrow morning, upon his return to Moscow, letter in hand, all would be different. The arch criminal would be removed from power. He did not expect him to go easily. There would be a confrontation. The man had many friends. He had spread his largesse wisely over the years. But now he must go. The evidence was too strong. Evidence of corruption. Of bribery. Of looting of the nation's rich patrimony.

And, finally, there was the letter. The indisputable proof of his villainy. Not only was the president of the Russian Federation a thief. He was a spy.

And spies, like all traitors to their country, must be put to death.

The door to the cockpit opened. The captain approached. "Landing in one hour," he said. "Ten minutes ahead of schedule."

Borodin thanked him and the captain returned to his controls.

One hour.

Borodin was not sure he could wait so long.

CHAPTER 64

They drove in two cars. Coluzzi in the lead, Nikki in the back seat, her gun aimed squarely at his solar plexus. Simon followed in the Ferrari. It was a ten-minute drive down to the Gineste in Les Calanques national park. They left the highway and navigated a macadam road that petered out into a single-lane dirt track leading across a bluff of red rock dotted with Aleppo pines and patches of coastal scrub, the azure expanse of the Mediterranean before them. There were no houses anywhere. No structures of any kind.

The track disappeared altogether, but Coluzzi continued another half kilometer, dodging the trees and bushes, before stopping. Simon parked behind him and grabbed the machine gun from the back seat, unwrapping it from a blanket and carrying it in one hand, safety on, finger above the trigger guard. He had no idea what Coluzzi had up his sleeve or why he was wearing the uniform. None of it mattered once he got the letter. Until then, he wasn't taking any chances.

"You did a good job," he said, surveying the area. "I can't spot it anywhere."

"That's the idea," said Coluzzi.

They walked across the bluff, winding through the scrub, then descended a series of rock steps, plates of stone laid atop one another, like playing cards fanned out on a table. The drop between the stone plates grew larger and Simon knew they were nearing one of the Calanques, the inlets cutting into the shoreline like a succession of long, crooked fingers.

A few more steps and they were standing on the cliff's edge, the sea a direct drop of a thousand feet. He leaned over and looked down, seeing the clear turquoise water, calm as a pond. To the right, there was a strip of beach and he could see a shack with a thatched roof and a few benches filled with guests.

"Le Bilboquet," he said, giving the name of the bar that was in the picture he'd found at Falconi's.

"So?"

"They had a good salade Niçoise."

"Still do."

Coluzzi turned to his left, and it was then that Simon discovered the shelter built into the surrounding rock. There was a stout wooden roof, sanded with red dust, a peasant's boarded door, and a terrace running to a vertical precipice. Like a mirage, it was there but not there. Blink twice and it was gone.

Coluzzi unlocked the door. Nikki followed close behind, her pistol aimed at a spot in the center of his back.

"Tea? Coffee? Something stronger?" Coluzzi called over his shoulder, as if inviting in his chums. "I've got some decent eau-de-vie for you, Ledoux, now that you've gone upper class on us."

"Let's get what we came for," Simon replied. "You can have happy hour at the station."

The hideout's furnishings were nicer than he'd

expected. There were carpets over wood floors, an old, flouncy sofa in the living area, a flat-screen TV plugged into a generator, and a few chairs and tables, staples of any second-hand furniture store. Coluzzi asked if he might open the door to the terrace. Simon said, "No."

"Where's the letter?" demanded Nikki.

"Why in such a hurry?" Coluzzi asked.

"We want to make sure you get a good night's sleep," said Simon. "Jails are such peaceful places." He had the machine gun in firing position. Coluzzi wasn't going without a fight.

"In the bedroom." Coluzzi turned and took a few paces to the rear of the shelter. "I've got a safe under my bed. I need to roll the carpet back."

"I'll give you a hand," said Simon.

"That would be nice."

Coluzzi stepped into a cramped room with low ceilings, no windows, a single bed pushed up against the wall. Simon handed Nikki the machine gun, and she set it down against the wall outside the room, quick to return to her alert position, gun raised, held with both hands.

Coluzzi got onto his knees and rolled back a tattered burgundy carpet. Simon kneeled next to him, peeling back the opposite corner. There was a door cut into the floorboards and a silver pull ring to one side.

"Easy," said Simon.

"Of course." Coluzzi gave the ring a yank and the door came free. He raised it slowly until it stood upright. "Hold it open. It tends to drop on my head."

Coluzzi bent lower to open the safe. "Funny, isn't it? We went to all that trouble to steal half a million euros, knocking off jewelry stores, banks, the big trucks.

Cops shooting at us, running like hell, driving like hell. I found a goddamned letter and it's worth ten million."

"Is that what they're offering?"

"Cash. On its way." He looked over his shoulder, hoping.

"That wasn't the original deal, though, was it?" said Simon.

"So you are working for him?"

"Open the safe, Tino."

Coluzzi returned his attention to the safe. "You know, it really isn't so difficult killing a man face-to-face," he said. "I didn't have a choice with you. Take you face-to-face and you would've killed me. I'm not stupid. I knew you'd come after me the moment I got put in Les Baums. It was survival, really. I couldn't have you telling everyone in the yard that I was a snitch. That would have been the end. Goodbye, Tino. That makes me smart, not a coward. Otherwise, it doesn't bother me. Looking a man in the eye and killing him." Coluzzi raised his head to look at Simon. "I didn't have a problem with the priest."

"Who?"

"Your buddy from the hole. Deschutes."

"He died from cancer."

"Really? That what you think?" Coluzzi smirked. "He was sick when they let him out of the hole, but he wasn't dead. Of course, you were back on the outside by then. You wouldn't have known."

"Paul Deschutes died from cancer three months after I was released. I asked about him."

"Last I checked prisons aren't as honest as they might be, reporting these kinds of things."

"You're lying. The monsignor never got out of solitary."

"Maybe I have him mixed up with someone else. Tall man, long hair he refused to cut. Spooky blue eyes. Oh…and he had great skill in martial arts even in his condition. He would teach some of the younger guys."

Simon felt his pulse racing. He'd never questioned how the monsignor had died. "You didn't?"

"I couldn't let him hang around the yard knowing he'd spent all that time with you. The way I see it, I just shortened his suffering."

Simon saw the taunting in his eyes, the casual cruelty. He didn't know if Coluzzi was telling the truth. Maybe. Maybe not. It didn't matter. Simon had spent years getting as far away as possible from him and those like him. He refused to go back.

"Open the safe," said Simon quietly, without rancor.

Coluzzi waited for a more heated reaction, and when none came he lowered his head and turned the dial a last time. Of course, it was the same combination as the other safe. He opened the door. There at the bottom was a buff-colored envelope.

"Here," he said. "Have a look."

Concerned, Nikki came closer. Simon said everything was all right. He studied the envelope, then opened it and read the note inside.

"What does it say?" Nikki asked.

"It's not what it says, it's who said it." Simon slipped the note back inside the envelope and prepared to hand it to Nikki.

He did not see Coluzzi dip back into the safe. He noted only a flash of motion from the corner of his eye. Then Coluzzi was raising his hand. Simon glimpsed a small silver canister. He shut his eyes tightly as Coluzzi shot the pepper spray into his face. The pain was immediate and devastating. Simon dropped the letter, his hands reflexively moving to his eyes. At the same time, Coluzzi kicked the door closed, then jumped to his feet and locked it.

"Simon!" Nikki pounded the door.

"Shoot him!" Simon fell to his side, the spray searing his eyes, burning, burning. He blinked and the pain worsened. He could see nothing.

"Lay down," shouted Nikki.

A moment passed and she fired three bullets into the lock. The door burst open. She was at his side. "Are you all right?"

"Where is he?"

"He's gone. There was a side door."

"Get him. I'll be okay."

CHAPTER 65

Those are gunshots."

Neill lay on his belly on a rock overlooking Coluzzi's hideout. Next to him, also in a prone position, Makepeace looked through the high-powered scope of a sniper's rifle.

"See anything?" Neill asked.

"Everyone's inside the house."

Neill stifled an expletive, his patience at an end. He didn't know how much longer he could stand back and watch from a distance. He'd followed Riske and the French policewoman to Coluzzi's house in Aubagne, losing sight of him time and again to maintain his cover. It had been the hardest decision in his life not to enter and end things there. He'd counted on Riske's calm, his maturity and devotion to doing his job properly. Ambassador Shea had said of him: "All I know about Riske is that you can count on him to do the right thing. He's got himself a backbone."

Neill had learned that all too well these past twenty-four hours.

"Sir, I've got something. It's our man."

"Riske?"

"No, the other one."

Just then, Coluzzi appeared among the rocks on the far side of the well-hidden structure. He ran awkwardly up the steepest section of the incline, stumbling, clawing at the ground. He wasn't terribly fast. Every few steps, he slowed to look over his shoulder.

A moment later, the female police officer emerged from the house, running after him. Even from this distance, he could see she was holding a pistol. She stopped after a few steps, took careful aim, and fired. The bullet sent up a spray of rock inches from Coluzzi, causing him to veer in another direction.

"Damn her," said Neill.

"What is it, sir?"

Neill watched the woman scramble up the hillside, nimbler than Coluzzi. She was gaining ground quickly. In no time, she'd have Coluzzi within range.

"I've got a clear shot," said Makepeace. "I can take him whenever you like."

Coluzzi crested the bluff. Now on flatter land, he was able to run more easily. The distance between them lengthened. The woman stopped and raised her gun.

"Shoot her, not him."

Makepeace took his eye from the scope. "Excuse me?"

"Do as I say."

Makepeace turned the rifle away from Tino Coluzzi, toward the woman. He laid his finger on the trigger, barely caressing the smooth metal crescent, and placed her in his sights. He drew a breath, feeling his heart slow, his vision sharpen.

Ever so gently, he squeezed the trigger.

He saw the woman fall before he heard the rifle's report and felt the butt dig into his shoulder. Next to him,

Neill had raised his head and was squinting against the glare of the late afternoon sun. The woman lay still, her body twisted beneath her, arms outstretched. Coluzzi slowed, seemingly caught between continuing his flight and seeking refuge where there was no refuge to be had. For a moment, he stopped entirely, staring at the woman, then he turned and ran toward his car.

"What about him?" asked Makepeace. "He's the one we want."

Barnaby Neill looked back at the house, waiting for Riske to appear. There had been three gunshots. Neither Coluzzi nor Perez had been hit. Had Riske?

Coluzzi cleared the ridge and disappeared from sight. There was no need to follow him. Taps had been placed on all the numbers Riske had found in Luca Falconi's apartment. Neill had heard every word Coluzzi had spoken since. He knew precisely where he was going.

"We can head him off at the car," said Makepeace, slipping the rifle strap from his arm, shifting to his side.

"Keep your eye on the house," said Neill sharply.

Makepeace retook his prone position, training the rifle on the hideout.

A minute passed. No one emerged. Neill breathed easier. It appeared that Coluzzi had made it easy for him. With Riske gone, there was nothing standing in the way between himself and ten million euros. He made a mental note to thank Coluzzi for that before he killed him.

"See anything?"

Makepeace pressed his eye to the scope. "No, sir."

Neill placed his pistol against the back of his head. "Sure?"

Chapter 66

Simon heard the gunshot, the report whistling forever over the dry bluffs.

Rifle. High caliber.

"Nikki!" he shouted. Then louder. "Nikki!"

No reply.

Essentially blind, he struggled to his feet, hands groping the wall. His eyes burned beyond description. Clenching his fists, he forced himself to blink repeatedly. Tears were the only antidote to pepper spray. Tears and more tears. He slammed into something heavy…a dresser? Shards of light guided him to the door through which Coluzzi had escaped.

"Nikki!"

He was outside, hands grasping the doorframe. Slowly, the tears lessened the pain. His vision returned. The sun was too bright. The glare too sharp. He stumbled up the hill, calling her name, worry hardening to despair. Then he saw her.

She lay on her side, eyes open, her breathing shallow but steady. He knelt beside her. There was blood. Lots of it. "Stay still," he said. "Let me look."

"What happened? Where is he?"

"Don't worry about him." He opened her blouse. The entry wound was the size of a penny.

"Your eyes," she said.

"We're a pair, the two of us."

"Who?" she whispered. "Was it Neill?"

Simon was not ready to give voice to his suspicions. He was still figuring the angles, what exactly might be motivating him. "Can you move your hands and legs?"

Nikki lifted her feet, then clenched her fists softly, drawing in the fingers one at a time.

With care, he examined the exit wound on her back. The hole was bigger, flesh torn, bone and ligament visible. If there were a place one could choose to be shot, this was it. High and to the right of the torso, directly below the clavicle, causing serious damage to the shoulder and upper back but avoiding major organs. It was a shot to put down a man, not kill him. Just three inches to the center and it would have been over.

He lifted his head and scanned his surroundings. Here, out in the open, with nothing to protect him, he was an easy target. He saw nothing he shouldn't, discerned no movement. Coluzzi was gone. And also whoever had shot Nikki, be it Barnaby Neill or parties unknown.

It took thirty minutes to get Nikki into the house and her wound dressed and cared for, if binding it with strips of bedsheets counted. During this time, he'd called emergency services and given their address as the bluff above Le Bilboquet. A helicopter was on its way. To help, he'd tied a blue duvet cover to a broomstick and stuck it on the roof, both wind sock and beacon.

"Go," she said as he sat on the bed beside her. "Get him."

"In due time," he said. "In due time." He ran a hand over her forehead, brushing away her matted hair.

"You didn't finish telling me about the letter."

"It said thank you." And he told her who had written it and to whom it was addressed.

"I guess that's pretty serious," she said. "He was the cowboy, right?"

"That's him."

"And he's dead?"

"Long time ago."

To Nikki, who hadn't yet been born when the letter was written, it was ancient history.

Simon squeezed her hand. He thought of Coluzzi's words about the monsignor. It was hard to feel more enmity toward him than he already did. Anger solved nothing. It was the sense of frustration more than anything that bothered him. He pictured Coluzzi in the gray uniform. Where was he going that he needed an armored car?

He grabbed his phone and punched in a number he knew as well as his own. A booming baritone answered. "Who the hell is this?"

"D'Art, it's Simon."

"Riske, that you?" asked D'Artagnan Moore. "Why are you calling on a French number?"

"I'll explain it to you later. Right now I need your help."

"That sounds ominous."

"It is."

"I was joking. So this is serious. Are you all right?"

"Yes, D'Art, I'm fine. I need to ask you a question. Do you ever work with security companies like Brink's?"

"Brink's? Of course we do. Can't transport a Van Gogh in the back of a Volkswagen. Why do you ask?"

"How about in France? Know anyone there?"

"Not offhand, but a friend of mine runs their European operations. Offices are just across the river at Canary Wharf, as a matter of fact."

"I need you to find out how many trucks are in service right now in and around Marseille."

"For Brink's?"

"For all of them."

"What is it, six o'clock there? Can't be too many. Banks are closed. Museums as well."

"That's what I'm thinking. Ask if they can drill down on those that are on the road and find out specifically who tasked them and where they are going."

"All trucks are equipped with individual location monitors these days. We can follow them every inch of the way, no matter where they go."

"That's what I thought."

"Anything you're looking for? Do we need to alert the police?"

"This isn't anything for the police. At least not yet. We're looking for a truck that is somewhere it shouldn't be. Something without a tasking or an assigned driver."

"A rogue armored car?"

"Something like that."

"Now you are scaring me."

"Make that call and get back to me as soon as possible. Oh, and D'Art, I owe you one."

As Simon ended the call, he heard the helicopter approaching. He touched Nikki's cheek. "Your ride is here."

He ran outside and signaled to the chopper, shielding his eyes from the spray of dirt and gravel as it set

CHRISTOPHER REICH

down. The attendants had Nikki on a stretcher and inside the passenger bay in five minutes. There was no room for Simon.

"Where are you going?" she asked, as the attendant finished strapping her in.

"Not sure."

Nikki squeezed his hand. "Hey," she said. "Come here." Simon came closer. "You never told me how you slipped my cigarette into the box without me seeing."

"That's a secret."

"I won't tell."

"Get better and I'll show you how I did it."

"Promise?"

"Promise."

Nikki lifted her head and kissed him. "I know you're not giving up."

"We'll see."

"When you find those bastards, give them my regards."

"Count on it."

Simon stepped away. The helicopter lifted off the stone butte. Its nose dipped and it dove over the cliff toward the blue water, then rose and flew into the setting sun.

He almost didn't hear the phone ringing. "D'Art?"

"Not much joy, I'm afraid. I called Garda, Securitas, and all the smaller shops. All their trucks are accounted for. Only Brink's had anything interesting."

"Go on."

"One of their trucks that was listed as 'under repair' left their lot a little while ago."

"Here in Marseille?"

"Nineteen Rue de la Paix. Know where that is?"

"Sure I do. Where is the truck now?"

"As of this moment, the truck appears to be on a highway heading northwest."

"To the airport?"

"Already past it, I'm afraid."

Simon sighed with frustration. If not the airport to meet Borodin, then where? "That's a start."

"Did I say I was finished? Clients like to follow the trucks transporting their valuables. I texted you a link to the truck's geo-locator. You can follow it yourself. If it's the right one…"

"It better be."

"Good luck, then. By the way, someone's been asking round about you."

"Client?"

"Never mind who," said D'Artagnan Moore in a lighter voice. "Call me as soon as you hit town. Right now it sounds as if you have your hands full enough."

Simon hung up.

He grabbed the assault rifle and retraced his path to the Ferrari. Five minutes later he was on the Gineste heading west. He kept one eye on the road and one on his phone and the blinking dot on the map. The Brink's truck had left the main highway ten kilometers past the airport and was headed north. Simon studied the map for possible locations. He spotted a name he hadn't thought of in almost twenty years. Suddenly, it made sense.

Returning his concentration to the road, he gripped the wheel lightly and depressed the accelerator. Ahead, the sun was setting over the sea, a brilliant fireball poised above a field of shimmering blue.

It was Coluzzi behind the wheel of the Brink's truck.

And Simon knew where he was headed.

Maybe…just maybe.

CHAPTER 67

Coluzzi had the feeling. The tingling at the tippy-tip of his fingers. The nervous rumble in his tummy. The unexplained desire to smile like an idiot, followed by the ferocious order to keep a straight face. It was the feeling he got when he was about to do a job and he knew it was going to come off.

And now, as he drummed his fingers on the steering wheel of the Brink's truck, guiding the heavy vehicle across the tarmac of the Aix-en-Provence aerodrome, he had it once again.

It was the feeling of fast money.

Coluzzi sat up straighter, gripping the wheel with both hands.

The aerodrome occupied a sprawling meadow bordered by a pine forest to the north, the highway to the east, and endless fields of wheat and barley to the south and west. There was one landing strip and a taxiway, nearly as long, running parallel to it. A few dozen private planes were parked near the control tower, all of them tethered to the tarmac. It was not uncommon for winds to reach triple digits.

A sleek jet sat on the apron at the far end of the runway. Six windows, blue stripe along the fuselage, winglets at the end of each wing. He didn't need to see the Russian tricolor painted high on its tail to know it was Borodin's. There wasn't another jet—private or commercial—at the aerodrome. The engines were spooling, trails of translucent exhaust visible against the backdrop of forest. This pleased Coluzzi. It meant Borodin wanted to make a quick exchange and get the hell out of here. He imagined Borodin had plans for the letter. Coluzzi had plans, too. Ten million euros' worth.

He drove past the squadron of aircraft to the north end of the field and stopped when he was at a safe distance from the jet. The aerodrome was shutting down for the night. There was little activity of note. A pair of mechanics in an old jeep bumped along toward the repair shed. A Piper Cub had just landed and was taxiing to its designated spot. The control tower closed at nine. Anyone wanting to land after that did it on his own visual reconnaissance.

He put the truck in park, leaving the engine running, and called Borodin.

"You're late," said the Russian. "Is everything in order?"

"Everything is fine," said Coluzzi. "Here's how it works. You'll come alone to my truck with the money. I'll open the back and you'll climb inside. After I count the money, I will give you the letter."

"Fine," said Borodin.

Fine? Coluzzi had expected more resistance, a request for a bodyguard to accompany him, proof he had the letter on his person. Something. He cursed Ledoux for causing him to be tardy. He had no idea when Borodin had arrived or if he'd had the chance to deploy any men. It made sense he wouldn't come alone or unprotected. Not the director of the SVR.

"Well?" asked the Russian.

"I'm waiting." Coluzzi unbuckled his safety belt. He had the air-conditioning on high, but he was sweating all the same. What he needed was some fresh air, but windows in armored cars didn't go down. There were only vents in the roof, which he knew about all too well because the first thing you did when you hit a truck was to clog them with towels soaked in ether to encourage the driver to abandon his post. You could block the vents to the cargo bay, too, but you couldn't count on that to force the guards to open the doors. It was usually necessary to take more proactive measures, namely a well-aimed RPG or a round from a Barrett .50 caliber rifle to blast open the lock.

The desire of armored car manufacturers to seal off the cargo bay had led them to install a steel bulkhead separating it from the driver's compartment. So it was that Coluzzi needed to exit the truck. This particular truck had its door on the side, a single panel like the door to an RV, but made from steel two inches thick.

He scanned the airfield, looking for signs of them lying in wait. The sun was touching the horizon. A soft wind rustled the pines. All was calm. Another look. He saw nothing to give him pause.

The jet's forward door opened inward. Stairs unfolded. A lone man descended the steps. He was short and thin, dressed in a dark suit. A runt if there ever was one. *Where was the money?* Another figure appeared in the doorway and handed down a suitcase. Borodin—at least he thought it was Borodin—took it by the handle and began to walk in his direction. After several steps, he set down the suitcase and stopped. Coluzzi shifted in his seat. What was wrong? Why had Borodin halted? Then the Russian freed the extendable handle and continued in his direction, wheeling the suitcase behind him.

Coluzzi opened the door and stepped outside into the warm evening air. With relish, he rubbed his hands together.

Payday.

Simon had never driven so fast.

As a boy, even before he was old enough for a license, he would take a car he'd boosted and give it a run through the hills outside the city. Speed limits meant nothing. He drove as fast as his skills allowed. If the car permitted it, he drove faster. The roads were narrow and winding with plenty of hairpin turns and more blind curves than not. Once in the mountains, there were no guardrails to keep you from sliding off the road and plummeting a few hundred meters down a sheer cliff. It went without saying, he preferred to drive at night.

Still, he had never driven like this, foot plastered to the floor, darting in and out of his lane, dodging oncoming traffic, daring others to hit him. Time and again, he met the blue flash of halogens, the fearful protest of a horn. Time and again, he ducked back into his lane by the skin of his teeth.

He crested a hill and came up much too quickly on a station wagon. There were three children in the rear. One of them, a boy, grew excited at the sighting of the Dino and began giving him thumbs-ups and other gestures of approbation.

Simon slipped the car to the left, edging into the oncoming lane. A Mercedes zipped by and another behind it, so close his wing mirror rattled. A patch of empty road beckoned. He downshifted and slid into the oncoming lane. The station wagon matched his acceleration. Simon refused to look at the driver and continued to build speed, the needle touching 160. The station wagon stayed with him. What the hell! There were children in the car. Simon dry-shifted, shoving the car into neutral for a split second while juicing the rpms, then throwing it back into fourth.

The Dino leapt ahead.

A truck rounded the bend and was coming at him, closing fast.

Simon was a nose in front of the station wagon, but still the driver refused to slow. The children's faces were glued to the window, unaware they were not simply spectators in a battle but unknowing participants. The Dino was underpowered by design, built as a more affordable entry into the Ferrari family. It didn't have a V-12 or even a turbo-charged V-8. Simon was handcuffed by a V-6 that could give him two hundred horses on a good day.

The truck sounded its horn.

Simon took a last look at the station wagon. For a moment, his foot moved to the brake, then he bit his lip and downshifted into third, skyrocketing the rpms. The engine howled in pain. The vehicle shot forward. He yanked the wheel to the right and retook his lane as the truck whizzed past him, the sudden and dramatic change in air pressure causing his ears to pop.

A green traffic sign passed in a blur.

AIX-EN-PROVENCE 10 KM

By now, Coluzzi was there.

Faster.

* * *

Alexei Ren sat in the copilot's seat of his helicopter, staring at the armored car. He'd landed at the aerodrome an hour earlier, sure to arrive before Borodin. He'd positioned his men strategically, knowing that Borodin would wish to leave as quickly as possible and that he would stay far from the main concourse. He saw them hiding among the private planes, fanned out evenly. There were six in all.

He was certain that Borodin had his own men positioned around the field, too, probably locals he'd brought for protection. Until now, however, no one besides Borodin had deplaned. Ren must assume the men were hidden on the far side of the field.

It made no difference.

All that mattered to Alexei Ren was that Vassily Borodin never again set foot in Moscow.

"Mr. Coluzzi."

"Call me Tino. Please."

Borodin looked up at Coluzzi standing in the bay of the armored truck, dressed in the Brink's uniform, a pistol in his hand. The man was clever. He'd grant him that. He was unsure if his men had a clear shot or if they'd even know this was the man they were after. "The letter is here?"

"Hand me the suitcase."

Borodin hoisted the suitcase into the truck, then followed it inside.

Coluzzi closed the door, then spun him around and frisked him. "Open the case. Take the money out and count it."

"Must we? I didn't fly all this way to engage in any last-minute tomfoolery. It's all there."

Coluzzi insisted. Borodin opened the case. He took out one packet of money and another, handing them over for inspection. "Ten thousand. Twenty."

Coluzzi pulled the suitcase toward him. "Sit still and shut up." He added an unctuous smile. "Please."

"As you wish."

The Corsican dug his hands into the case and removed the packets at random, fanning each to check against any padding, freeing one or two notes and holding them to the weak interior bulb.

"Happy?" asked Borodin.

"Ten million euros," said Coluzzi, with smug satisfaction. "It really does look bigger."

"Excuse me?"

Coluzzi closed the suitcase. "Never mind."

"The letter?"

Coluzzi unbuttoned his chest pocket and withdrew the envelope, the rear flap embossed with an image of the White House. He watched Borodin's eyes light up, his cheeks fire with a rosy glow.

With care, Borodin slipped the letter from the envelope. Here it was, then. The grail itself. Relief, satisfaction, and venom—in that order—coursed through his veins as he read the short message.

"Happy?" asked Coluzzi.

Borodin gestured at the door. "Our business is concluded. May I?"

Coluzzi threw it open and Borodin left the truck. When he had covered a few steps, he heard his deputy's voice in his earpiece. "We can take him when he shows himself. We have a clear shot."

"Leave him be," said Borodin.

"But we cannot—"

"We have what we came for. The last thing we need

is a fiasco. It will be bad enough if Major Asanova is tied to us."

"Yes, sir."

Borodin breathed deeply of the warm, scented air. He felt a lightness to his step that was entirely new to him. A sense of optimism he'd made a point to guard against. One day, he mused, it would be nice to vacation in the area. Perhaps, once he repatriated some of the billions the president had stolen, he would allow himself to borrow a bit off the top and bring his family. Nothing too much, mind you. No lordly sums. A million or two, at most. There were many lovely hotels. He'd heard the Hôtel du Cap was especially nice, a favorite of his countrymen. The minutest of smiles creased his lips. How sweet, revenge.

"Tell the pilot to fire up the engines," he said. "Let's go home."

Just then he felt something strike his leg. Something sharp and fleeting. A wasp sting on his thigh. Inexplicably, he fell to the ground. His vision blurred. His head spun. It all happened so fast.

Only then did Vassily Borodin hear the gunshot.

Slowing as he neared the gated entry to the aerodrome, Simon made out the unmistakable snap-crackle-and-pop of fireworks. Not fireworks. Gunshots. The crack of high-caliber rifles and the frenetic patter of automatic weapons. A man ran toward him, hands waving.

"Turn around," the gate attendant blurted, pausing for the shortest of moments at Simon's window. "It's a war. Get out now."

With the engine idling, Simon could hear more clearly. The pops and bangs were coming fast and furious.

Simon accelerated and crashed through the pole barrier. He rounded the main building and immediately spotted a Brink's truck at the far side of the field. *Coluzzi*. Not far from the truck, a private jet was parked, taxi lights flashing, front door open, stairs extended. *Enter Vassily Borodin*. Dusk was falling. Against the violet hues of fading day, the muzzle flash of machine-gun fire popped like fireflies.

He braked hard and skidded to a halt.

It was a pitched battle. He counted two men down on the tarmac near the jet. Another two fired automatic weapons from the protection of the jet's landing gear. Return fire came from a helicopter parked a distance to the right and several small propeller planes.

Who were they? Friends of Coluzzi? Or was it Neill?

A man broke from the cover of the jet—*one of Borodin's?*—unleashing a spray of gunfire while shouting exhortations to an unseen comrade. One of the men lying on the tarmac rose to his feet and limped toward the plane. A second man broke from the landing gear and ran to help, shooting from the hip, throwing the limping man's arm over his shoulder.

Amid this, the Brink's truck had begun to move, slowly at first but now gathering speed, executing a violent U-turn and barreling down the runway.

Heading directly at Simon.

He was getting away.

Alexei Ren had abandoned the safety of his helicopter to be with his men. He took cover behind the struts of a large Pilatus turboprop and watched as Borodin struggled to his feet. "Get him," he shouted. Three of his men were dead and the other two pinned down by fire. He wasn't sure what the tally was on the other side, but they'd lost a few of their own, too, and he was damned happy about it.

Several bullets struck the engine cowling above him, pinging madly. The shooting had been going on for an eternity, though it was probably no more than a minute. Already he was growing accustomed to the gunfire. It was easy to forget how loud and frightening an automatic weapon could be.

On the landing strip, one of Borodin's men dashed to his side. The two made an easy target, but suddenly the gunfire had stopped. The air was still. Ren craned his neck but could no longer see his men. *Were they dead? All of them?*

A tall thin man appeared in the doorway of the jet, then ran down the stairs and hurried to Borodin.

Ren looked on, seized by a spasm of injustice. No, he protested impotently. He can't get away. He can't.

He remembered the time he'd spent in Siberia, the countless humiliations, the endless discomfort, the constant beatings, the unimaginable filth, the cold, oh yes, the cold. And, of course, the loss of his money, stolen by the government. Stolen by Borodin. The loss of precious years of his life. Stolen by Borodin.

His eye fell to his forearm and the daggers tattooed there. He'd killed three men in prison. And now? Who was he? A businessman? A yachtsman? A husband? The words sickened him. He'd allowed time and money and the easy life to soften him. To shelter him from his true self.

Enough.

Ren raised his submachine gun to his shoulder and charged. "Borodin!" he screamed at the top of his lungs, running toward the jet.

One of Borodin's men lifted his rifle and fired.

Ren thrust out his arm and fired back, one-handed.

The man threw up his arms and fell.

"Borodin!" Ren shouted again, still running. He could see the weasel now, his face turned toward him, whiter than white, a death mask.

Here I am, he said to himself. *You put me through hell and now I'm returning the favor.*

Ren raised the weapon, the barrel pointing at the man he despised more than any other. Twenty meters separated them. He squeezed the trigger joyously, wildly happy. He had him!

A blow struck his chest. His breath left him, and he stopped at once, wondering who had shot him. Borodin was fleeing, climbing the stairs to the plane. His men were closing ranks behind him. Who?

Ren collapsed onto the tarmac. He could not move. His hands refused his commands, as did his feet. He wanted to blink but he could not even manage that. He felt the life running out of him as water spirals down a drain, circling ever faster. He saw Borodin's pale face leering at him. Not for a moment did he regret his actions. He only wished that he'd fired more quickly. He'd wanted very badly to stand over his foe and spit in his face.

Ren stared into the sky. The light was fading so quickly. Impossible. The sun had only just gone down. He saw no stars. Only darkness as death wrapped him in its cold grip and carried him away.

He'll never do it.

Simon gunned the Dino down the center of the landing strip, the painted white stripes disappearing beneath the hood as one long blur. He had the accelerator to the floor. He kept extra weight upon it, in case it might go a little bit further. The needle on the speedometer edged close to its limit. The Dino, though it looked like a million bucks, wasn't built to run at high speed. Everything in the car rattled and jumped as if the screws were loose. He had the absurd and fleeting thought that the owner needed to bring it into his shop for a once-over.

He kept his eyes on the asphalt rushing toward him. Somewhere out there, barreling at him, was a ten-ton fist of reinforced, impregnable steel. He didn't see the vehicle. He saw only the man inside. And that man was weak.

Playing chicken was not Simon's first idea. He had the AK-47 in the back seat and three clips of ammunition. He'd considered trying to stop Coluzzi with concentrated bursts of fire. The problem was that it wouldn't work. The truck's engine was protected by a steel cowling. The windows were bulletproof. And the tires were run flat. Armored cars were designed to withstand precisely that kind of attack. The machine gun was out.

A second option was to follow Coluzzi from the airport to his destination. Sooner or later he would have to stop, and when he did, Simon would be there. If he wanted to use the machine gun at that point, he could have at it. Unlike the armored car, Coluzzi was not designed to withstand concentrated bursts of automatic weapons fire. This option was more feasible but equally unsatisfactory. Too much could happen once they left the aerodrome. A look at the fuel gauge put an end to the discussion. Simon was running on fumes.

Or he could simply let Coluzzi go and track him down another day. That was the simplest option and the safest for all concerned. If Simon could find him once, he could find him again. But in that time Coluzzi would have taken the money—however many million euros Borodin had paid him—and socked it away somewhere safe. The idea alone rankled him. Besides, who knew where he might get to?

This last option, he decided, was the dumbest of all. Not because it had the best chance of success—because it did—but because the mere thought of it made him ill. The bad guys did not get away with it. Not even for a day. And certainly not if their name was Coluzzi. Full stop.

Which brought Simon back to the present and the mass of gray steel filling up more and more of his windshield.

This was happening here. And it was happening now.

Simon's fingers tightened on the wheel. He noted that his palms were as dry as dirt. By all rights his heart should be jumping out of his chest. Instead, it was beating quickly but rhythmically and, he was certain, half as fast as Tino Coluzzi's was at this instant.

Simon lifted his eyes from the asphalt to the armored truck driving straight for him. If either of them was going to swerve, this was the moment. Twenty meters separated them. His arms tightened, his wrist locked into position. Somewhere he heard a horn blaring, growing louder, louder even than the bloody thoughts that had knocked all the others from his mind. The halogens flashed repeatedly.

Simon raised his gaze to Coluzzi, and for a moment the two looked at each other. In the eye. Man to man.

The next, Coluzzi threw the wheel to one side and steered the truck off the landing strip and into the grassy median.

The truck bounced over the tall grass, drifted into

a shallow dip, then bounded up the other side, listing dangerously to one side. The wheels lifted off the ground, and for a few seconds the truck continued on two wheels, balancing precariously as if on a high wire. Then gravity asserted its domain and the armored truck fell onto its side and skidded to a long, slow halt.

Simon saw none of this.

The moment Coluzzi had veered off the runway, something else had demanded his attention. Not a truck, but a plane. His eyes were focused once again directly in front of him, where Vassily Borodin's jet was advancing toward him like an arrow to its target. Simon braked and made a controlled one hundred eighty degree turn, leaving half his tires on the road. As he came to a halt, he felt the jet pass overhead, its weight pressing down upon him, its shadow blocking out the setting sun. He looked up. The plane was so close he could see the tires spinning, the grease slathered on the metal struts holding the landing gear, so close he could lift his hand and scratch the underbelly.

And then, as the sun came back into view and the plane rose into the air and he finally saw the truck lying on its side, Simon knew that he was going to die.

The thrust of the Gulfstream's engines struck exactly two seconds later. The Dino was not a heavy car. Its weight with Simon, the machine gun, and the quarter gallon of gasoline remaining in the tank came to less than three thousand pounds. Each of the jet's two Rolls-Royce turbine engines was capable of producing a maximum of fourteen thousand pounds of thrust. At the moment of takeoff, when the engines were tasked with lifting a forty-thousand-pound object off the earth and propelling it high into the sky, each was working at eighty percent of capacity, creating a combined thrust of nearly twenty-five thousand pounds per square inch. It was this miracle of engineering that picked up the Ferrari and flung it bodily into the air, spinning it head over tail, side over side, like a toy in a dryer.

Simon wrapped his hands around the steering wheel and braced both feet against the floorboard. It was no use. Everything was moving too rapidly, too wildly. He saw the earth and the sky and the earth and the sky. At some point he lost hold of the wheel. There was a terrific collision. Something knocked the wind out of him. He struck his head.

Then he saw nothing at all.

CHAPTER 68

Barnaby Neill steered his car along the auxiliary road
that ringed the aerodrome. He kept one hand on the
wheel while the other massaged his aching shoulder.
Years had passed since he'd fired a rifle, and he'd failed
to hold it as tightly as needed. Still, he was pleased with
his aim. He'd needed one shot to neutralize Ren. Makepeace could not have done any better, rest his soul.

He slowed as he came abreast of the Ferrari, lying
on its roof a hundred meters to his left. The car
looked more like a recycled Coke can than a mas-
terpiece of Italian design. He could not see Riske
inside or, for that matter, anywhere in the grass. It
was doubtful he could have escaped unscathed. If he
wasn't dead, he was badly injured. Under normal circumstances, he could simply dismiss him as a factor
to be reckoned with. But Riske was anything but normal. He was a cockroach. You could step on him with
your boot, you could grind him with your heel, and
still he managed to survive.

Enough was enough.

Neill threw the car into park. Opening the door, he

unholstered his pistol, chambered a round, then stepped outside. The road was covered with pine needles and he took a deep breath of the warm, fragrant air. A new resolve filled him. It was time to neutralize Mr. Riske just as he'd neutralized Mr. Ren.

He started out across the grass, searching for some sign of the investigator. It was common for people to be expelled from their vehicles in rollover crashes. He kept his eyes on the ruined car and the area nearby. A flurry of activity out of the corner of his eye drew his attention. Not Riske, Coluzzi. With evident difficulty, the Corsican was climbing out of the cab of the armored truck. His face was a bloody mess, his clothing askew. He pulled himself over the foot rail and slid indecorously down the side of the truck, falling into the grass and lying still.

Neill stopped to assess the situation. A moment ago he'd caught the first dissonant wails of a police siren. He could see the flashing blue lights deep in the trees as they neared the aerodrome. Not a single pair, but a dozen. His eyes studied the Ferrari, then dashed to the truck. It was one or the other.

Neill returned to his car at a jog. A minute later he was parked near the truck, using it to shield his presence as best as possible. He approached with caution, pistol in hand.

"Mr. Coluzzi, we meet again."

"Mr. Neill, is it? I was wondering when I'd see you."

Up close, Neill could see that Coluzzi had suffered a gash on the forehead as well as a broken nose. He was a mess. "I'm guessing our mutual friend told you my name."

"Is it Ledoux or Riske? I'm confused."

"Do you have my letter?"

Coluzzi pointed at the sky. "Airmail to Moscow." He coughed, expelling a wad of bloody phlegm.

"At least I've earned a consolation prize."

"I don't suppose you'd care to split it? We make a good team. Next time, though, tell me the rules in advance."

"You have your six hundred thousand euros. Or, rather, you did."

"It was the money you were after all along, not the letter."

"It's more complicated than that. Let's just say I knew who I was dealing with."

"I'm glad I didn't disappoint you."

"Only a little. You could have killed Riske."

Coluzzi sighed, a mistake he rued as well. "How are we going to settle things?"

"Get me my money. Then we'll talk."

"I can't," said Coluzzi. "Knee. It's ruined."

"Up," said Neill, not buying it. "On your feet."

Coluzzi forced himself to his good knee, then attempted to stand. He managed, just, and wobbled unsteadily. Neill motioned with the pistol for him to walk. Coluzzi took a step and collapsed to the ground, moaning unpleasantly. Neill grabbed his leg below the kneecap. With thumb and forefinger, he squeezed. Coluzzi cried out.

"You really are hurt," said Neill.

Grimacing, Coluzzi sat up, rubbing his knee. One hand moved slowly toward his ankle. His fingers tugged at his pant leg. The stiletto flashed through the air, its razor-sharp blade angling for Neill's fleshy neck.

But Neill saw it coming. He caught Coluzzi's wrist, stopping the blade a breath from its target. He stared at Coluzzi, tightening his grasp, slowly turning the wrist backward on itself. Coluzzi clenched his jaw. His body began to shake. Still, he said nothing. Neill wrenched the wrist violently, snapping bone and tearing cartilage. The stiletto fell to the ground. Coluzzi cried out. Neill cuffed him with the butt of his pistol for good measure.

"Is the truck unlocked?" he asked, and when Coluzzi refused to answer, he asked again, with menace.

"See for yourself."

"I'll take that as a yes." Neill walked to the rear of the truck and put a foot on the bumper, reaching a hand to the roof, and hauling himself up onto the side of the truck. He remained prone, as the first police cars entered the aerodrome. One after another, they made a sharp right turn and drove pell-mell to the far end of the field, where Borodin and Ren had engaged in their version of the shootout at the OK Corral. Finally, the sirens died off. He watched as the officers poured from their cars and surveyed the scene. Not one glanced in his direction.

He scuttled crab-like to the cargo door. It opened outward and he lowered himself into the rear bay. It was more cramped than he had expected, with a bench and an enclosed container to accept deposits. He noted how stuffy the air was, how stale and sour. The thought of spending an eight-hour day trapped in such unpleasant confines made him claustrophobic. But that was another man's fate.

Neill picked up the suitcase, guessing its weight to be close to forty pounds. He saw that there was no combination and that it was unlocked.

Ten million euros.

How long had he waited?

The idea had come to him years before. He had grown tired of this life. He was doing an all-star's job for a journeyman's wages. The world was an expensive place and there was money to be had. At some point, between all the cars he'd never drive, the suits he'd never wear, the meals he'd never eat, and the women he'd never screw—out there between Belgrave Square and Rodeo Drive—he decided he wanted a piece. A government salary wasn't going to cut it. And so he'd set about planning.

He'd started his career as a Russia hand. He'd been a young man when Reagan had visited Red Square as a guest of Mikhail Gorbachev. He'd been in the room when his superior had suggested making a pass at the young KGB officer shipped in from Dresden, along with a hundred others, to populate Red Square. The First Gulf War broke out barely eighteen months later and he was transferred to the Middle East desk. Off he went to Kuwait and an assignment with the Special Activities Division. Russia was a memory.

But over the years, he'd heard whispers about "their man" in Moscow. Whatever the Agency was doing, it worked. From 1990 to 2000, Russia went from being the "main enemy," a vaunted military power and feared rival, to the closest thing to a failed state. The old USSR broke up into a dozen pieces, most of which—not coincidentally—hated one another. What remained of Russia proper was ruled by the greediest bunch of plutocrats since Nero and his violin had plundered Rome. And presiding over this wholesale pillage was "their man in Moscow," Vladimir Vladimirovich Putin. First as a bagman for the mayor of Moscow, then as an assistant to President Boris Yeltsin (who else could have slipped Yeltsin the bottle of vodka he was forbidden during the fated visit to Washington, DC, when he escaped the White House in his pajamas and was found wandering down Pennsylvania Avenue at three a.m. singing "The Internationale"?), and then as president of Russia himself, a position he had held, on and off, for two decades.

At some point the Agency lost its man, which was par for the course. Putin accumulated too much power, too much money. He decided to be his own man. No one minded much. Russia needed a strong hand. Worse than a dictator was a weak democracy. The West required a reliable bulwark against the Chinese hordes. It also required an enemy with sharp teeth and a set of claws. Of late, however, he had grown too headstrong. It was decided he needed to be reined in. No one suggested replacing him. God, no. Just a slap on the hand to remind him who was "daddy," to use the vernacular.

Vassily Borodin had been marked as a comer for some time. His rise through the ranks of the SVR had been rapid and without pause. He was smart, capable, ruthless, cunning, and very, very ambitious. For the first time in recent memory, Russia had spawned a man capable not only of replacing Vladimir Putin but of returning Mother Russia to some semblance of her former glory. For Vassily Borodin possessed another quality in even rarer supply. He was an honest man.

And so the letter.

It had been Neill's idea. An ingenious means to draw the attention of a man with righteousness in his heart and treachery in his blood. A born usurper. The West had operatives by the dozens inside the Kremlin. The United States had operatives, the United Kingdom, France, Germany, Australia. It was just a matter of having one drop a hint here and there. The rest they left to Borodin.

The goal was not to depose the sitting president but

to weaken him. And at the same time, to remove an unwelcome successor. For there was one hitch that Vassily Borodin could not know.

The letter was a fake.

Everything up to this point had been done to make him think otherwise.

But one of the graphologists in the Kremlin would know better. The error was in Reagan's signature. A loop that was too big. Or was it a curl that was too tight? Neill couldn't remember which. Anyway, they would compare it to others and they would know. Goodbye, Borodin.

The money was Neill's reward for a job well done.

He had an urge to open the case, to look at the piles and piles of currency, to wallow in a few moments of wanton greed. Another time.

He hoisted the case up and out of the truck, sliding it to one side of the door. He began to think ahead. His first order of business would be to kill Coluzzi. From there it was an hour's drive to the ferry in Marseille. He had just enough time to make the eleven p.m. boat to Ajaccio. He'd be sure to bid Coluzzi's family a silent hello and thank you. He couldn't have done it without their son. From Ajaccio, he'd take a plane to Morocco. He had a friendly banker in Marrakech and enough passports to stay hidden for the next fifty years. From there, he would disappear.

Neill smiled at the thought. He'd done it. He'd pulled it off.

He needed a boost to pull himself out of the truck and searched the compartment for a platform where he might stand. The bench would do nicely. He put a foot on it and raised a hand to the doorway. When he looked up, Simon Riske was there, staring down at him.

"Go away," said Neill. "You've done your job."

"And yours, too."

"What do you want?"

"You should know. I wanted him. Coluzzi. Now I want something else."

"The money? Fine. We can discuss it. First, let's get out of here. I'm sure we can come to a reasonable agreement."

"Not the money."

"There's ten million euros in that case."

"That's a lot."

"Plenty to keep that shop of yours going. You can buy yourself a car. Buy two, even."

"This whole thing was your plan, wasn't it? The letter, Borodin, Coluzzi, the money."

Neill was growing impatient. "Is this about the girl?"

"She's alive, in case you're interested."

"I'm glad to hear that. I never like it when there's collateral damage."

"You're a real caring soul."

"What's done is done. Now let me out of here."

"I can't do that."

"What do you mean?"

"I'm still figuring that out. I'm a little shaken up, to tell you the truth. My collarbone's busted and I think my arm is, too. All I know is that I'm not letting you walk away from here with all this money."

"So it is about the money?" said Neill, desperation growing. "I knew it. You've been after it all along."

"Sit down and take a rest," said Simon, pushing the door closed. "I'll be back to you soon."

"Don't you…" Neill went for his pistol and fired a round as the door slammed shut. The bullet ricocheted and penetrated the floorboard. The armored truck was built to withstand automatic weapons fire, rocket-propelled grenades, even smaller improvised explosive devices. But all those delivered their charge to the outside of the vehicle. The truck was not designed to guard against a weapon fired inside it. The floorboard was built of standard sheet metal. The nine-millimeter bullet bounced off the reinforced steel door and passed through the quarter-inch metal plate into the gasoline tank, also armored exclusively on its exterior facing side.

The heat of the bullet and the friction it generated as it passed through the metal caused a spark. The gasoline exploded instantaneously, the force of the blast deflected entirely into the cargo bay.

At once, the truck was enveloped in flames.

Simon leapt from the truck and rolled in the grass, extinguishing his clothing. Coluzzi struggled to distance himself from the flames. Simon got to his feet and dragged him a safe distance from the burning truck. Neill's screams lasted for a minute.

By now, police were streaming in their direction, drawn by the explosion.

Coluzzi pointed to the suitcase, which had landed perfectly upright a stone's throw away. "Pity to give it to the authorities."

"What do you suggest?"

Coluzzi looked at Riske and lay back in the grass. He shook his head, disconsolately. "Where did you go wrong?"

Friday

Chapter 69

The Cimetière de Saint-Paul et Saint-Pierre was where the poor, the unwanted, the unloved and unidentified of Marseille were sent to spend eternity, or at least the twenty-five years they were granted until each was dug up, incinerated, and another put in their place. It was the French version of Potter's Field, and the worse for it. It sat on an untended plot of land a few kilometers outside the city, squeezed between a landfill and a recycling plant.

Rain was coming. He could smell it on the wind. A few drops landed on Simon's coat as he made his way down row after row, reading the names of those buried here. He found the monsignor's grave at the far corner of the cemetery, his final resting place marked by a stone cross that had originally been white but after years of neglect had faded to a mottled yellow where the paint had not chipped away altogether.

PAUL DESCHUTES
1931–2004

There were no last words, nothing to offer a hint of a life lived or advice to those still inhabiting the earthly plane.

Simon placed a bouquet of flowers at its base. He was not a religious man, at least not in the formal sense. He didn't know what prayer he should say. The monsignor wouldn't mind. Religion was a matter of the heart, he'd taught Simon. Every man was born with God inside him. It was easy enough to find him. All you had to do was ask.

So Simon thanked God for bringing this man into his life and asked that he bless his soul for all that he had given him.

Then he kneeled and, with his good arm, pulled out the tall, untamed grass around the marker so that others could read the monsignor's name.

"Did you find him?" Nikki was standing at the end of the row, her arm in a sling.

Simon stood, brushing off his hands. "Yes. Thanks again."

"Wish it were nicer."

"It's fine enough," said Simon, though of course it wasn't. "He was a tough guy."

"Like you."

"Look who's talking."

Nikki smiled. "We're a pair."

Already, she was getting the color back in her face. The bullet had been a "through and through." She'd lost a lot of blood and suffered some fairly significant muscular damage, but that was it. Turned out they didn't keep people in the hospital any longer in France than they did in the UK.

They walked back to the car, shoulder touching shoulder. Frank Mazot held the door, and Nikki slid gingerly into the back seat. Simon walked to the other side and got in. Mazot guided the car through the cemetery gates. In minutes, they were on the downhill run into Marseille.

Nikki took his hand. "I got a call from Marc Dumont."

"He's still talking to you?"

"I'm officially off administrative duty."

"Good news." Simon cocked his head. "You know something? You never told me what you did to get suspended."

"It never came up."

"Well?"

"I don't want to talk about it."

Simon nudged her with his good shoulder.

"Crazy glue," she said, then explained about her work on the Zenstrom case, nailing the gang of credit card thieves and how her boss took all the credit. "I got tired of him bragging. He always had these chapped lips. I went into his office after work one night, broke into his desk, and replaced his stick of Chap Stick with crazy glue, made it look just the same. He came in the next day, hung over like usual, opened his desk drawer, and that was that. He glued his big mouth shut."

"Ouch," said Simon.

Nikki shrugged, suppressing a grin. "Sometimes a girl has to do what she has to do."

"Guess so."

"Oh, and about Marc Dumont. He asked me to tell you that the next time you're in Paris, you should not bother getting in touch."

Simon laughed. "And Mr. Coluzzi?"

"He arrived in Paris this morning and was taken into custody. They pulled in Giacomo, as well. 'Jack,' you remember?"

Simon ran a hand along his stitches. "How could I forget?"

"Jack's going to testify against him for a reduced sentence. He's spilling the beans."

"Give Coluzzi a taste of his own medicine. About time."

"The prosecutor is asking for twenty years. He'll be lucky if he gets five. Armed robbery doesn't count for much these days. Besides, Coluzzi is spinning some story that he was actually working for our intelligence services all along."

Simon shook his head. With the right lawyer, Coluzzi could probably get someone to believe it, too. Even so, five years was five years. A long time when you were on the starting end of it. If only they'd send him back to Les Baums. He'd have a word with Dumont to that effect. He looked at Nikki. "So you're staying in?"

"Sure," she said brightly, and it was clear she'd never considered doing otherwise. "I'll leave the private sector to you. I like being a cop."

"You're a good one."

Nikki nodded, not quite convinced. "Getting there. And you? Heading back to London soon?"

"There's a flight at four."

"*Today?*"

"Today. Business."

"Of course," said Nikki, lowering her eyes. "I mean…sure. Good for you. I understand."

"Come and visit?"

"Less than three hours by train, right?"

"Blink and you're there," said Simon.

Nikki smiled suddenly. "I've never been."

"To London? You're kidding me."

She said, "No," and appeared embarrassed by it. "Give me a tour?"

"I'd like that," said Simon. He touched her cheek and kissed her.

"Promise?" she asked.

"Promise."

The car crested a rise, and the old port came into view, protected by Fort Saint-Jean and Fort Saint-Nicolas. A very large yacht was entering the harbor, navy-blue with a sharp, proud bow, dwarfing the boats around it.

Frank Mazot looked over his shoulder. "Where to?"

"I'm hungry," said Simon. "You?"

Nikki nodded. "I could eat. But not a ham and cheese sandwich."

"Who wants ham and cheese?" said Simon. "How 'bout some bouillabaisse. What do you say, Frank?"

"I know just the place."

EPILOGUE

London
Three days later

"Finished yet?" asked Simon.

Lucy Brown was crouched beside the Dino, blasting a section of the passenger door with her heat gun. She wore her usual ratty gray coverall, her hair tucked inside a baseball cap. "Finished? You're not serious?"

"Seven days. That's plenty of time."

"Says who? The boss now that he's—" Lucy's smile disappeared the moment she saw him. She pulled off her safety goggles and rushed toward him. "What happened to you?"

"I swam with some piranhas," said Simon.

"Did they break your arm?"

"And collarbone." He didn't mention the stitches in his side. "But the other guys got worse."

"Well," said Lucy, looking aghast. "If that's what happens when you travel to France, count me out. I'd rather go to Brighton."

Simon circled the automobile, running a critical hand across the chassis, now and again checking his fingertips for paint speckles. "You did all of this?"

"I did."

He eyed her with suspicion. "By yourself?"

Lucy placed her hands on her hips. "I did."

Simon gave the car a final once-over. "Not bad," he said, as if he only half meant it.

"Not bad?" Lucy put down her heat gun and scraper. "It's immaculate."

"That's one of my words."

"Well, is it?"

Simon nodded grudgingly. "Getting there."

Lucy beamed with pride, a victory won. She took off her cap and shook loose her hair, then touched his cast gingerly. "Hurt much?"

"No."

She ran a hand up his arm toward his shoulder. "And this?"

"Careful," he said, wincing.

She ran her fingers over his bruised cheek. "Bring me back a present?"

"I might have a snow globe for you."

"You were in Paris. That's where all the designers are."

"Do you think I brought Harry Mason a present?"

"He wouldn't look as nice in a silk camisole as I would."

Simon considered this. "You have me there."

"Besides, I could be more."

"More than what?"

Lucy smiled, her head tilted toward him. "More than just your favorite mechanic."

Simon took her hand and guided it to her side. "Who

says you're my favorite?" he said firmly. "Now, give me the heat gun. You missed a spot."

Lucy crossed her arms furiously. "I did not!"

A commotion in the main shop interrupted them. He heard raised voices. Harry Mason shouted. A toolbox overturned, scattering its contents.

"Riske," a man called. "Simon Riske!"

The voice was too loud, the words too clearly enunciated, to mistake the accent. Not again, thought Simon.

"Don't!" said Lucy, grabbing his arm.

"Stay here." Simon hurried back to the shop floor. There were five large men he didn't know and one fat man he did.

"You asked me to look you up," said Boris Blatt. "Here I am."

One of Blatt's men held Harry Mason in a headlock with a gun stuck into his side.

"And here I am," said Simon. "Let Mr. Mason go."

Blatt barked an order in Russian and the man released Mason.

"Everyone keep calm," said Simon. "I know why Mr. Blatt is here. You guys can go back to work."

Blatt carved a path through the sports cars, appraising each in turn. "Nice, but nothing special."

"No 275s," said Simon, referring to the automobile Blatt had purchased the Sunday before. "I told you not a dollar over twenty million."

"What's five million here or there?" Blatt shrugged, but his sour expression said he wasn't happy to be reminded of his rash expenditure.

"I don't suppose you've come to see about some work it might need?"

"I suppose not." Blatt made a show of extending his

left arm. He was wearing a Casio G-Shock. "Feel free to take this one."

Simon spoke earnestly. "I was simply repossessing stolen property."

"You are saying I stole the watch?" Blatt's pale face had gone a vivid shade of crimson at the drop of a hat.

"I'm sure it was an honest mistake," said Simon. "Watches aren't like cars. Much harder to keep track of past owners."

"This is true," said Blatt, mollified. "One never knows where a watch has been. A person buys it. Perhaps he gives it to a friend. Someone else loses it. Over the years, anything can happen."

"Anything." Simon nodded obediently. Blatt's men had formed a circle around him, and he could feel their enmity radiating like heat off a blacktop.

"However," Blatt continued, rubbing his little gray head, "that does not change the reason for my visit. It seems you owe me five million dollars."

"I do?"

"We already agree that you took my watch. Its value is given as three million and change. You do the math."

Simon already had and he didn't like the result. "And the additional sum?"

"For my time, my efforts to find you, and my *forbearance*."

"Quite an hourly rate. I didn't know you were an attorney."

"Five million dollars, Mr. Riske."

One of Blatt's thugs emerged from the paint studio, manhandling Lucy.

"Ah," said Blatt, eyes undressing her. "Your lovely assistant." He nodded at her. "I believe we met the other night."

To her credit, Lucy held her tongue.

Simon assessed the situation. He was not in what one might call a good bargaining position. He guessed that Lucy was to be their hostage until he ponied up the money or they came to some other agreement. He did not want to imagine what might happen to her once Blatt turned his back. "What do you suggest, Mr. Blatt?"

"*Boris,* please. We are all friends here." He smiled theatrically, then approached Simon, one man speaking to another. "I would like you to come work for me."

"Really?"

"I could use a man with your skills."

Simon smiled faintly, as if not entirely averse to the proposition. "In what capacity?"

"In whatever capacity I say."

The smile faded. "And my work here?"

"Oh, the shop will be mine, too," Blatt went on, speaking the words softly, inches from his face, enjoying himself far too much for Simon's taste. "Did I forget to mention that?"

Simon looked around the floor. At Harry and Lucy. At his crew of mechanics. At the cars in varied states of restoration and rebuilding. He loved this place. The people. The cars. The lingering scents of oil and grease and the smell of good old-fashioned sweat. The day he turned his shop over to Blatt was the day he...Well, he'd *never* turn it over to Blatt.

"Would you excuse me a moment?" he said, far too politely.

"Where are you going?"

"To get you your money."

"You have it here?" asked Blatt.

Simon stared back at the Russian. Blatt nodded to an underling. "Go with him."

Simon climbed the stairs to his flat. He'd left his bags in the living room. Happily, the French railway had taken his bags from the TGV and stored them in the Marseille Lost and Found. He now pointed to Borodin's suitcase and instructed the thug to carry it into his bedroom. "Put it there," he said, indicating his bed.

Simon unlocked the case, allowing the thug to get a look at the money. "I've got to use the men's room," he said. "Don't even think of taking any. I know exactly how much there is. Understand? Give me a minute."

"Just hurry up."

In fact, Simon needed two minutes to complete his business. When he emerged from the washroom, the thug and his suitcase were gone. Simon put on his angriest face and puffed his cheeks, then ran after him. "Hey!" he shouted as desperately as he knew. "Bring that back. It's not yours!"

Blatt and his thugs had retreated to the front door. Lucy Brown had been freed and stood next to Harry Mason.

"Where do you think you're going?" asked Simon, skidding to a halt.

"I've decided that you may keep your shop," said Blatt. "I'm not one for manual labor."

Simon gathered his breath. "That's more than we agreed," he said, pointing at the suitcase.

"May I ask how much is in it? It would save me time."

"Count it yourself."

"As you wish." Blatt buttoned his jacket. "I'll make it a point to visit more often."

Simon rushed the man, grabbing one lapel with his good hand. "That's not yours."

Two of Blatt's bodyguards grabbed Simon and tossed him onto the floor. He lay there, beaten and defeated.

"Goodbye, Mr. Riske. Let this be the end of our relationship. Unless, of course, I need some work done on my car."

Simon waited until Blatt had departed, then jumped to his feet and dusted himself off. After assuring his staff that he was fine and that Blatt hadn't taken that much money, he returned to his flat. He walked at once to his bathroom. He looked at himself in the mirror. "'That's not yours,'" he repeated, pointing a finger at his reflection. Then angrier: " *'That's not yours!'* " He shook his head with dismay. "Boy, that's weak. Sad, really."

He emptied his pockets and set a small black SIM card on the counter. The card held the entire contents of Boris Blatt's phone—his mail, his texts, his photographs, and all the websites he'd ever visited, including the passwords to his bank accounts. He'd borrowed the phone when Blatt had made his generous offer of employment and returned it when he'd accosted the vile Russian. During his visit to the men's room, he'd duplicated the SIM card. Amazing what could be done in two minutes these days.

Simon grabbed a beer from the fridge and dropped onto the couch. Holding the little card between his fingers, he placed a call.

"Hello, D'Art. It's Simon. Remember last week you mentioned your friends at Scotland Yard? Good news. I have a little something that might interest them."

ACKNOWLEDGMENTS

My sincere thanks to my editor, Josh Kendall; Emily Giglierano; Pam Brown; and of course Reagan Arthur, as well as the entire team at Mulholland Books.

At InkWell Management, thanks to my agent, Richard Pine, and his assistant, Eliza Rothstein.

ABOUT THE AUTHOR

Christopher Reich is the *New York Times* bestselling author of *Numbered Account, Rules of Deception, Rules of Vengeance, Rules of Betrayal, The Devil's Banker,* and many other thrillers. His novel *The Patriots Club* won the International Thriller Writers Award for Best Novel in 2006. He lives in Encinitas, California.

...AND *CROWN JEWEL*

Following is an excerpt from the next Simon Riske novel.

CHAPTER 1

Lyceum Alpinum Zuoz
Engadin, Switzerland

The men were watching again.

There were two of them, up by the monastery on the hill overlooking the athletic field. They stayed in the shadows of the gallery, popping out to take a photograph, then ducking back again. The boy could tell they thought he hadn't spotted them.

But he had.

He always did.

"Look out!" someone shouted. "Robby! Tackle him!"

Robby returned his attention to the scrimmage in time to see the scrum-half—it was Karl Marshal, the best player on the team—lower his shoulder and plow into him. Robby's feet left the ground and he landed flat on his back, the wind knocked out of him, sure he'd never take a breath again. The other players ran past, laughing.

"Might as well make a mud castle while you're down there."

"Only one you'll ever have."

He heard a whistle. Karl Marshal had scored a try.

Robby climbed to his feet and wiped the dirt from his face. When he'd regained his breath, he set off down the field, limping at first, then shaking it off and running as fast as he could. He was small for a sixth-former and thin, with pale skin, a mop of curly blond hair, and questioning blue eyes. His size didn't bother him. His father was tall. One day he'd grow. He might not be as big as the others yet, or as strong, but he was no quitter. One of his teachers had remarked upon his determination and called him Das Krokodil. For a few days, the nickname stuck. He liked being called Krok. A week later, everyone had forgotten it.

He caught up to the game in time to run into a ruck. He got knocked down two more times, but he caught a pass and almost tackled Karl Marshal. Robby was practical. He knew it would be foolish to expect anything more. Finally, the whistle blew. The scrimmage ended.

Walking back to the athletic center, he glanced at the monastery. It was nearly dusk, the gallery cloaked in shadow. The men were nowhere to be seen. Robby wasn't concerned one way or the other. People had been watching him his entire life. The best thing to do was simply to ignore them.

It wasn't until later that night, as he got ready for bed, that he thought about the two men again. He realized that this was the fourth time in the past week or so that he'd seen them. One had a large nose that looked like an eagle's beak and black hair. The other was bald and never took his hands out of his pockets. Robby had exceptional vision. It ran in the family. It bothered him that the men stayed so far away.

Farther than the distance prescribed by the school for journalists and photographers. This was odd, Robby concluded, in his methodical manner. "Rum," Mr. Bradshaw-Mack, his English teacher, would say. "Very rum, indeed."

Robby went to the window and peered outside. Down the hill, the lights from the village of Zuoz glowed warmly, a spot illuminating the tall, rectangular spire of the Protestant church. A crescent moon sat low in the sky and he could just make out the silhouette of the jagged peaks all around. The Piz Blaisun, Cresta Mora, and, further west, near St. Moritz, the Corvatsch.

He closed the window and secured the lock, then crawled into bed. His roommate, Alain, was reading an *Astérix* comic book his father had sent him from Paris. Robby wished he had a father to send him comics, or, preferably, a book about rugby, which was his favorite sport. It was hard to be too sad, though, because he'd never really known his dad, and besides, he had a wonderful mother.

Robby picked up his phone and considered calling her. The more he thought about the watchers, the more they bothered him. He refused to use the word "scared," because people like Robby were not allowed to be scared. It was a question of setting the right example. He heard Alain snore and decided against calling. Good manners were part of that example, too.

Robby turned out the light and lay his head on the pillow. There was math first period tomorrow, then history, and rugby again after school. As he drifted off to sleep, his eyes opened for a second, less even, and he thought he saw a shadow in the window. *The watchers*.

Maybe it was just a dream or a figment of his imagination. Either way, the image didn't register. He turned over and fell into a deep slumber.

It had been a long day, and a twelve-year-old boy got very tired.

CHAPTER 2

Les Ambassadeurs
London, England

Simon Riske did not like losing money.

Seated at the center of a card table in the high-rollers room of Les Ambassadeurs, London's most exclusive gaming establishment, he peeked at his cards, then lifted his eyes to the dwindling stacks of chips before him. He wondered how much longer his bad luck could continue.

"Well," said Lucy Brown, seated at his shoulder so she could view his cards, "what do we do?"

"What do you think?"

"Both cards are different."

"So they are."

"Neither matches the cards in front of the dealer."

"And so?"

Lucy screwed up her face, and Simon allowed her a moment to figure things out.

It wasn't normal for players to discuss their hands, especially when large sums of money were at stake. But Lucy was young and blond and pretty, and upon sitting down, Simon had explained to all present that he would be teaching her a thing or two about poker. The other players—all male—had taken a glance (some discreet, some not so) at Lucy's black dress, her figure, and her blue eyes. If anyone had voiced an objection, Simon hadn't heard it.

"Fold?" said Lucy.

"Fold," he said, sliding his cards to the center of the table.

"Darn," said Lucy.

Simon had a more colorful word in mind. Instead, he offered his best "not to worry" smile and signaled for a drink—a Fanta for Lucy and a grapefruit and soda for himself. Alcohol and gambling were as combustible as matches and gasoline.

It was an ordinary Friday night at "Les A" (as the club was known to habitués). Downstairs, a lively crowd milled about the gaming tables, the atmosphere one of a posh Georgian country house. The play was spread evenly between roulette, blackjack, and baccarat. Slot machines were the province of the lower classes and strictly verboten.

But the real action took place in the private rooms on the second floor.

It had been Simon's plan to observe from afar while explaining the rules of the game. The idea vanished approximately five seconds after he witnessed a player win a five-thousand-pound pot on a weak hand. Being a modest and unassuming sort, Simon had reasoned he could do better. That was two hours and twenty thousand pounds ago.

"Another hand," said Lucy cheerily. "Our luck's bound to change."

Simon looked at her expectant gaze, her adventurous posture. Lucy was twenty-three and gifted with what some might call, in the polite confines of Les Ambassadeurs, a curvy figure. Like most girls her age, she liked showing off her assets. Simon's relationship with her was purely platonic, somewhere between father and friend. It was nebulous territory. In fact, he was her employer. Lucy worked as an apprentice in his automotive repair shop, learning to restore vintage Italian sports cars, primarily Ferraris with a Lamborghini thrown in here and there. In a sense, she was his own restoration project. But that was another story.

As for himself, Simon was dressed in a black suit and white open-collar shirt, both fresh from the cleaner. His nails were neatly trimmed and he'd spent ten minutes scrubbing them with steel wool to clean the grease from beneath them. He collected cuff links, and tonight, for luck, he'd chosen his favorites, a pair he'd been given by MI5, the British Security Service, as a thank-you for a job undertaken on their behalf a year earlier. His eye fell on the puny stack of chips and he scowled. So much for talismans. His hair was in the sleekest order, cut short and therefore in need of a brush, never a comb, which was the polite way to say that it was receding faster than the Greenland ice shelf. Unlike the man a few places to his left—a wan, unsavory sort who'd taken too much of Simon's money—he'd shaven and treated himself to a splash of Acqua di Parma. His bespoke lace-ups were polished and only his beryl-green eyes shone brighter.

But all his finery couldn't disguise his true nature. Simon had spent too much time on the wrong side of the tracks to ever be a real gentleman. Some things you could never wash from beneath your nails.

"Well?" Lucy demanded, her lip thrust out petulantly.

"That's plenty for tonight," said Simon. "We've done enough damage."

"But you still have some chips."

"The idea is to leave with a few in your pocket," he said. "More rather than less."

Lucy appeared crestfallen.

"There's just enough to buy us a fancy dinner," he continued. "How about the Ivy?"

"That's for old people."

"It's the princes' favorite place."

"Exactly."

Simon considered this, realizing that "old" for Lucy meant anyone over twenty-five. "How about fish-and-chips at the pub 'round the corner?"

"I'm not hungry." Lucy crossed her arms and pouted. It was an inviting pout, and Simon felt sorry for her boyfriend.

"One last hand," he said. "But I mean it."

Lucy brightened, clutching his arm and scooting closer. "We're going to win. I know it!" She kissed his cheek and Simon said that was close enough and scooted her back a few inches.

It was then that the tenor of the evening took a dramatic turn.

Simon ponied up his chips. The cards were dealt. Simon's were as miserable as usual. The players called and raised and called again. The dealer tossed out the last cards.

And that was when Simon saw it again. A flick of the wrist. A rustle of the sleeve. A flash of white. The player two seats to his left—the unkempt man who'd been winning the entire evening—was cheating. Twice now, he'd caught it. The man was good, a professional, or "sharp" in the parlance, but Simon knew a thing or two about cards himself, and about unfair advantages.

"What is it?" Lucy nudged him, sensing something amiss.

"Nothing."

Lucy held his gaze and he gave her the subtlest of looks—eyes harder, jaw steeled—and she looked away, knowing better than to ask any question. If he ever had a daughter, he hoped she'd turn out something like Lucy, though he'd never in his life allow her to go out dressed as she was.

Simon signaled to the server. "Jack Daniel's," he said. "Straightaway."

Lucy tugged at his sleeve. "You said only a fool drinks while gambling."

"Did I?"

Lucy nodded urgently.

"That was before we lost your annual salary."

"Maybe we should go."

"Nonsense," he said. "Not when we're just starting to have fun." He turned to the dealer. "Five thousand pounds...no, make it ten."

The dealer shot a discreet glance to Ronnie, the casino boss, who stood at the door. Ronnie was a friend. He and Simon played on the same rugby team Saturdays during the fall. He was forty, tall, and dapper in a white dinner jacket, red carnation in his lapel. A black Clark Gable, with the same gambler's mustache and rakish air. Ronnie nodded, shooting Simon a cautionary look, then left the room.

Ten stacks of chips came Simon's way.

The server arrived with his cocktail. Simon stole it off the tray and downed it. "Another," he said, returning the empty to the tray, flipping her a fifty-pound chip for good measure. "And one for my friend, too."

Lucy took a judicious step from Simon. She'd worked with him for three years. She knew his moods. She knew when a bomb was about to go off.

Simon noted the cheat shift in his chair, the corners of his mouth lift in anticipatory delight.

The dealer called for bets. Simon ponied up five hundred pounds, the minimum.

There were two ways this could go. He could wait and take matters into his own hands. Or he could act now, expose the cheat, and let Ronnie sort things out.

Simon preferred the first choice. A confrontation in the alley followed by a full and frank exchange of views. He would take back his money and the cheat would pick himself up off the ground and get to a hospital to look after his missing teeth and broken bones.

But, of course, there was Lucy to think of.

The game progressed. For once, Simon had a decent hand. He called and raised and called and raised.

The dealer turned over the last card, known as "the river." An eight of spades.

Simon was holding two kings and an eight of hearts. The eight of spades gave him two pair. His best hand all evening.

The room went quiet, the only noise the *clack, clack, clack* of the roulette ball skipping across the wheel in the outer room.

The player next to Simon tossed in his cards. "I'm out."

"Raise two thousand pounds," said Simon.

The man next to him tossed in his cards. "Out."

"Call," said the cheat, picking up four blue chips and tossing them into the pot.

It was the moment of truth.

"Two pair," announced Simon. "Kings and eights."

Simon's eyes went to the cheat, who coolly deflected the gaze. To his credit, he didn't flinch. One hand went to his kingdom of chips, fingers racing between spires, touching each in turn. It was a distraction, a motion to lure the eye. He lifted the cards off the table. Fanned them deftly. And in the downward motion he made the switch. A flick of the wrist. A rustling of the cuff. A flash of white, though this time his motion was so expert that even Simon, eyes trained on him, did not catch it.

"Full house," the cheat announced, spreading his cards on the table.

Shouts went up. Exhortations of amazement and disbelief.

"Damn," said the player to Simon's right. The other players simply shook their heads.

And, as the cheat extended his hands for the pot, Simon lashed out and grabbed one wrist, closing his fingers around it in a vice. Their eyes met. Instead of protesting, of calling out Simon, the man stood, wrenching his hand free, the violent motion knocking over his chair. He stumbled backward, head turned, plotting a way out.

Simon was up, too, and a half step behind. A dozen people ringed the table. All remained glued to the spot, their expressions as immobile as their feet. The cheat shoved the man nearest him hard enough to topple him into the woman behind him. The two fell unceremoniously to the floor. He dashed through the gap between them and out the door, heading toward the staircase that descended to the main floor. Simon gave chase, leaping over the two, pausing at the top of the stairs before vaulting the balustrade and landing in the center of the blackjack table eight feet below. He jumped to the floor, cutting off the cheat's path. Seeing his escape ruined, the man slowed. He started left, then went right, then stopped altogether.

Simon crashed into him before he could make it a step. He led with his shoulder, aiming for the sternum but striking the man's collarbone, feeling it crack as they hit the floor. The man grunted, his face inches from Simon's, and Simon saw that he had bad teeth and worse dental work, and his breath reeked of the Brandy Alexanders he'd been drinking all night.

But if Simon expected him to give up, he was mistaken. A knee to the groin signaled his resistance, followed by a head butt glancing off the bridge of Simon's nose. Stunned, breathless, and momentarily paralyzed, Simon was unable to stop the man from climbing to his feet. In desperation, he threw out a hand and grasped hold of his ankle. Unfortunately, it was the wrong ankle and belonged to a horrified Asian woman. The woman screamed and her cry roused Simon. He was on his feet as the cheat navigated his way through the crowd of gamblers.

By now, security had mobilized in response to the incident. Two men in maroon jackets blocked the only path out of the casino. The cheat spun and pointed at Simon. "It's him," he said, in accented English whose origin Simon would place only later.

The guards hesitated long enough for the cheat to lash out with a cosh, striking the first man squarely on the jaw, dropping him, before backhanding the second, the cosh caroming off his temple. His route to the entrance clear, the cheat bolted. He grabbed at the door handle, pulling it toward him, unaware that Simon was close behind. In England, exit doors pivot outward, and in that moment, Simon had him. He grabbed the collar of his jacket and yanked the man backward. Ready for a blow, Simon ducked as the cosh cut a path above his head, noting that a nail extended from the business end of the leather cudgel. He thrust an open palm upward, landing it on the man's jaw, snapping his head backward. His other hand latched onto the man's wrist. He dropped to a knee, wrenching the wrist and the arm attached to it with all his might. There was a pop—loud as a champagne cork—as the shoulder dislocated. The man cried out. The cosh dropped into Simon's hand and he spun it so the nail was facing outward. It was a killing weapon.

"No!" a man shouted. "Simon, stop!" It was Ronnie, the casino boss, emerging from his private office across the floor, barreling toward him.

Simon didn't hear him, or didn't want to. He wanted to punish the man, to hurt him badly. Turning, he lashed out toward the cheat's undefended face.

A woman screamed. It was Lucy. He saw her from the corner of his eye.

The nail stopped a millimeter from the man's eye. "You got lucky," he said, throwing the man against the wall. "Say 'thank you' to the lady."

The cheat said nothing. His silence riled Simon all over again, and he hit the man in the stomach. "I won't ask again."

The man fought for his breath, his eyes cursing Simon. His gaze shifted, focusing on something...*or someone*.

Simon began to turn as a fist slammed into his kidney. It was a professional punch, knuckles first, delivered with force and accuracy. A second followed to the opposite side, harder still.

Simon bent double at the waist, tears fouling his vision. That was that. He was officially out of the game. TKO.

He dropped to one knee, aware of a commotion around him, Ronnie going after the cheat and his secret accomplice, but not much else. He tried not to move, the pain exquisite and relentless. He heard Lucy shout, "Stop him…don't let him leave! Come back, you fucking thief."

They left Les Ambassadeurs an hour later. Simon walked out the front door, pushing it, not pulling, under his own power. His car was brought up and he held the door for Lucy, declining her offer to drive. Once behind the wheel, he made a circuit of Sloane Square and headed east.

"You're not taking me home," said Lucy. "Not after all that."

Simon kept his eyes on the road. He was in no mood to take orders. His side ached like hell. He'd washed up and used the men's room. As expected, there was blood in his urine. It wasn't the first time. If it persisted, he'd see a doctor. His head throbbed and there was a noticeable knot above the bridge of his nose. Hoping to keep it from swelling, he'd pressed an old fifty p coin against it for a minute, then given up. Que será, será. But it was his pride that hurt worst of all. He'd brought the operations of London's best gaming house to a halt only to allow the cheats who'd robbed him of twenty thousand pounds to escape. The loss was hypothetical. The cheats hadn't been able to pocket their ill-gotten gains. Ronnie had returned his original stake. Somehow, the thought did little to console him.

"I want to do something," Lucy went on. "I'm too excited to sleep. Where shall we go?"

"It's eleven," said Simon. "You're twenty-three years old. You have work tomorrow. If I hear you set foot outside your door before six a.m. tomorrow, you can find yourself another job."

Lucy looked at him as if he'd slapped her. "What?"

"You heard me."

"You have no right," she exclaimed. "I can do whatever I choose."

"Feel free."

Simon continued across town, thankful that traffic was only bad, not miserable. All the way Lucy carped and complained, but he said nothing more until they arrived at her flat. "Here we are. Go upstairs straightaway. Get into bed and go to sleep. It's been enough of a night for both of us."

Lucy unclasped her safety belt. She motioned as if she were going to start up again, then thought better of it. "Not fair," she said, then climbed out of the car.

To her credit, she did not slam the door.

Maybe she was finally growing up.

Simon waited until she was inside and disappeared into the vestibule before slipping the car into first and making a U-turn. His home and business lay in southwest London, a stone's throw from Wimbledon. It was a thirty-minute drive in the best of conditions. Tonight, it would be double that. But traffic didn't play into Simon's thinking. Not a wit.

He was too jacked up to go home. Nothing revved his juices more than a little physical violence, even if he had been on the losing end of it. All measure of good sense had gone out the window the moment he'd given chase to the cheat. At that instant, his world had boiled down to him versus the bad guy, good versus evil, though it was a question of his ego run riot, not anything so grandiose as maintaining the universe's order. Mess with me and you're going to pay. It was as simple as that. It was not a motto by which to live any kind of successful life. But at that moment, Simon hadn't cared about mottoes or, to tell the truth, *anything* except catching the thief and inflicting punishment upon him.

Two hours later, those same wild and ungovernable instincts raced through his blood. If he'd been hard on Lucy, it was because he feared she shared his affinity for mayhem. He couldn't control himself, but he could control her. He was a hypocrite. So what?

Instead of driving east along Brompton Road, he pointed the car north toward Southwark Bridge and the city. He rolled down the window, enjoying the warm, fetid air, the scent of the River Thames hidden somewhere inside the exhaust and grit of central London. He was navigating to that part of the map where borders lay undefined and lands undiscovered, to the hazy, unmarked section labeled "Where Dragons Lie."

Simon Riske headed into the night.

MULHOLLAND BOOKS

You won't be able to put down these Mulholland books.